JEFFERY DEAVER

THE VANISHED MAN

A LINCOLN RHYME NOVEL

DOUBLEDAY LARGE PRINT HOME LIBRARY EDITION

Simon & Schuster

NEW YORK • LONDON • TORONTO
SYDNEY • SINGAPORE

This Large Print Edition, prepared especially for Doubleday Large Print Home Library, contains the complete, unabridged text of the original Publisher's Edition.

SIMON & SCHUSTER
Rockefeller Center
1230 Avenue of the Americas
New York, NY 10020

SIMON & SCHUSTER and colophon are registered trademarks of Simon & Schuster, Inc.

Manufactured in the United States of America

ISBN 0-7394-3371-7

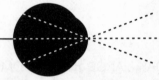

This Large Print Book carries the Seal of Approval of N.A.V.H.

To Madelyn Warcholik

"A conjuring trick is generally regarded by magicians as consisting of an effect and a method. The effect is what the spectator sees. . . . The method is the secret behind the effect and allows the effect to take place."

—Peter Lamont and Richard Wiseman,
Magic in Theory

I
EFFECT

"The expert magician seeks to deceive the mind, rather than the eye."

Marvin Kaye,
The Creative Magician's Handbook

Chapter One

Greetings, Revered Audience. Welcome.
Welcome to our show.

We have a number of thrills in store for you over the next two days as our illusionists, our magicians, our sleight-of-hand artists weave their spells to delight and captivate you.

Our first routine is from the repertoire of a performer everyone's heard of: Harry Houdini, the greatest escape artist in America, if not the world, a man who performed before crowned heads of state and U.S. presidents. Some of his escapes are so difficult no one has dared attempt them, all these years after his untimely death.

Today we'll re-create an escape in which he risked suffocation in a routine known as the Lazy Hangman.

In this trick, our performer lies prone on the belly, hands bound behind the back with classic Darby handcuffs. The ankles are tied together and another length of rope is wound around the neck, like a noose, and tied to the ankles. The tendency of the legs to straighten pulls the noose taut and begins the terrible process of suffocation.

Why is it called the "Lazy" Hangman? Because the condemned executes himself.

In many of Mr. Houdini's more dangerous routines, assistants were present with knives and keys to release him in the event that he was unable to escape. Often a doctor was on hand.

Today, there'll be none of these precautions. If there's no escape within four minutes, the performer will die.

We begin in a moment . . . but first a word of advice:

Never forget that by entering our show you're abandoning reality.

What you're absolutely convinced you see might not exist at all. What you know has to be an illusion may turn out to be God's harsh truth.

Your companion at our show might turn out to be a total stranger. A man or woman in the audience you don't recognize may know you far too well.

What seems safe may be deadly. And the dangers you guard against may be nothing more than distractions to lure you to greater danger.

In our show what can you believe? Whom can you trust?

Well, Revered Audience, the answer is that you should believe nothing.

And you should trust no one. No one at all.

Now, the curtain rises, the lights dim, the music fades, leaving only the sublime sound of hearts beating in anticipation.

And our show begins. . . .

The building looked as if it'd seen its share of ghosts.

Gothic, sooty, dark. Sandwiched between two high-rises on the Upper West Side, capped with a widow's walk and many shuttered windows. The building dated from the Victorian era and had been a boarding school at one point and later a sanatorium, where the criminally insane lived out their frazzled lives.

The Manhattan School of Music and Performing Arts could have been home to dozens of spirits.

But none so immediate as the one who might be hovering here now, above the warm body of the young woman lying, stomach down, in the dim lobby outside a small recital hall. Her eyes were still and wide but not yet glassy, the blood on her cheek was not yet brown.

Her face was dark as plum from the constriction of the taut rope connecting her neck to her ankles.

Scattered around her were a flute case, sheet music and a spilled grande cup from Starbucks, the coffee staining her jeans and green Izod shirt and leaving a comma of dark liquid on the marble floor.

Also present was the man who'd killed her, bending down and examining her carefully. He was taking his time and felt no urge to rush. Today was Saturday, the hour early. There were no classes in the school on the weekends, he'd learned. Students did use the practice rooms but they were in a different wing of the building. He leaned closer to the woman, squinting, wondering if he could see some essence, some spirit rising from her body. He didn't.

He straightened up, considering what else he might do to the still form in front of him.

"You're sure it was screaming?"

"Yeah. . . . No," the security guard said. "Maybe not screaming, you know. Shouting. Upset. For just a second or two. Then it stopped."

Officer Diane Franciscovich, a portable working out of the Twentieth Precinct, continued, "Anybody else hear anything?"

The heavy guard, breathing hard, glanced at the tall, brunette policewoman, shook his head and flexed and opened his huge hands. He wiped his dark palms on his blue slacks.

"Call for backup?" asked Nancy Ausonio, another young patrol officer, shorter than her partner, blonde.

Franciscovich didn't think so, though she wasn't sure. Portables walking the beat in this part of the Upper West Side dealt mostly with traffic accidents, shoplifting and car theft (as well as holding the hands of distraught muggees). This was a first for them—the two women officers, on their Saturday morning watch, had been spotted on the sidewalk and motioned urgently inside by the guard to help check out the screaming. Well, upset shouting.

"Let's hold off," the calm Franciscovich said. "See what's going on."

The guard said, "Sounded like it was comin' from 'round here somewhere. Dunno."

"Spooky place," Ausonio offered, oddly uneasy; she was the partner most likely to leap into the middle of a dispute, even if it involved combatants twice her size.

"The sounds, you know. Hard to tell. You know what I'm sayin'? Where they're coming from."

Franciscovich was focusing on what her partner had said. *Damn* spooky place, she added silently.

Seeming miles of dim corridors later, finding nothing out of the ordinary, the security guard paused.

Franciscovich nodded to a doorway in front of them. "What's through here?"

"Be no reason for students t'be there. It's only—"

Franciscovich pushed the door open.

Inside was a small lobby that led to a door labeled Recital Hall A. And near *that* door was the body of a young woman, trussed up, rope around her neck, hands in cuffs. Eyes open in death. A brown-haired, bearded man in his early fifties crouched over her. He looked up, surprised at their entry.

"No!" Ausonio cried.

"Oh, Christ," the guard gasped.

The officers drew their weapons and Franciscovich sighted down on the man with what she thought was a surprisingly steady hand. "You, don't move! Stand up slow, move away from her and put your hands in the air." Her voice was much less firm than the fingers gripping the Glock pistol.

The man did as he was told.

"Lie face down on floor. Keep your hands in sight!"

Ausonio started forward to the girl.

It was then Franciscovich noticed that the man's right hand, over his head, was closed in a fist.

"Open your—"

Pop . . .

She went blind as a flash of searing light filled the room. It seemed to come directly from the suspect's hand and hovered for a moment before going out. Ausonio froze and Franciscovich went into a crouch, scrabbling backward and squinting, swinging the gun back and forth. Panicked, she knew the killer had kept his eyes shut when the flash went off and would be aiming his own weapon at them or charging forward with a knife.

"Where, where, where?" she shouted.

Then she saw—vaguely thanks to her frizzled vision and the dissipating smoke—the killer running into the recital hall. He slammed the door shut. There was a thud inside as he moved a chair or table against the door.

Ausonio dropped to her knees in front of the girl. With a Swiss army knife she cut the rope off her neck, rolled her over and, using a disposable mouthpiece, started CPR.

"Any other exits?" Franciscovich shouted to the guard.

"Only one—in the back, around the corner. To the right."

"Windows?"

"No."

"Hey," she called to Ausonio as she started sprinting. "Watch this door!"

"Got it," the blonde officer called and blew another breath into the victim's pale lips.

More thuds from inside as the killer beefed up his barricade; Franciscovich sprinted around the corner, toward the door the guard had told them about, calling for backup on her Motorola. As she looked ahead she saw someone standing at the end of the corridor. Franciscovich stopped fast, drew a target on the man's chest and shone the brilliant beam from her halogen flashlight on him.

"Lord," croaked the elderly janitor, dropping the broom he held.

Franciscovich thanked God she'd kept her finger outside the trigger guard of the Glock. "You see somebody come out of that door?"

"What's going on?"

"You *see* anybody?" Franciscovich shouted.

"No, ma'am."

"How long you been here?"

"I don't know. Ten minutes, I'd guess."

There was another thud of furniture from

inside as the killer continued to blockade the door. Franciscovich sent the janitor into the main corridor with the security guard then eased up to the side door. Gun held high, eye level, she tested the knob gently. It was unlocked. She stepped to the side so she wouldn't be in the line of fire if the perp shot through the wood. A trick she remembered from *NYPD Blue,* though an instructor might've mentioned it at the Academy too.

Another thump from inside.

"Nancy, you there?" Franciscovich whispered into her handy-talkie.

Ausonio's voice, shaky, said, "She's dead, Diane. I tried. But she's dead."

"He didn't get out this way. He's still inside. I can hear him." Silence.

"I tried, Diane. I tried."

"Forget it. Come on. You on this? You *on* it?"

"Yeah, I'm cool. Really." The officer's voice hardened. "Let's go get him."

"No," Franciscovich said, "we'll keep him contained till ESU gets here. That's all we've got to do. Sit tight. Stay clear of the door. And sit tight."

Which is when she heard the man shout

from inside, "I've got a hostage. I've got a girl in here. Try to get in and I'll kill her!"

Oh, Jesus . . .

"You, inside!" Franciscovich shouted. "Nobody's going to do anything. Don't worry. Just don't hurt anybody else." Was this procedure? she wondered. Neither prime-time television nor her Academy training was any help here. She heard Ausonio call Central and report that the situation was now a barricade and hostage-taking.

Franciscovich called to the killer, "Just take it easy! You can—"

A huge gunshot from inside. Franciscovich jumped like a fish. "What happened? Was that you?" she shouted into her radio.

"No," her partner replied, "I thought it was you."

"No. It was him. You okay?"

"Yeah. He said he's got a hostage. You think he shot her?"

"I don't know. How do I know?" Franciscovich, thinking: Where the *hell* is the backup?

"Diane," Ausonio whispered after a moment. "We've gotta go in. Maybe she's hurt.

Maybe she's wounded." Then, shouting: "You, inside!" No answer. "You!"

Nothing.

"Maybe he killed himself," Franciscovich offered.

Or maybe he fired the shot to make us *think* he'd killed himself and he's waiting inside, drawing a target gut high on the doorway.

Then that terrible image returned to her: the seedy door to the recital lobby opening, casting the pale light on the victim, her face blue and cold as winter dusk. Stopping people from doing things like this was why she'd become a cop in the first place.

"We have to go in, Diane," Ausonio whispered.

"That's what I'm thinking. Okay. We'll go in." Speaking a bit manically as she thought of both her family and how to curl her left hand over her right when firing an automatic pistol in a combat shooting situation. "Tell the guard we'll need lights inside the hall."

A moment later Ausonio said, "The switch is out here. He'll turn 'em on when I say so." A deep breath that Franciscovich heard through the microphone. Then Ausonio said, "Ready. On three. You count it."

"Okay. One . . . Wait. I'll be coming in from your two o'clock. Don't shoot me."

"Okay. Two o'clock. I'll be—"

"You'll be on my left."

"Go ahead."

"One." Franciscovich gripped the knob with her left hand. "Two."

This time her finger slipped inside the guard of her weapon, gently caressing the second trigger—the safety on Glock pistols.

"Three!" Franciscovich shouted so loud that she was sure her partner heard the call without the radio. She shoved through the doorway into the large rectangular room just as the glaring lights came on.

"Freeze!" she screamed—to an empty room.

Crouching, skin humming with the tension, she swung her weapon from side to side as she scanned every inch of the space.

No sign of the killer, no sign of a hostage.

A glance to her left, the other doorway, where Nancy Ausonio stood, doing the same frantic scan of the room. "Where?" the woman whispered.

Franciscovich shook her head. She noticed about fifty wooden folding chairs arranged in neat rows. Four or five of them were lying on their backs or sides. But they didn't seem to be a barricade; they were randomly kicked over. To her right was a low stage. On it sat an amplifier and two speakers. A battered grand piano.

The young officers could see virtually everything in the room.

Except the perp.

"What happened, Nancy? Tell me what happened."

Ausonio didn't answer; like her partner she was looking around frantically, three-sixty, checking out every shadow, every piece of furniture, even though it was clear the man wasn't here.

Spooky . . .

The room was essentially a sealed cube. No windows. The air-conditioning and heating vents were only six inches across. A wooden ceiling, not acoustic tile. No trapdoors that she could see. No doors other than the main one Ausonio had used and the fire door that Franciscovich had entered through.

Where? Franciscovich mouthed.

Her partner mouthed something back. The policewoman couldn't decipher it but the message could be read in her face: I don't have a clue.

"Yo," a loud voice called from the doorway. They spun toward it, drawing targets on the empty lobby. "Ambulance and some other officers just got here." It was the security guard, hiding out of sight.

Heart slamming from the fright, Franciscovich called him inside.

He asked, "Is it, uhm . . . I mean, you get him?"

"He's not here," Ausonio said in a shaky voice.

"What?" The man peeked cautiously into the hall.

Franciscovich heard the voices of the officers and EMS techs arriving. The jangle of equipment. Still, the women couldn't bring themselves to join their fellow cops just yet. They stood transfixed in the middle of the recital space, both uneasy and bewildered, trying vainly to figure out how the killer had escaped from a room from which there *was* no escape.

Chapter Two

"He's listening to music."

"I'm not *listening* to music. The music happens to be on. That's all."

"Music, huh?" Lon Sellitto muttered as he walked into Lincoln Rhyme's bedroom. "That's a coincidence."

"He's developed a taste for jazz," Thom explained to the paunchy detective. "Surprised me, I have to tell you."

"As I said," Lincoln Rhyme continued petulantly, "I'm working and the music happens to be playing in the background. What do you mean, coincidence?"

Nodding at the flat-screen monitor in front of Rhyme's Flexicair bed, the slim, young aide, dressed in a white shirt, tan slacks and solid purple tie, said, "No, he's not working. Unless staring at the same page for an hour is work. He wouldn't let *me* get away with work like that."

"Command, turn page." The computer recognized Rhyme's voice and obeyed his order, slapping a new page of *Forensic Science Review* onto the monitor. He asked Thom acerbically, "Say, you want to quiz me on what I've been *staring* at? The composition of the top five exotic toxins found in recent terrorist laboratories in Europe? And how 'bout we put some money on the answers?"

"No, we have other things to do," the aide replied, referring to the various bodily functions that caregivers must attend to several times a day when their patients are quadriplegics like Lincoln Rhyme.

"We'll get to that in a few minutes," the criminalist said, enjoying a particularly energetic trumpet riff.

"We'll get to that *now.* If you'll excuse us for a moment, Lon."

"Yeah, sure." Large, rumpled Sellitto stepped into the corridor outside the second-floor bedroom of Rhyme's Central Park West town house. He closed the door.

As Thom expertly performed his duties

Lincoln Rhyme listened to the music and wondered: Coincidence?

Five minutes later Thom let Sellitto back into the bedroom. "Coffee?"

"Yeah. Could use some. Too fucking early to work on a Saturday."

The aide left.

"So, how do I look, Linc?" asked the pirouetting middle-aged detective, whose gray suit was typical of his wardrobe— made apparently from permanently wrinkled cloth.

"A fashion show?" Rhyme asked.

Coincidence?

Then his mind slipped back to the CD. How the hell does somebody play the trumpet so smoothly? How can you get that kind of sound from a metal instrument?

The detective continued: "I lost sixteen pounds. Rachel has me on a diet. Fat's the problem. You cut out fat, you'd be amazed how much weight you can lose."

"Fat, yes. I think we knew that, Lon. So . . . ?" Meaning, get to the point.

"Gotta bizarre case. Found a body a half hour ago at a music school up the street from here. I'm case officer and we could use some help."

Music school. And I'm listening to *music.* That's a piss-poor coincidence.

Sellitto ran through some of the facts: student killed, the perp was nearly collared but he got away through some kind of trapdoor that nobody could find.

Music was mathematical. That much Rhyme, a scientist, could understand. It was logical, it was perfectly structured. It was also, he reflected, infinite. An unlimited number of tunes could be written. You could never be bored writing music. He wondered how one went about it. Rhyme believed he had no creativity. He'd taken piano lessons when he was eleven or twelve but, even though he'd developed an enduring crush on Miss Osborne, the lessons themselves were a write-off. His fondest memories of the instrument were taking stroboscopic pictures of the resonating strings for a science-fair project.

"You with me, Linc?"

"A case, you were saying. Bizarre."

Sellitto gave more of the details, slowly corralling Rhyme's attention. "There's got to be some way outta the hall. But nobody from the school or our team can find it."

"How's the scene?"

"Still pretty virgin. Can we get Amelia to run it?"

Rhyme glanced at the clock. "She's tied up for another twenty minutes or so."

"That's not a problem," Sellitto said, patting his stomach as if he were searching for the lost weight. "I'll page her."

"Let's not distract her just yet."

"Why, what's she doing?"

"Oh, something dangerous," Rhyme said, concentrating once more on the silken voice of the trumpet. "What else?"

She smelled the wet brick of the tenement wall against her face.

Her palms sweated and, beneath the fiery red hair shoved up under her dusty issue hat, her scalp itched fiercely. Still, she remained completely motionless as a uniformed officer slipped up close beside her and planted his face against the brick too.

"Okay, here's the situation," the man said, nodding toward their right. He explained that just around the corner of the tenement was a vacant lot, in the middle of which was a getaway car that'd crashed a few minutes ago after a high-speed pursuit.

"Drivable?" Amelia Sachs asked.

"No. Hit a Dumpster and's out of com-mission. Three perps. They bailed but we got one in custody. One's in the car with some kind of Jesus-long hunting rifle. He wounded a patrolman."

"Condition?"

"Superficial."

"Pinned down?"

"No. Out of the perimeter. One building west of here."

She asked, "The third perp?"

The officer sighed. "Hell, he made it to the first floor of this building here." Nodding toward the tenement they were hugging. "It's a barricade. He's got a hostage. Preg-nant woman."

Sachs digested the flood of information as she shifted her weight from one foot to the other, to ease the pain of the arthritis in her joints. Damn, that hurt. She noticed her companion's name on his chest. "The hostage-taker's weapon, Wilkins?"

"Handgun. Unknown type."

"Where's our side?"

The young man pointed out two officers behind a wall at the back of the lot. "Then two more in front of the building, containing the H-T."

"Anybody call ESU?"

"I don't know. I lost my handy-talkie when we started taking fire."

"You in armor?"

"Negative. I was doing traffic stops. . . . What the hell're we going to do?"

She clicked her Motorola to a particular frequency and said, "Crime Scene Five Eight Eight Five to Supervisor."

A moment later: "This is Captain Seven Four. Go ahead."

"Ten-thirteen at a lot east of six-oh-five Delancey. Officer down. Need backup, EMS bus and ESU immediately. Two subjects, both armed. One with hostage; we'll need a negotiator."

"Roger, Five Eight Eight Five. Helicopter for observation?"

"Negative, Seven Four. One suspect has a high-powered rifle. And they're willing to target blues."

"We'll get backup there as soon as we can. But the Secret Service's closed up half of downtown 'cause the vice president's coming in from JFK. There'll be a delay.

Handle the situation at your discretion. Out."

"Roger. Out."

Vice president, she thought. Just lost *my* vote.

Wilkins shook his head. "But we can't get a negotiator near the apartment. Not with the shooter still in the car."

"I'm working on that," Sachs replied.

She edged to the corner of the tenement again and glanced at the car, a cheap low-rider with its nose against a Dumpster, doors open, revealing a thin man holding a rifle.

I'm working on that. . . .

She shouted, "You in the car, you're surrounded. We're going to open fire if you don't drop your weapon. Do it now!"

He crouched and aimed in her direction. She ducked for cover. On her Motorola she called the two officers in the back of the lot. "Are there hostages in the car?"

"None."

"You're sure?"

"Positive" was the officer's reply. "We got a good look before he started shooting."

"Okay. You got a shot?"

"Probably through the door."

"No, don't shoot blind. Go for position. But only if you've got cover all the way."

"Roger."

She saw the men move to a flanking position. A moment later one of the officers said, "I've got a shot to kill. Should I take it?"

"Stand by." Then she shouted, "You in the car. With the rifle. You have ten seconds or we'll open fire. Drop your weapon. You understand?" She repeated this in Spanish.

"Fuck you."

Which she took to be affirmative.

"Ten seconds," she shouted. "We're counting."

To the two officers she radioed, "Give him twenty. Then you're green-lighted."

At close to the ten-second mark, the man dropped the rifle and stood up, hands in the air. "No shoot, no shoot!"

"Keep those hands straight up in the air. Walk toward the corner of the building here. If you lower your hands you will be shot."

When he got to the corner Wilkins cuffed and searched him. Sachs remained crouched down. She said to the suspect, "The guy inside. Your buddy. Who is he?"

"I don't gotta tell you—"

"Yeah, you do gotta. Because if we take him out, which we *are* going to do, you'll go down for felony murder. Now, is that man in there worth forty-five years in Ossining?"

The man sighed.

"Come on," she snapped. "Name, address, family, what he likes for dinner, what's his mother's first name, he have relatives in the system—you can think of all kinds of real helpful stuff about him, I'll bet."

He sighed and started to talk; Sachs scribbled down the details.

Her Motorola crackled. The hostage negotiator and the ESU team had just showed up in front of the building. She handed her notes to Wilkins. "Get those to the negotiator."

She read the rifleman his rights, thinking, Had she handled the situation the best way she could? Had she endangered lives unnecessarily? Should she have checked on the wounded officer herself?

Five minutes later, the supervising captain walked around the corner of the building. He smiled. "The H-T released the woman. No injuries. We've got three collared. The wounded officer'll be okay. Just a scratch."

A policewoman with short blond hair poking out from under her regulation hat joined them. "Hey, check it out. We got a bonus." She held up a large Baggie full of white powder and another containing pipes and other drug paraphernalia.

As the captain looked it over, nodding with approval, Sachs asked, "That was in their car?"

"Naw. I found it in a Ford across the street. I was interviewing the owner as a witness and he started sweating and looking all nervous so I searched his car."

"Where was it parked?" Sachs asked.

"In his garage."

"Did you call in a warrant?"

"No. Like I say, he was acting nervous and I could see a corner of the bag from the sidewalk. That's probable cause."

"Nope." Sachs was shaking her head. "It's an illegal search."

"Illegal? We pulled this guy over last week for speeding and saw a kilo of pot in the back. We busted *him* okay."

"It's different on the street. There's a lesser expectation of privacy in a mobile vehicle on public roads. All you need for an arrest then is probable cause. When a car's on private property, even if you see drugs, you need a warrant."

"That's crazy," the policewoman said defensively. "He's got ten ounces of pure coke here. He's a balls-forward dealer. Narcotics spends months trying to collar somebody like this."

The captain said to Sachs, "You sure about this, Officer?"

"Positive."

"Recommendation?"

Sachs said, "Confiscate the stuff, put the fear of God into the perp and give his tag number and stats to Narcotics." Then she glanced at the policewoman. "And you better take a refresher course in search and seizure."

The woman officer started to argue but Sachs wasn't paying attention. She was surveying the vacant lot, where the perps' car rested against the Dumpster. She squinted at the vehicle.

"Officer—" the captain began.

She ignored him and said to Wilkins, "You said *three* perps?"

"That's right."

"How do you know?"

"That was the report from the jewelry store they hit."

She stepped into the rubble-filled lot, pulling out her Glock. "Look at the getaway car," she snapped.

"Jesus," Wilkins said.

All the doors were open. *Four* men had bailed.

Dropping into a crouch, she scanned the lot and aimed her gun toward the only possible hiding place nearby: a short cul-de-sac behind the Dumpster.

"Weapon!" she cried, almost before she saw the motion.

Everyone around her turned as the large, T-shirted man with a shotgun jogged out of the lot, making a run for the street.

Sachs's Glock was centered on his chest as he broke cover. "Drop the weapon!" she ordered.

He hesitated a moment then grinned and began to swing it toward the officers.

She pushed her Glock forward.

And in a cheerful voice, she said, "Bang, bang. . . . You're dead."

The shotgunner stopped and laughed. He shook his head in admiration. "Damn good. I thought I was home free." The stubby gun over his shoulder, he strolled to the cluster of fellow cops beside the tenement. The other "suspect," the man who'd been in the car, turned his back so that the cuffs could be removed. Wilkins released him.

The "hostage," played by a very unpregnant Latina officer Sachs had known for years, joined them too. She clapped Sachs on the back. "Nice work, Amelia, saving my ass."

Sachs kept a solemn face, though she was pleased. She felt like a student who'd just aced an important exam.

Which was, in effect, exactly what had happened.

Amelia Sachs was pursuing a new goal. Her father, Herman, had been a portable, a beat cop in the Patrol Services Division, all his life. Sachs now had the same rank and might've been content to remain there for another few years before moving up in the department but after the September 11 attacks she'd decided she wanted to do more for her city. So she'd submitted the paperwork to be promoted to detective sergeant.

No group of law enforcers has fought crime like NYPD detectives. Their tradition went back to tough, brilliant Inspector

Thomas Byrnes, named to head up the fledgling Detective Bureau in the 1880s. Byrnes's arsenal included threats, head-knocking and subtle deductions—he once broke a major theft ring by tracing a tiny fiber found at a crime scene. Under Byrnes's flamboyant guidance the detectives in the bureau became known as the Immortals and they dramatically reduced the level of crime in a city as freewheeling back then as the Wild West.

Officer Herman Sachs was a collector of police department memorabilia, and not long before he died he gave his daughter one of his favorite artifacts: a battered notebook actually used by Byrnes to jot notes about investigations. When Sachs was young—and her mother wasn't around—her father would read aloud the more legible passages and the two of them would make up stories around them.

October 12, 1883. The other leg has been found! Slaggardy's coal bin, Five Pts. Expect Cotton Williams's confession forthwith.

Given its prestigious status (and lucrative pay for law enforcement), it was ironic that women found *more* opportunities in the Detective Bureau than in any other division of the NYPD. If Thomas Byrnes was the male detective icon, Mary Shanley was the female—and one of Sachs's personal heroines. Busting crime throughout the 1930s, Shanley was a boisterous, uncompromising cop, who once said, "You have the gun to use, and you may as well use it." Which she did with some frequency. After years of combating crime in Midtown she retired as a detective first-grade.

Sachs, however, wanted to be more than a detective, which is just a job specialty; she wanted rank too. In the NYPD, as in most police forces, one becomes a detective on the basis of merit and experience. To become a sergeant, though, the applicant goes through an arduous triathlon of exams: written, oral and—what Sachs had just endured—an assessment exercise, a simulation to test practical skills at personnel management, community sensitivities and judgment under fire.

The captain, a soft-spoken veteran who resembled Laurence Fishburne, was the primary assessor for the exercise and had been taking notes on her performance.

"Okay, Officer," he said, "we'll write up our results and they'll be attached to your review. But let me just say a word unofficially." Consulting his notebook. "Your threat assessment regarding civilians and officers was perfect. Calls for backup were timely and appropriate. Your deployment of personnel negated any chance the perpetrators would escape from the containment situation and yet minimized exposure. You called the illegal drug search right. And getting the personal information from the one suspect for the hostage negotiator was a nice touch. We didn't think about making that part of the exercise. But we will now. Then, at the end, well, frankly, we never thought you'd determine there was another perp in hiding. We had it planned that he'd shoot Officer Wilkins here and then we'd see how you'd handle an officer-down situation and organize a fleeing felon apprehension."

The officialese vanished and he smiled. "But you nailed the bastard."

Bang, bang.

Then he asked, "You've done the written and orals, right?"

"Yessir. Should have the results any day now."

"My group'll complete our assessment

evaluation and send that to the board with our recommendations. You can stand down now."

"Yessir."

The cop who'd played the last bad guy—the one with the shotgun—wandered up to her. He was a good-looking Italian, half a generation out of the Brooklyn docks, she judged, and had a boxer's muscles. A dirty stubble of beard covered his cheeks and chin. He wore a big-bore chrome automatic high on his trim hip and his cocky smile brought her close to suggesting he might want to use the gun's reflection as a mirror to shave.

"I gotta tell ya—I've done a dozen as-sessments and that was the best I ever seen, babe."

She laughed in surprise at the word. There were certainly cavemen left in the de-partment—from Patrol Services to corner offices at Police Plaza—but they tended to be more condescending than openly sexist. Sachs hadn't heard a "babe" or "honey" from a male cop in at least a year.

"Let's stick with 'Officer,' you don't mind."

"No, no, no," he said, laughing. "You can chill now. The AE's over."

"How's that?"

"When I said 'babe,' it's not like it's a part of the assessment. You don't have to, you know, deal with it official or anything. I'm just saying it 'cause I was impressed. And 'cause you're . . . you know." He smiled into her eyes, his charm as shiny as his pistol. "I don't do compliments much. Coming from me, that's something."

'Cause you're you know.

"Hey, you're not pissed or anything, are you?" he asked.

"Not pissed at all. But it's still 'Officer.' That's what you call me and what I'll call you."

At least to your face.

"Hey, I didn't mean any offense or anything. You're a pretty girl. And I'm a guy. You know what that's like. . . . So."

"So," she replied and started away.

He stepped in front of her, frowning. "Hey, hold on. This isn't going too good. Look, let me buy you a coffee. You'll like me when you get to know me."

"Don't bet on it," one of his buddies called, laughing.

The Babe Man good-naturedly gave him the finger then turned back to Sachs.

Which is when her pager beeped and she looked down to see Lincoln Rhyme's number on the screen. The word "URGENT" appeared after it.

"Gotta go," she said.

"So no time for that coffee?" he asked, a fake pout on his handsome face.

"No time."

"Well, how 'bout a phone number?"

She made a pistol with her index finger and thumb and aimed it at him. "Bang, bang," she said. And trotted toward her yellow Camaro.

Chapter Three

This is a school?

Wheeling a large black crime-scene suitcase behind her, Amelia Sachs walked through the dim corridor. She smelled mold and old wood. Dusty webs had coagulated near the high ceiling and scales of green paint curled from the walls. How could anybody study music here? It was a setting for one of the Anne Rice novels that Sachs's mother read.

"Spooky," one of the responding officers had muttered, only half jokingly.

That said it all.

A half-dozen cops—four patrol officers and two in soft clothes—stood near a double doorway at the end of the hall. Disheveled Lon Sellitto, head down and hand clutching one of his notepads, was talking to a guard. Like the walls and floors the guard's outfit was dusty and stained.

Through the open doorway she glimpsed another dim space, in the middle of which was a light-colored form. The victim.

To the CS tech walking beside her she said, "We'll need lights. A couple of sets." The young man nodded and headed back to the RRV—the crime scene rapid response vehicle, a station wagon filled with forensic collection equipment. It sat outside, half on the sidewalk, where he'd parked it after the drive here (probably at a more leisurely pace than Sachs in her 1969 Camaro SS, which had averaged 70 mph en route to the school from the assessment exercise).

Sachs studied the young blonde woman, lying on her back ten feet away, belly arched up because her bound hands were underneath her. Even in the dimness of the school lobby Sachs's quick eyes noted the deep ligature marks on her neck and the blood on her lips and chin—probably from biting her tongue, a common occurrence in strangulations.

Automatically she also observed: emerald-colored studs for earrings, shabby running shoes. No apparent robbery, sexual molestation or mutilation. No wedding ring.

"Who was first officer?"

A tall woman with short brunette hair, her name tag reading D. FRANCISCOVICH, said, "We were." A nod toward her blonde partner. N. AUSONIO. Their eyes were troubled and Franciscovich played a brief rhythm on her holster with thumb and fingers. Ausonio kept glancing at the body. Sachs guessed this was their first homicide.

The two patrol officers give their account of what had happened. Finding the perp, a flash of light, his disappearing, a barricade. Then he was gone.

"You said he claimed to have a hostage?"

"That's what he said," Ausonio offered. "But everybody in the school's accounted for. We're sure he was bluffing."

"Victim?"

"Svetlana Rasnikov," Ausonio said. "Twenty-four. Student."

Sellitto turned away from the security guard. He said to Sachs, "Bedding and Saul're interviewing everybody in the building here this morning."

She nodded toward the scene. "Who's been inside?"

Sellitto said, "The first officers." Nodding toward the women. "Then two medics and two ESU. They backed out as soon as they cleared it. Scene's still pretty clean."

"The guard was inside too," Ausonio said. "But only for a minute. We got him out as soon as we could."

"Good," Sachs said. "Witnesses?"

Ausonio said, "There was a janitor outside the room when we got here."

"He didn't see anything," Franciscovich added.

Sachs said, "I still need to see the soles of his shoes for comparison. Could one of you find him for me?"

"Sure." Ausonio wandered off.

From one of the black suitcases Sachs extracted a zippered clear plastic case. She opened it and pulled out a white Tyvek jumpsuit. Donning it, she pulled the hood over her head. Then gloves. The outfit was standard issue now for all forensics techs at the NYPD; it prevented substances—trace, hair, epithelial skin cells and foreign matter—from sloughing off her body and contaminating the scene. The suit had booties but she still did what Rhyme always insisted on—put rubber bands on her feet to distinguish her prints from the victim's and the perp's.

Mounting the earphones on her head and adjusting the stalk mike, she hooked up her Motorola. She called in a landline patch and a moment later a complex arrangement of communications systems brought the low voice of Lincoln Rhyme into her ear.

"Sachs, you there?"

"Yep. It was just like you said—they had him cornered and he disappeared."

He chuckled. "And now they want us to find him. Do we have to clean up for everybody's mistakes? Hold on a minute. Command, volume lower . . . lower." Music in the background diminished.

The tech who'd accompanied Sachs down the gloomy corridor returned with tall lamps on tripods. She set them up in the lobby and clicked the switch.

There's a lot of debate about the proper way to process a scene. Generally investigators agree that less is more, though most departments still use teams of CS searchers. Before his accident Lincoln Rhyme, however, had run most scenes alone and he insisted that Amelia Sachs do the same. With other searchers around, you tend to be distracted and are often less vigilant because you feel—even if only subconsciously—that your partner will find what you miss.

But there was another reason for solitary searching. Rhyme recognized that there's a macabre intimacy about criminal violation. A crime scene searcher working alone is better able to forge a mental relationship with the victim and the perpetrator, gather better insights into what is the relevant evidence and where it might be found.

It was into this difficult state of mind that Amelia Sachs now slipped as she gazed at the body of the young woman, lying on the floor, next to a fiberboard table.

Near the body were a spilled cup of coffee, sheet music, a music case and a piece of the woman's silver flute, which she'd apparently been in the act of assembling when the killer flipped the rope around her neck. In her death grip she clutched another cylinder of the instrument. Had she intended to use it as a weapon?

Or did the desperate young woman just want to feel something familiar and comforting in her fingers as she died?

"I'm at the body, Rhyme," she said as she snapped digital pictures of the corpse.

"Go ahead."

"She's on her back—but the respondings found her on her abdomen. They turned her over to give her CPR. Injuries consistent with strangulation." Sachs now delicately rolled the woman back onto her belly. "Hands're in some kind of old-fashioned cuffs. I don't recognize them. Her watch is broken. Stopped at exactly eight A.M. Doesn't look accidental." She closed her gloved hand around the woman's narrow wrist. It was shattered. "Yep, Rhyme, he stomped on it. And it's nice. A Seiko. Why break it? Why not steal it?"

"Good question, Sachs. . . . Might be a clue, might be nothing."

Which was as good a slogan for forensic science as any, she reflected.

"One of the respondings cut the rope around her neck. She missed the knot." Officers should never cut through the knot to remove a cord from a strangulation victim; it can reveal a great deal of information about the person who tied it.

Sachs then used a tape roller to collect trace evidence—recent forensic thinking was that a portable vacuum cleaner, which resembled a Dustbuster, picked up too much trace. Most CS teams were switching to rollers similar to dog-hair removers. She bagged the trace and used a vic kit to take hair combings and nail scraping samples from the woman's body.

Sachs said, "I'm going to walk the grid."

The phrase—of Lincoln Rhyme's own creation—came from his preference for searching a crime scene. The grid pattern is the most comprehensive method: back and forth in one direction, then turning perpendicular and covering the same ground again, always remembering to examine the ceiling and walls as well as the ground or floor.

She began the search now, looking for discarded or dropped objects, rolling for trace, taking electrostatic prints of shoe-prints and digital photos. The photo team would make a comprehensive still and video record of the scene but getting those images took time and Rhyme always insisted on having some photographic record available instantly.

"Officer?" Sellitto called.

She glanced back.

"Just wondering. . . . Since we don't know where this asshole got to, you want some backup in there?"

"Nope," she said, silently thanking him for reminding her that there was a missing murderer last seen nearby. Another of Lincoln Rhyme's crime scene aphorisms: search well but watch your back. She tapped the butt of her Glock to remind herself exactly where it was in case she needed to draw fast—the holster rode slightly higher when she wore the Tyvek jumpsuit—and continued the search.

"Okay, got something," she told Rhyme a moment later. "In the lobby. About ten feet away from the victim. Piece of black cloth. Silk. I mean, it *appears* to be silk. It's on top of a part of the vic's flute so it has to be his or hers."

"Interesting," Rhyme mused. "Wonder what *that's* about."

The lobby yielded nothing else and she entered the performance space itself, her hand continuing to stray to the butt of her Glock. She relaxed momentarily, seeing that there was in fact absolutely no hiding place where a perp could be, no secret doorways or exits. But as she started on the grid here she felt a growing sense of discomfort.

Spooky . . .

"Rhyme, this is strange. . . ."

"I can't hear you, Sachs."

She realized that in her uneasiness she'd been whispering.

"There's burned string tied around the chairs that're lying on the ground. Fuses too, it looks like. I smell nitrate and sulfur residue. The reportings said he fired a round. But it's not the smell of smokeless powder. It's something else. Ah, okay. . . . It's a little gray firecracker. Maybe that was the gunshot they heard. . . . Hold on. There's something else—under a chair. It's a small green circuit board with a speaker attached to it."

"'Small'?" Rhyme asked caustically. "A foot is small compared with an acre. An acre's small compared with a hundred acres, Sachs."

"Sorry. Measures about two inches by five."

"That'd be big compared with a dime, now, wouldn't it?"

Got the message, thank you very much, she replied silently.

She bagged everything, then left by the second door—the fire door—and electro-staticked and photographed the footprints she found there. Finally, she took control samples to compare against the trace found on the victim and where the unsub had walked. "Got everything, Rhyme. I'll be back in a half hour."

"And the trapdoors, the secret passages everybody's talking about?"

"I can't find any."

"All right, come on home, Sachs."

She returned to the lobby and let Photo and Latents take over the scene. She found Franciscovich and Ausonio by the doorway. "You find the janitor?" she asked. "I need to look at his shoes."

Ausonio shook her head. "He told the guard he had to take his wife to work. I left a message with maintenance for him to call."

Her partner said solemnly, "Hey, Officer, we were talking, Nancy and me? And we don't want this scumbag to get away. If there's anything more we can do, you know, to follow up, let us know."

Sachs understood exactly how they felt. "I'll see what I can do," she told them.

Sellitto's radio crackled and he took the call. Listened for a moment. "It's the Hardy Boys. They've finished interviewing the wits and're in the main lobby."

Sachs, Sellitto and the two patrolwomen returned to the front of the school. There they joined Bedding and Saul, one of them tall, one short, one with freckles, one with a clear complexion. These were detectives from the Big Building who specialized in canvassing—post-crime interviewing of witnesses.

"We talked to the seven people here this morning."

"Plus the guard."

"No teachers—"

"—only students."

Also called the Twins, despite very different appearances, the duo were skilled at double-teaming perps and witnesses alike. It got too confusing if you tried to tell them apart. Lump them together and consider them one person, they were a lot easier to understand.

"The information was not the most illuminating."

"For one thing everybody was freaked out."

"The location's not helping." A nod toward a wad of cobwebs hanging from the dark, water-stained ceiling.

"Nobody knew the victim very well. When she got here this morning she walked to the recital room with a friend. She—"

"The friend."

"—didn't see anybody inside. They stood in the lobby for five, ten minutes, talking. The friend left around eight."

"So," said Rhyme, who'd overheard on the radio, "he was inside the lobby waiting for her."

"The victim," the shorter of the two sandy-haired detectives said, "had come over here from Georgia—"

"That's the Russia Georgia, not the peachtree Georgia."

"—about two months ago. She was kind of a loner."

"The consulate's contacting her family."

"All the other students were in different practice rooms today and none of them heard anything or saw anybody they didn't know."

"Why wasn't Svetlana in a practice room?" Sachs asked.

"Her friend said Svetlana liked the acoustics better in the hall."

"Husband, boyfriend, girlfriend?" Sachs asked, thinking of rule number one in homicide investigations: the doer usually knows the doee.

"None that the other students knew."

"How'd he get into the building?" Rhyme asked and Sachs relayed the question.

The guard said, "Only door's open is the front one. We got fire doors, course. But you can't open them from the outside."

"And he'd have to walk past you, right?"

"And sign in. *And* get his picture took by the camera."

Sachs glanced up. "There's a security camera, Rhyme, but it looks like the lens hasn't been cleaned in months."

They gathered behind the desk. The guard punched buttons and played the tape. Bedding and Saul had vetted seven of the people. But they agreed that one person—a brown-haired, bearded older man in jeans and bulky jacket—hadn't been among those they'd talked to.

"That's him," Franciscovich said. "That's the killer." Nancy Ausonio nodded.

On the fuzzy tape he was signing the register book then walking inside. The guard glanced at the book, but not at the man's face, as he signed it.

"Did you get a look at him?" Sachs asked.

"Didn't pay no attention," he said defensively. "If they sign I let them in. That's all I gotta do. That's my job. I'm here mostly to keep folk from walking *out* with our stuff."

"We've got his signature at least, Rhyme. And a name. They'll be fake but at least it's a handwriting sample. Which line did he sign on?" Sachs asked, picking up the sign-in book with latex-clad fingers.

They ran the tape, fast-forward, from the beginning. The killer was the fourth person to sign the book. But in the fourth slot was a woman's name.

Rhyme called, "Count all the people who signed."

Sachs told the guard to do so and they watched nine people fill in their names—eight students, including the victim, and her killer.

"Nine people sign, Rhyme. But there are only eight names on the list."

"How'd that happen?" Sellitto asked.

Rhyme: "Ask the guard if he's sure the perp signed. Maybe he faked it."

She put the question to the placid man.

"Yeah, he did. I saw it. I don't always look at their faces but I make sure they sign."

That's all I gotta do. That's my job.

Sachs shook her head and dug into the cuticle of her thumb with another nail.

"Well, bring me the sign-in book with everything else and we'll have a look at it here," Rhyme said.

In the corner of the room a young Asian woman stood hugging herself and looking out the uneven leaded glass. She turned and looked at Sachs. "I heard you talking. You said, I mean, it sounded like you didn't know if he got out of the building after he . . . afterward. You think he's still here?"

"No, I don't," Sachs said. "I just meant we're not sure *how* he escaped."

"But if you don't know that, then it means he *could* still be hiding here, somewhere. Waiting for somebody else. And you don't have any idea where he is."

Sachs gave her a reassuring smile. "We'll have plenty of officers around until we get to the bottom of what happened. You don't have to worry."

Though she was thinking: The girl was

absolutely right. Yes, he could be here, waiting for somebody else.

And, no, we don't have a clue who or where he is.

Chapter Four

And now, Revered Audience, we'll take a short intermission.

Enjoy the memory of the Lazy Hangman . . . and relish the anticipation of what's coming up soon.

Relax.

Our next act will begin shortly. . . .

The man walked along Broadway on the Upper West Side of Manhattan. When he reached one street corner he stopped, as if he'd forgotten something, and stepped into the shadow of a building. He pulled his cell phone off his belt and lifted it to his ear. As he spoke, smiling from time to time, the way people do on mobiles, he gazed around him casually, also a common practice for cell-phone users.

He was not, however, actually making a

call. He was looking for any sign that he'd been followed from the music school.

Malerick's present appearance was very different from his incarnation when he'd escaped from the school earlier that morning. He was now blond and beardless and wearing a jogging outfit with a high-necked athletic shirt. Had passersby been looking they might have noticed a few oddities in his physique: leathery scar tissue peeked over the top of his collar and along his neck, and two fingers—little and ring—of his left hand were fused together.

But no one *was* looking. Because his gestures and expressions were natural, and—as all illusionists know—acting naturally makes you invisible.

Finally content that he hadn't been followed, he resumed his casual gait, turning the corner down a cross street, and continued along the tree-lined sidewalk to his apartment. Around him were only a few joggers and two or three locals returning home with the *Times* and Zabar's bags, looking forward to coffee, a leisurely hour with the newspaper and perhaps some unhurried weekend morning sex.

Malerick walked up the stairs to the apartment he'd rented here a few months ago, a dark, quiet building very different from his house and workshop in the desert outside Las Vegas. He made his way to the apartment in the back.

As I was saying, our next act will begin shortly.

For now, Revered Audience, gossip about the illusion you've just seen, enjoy some conversation with those around you, try to guess what's next on the bill.

Our second routine will involve very different skills to test our performer but will be, I assure you, every bit as compelling as the Lazy Hangman.

These words and dozens more looped automatically through Malerick's mind. *Revered Audience. . . .* He spoke to this imaginary assembly constantly. (He sometimes heard their applause and shouts of laughter and, occasionally, gasps of horror.) A white noise of words, in that broad theatrical intonation a greasepainted ringmaster or a Victorian illusionist would use. Patter, it was called—a monologue directed to the audience to give them information they need to know to make a trick work, to build rapport with the audience. And to disarm and distract them too.

After the fire, Malerick cut off most contact with fellow human beings, and his imagined Revered Audience slowly replaced them, becoming his constant companions. The patter soon began to fill his waking thoughts and dreams and threatened, he sometimes felt, to drive him completely insane. At the same time, though, it gave him intense comfort, knowing that he hadn't been left completely alone in life after the tragedy three years ago. His revered audience was always with him.

The apartment smelled of cheap varnish and a curious meaty aroma rising from the wallpaper and floors. The place had come lightly furnished: inexpensive couches and armchairs, a functional dining room table, currently set for one. The bedrooms, on the other hand, were packed—filled with the tools of the illusionist's trade: props, rigs, ropes, costumes, latex molding equipment, wigs, bolts of cloth, a sewing machine, paints, squibs, makeup, circuit boards, wires, batteries, flash paper and cotton, spools of fuse, woodworking tools . . . a hundred other items.

He made herbal tea and sat at the dining room table, sipping the weak beverage and eating fruit and a low-fat granola bar. Illusion is a physical art and one's act is only as good as one's body. Eating healthy food and working out were vital to success.

He was pleased with this morning's act. He'd killed the first performer easily—recalling with shivery pleasure how she'd stiffened with shock when he'd appeared behind her and slipped the rope around her neck. Never a clue he'd been waiting in the corner, under the black silk, for a half hour. The surprise entrance by the police—well, that'd shaken him. But like all good illusionists Malerick had prepared an out, which he'd executed perfectly.

He finished his breakfast and took the cup into the kitchen, washed it carefully and set it in a rack to dry. He was meticulous in all his ways; his mentor, a fierce, obsessive, humorless illusionist, had beaten discipline into him.

The man now went into the larger of the bedrooms and put on the videotape he'd made of the site of the next performance. He'd seen this tape a dozen times and, though he virtually had it memorized, he was now going to study it again. (His mentor had also beaten into him—literally sometimes—the importance of the 100:1 rule. You rehearse one hundred minutes for every one minute onstage.)

As he watched the tape he pulled a velvet-covered performing table toward him. Not watching his hands, Malerick practiced some simple card maneuvers: the False Dovetail Shuffle, the Three-Pile False Cut then some trickier ones: the Reverse Sliparound, the Glide and the Deal-Off Force. He ran through some actual tricks, complicated ones, like Stanley Palm's Ghost Cards, Maldo's famous Six-Card Mystery and several others by the famous card master and actor Ricky Jay, others by Cardini.

Malerick also did some of the card tricks that had been in Harry Houdini's early repertoire. Most people think of Houdini as an escapist but the performer had actually been a well-rounded magician, who performed illusion—large-scale stage tricks like vanishing assistants and elephants—as well as parlor magic. Houdini had been an important influence in his life. When he first started performing, in his teens, Malerick used as a performing name "Young Houdini." The "erick" portion of his present name was both a remnant of his former life—his life before the fire—and an homage to Houdini himself, who'd been born Ehrich Weisz. As for the prefix "Mal" a magician might suspect that it was taken from another world-famous performer, Max Breit, who performed under the name Malini. But in fact, Malerick had picked the three letters because they came from the Latin root for "evil," which reflected the dark nature of his brand of illusion.

He now studied the tape, measuring angles, noting windows and the location of possible witnesses, blocking out his positions as all good performers do. And as he watched, the cards in his fingers riffled together in lightning-fast shuffles that hissed like snakes. The kings and jacks and queens and jokers and all the rest of the cards slithered onto the black velvet and then seemed to defy gravity as they leaped back into his strong hands, where they vanished from sight. Watching this impromptu performance, an audience would shake their heads, half-convinced that reality had given way to delusion, that a human being couldn't possibly do what they were observing.

But the truth was the opposite: the card tricks Malerick was now performing absently on the plush black cloth were not miraculous at all; they were merely carefully rehearsed exercises in dexterity and perception, governed by mundane rules of physics.

Oh, yes, Revered Audience, what you've seen and what you're about to see are very real.

As real as fire burning flesh.

As real as a rope knotted around a young girl's white neck.

As real as the circuit of the clock hands moving slowly toward the horror that our next performer is about to experience.

"Hey, there."

The young woman sat down beside the bed where her mother lay. Out the window in the manicured courtyard she saw a tall oak tree on the trunk of which grew a tentacle of ivy in a shape that she'd had interpreted a number of ways over the past months. Today the anemic vine wasn't a dragon or a flock of birds or a soldier. It was simply a city plant struggling to survive.

"So. How you feeling, Mum?" Kara asked.

The appellation grew out of one of the family's many vacations—this one to England. Kara had given them all nicknames: "His Kingness" and the "Queenly Mum" for her parents. She herself had been the "Royal Kid."

"Just fine, darling. And how's life treating you?"

"Better than some, not as good as others. Hey, you like?" Kara held up her hand to show off her short, evenly filed fingernails, which were black as a grand piano's finish.

"Lovely, darling. I was getting a bit tired of the pink. You see it everywhere nowadays. Awfully conventional."

Kara stood and adjusted the down pillow under her mother's head. Then sat again and sipped from the large Starbucks container; coffee was her sole drug but the addiction was intense, not to mention expensive, and this was her third cup of the morning.

Her hair was cut in a boyish style, currently colored auburn-purple, having been pretty much every color of the spectrum at some point in her years in New York City. Pixieish, some people said of the cut, a description she hated; Kara herself described the do simply as "convenient." She could be out her door minutes after stepping from the shower—a true benefit for someone who tended not to get to bed before 3:00 A.M. and who was definitely not a morning person.

Today she wore black stretch pants and, though she was not much over five feet, flat shoes. Her dark purple top was sleeveless and revealed taut, cut muscles. Kara had attended a college where art and politics took precedence over the cult of the physique but after graduating from Sarah Lawrence she'd joined Gold's Gym and was now a regular weight-pumper and treadmill runner. One would expect an eight-year resident of bohemian Greenwich Village, hovering somewhere in her late twenties, to dabble in body art or to sport at least a latent ring or stud but Kara's very white skin was tattoo-free and unpierced.

"Now, check this out, Mum. I've got a show tomorrow. One of Mr. Balzac's little things. You know."

"I remember."

"But this time it's different. This time he's letting me go on solo. I'm warm-up and main bill rolled into one."

"Really, honey?"

"True as toast."

Outside the doorway Mr. Geldter shuffled past. "Hello, there."

Kara nodded at him. She recalled that when her mother had first come to Stuyvesant Manor, one of the city's best aging facilities, the woman and the widower had caused quite a stir.

"They think we're shacking up," she'd told her daughter in a whisper.

"Are you?" Kara had asked, thinking it was about time her mother struck up a relationship with a man after five years of widowhood.

"Of course not!" her mother had hissed, truly angry. "What a thing to suggest." (The incident defined the woman perfectly: a hint of the bawdy was fine but there was a very clear line—established arbitrarily—past which you would become The Enemy, even if you were her flesh and blood.)

Kara continued, rocking forward excitedly and telling her mother in an animated way about what she planned for tomorrow. As she spoke she studied her mother closely, the skin oddly smooth for a woman in her mid-seventies and as healthy pink as a crying baby's, hair mostly gray but with plenty of defiant wiry black strands scattered throughout. The staff beautician had done it up in a stylish bun. "Anyway, Mum, some friends'll be there and it'd be great if you could come too."

"I'll try."

Kara, now sitting on the very edge of the armchair, realized suddenly that her fists were clenched, her body a knot of tension. Her breath was coming in shallow sibilant gasps.

I'll try. . . .

Kara closed her eyes, filling with slivers of tears. Goddamnit!

I'll try. . . .

No, no, no, that's all wrong, she thought angrily. Her mother wouldn't say, "I'll try." That wasn't her sort of dialogue. It might be: "I'll be there, hons. In the first row." Or she'd say frostily, "Well, I *can't* tomorrow. You should've let me know earlier."

Whatever else about her mother, there was nothing I'll-try about her. Balls-out for you, or hell-to-pay against.

Except now—when the woman was hardly a human being at all. At most a child, sleeping with her eyes open.

The conversation Kara had just had with the woman had occurred only in the girl's hopeful imagination. Well, Kara's portion had been real. But her mother's, from the *Just fine, darling. And how's life treating you?* to the glitch of *I'll try,* had been ginned up by Kara herself.

No, her mother hadn't said a single word today. Or during yesterday's visit. Or the one before. She'd lain beside the ivy window in some kind of waking coma. Some days she was like that. On others, the woman might be fully awake but babbling scary nonsense that only attested to the success of the invisible army moving relentlessly through her brain, torching memory and reason.

But there was a more pernicious part of the tragedy. Once in a rare while, there'd be a fragile moment of clarity, which, brief though it was, perfectly negated her despair. Just when Kara had come to accept the worst—that the mother she knew was gone forever—the women would return, just like in the days before the cerebral hemorrhage. And Kara's defenses vanished, the same way an abused woman forgives her slugging husband at the slightest hint of contrition. At moments like that she'd convince herself that her mother was improving.

The doctors said that there was virtually no hope for this, of course. Still, the doctors hadn't been at her mother's bedside when, several months ago, the woman woke up and turned suddenly to Kara. "Hi there, hons. I ate those cookies you brought me yesterday. You put in extra pecans the way I like them. And heck with the calories." A girlish smile. "Oh, I'm glad you're here. I wanted to tell you what Mrs. Brandon did last night. With the remote control."

Kara had blinked, stunned. Because, damn, she *had* brought her mother pecan sandies the day before and *had* stocked them with extra nuts. And, yes, crazy Mrs. Brandon from the fifth floor *had* copped a remote and bounced the signal off the windows next door into the nursing home's lounge, confounding the residents for a half hour by changing channels and volume like a poltergeist.

There! Who needed better evidence than

this that her vibrant mother, her *real* mother remained within the injured shell of a body and could someday escape.

But the next day Kara had found the woman staring at her daughter suspiciously, asking why she was there and what she wanted. If this was about the electric bill for twenty-two dollars and fifteen cents she'd paid it and had the canceled check for proof. Since the pecan-sandy/remote-control performance there'd been no encores.

Kara now touched her mother's arm, warm, wrinkle-free, baby pink. Sensing what she always did here on her daily visits: the numbing trilogy of wishing that the woman would mercifully die, wishing that she'd come back to her vibrant life—and wishing that Kara herself could escape from the terrible burden of wanting both of those irreconcilable choices.

A glance at her watch. Late for work, as always. Mr. Balzac would *not* be happy. Saturday was their busiest day. She drained the coffee cup, pitched it out and walked into the hallway.

A large black woman in a white uniform lifted a hand in greeting. "Kara! How long you been here?" A broad smile in a broad face.

"Twenty minutes."

"I would've come by and visited," Jaynene said. "She still awake?"

"No. She was out when I got here."

"Oh, I'm sorry."

"Was she talking before?" Kara asked.

"Yep. Just little things. Couldn't tell if she was with us or not. Seemed like it. . . . This is some gorgeous day, hm? Sephie and me, we're gonna take her walking in the court-yard later if she's awake. She likes it. She always does better after that."

"I've gotta get to work," Kara told the nurse. "Hey, I'm doing a show tomorrow. At the store. Remember where it is?"

"Sure do. What time?"

"Four. Come on by."

"I'm off early tomorrow. I'll be there. We'll drink some more of those peach margaritas after. Like last time."

"That'll work," Kara replied. "Hey, bring Pete."

The woman scowled. "Girl, nothing per-sonal, but th'only way that man'll see you on Sunday is if you're playing the halftime show for the Knicks or the Lakers an' it's on network TV."

Kara said, "From your mouth to God's ear."

Chapter Five

One hundred years ago a moderately successful financier might've called this place home.

Or the owner of a small haberdashery in the luxurious shopping neighborhood of Fourteenth Street.

Or possibly a politician connected with Tammany Hall, savvy in the timeless art of growing rich through public office.

The present owner of the Central Park West town house, however, didn't know, or care, about its provenance. Nor would the Victorian furnishings or subdued fin de siècle objets d'art that had once graced these rooms appeal to Lincoln Rhyme at all. He enjoyed what surrounded him now: a disarray of sturdy tables, swivel stools, computers, scientific devices—a density gradient rack, a gas chromatograph/mass spectrometer, microscopes, plastic boxes in myriad colors, beakers, jars, thermometers, propane tanks, goggles, latched black or gray cases of odd shapes, which suggested they contained esoteric musical instruments.

And wires.

Wires and cables everywhere, covering much of the limited square footage of the room, some tidily coiled and connecting adjacent pieces of machinery, some disappearing through ragged holes shamefully cut into the hard-earned smoothness of century-old plaster-and-lath walls.

Lincoln Rhyme himself was largely wireless now. Advances in infrared and radio technology had linked a microphone on his wheelchair—and on his bed upstairs—to environmental control units and computers. He drove his Storm Arrow with his left ring finger on an MKIV touchpad but all the other commands, from phone calls to email to slapping the image from his compound microscope onto computer monitors, could be accomplished by using his voice.

It could also control his new Harmon Kardon 8000 receiver, which was currently piping a pleasant jazz solo through the lab.

"Control, stereo off," Rhyme reluctantly ordered, hearing the front door slam.

The music went silent, replaced by the erratic beat of footsteps in the front hall and the parlor. One of the visitors was Amelia Sachs, he knew; for a tall woman she had a decidedly light footfall. Then he heard the distinctive clump of Lon Sellitto's big, perpetually out-turned feet.

"Sachs," he muttered as she entered the room, "was it a big scene? Was it huge?"

"Not so big." She frowned at the question. "Why?"

His eyes were on the gray milk crates containing evidence she and several other officers carried. "I was just wondering because it seemed to take a long time to search the scene and get back here. It *is* okay for you to use that flashing light on your car. That's why they make them, you know. Sirens are allowed too." When Rhyme was bored he grew testy. Boredom was the biggest evil in his life.

Sachs, however, was impervious to his sourness—she seemed in a particularly good mood—and said merely, "We've got ourselves some mysteries here, Rhyme."

He recalled that Sellitto had used the word "bizarre" about the killing.

"Give me the scenario. What happened?"

Sachs offered a likely account of the events, culminating in the perp's escape from the recital hall.

"The respondings heard a shot inside the hall then they did a kick-in. Timed it together, went in through the only two doors in the room. He was gone."

Sellitto consulted his notes. "The patrol officers put him in his fifties, medium height, medium build, no distinguishings other than a beard, brown hair. There was a janitor who says he didn't see anybody go in or out of the room. But maybe he got witnessitis, you know. The school's gonna call with his name and number. I'll see if I can refresh his memory."

"What about the vic? What was the motive?"

Sachs said, "No sexual assault, no robbery."

Sellitto added, "Just talked to the Twins. She hasn't got any present or recent boyfriends. Nobody in the past that'd be a problem."

"She was a full-time student?" Rhyme asked. "Or did she work?"

"Full-time student, yeah. But apparently she did some performing on the side. They're finding out where."

Rhyme recruited his aide, Thom, to act as a scribe, as he often did, jotting down the evidence in his elegant handwriting on one of the large whiteboards in the lab. The aide took the marker and began to write.

There was a knock on the door and Thom disappeared momentarily from the lab.

"Incoming visitor!" he called from the hall-way.

"Visitor?" Rhyme asked, hardly in the mood for company. The aide, though, was being playful. Into the room walked Mel Cooper, the slim, balding lab technician whom Rhyme, then head of NYPD foren-sics, had met some years ago on a joint burglary/kidnapping case with an upstate New York police department. Cooper had disputed Rhyme's analysis of a particular type of soil and had been right, it turned out. Impressed, Rhyme had dug into the tech's credentials and found that, like Rhyme, he

was an active and highly respected member of the International Association for Identification—experts at identifying individuals from friction ridges, DNA, forensic reconstruction and dental remains. With degrees in math, physics and organic chemistry, Cooper was also top-notch at physical evidence analysis.

Rhyme mounted a campaign to get the man to return to the city where he'd been born and he finally agreed. The soft-spoken forensic tech/champion ballroom dancer was based in the NYPD crime lab in Queens but he often worked with Rhyme when the criminalist was consulting on an active case.

Greetings all around and then Cooper shoved his thick, Harry Potter–style glasses high on his nose and squinted a critical eye at the crates of evidence like a chess player sizing up his opponent. "What do we have here?"

"'Mysteries,'" Rhyme said. "To use our Sachs's assessment. Mysteries."

"Well, let's see if we can't make them a little less mysterious."

Sellitto ran through the scenario of the killing for Cooper as he donned latex gloves and began looking over the bags and jars. Rhyme wheeled up close to him. "There." He nodded. "What's *that?*" He was gazing at the green circuit board with a speaker attached.

"The board I found in the recital hall," Sachs said. "No idea what it is. Only that the unsub put it there—I could tell by his footprints."

It looked like it'd come from a computer, which didn't surprise Rhyme; criminals have always been in the forefront of technological development. Bank robbers armed themselves with the famous 1911 Colt .45 semi-automatic pistols within days of their release even though it was illegal for anyone but the military to possess one. Radios, scrambled phones, machine guns, laser sights, GPS, cellular technology, surveillance equipment and computer encryption ended up in the arsenal of criminals often before they were added to law enforcers'.

Rhyme was the first to admit that some subjects were beyond his realm of expertise. Clues like computers, cell phones and this curious device—all of which he called "NASDAQ evidence"—he farmed out to the experts.

"Get it downtown. To Tobe Geller," he instructed.

The FBI had a talented young man in its New York computer crimes office. Geller had helped them in the past and Rhyme knew that if anyone could tell them what the device was and where it might've come from Geller could do it.

Sachs handed off the bag to Sellitto, who in turn gave it to a uniformed policeman for transport downtown. But aspiring sergeant Amelia Sachs stopped him. She made sure he filled out a chain-of-custody card, which documents everyone who's handled each piece of evidence from crime scene to trial. She checked the card carefully and sent him on his way.

"And how *was* the assessment exercise, Sachs?" Rhyme asked.

"Well," she said. A hesitation. "I think I nailed it."

Rhyme was surprised at this response. Amelia Sachs often had a difficult time accepting praise from others and hardly ever bestowed it on herself.

"I didn't doubt you would," he said.

"*Sergeant* Sachs," Lon Sellitto pondered. "Gotta good ring to it."

They turned next to the pyrotechnic items found at the music school: the fuses and the firecracker.

Sachs had figured out one mystery, at least. The killer, she explained, had leaned chairs backward on two legs, balancing them in that position with thin pieces of cotton string. He'd tied fuses to the middle of the strings and lit them. After a minute or so the flame in the fuses hit the strings and burned through them. The chairs tumbled to the floor, making it sound like the killer was still inside. He'd also lit a fuse that ultimately set off the squib they mistook for a gunshot.

"Can you source any of it?" Sellitto asked.

"Generic fuse—untraceable—and the squib's destroyed. No manufacturer, nothing." Cooper shook his head. All that was left, Rhyme could see, were tiny shreds of paper with a burned metal core of fuse attached. The strings turned out to be narrow-gauge 100 percent cotton, generic and thus also impossible to source.

"There was that flash too," Sachs said, looking over her notes. "When the officers saw him with the victim he held up his hand

and there was a brilliant light. Like a flare. It blinded both of them."

"Any trace?"

"None that I could find. They said it just dissolved in the air."

Okay, Lon, you said it: bizarre.

"Let's move on. Footprints?"

Cooper pulled up the NYPD database on shoe-tread prints, a digitized version of the hard-copy file Rhyme had compiled when he'd been head of NYPD forensics. After a few minutes of perusal he said, "Shoes are slip-on black Ecco brand. Appear to be a size ten."

"Trace evidence?" Rhyme asked.

Sachs picked several plastic bags out of a milk crate. Inside were strips of adhesive tape, torn off the trace pick-up roller. "These're from where he walked and next to the body."

Cooper took the plastic bags and extracted the adhesive tape rectangles, one by one, over separate examining trays, to avoid cross-contamination. Most of the trace adhering to the squares was dust that matched Sachs's control samples, meaning that its source was neither the perp nor the victim but was found naturally at the crime scene. But on several of the pieces of tape were some fibers that Sachs had found only in places where the perp had walked or on objects that he'd touched.

"Scope 'em."

The tech lifted them off with a pair of tweezers and mounted them on slides. He put them under the stereo binocular microscope—the preferred instrument for analyzing fibers—and then hit a button. The image he was looking at through the eyepiece popped onto the large flat-screen computer monitor for everyone to see.

The fibers appeared as thick strands, grayish in color.

Fibers are important forensic clues because they're common, they virtually leap from one source to another and they can be easily classified. They fall into two categories: natural and man-made. Rhyme noted immediately that these weren't viscous rayon or polymer based and therefore had to be natural.

"But what kind specifically?" Mel Cooper wondered aloud.

"Look at the cell structure. I'm betting it's excremental."

"Whatsat?" Sellitto asked. "Excrement? Like shit?"

"Excrement, like *silk.* It comes from the digestive tract of worms. Dyed gray. Processed to a matte finish. What's on the other slides, Mel?"

He ran these through the scope too and found they were identical fibers.

"Was the perp wearing gray?"

"No," Sellitto reported.

"The vic wasn't either," Sachs said.

More mysteries.

"Ah," Cooper said, peering into the eyepiece, "might have a hair here."

On the screen a long strand of brown hair came into focus.

"Human hair," Rhyme called out, noting hundreds of scales. An animal hair would have at most dozens. "But it's fake."

"Fake?" Sellitto asked.

"Well," he said impatiently, "it's real hair but it's from a wig. *Obviously.* Look—at the end. That's not a bulb. It's *glue.* Might not be his, of course, but it's worth putting on the chart."

"That he's not brown-haired?" Thom asked.

"The facts," Rhyme said tersely, "are all

we care about. Write that the unsub is possibly wearing a brown wig."

"Okay, bwana."

Cooper continued his examination and found that two of the adhesive squares revealed a minuscule bit of dirt and some plant material.

"Scope the plant first, Mel."

In analyzing crime scenes in New York, Lincoln Rhyme had always placed great importance on geologic, plant and animal evidence because only one-eighth of the city is actually on the North American mainland; the rest is situated on islands. This means that minerals, flora and fauna tend to be more or less common to particular boroughs and even neighborhoods within them, making it easier to trace substances to specific locations.

A moment later a rather artistic image of a reddish twig and a bit of leaf appeared on the screen.

"Good," Rhyme announced.

"What's good about it?" Thom asked.

"It's good because it's rare. It's a red pignut hickory. You hardly ever find them in the city. The only place I know of are Central and Riverside Parks. And . . . oh, look at that. That little blue-green mass?"

"Where?" Sachs asked.

"Can't you see it? It's right there!" Feeling painfully frustrated that he couldn't leap from his chair and tap the screen. "Lower right-hand corner. If the twig's Italy then the mass is Sicily."

"Got it."

"What do you think, Mel? Lichen, right? And I'd vote for *Parmelia conspersa.*"

"Could be," the tech said cautiously. "But there're a lot of lichens."

"But there aren't a lot of *blue-green and gray* lichens," Rhyme replied dryly. "In fact, hardly any. And this one is most abundant in Central Park. . . . We've got two links to the park. Good. Now let's look at the dirt."

Cooper mounted another slide. The image in the microscope—grains of dirt like asteroids—wasn't forensically revealing and Rhyme said, "Run a sample through the GC/MS."

The gas chromatograph/mass spectrometer is a marriage of two chemical analysis instruments, the first of which breaks down an unknown substance into its component parts with the second determining what each of those parts is. White powder that appears uniform, for instance, might be a dozen different chemicals: baking soda, arsenic, baby powder, phenol and cocaine. The chromatograph has been compared to a horse race: the substances start out moving through the instrument together but they progress at different rates, becoming separated. At the "finish line" the mass spectrometer compares each one with a huge database of known substances to identify it.

The results of Cooper's analysis showed that the dirt Sachs had recovered was impregnated with an oil. The database, though, reported only that it was mineral based—not plant or animal—and couldn't identify it specifically.

Rhyme commanded, "Send it to the FBI. See if their lab people've run across it." Then he squinted into a plastic bag. "That's the black cloth you found?"

Might be a clue, might be nothing . . .

She nodded. "It was in the corner of the lobby where the victim was strangled."

"Was it hers?" Cooper wondered.

"Maybe," Rhyme said, "but for the time being let's go on the assumption it's the killer's."

Cooper carefully lifted out the material. He examined it. "Silk. Hemmed by hand."

Rhyme observed that even though it could be folded into a tiny wad it opened up to be quite large, about six by four feet.

"We know from the timing he was waiting for her in the lobby," Rhyme said. "I'll bet that's how he did it: hid in the corner with that cloth draped over him. He'd be invisible. He probably would've taken it with him except the officers showed up and he had to get away."

What the poor girl must've felt when the killer materialized as if by magic, cuffed her and strung the rope around her neck.

Cooper found several flecks adhering to the black cloth. He mounted them on a slide. An image soon popped up on the screen. Under magnification the flecks resembled ragged pieces of flesh-colored lettuce. He touched one with a fine probe. The material was springy.

"What the hell is *that?*" Sellitto asked.

Rhyme suggested, "Rubber of some kind. Shred of balloon—no, too thick for that. And look at the slide, Mel. Something smeared off. Flesh-colored too. Run it through the GC."

While they waited for the results the doorbell rang.

Thom stepped out of the room to open the door and returned with an envelope.

"Latents," he announced.

"Ah, good," Rhyme said. "Fingerprints are back. Run them through AFIS, Mel."

The powerful servers of the FBI's automated fingerprint identification system, located in West Virginia, would search digitized images of friction ridges—fingerprints—throughout the country and return the results in hours, possibly even minutes if the latents team had found good, clear prints.

"How do they look?" Rhyme asked.

"Pretty clean." Sachs held up the photos for him to see. Many were just partials. But they had a good print of his whole left hand. The first thing Rhyme noticed was that the killer had two deformed fingers on that hand—the ring and little fingers. They were joined, it seemed, and ended in smooth skin, without prints. Rhyme had a working knowledge of forensic pathology but couldn't tell whether this was a congenital condition or the result of an injury.

Ironic, Rhyme thought, gazing at the picture, the unsub's left ring finger is damaged;

mine is the only extremity below my neck that can move at all.

Then he frowned. "Hold off on the scan for a minute, Mel. . . . Closer, Sachs. I want to see them closer."

She stepped next to Rhyme and he examined the prints again. "Notice anything unusual about them?"

She said, "Not really. . . . Wait." She laughed. "They're the same." Flipping through the pictures. "All his fingers—they're the *same.* That little scar, it's in the same position on every one of them."

"He must be wearing some kind of glove," Cooper said, "with fake friction ridges on them. Never seen *that* before."

Who the hell *was* this perp?

The results from the chromatograph/spectrometer popped onto a computer screen. "Okay, I've got pure latex . . . and what's this?" he pondered. "Something the computer identifies as an alginate. Never heard of—"

"Teeth."

"What?" Cooper asked Rhyme.

"It's a powder you mix with water to make molds. Dentists use it for crowns and dental work. Maybe our doer'd just been to the dentist."

Cooper continued to examine the computer screen. "Then we have very minute traces of castor oil, propylene glycol, cetyl alcohol, mica, iron oxide, titanium dioxide, coal tar and some neutral pigments."

"Some of those're found in makeup," Rhyme said, recalling a case in which he'd placed a killer at the scene after the man wrote obscene messages on the victim's mirror with a touch-up stick, smears of which were found on his sleeve. Running the case, he'd made a study of cosmetics.

"Hers?" Cooper asked Sachs.

"No," the policewoman answered. "I took swabs of her skin. She wasn't wearing any."

"Well, put it on the board. We'll see if it means anything."

Turning to the rope, the murder weapon, Mel Cooper looked up from his slump over a porcelain examining board. "It's a white sheath of rope around a black core. They're both braided silk—real light and thin— which is why it doesn't look any thicker than a normal rope even though it's really two put together."

"What's the point of that? Does the core

make it stronger?" Rhyme asked. "Easier to untie? *Harder* to untie? What?"

"No idea."

"It's getting mysteriouser," Sachs said with a dramatic flair that Rhyme would have found irritating if he hadn't agreed with her.

"Yup," he confirmed, disconcerted. "That's a new one to me. Let's keep going. I want something *familiar,* something we can *use.*"

"And the knot?"

"Tied by an expert but I don't recognize it," Cooper said.

"Get a picture of it to the bureau. And . . . don't we know somebody at the Maritime Museum?"

"They've helped us with knots a few times," Sachs said. "I'll upload a picture to them too."

A call came in from Tobe Geller at the Computer Crimes Unit at New York's FBI headquarters. "This is fun, Lincoln."

"Glad we're keeping you amused," Rhyme murmured. "Anything *helpful* you might be able to tell us about our *toy?*"

Geller, a curly-haired young man, was impervious to Rhyme's edge, especially since there was a computer product involved. "It's a digital audio recorder. Fascinating little thing. Your unsub recorded something on it, stored the sounds on a hard drive then programmed it to play back after some delay. We don't know what the sound was—he built in a wiping program so that it destroyed the data."

"It was his voice," Rhyme muttered. "When he said he had a hostage it was just a recording. Like the chairs. It was to make us think he was still in the room."

"That makes sense. It had a special speaker—small but excellent bass and midtone range. It'd mimic a human voice pretty well."

"There's nothing left on the disk?"

"Nope. Gone for good."

"Damn. I wanted a voiceprint."

"Sorry. It's gone."

Rhyme sighed in frustration and rolled back to the examination trays; it was left to Sachs to tell Geller how much they appreciated the help.

The team then examined the victim's wristwatch, which had been shattered for reasons none of them could figure out. It yielded no evidence except the time it was broken. Perps occasionally broke watches or clocks at crime scenes after they'd set them to the wrong time to mislead investigators. But this was stopped at close to the actual time of death. What should they make of that?

Mysteriouser . . .

As the aide wrote their observations on the whiteboard Rhyme looked over the bag containing the sign-in book. "The missing name in the book." He mused, "Nine people signed but there're only eight names in the log. . . . I think we need an expert here." Rhyme ordered into the microphone, "Command, telephone. Call Kincaid comma Parker."

Chapter Six

On the screen the display showed a 703 area code, Virginia, then the number being dialed.

A ring. A young girl's voice said, "Kincaid residence."

"Uhm, yes. Is Parker there? Your father, I mean."

"Who's calling?"

"Lincoln Rhyme. In New York."

"Hold on, please."

A moment later the laid-back voice of one of the country's preeminent document examiners came on the line. "Hey, Lincoln. Been a month or two, hasn't it?"

"Busy time," Rhyme offered. "And what're you up to, Parker?"

"Oh, getting into trouble. Nearly caused an international incident. The British Cultural Society in the District wanted me to authenticate a notebook of King Edward's they'd purchased from a private collector. Note the tense of the verb, Lincoln."

"They'd already paid for it."

"Six hundred thousand."

"Little pricey. They wanted it that badly?"

"Oh, it had some real nice juicy gossip about Churchill and Chamberlain. Well, not in *that* sense, of course."

"Of course not." As usual Rhyme tried to be patient with those from whom he was seeking gratuitous help.

"I looked it over and what could I do? I had to question it."

The innocuous verb, from a respected document examiner like Kincaid, was synonymous with branding the diary a bad-ass forgery.

"Ah, they'll get over it," he continued. "Though, come to think of it, they haven't paid my bill yet. . . . No, honey, we don't make the frosting till the cake cools. . . . Because I said so."

A single father, Kincaid was the former head of the FBI's documents department at headquarters. He'd left the bureau to run his own document examination service so he could spend more time with his children, Robby and Stephanie.

"How's Margaret?" Sachs called into the speaker.

"That you, Amelia?"

"Yup."

"She's fine. Haven't seen her for a few days. We took the kids to Planet Play on Wednesday and I was just starting to beat her at laser tag when her pager goes off. She had to go kick in somebody's door and arrest them. Panama or Ecuador or someplace like that. She doesn't give me the details. So, what's up?"

"We're running a case and I need some help. Here's the scenario: perp was seen writing his name in a security desk sign-in book. Okay?"

"Got it. And you need the handwriting analyzed?"

"The problem is we don't *have* any handwriting."

"It disappeared?"

"Yep."

"And you're sure the writer wasn't faking?"

"Positive. There was a guard who saw ink going on paper, no question."

"Anything visible now?"

"Nothing."

Kincaid gave a grim laugh. "That's smart. So there was no record of the perp entering the building. And then somebody else wrote their name *over* the blank space and ruined whatever impression there might've been of his signature."

"Right."

"Anything on the sheet below the top one?"

Rhyme glanced at Cooper, who shone a bright light at an acute angle on the second sheet in the log—this, rather than covering the page with pencil lead, was the preferred method to raise impression evidence. He shook his head.

"Nothing," Rhyme told the document examiner. Then asked, "So how'd he pull that off?"

"He Ex-Laxed it," Kincaid announced.

"How's that?" Sellitto called.

"Used disappearing ink. We call it Ex-laxing in the business. The old Ex-Lax contained phenolphthalein. Before it was banned by the FDA. You'd dissolve a pill in alcohol and make a blue ink. It had an alkaline pH. Then you'd write something. After a while, exposure to the air would make the blue disappear."

"Sure," said Rhyme, recalling his basic chemistry. "The carbon dioxide in the air turns the ink acidic and that neutralizes the color."

"Exactly. You don't see phenolphthalein much anymore. But you can do the same thing with thymolphthalein indicator and sodium hydroxide."

"Can you buy this stuff anyplace in particular?"

"Hm," Kincaid considered. "Well. . . . Just a minute, honey. Daddy's on the phone. . . . No, it's okay. All cakes look lopsided when they're in the oven. I'll be there soon. . . . Lincoln? What I was going to say was that it's a great idea in theory but when I was in the bureau there were never any perps or spies who actually *used* disappearing ink. It's more of a novelty, you know. Entertainers'd use it."

Entertainment, Rhyme thought grimly, looking at the board on which were taped the pictures of poor Svetlana Rasnikov. "Where would our doer find ink like that?"

"Most likely toy stores or magic shops."

Interesting . . .

"Okay, well, that's helpful, Parker."

"Come and visit sometime," Sachs called. "And bring the kids."

Rhyme grimaced at the invitation. He whispered to Sachs, "And why don't you invite all their friends too. The whole school . . ."

Laughing, she shushed him.

After he disconnected the call Rhyme said grumpily, "The more we learn, the less we know."

Bedding and Saul called in and reported that Svetlana seemed to be well liked at the music school and had no enemies there. Her part-time job wasn't likely to have produced any stalkers either; she led sing-alongs at kids' birthday parties.

A package arrived from the medical examiner's office. Inside was a plastic evidence bag containing the old handcuffs the victim had been restrained with. They were unopened, as Rhyme had ordered. He'd told the M.E. to compress the victim's hands to remove them since drilling out the locks could destroy valuable trace.

"Never seen anything like this," Cooper said, holding them up, "outside of a movie."

Rhyme agreed. They were antique, heavy and made of unevenly forged iron.

Cooper brushed and tapped all around the lock mechanisms but he found no significant trace. The fact they were antique, though, was encouraging because it would limit the sources they might've come from. Rhyme told Cooper to photograph the cuffs and print out pictures to show to dealers.

Sellitto received another phone call. He listened for a moment then, looking bewildered, said, "Impossible. . . . You're sure? . . . Yeah, okay. Thanks." Hanging up, the detective glanced at Rhyme. "I don't get it."

"What's that?" Rhyme asked, in no mood for any more mysteries.

"That was the administrator of the music school. There *is* no janitor."

"But the patrol officers saw him," Sachs pointed out.

"The cleaning staff doesn't work on Saturday. Only weekday evenings. And none of 'em look like the guy the respondings saw."

No janitor?

Sellitto looked through his notes. "He was right outside the second door, sweeping up. He—"

"Oh, goddamn," Rhyme snapped. "It was him!" A glance at the detective. "The janitor looked completely different from the perp, right?"

Sellitto consulted his notebook. "He was in his sixties, bald, no beard, wearing gray coveralls."

"*Gray* coveralls!" Rhyme shouted.

"Yeah."

"That's the silk fiber. It was a costume."

"What're you talking about?" Cooper asked.

"Our unsub killed the student. When he was surprised by the respondings he blinded them with the flash and ran into the performance space, set up the fuses and the digital recorder to make them think he was still inside, changed into the janitor out-fit and ran out the second door."

"But he didn't just strip off throwaway sweats like some chain-snatcher on the A train, Linc," the rotund policeman pointed out. "How the hell could he've done it? He was out of sight for, what, sixty seconds?"

"Fine. If you have an explanation that doesn't involve divine intervention I'm will-ing to listen."

"Come on. There's no fucking way."

"No way?" Rhyme mused cynically as he wheeled closer to the whiteboard on which Thom had taped the printouts of the digital photos Sachs had taken of the footprints. "Then how 'bout some *evidence?*" He examined the perp's footprints and then the ones that she'd lifted in the corridor near where the janitor had been.

"Shoes," he announced.

"They're the same?" the detective asked.

"Yep," Sachs said, walking to the board. "Ecco, size ten."

"Christ," Sellitto muttered.

Rhyme asked, "Okay, what do we have? A perp in his early fifties, medium build, medium height and beardless, two deformed fingers, probably has a record 'cause he's hiding his prints—and that's *all* we goddamn know." But then Rhyme frowned. "No," he muttered darkly, "that's *not* all we know. There's something else. He had a change of clothes with him, murder weapons. . . . He's an organized offender." He glanced at Sellitto and added, "He's going to do this again."

Sachs nodded her grim agreement.

Rhyme gazed at Thom's flowing lettering

on the evidence whiteboards and he wondered: What ties this all together?

The black silk, the makeup, the costume change, the disguises, the flashes and the pyrotechnics.

The disappearing ink.

Rhyme said slowly, "I'm thinking that our boy's got some magic training."

Sachs nodded. "Makes sense."

Sellitto nodded. "Okay. Maybe. But whatta we do now?"

"Seems obvious to me," Rhyme said. "Find our own."

"Our own what?" Sellitto asked.

"Magician of course."

"Do it again."

She'd done it eight times so far.

"Again?"

The man nodded.

And so Kara did it again.

The Triple Handkerchief Release—developed by the famous magician and teacher Harlan Tarbell—is a sure-fire audience-pleaser. It involves separating three different colored silks that seem hopelessly knotted together. It's a hard trick to perform smoothly but Kara felt good about how it'd gone.

David Balzac didn't, however. "Your coins were talking." He sighed—harsh criticism, meaning that an illusion or trick was clumsy and obvious. The heavyset older man with a white mane of hair and tobacco-stained goatee shook his head in exasperation. He removed his thick glasses, rubbed his eyes and replaced the specs.

"I think it was smooth," she protested. "It seemed smooth to me."

"But you weren't the audience. I was. Now again."

They stood on a small stage in the back of Smoke & Mirrors, the store that Balzac had bought after he'd retired from the international magic and illusion circuit ten years ago. The grungy place sold magic supplies, rented costumes and props and presented free, amateur magic shows for customers and locals. A year and a half ago Kara, doing freelance editing for *Self* magazine, had finally worked up her courage to get up on stage—Balzac's reputation had intimidated her for months. The aging magician had watched her act and called her into his office afterward. The Great Balzac himself had told her in his gruff but silky voice that she had potential. She could be a great illusionist—with the proper training—and proposed that she come work in the shop; he'd be her mentor and teacher.

Kara had moved to New York from the Midwest years before and was savvy about city life; she knew immediately what "mentor" might entail, especially when he was a quadruple divorcé and she was an attractive woman forty years younger than he. But Balzac was a renowned magician—he'd been a regular on Johnny Carson and had been a headliner in Las Vegas for years. He'd toured the world dozens of times and knew virtually every major illusionist alive. Illusion was her passion and this was a chance of a lifetime. She accepted on the spot.

At the first session her guard was up and she was ready to repel boarders. The lesson indeed turned out to be upsetting to her—though for an entirely different reason.

He tore her to shreds.

After an hour of criticizing virtually every aspect of her technique Balzac had looked at her pale, tearful face and barked, "I said you have *potential.* I didn't say you were good. If you want somebody to polish your ego you're in the wrong place. Now, are you going to run home crying to mommy or are you going to get back to work?"

They got back to work.

And so began an eighteen-month love-hate relationship between mentor and apprentice, which kept her up until the early hours of the morning six or seven days a week, practicing, practicing, practicing. While Balzac had had many assistants in his years as a performer he'd been a mentor to only two apprentices and in both cases, it seemed, the young men had proved to be disappointments. He wasn't going to let that happen with Kara.

Friends sometimes asked her where her love of—and obsession with—illusion came from. They were probably expecting a movie-of-the-week tormented childhood filled with abusive parents and teachers or, at least, a little slip of a mousy girl escaping from the cruel cliques at school into the world of fantasy. But they got Normal Girl instead—a cheerful A student, gymnast, cookie baker and school-choir singer, who started on the path of entertainment undramatically by attending a Penn and Teller performance in Cleveland with her grand-parents, followed a month later by a coinci-dental family trip to Vegas for one of her father's turbine-manufacturing conventions, the trip exposing her to the thrill of flying tigers and fiery illusions, the exhilaration of magic.

That's all it took. At thirteen she founded the magic club at JFK Junior High and was soon sinking every penny of baby-sitting money into magic magazines, how-to videos and packaged tricks. She later ex-panded her entrepreneurial efforts to yard work and snow shoveling in exchange for rides to the Big Apple Circus and Cirque du Soleil whenever they were appearing within a fifty-mile radius.

Which is not to say that there wasn't an important motive that set—and kept—her on this course. No, what drove Kara could be easily found in the blinks of delighted surprise on the faces of the audience—whether they were two-dozen of her rela-tives at Thanksgiving dinner (a show com-plete with quick-change routines and a levitating cat, though without the trapdoor her father wouldn't let her cut in the living room floor) or the students and parents at the high school senior talent show, where she did two encores to a standing ovation.

Life with David Balzac, though, was quite different from that triumphant show; over the past year and a half she sometimes felt she'd lost whatever talent she'd once had.

But just as she'd be about to quit he'd nod and offer the faintest of smiles. Several times he actually said, "That was a tight trick."

At moments like that her world was complete.

Much of the rest of her life, though, blew away like dust as she spent more and more time at the store, handling the books and inventory for him, the payroll, serving as webmaster for the store's website. Since Balzac wasn't paying her much she needed other work and she took jobs that were at least marginally compatible with her English degree—writing content for other magic and theater websites. Then about a year ago her mother's condition had began to worsen and only-child Kara spent her little remaining free time with the woman.

An exhausting life.

But she could handle it for now. In a few years Balzac would pronounce her fit to perform and off she'd go with his blessing *and* his contacts with producers around the world.

Hold tight, girl, as Jaynene might say, and stay on top of the galloping horse.

Kara now finished Tarbell's three-silk trick again. Tapping his cigarette ash onto the floor, Balzac frowned. "Left index finger slightly higher."

"You could see the tie?"

"If I couldn't see it," he snapped angrily, "why would I ask you to lift your finger higher? Try again."

Once more.

The goddamn index finger slightly goddamn higher.

Wshhhhhh . . . the entangled silks separated and flew into the air like triumphant flags.

"Ah," Balzac said. A faint nod.

Not traditional praise exactly. But Kara had learned to make do with *ah*'s.

She put the trick away and stepped behind the counter in the cluttered business area of the store to log in the merchandise that had arrived in Friday's afternoon shipment.

Balzac returned to the computer, on which he was writing an article for the store's website about Jasper Maskelyne, the British magician who created a special military unit in World War Two, which used illusionist techniques against the Germans in North Africa. He was writing it from memory, without any notes or research; that was one thing about David Balzac—his knowledge of magic was as deep as his temperament was unstable and fiery.

"You hear that the Cirque Fantastique's in town?" she called. "Opens tonight."

The old illusionist grunted. He was exchanging his glasses for contact lenses; Balzac was extremely aware of the importance of a performer's image and always looked his best for any audience, even his customers.

"You going to go?" she persisted. "I think we should go."

Cirque Fantastique—a competitor to the older and bigger Cirque du Soleil—was part of the next generation of circuses. It combined traditional circus routines, ancient commedia dell'arte theater, contemporary music and dance, avant-garde performance art and street magic.

But David Balzac was old school: Vegas, Atlantic City, *The Late Show.* "Why change something that works?" he'd grumble.

Kara loved Cirque Fantastique, though, and was determined to get him to a performance. But before she could pitch her case to convince him to accompany her the store's front door opened and an attractive, redheaded policewoman walked in, asking for the owner.

"That's me. I'm David Balzac. What can I do for you?"

The officer said, "We're investigating a case involving someone who might've had some training in magic. We're talking to magic supply stores in town, hoping you might be able to help us."

"You mean, somebody's running a scam or something?" Balzac asked. He sounded defensive, a feeling Kara shared. In the past magic has often been linked to crooks—sleight-of-hand artists as pickpockets, for instance, and charlatan clairvoyants using illusionist techniques to convince bereaved family members that the spirits of their relatives are communicating with them.

But the policewoman's visit, it turned out, was prompted by something else.

"Actually," she said, glancing at Kara then back to Balzac. "The case is a homicide."

Chapter Seven

"I have a list of some items we found at a crime scene," Amelia Sachs told the owner, "and was wondering if you might've sold them."

He took the sheet she handed him and read it as Sachs looked over Smoke & Mirrors. The black-painted cavern of a store in the photo district, part of Manhattan's Chelsea neighborhood, smelled of mold and chemicals—plastic too, the petrochemical body odor from the hundreds of costumes that hung like a limp crowd from racks nearby. The grimy glass counters, half of them cracked and taped together, were filled with card decks and wands and phony coins and dusty boxes of magic tricks. A full-size replica of the creature from the *Alien* movies stood next to a Diana mask and costume. (BE THE PRINCESS OF THE PARTY! a card read. As if no one in the store even knew she was dead.)

He tapped the list and then nodded at the counters. "I don't think I can help. We sell some of this, sure. But so does every magic store in the country. A lot of toy stores too."

She observed he hadn't spent more than a few seconds looking it over. "How about these?" Sachs showed him the printout of the photo of the old handcuffs.

He glanced at it quickly. "I don't know anything about escapology."

Was this an answer? "So that means you don't recognize them?"

"No."

"It's very important," Sachs persisted.

The young woman, with striking blue eyes and black fingernails, looked at the picture. "They're Darbys," she said. The man glanced at her coolly. She fell silent for a moment then: "Regulation Scotland Yard handcuffs from the eighteen hundreds. A lot of escapists use them. They were Houdini's favorites."

"Where could they've come from?"

Balzac rocked impatiently in his office chair. "We wouldn't know. Like I was saying, that's not a field we have any experience with."

The woman nodded, agreeing with him. "There're probably escapology museums somewhere you could get in touch with."

"And after you restock," Balzac said to his assistant, "I need you to process those orders. There were a dozen came in last night after you left." He lit a cigarette.

Sachs offered him the list again. "You did say you sold *some* of these products. Do you have records of customers?"

"I meant, products *like* them. And, no, we don't keep customer records."

After some questioning, Sachs finally got him to admit that there were recent records of mail-order and on-line sales. The young woman checked these, though, and found that nobody had bought any of the items on the evidence list.

"Sorry," Balzac said. "Wish we could be more help."

"You know, I wish you could be more help too," Sachs said, leaning forward. "Because, see, this guy killed a woman and escaped by using magic tricks. And we're afraid he's going to do it again."

Giving a frown of concern, Balzac said,

"Terrible. . . . You know, you might try East Side Magic and Theatrical. They're bigger than us."

"We have another officer over there now."

"Ah, there you go."

She let a moment pass, silent. Then: "Well, if you can think of anything else, I'd appreciate a call." A good civil servant's smile, an NYPD sergeant's smile ("Remember: community relations are as important as criminal investigations").

"Good luck, Officer," Balzac said.

"Thanks," she said.

You apathetic son-of-a-bitch.

She nodded farewell to the young woman and glanced at a cardboard cup she was sipping from. "Hey, there anyplace around here to get some decent coffee?"

"Fifth and Nineteenth," she replied.

"Good bagels too," Balzac said, helpful now that there was no risk, or effort, involved.

Outside, Sachs turned toward Fifth Avenue and found the recommended coffee shop. She walked inside, bought a cappuccino. She leaned against a narrow mahogany bar in front of the flecked window, sipping the hot drink and watching the Saturday morning populace here in Chelsea—salespeople from the clothing stores in the area, commercial photographers and their assistants, rich yuppies who lived in the massive lofts, poor artists, lovers young and lovers old, a wacky notebook scribbler or two.

And one magic store clerk, now entering the shop.

"Hi," said the woman with short reddish-purple hair, carrying a battered faux zebra-skin purse over her shoulder. She ordered a large coffee, filled it with sugar and joined Sachs at the bar.

Back at Smoke & Mirrors the police-woman had asked about a venue for coffee because of a conspiratorial glance the assistant had shot Sachs; it seemed that she'd wanted to say something out of Balzac's presence.

Sipping her coffee thirstily, the woman said, "The thing about David is—"

"He's uncooperative?"

A frown of consideration. "Yeah. That says it pretty well. Anything outside his world he doesn't trust or want any part of. He was afraid we'd have to be witnesses or something. I'm not supposed to be distracted."

"From what?"

"From the profession."

"Magic?"

"Right. See, he's sort of my mentor more than my boss."

"What's your name?"

"Kara—it's my stage name but I use it most of the time." A pained smile. "Better than the one my parents were kind enough to give me."

Sachs lifted a curious eyebrow.

"We'll keep that a secret."

"So," Sachs said, "why'd you give me that look back at the store?"

"David's right about that list. You can buy those things anywhere, in any store. Or on the Internet in hundreds of places. But about the Darbys, the handcuffs? Those're rare. You should call the Houdini and Escapology Museum in New Orleans. It's the best in the world. Escapism's one of my things. I don't tell him, though." Reverent emphasis on the third-person pronoun. "David's kind of opinionated. . . . Can you tell me what happened? With that murder?"

Normally circumspect about what she

gave away on an active case, Sachs knew they needed help and gave Kara an outline of the killing and the escape.

"Oh, that's horrible," the young woman whispered.

"Yeah," Sachs replied softly. "It is."

"The way he disappeared? There's something you ought to know, Officer— Wait, do I call you 'officer'? Or are you like a detective or something?"

"Amelia's fine." Enjoying a brief memory of how she'd aced the assessment exercise.

Bang, bang . . .

Kara sipped more coffee, decided that it wasn't sweet enough and unscrewed the top of the sugar bottle then poured more in. Sachs watched the young woman's deft hands then glanced down at her own fingernails, two of which were torn, the cuticles bloody. The girl's were perfectly filed and the glossy black finish reflected the overhead lights in exact miniature. A jealous twinge—at the nails and the self-control that kept them so perfect—flared momentarily and then was put quickly to sleep by Amelia Sachs.

Kara asked, "You know what illusion is?"

"David Copperfield," Sachs replied, shrugging. "Houdini."

"Copperfield, yes. Houdini, no—he was an escapist. Well, illusion's different from sleight of hand or close-in magic, we call it. Like . . ." Kara held up a quarter in her fingers, change from the coffee. She closed her palm and when she opened it again the coin was gone.

Sachs laughed. Where the hell had it gone?

"That was sleight of hand. Illusion is tricks involving large objects or people or animals. What you just described, what that killer did, is a classic illusionist trick. It's called the Vanished Man."

"Vanishing Man?"

"No, the Vanished Man. In magic we use 'vanish' to mean 'to make disappear.' Like, 'I just vanished the quarter.'"

"Go on."

"The way it's performed usually is a little different from what you described but basically it involves the illusionist getting out of a locked room. The audience sees him step into this little room onstage—they can see the back because of a big mirror behind it. They hear him pound on the walls. The assistants pull the walls down and he's gone. Then one of the assistants turns around and it's the illusionist."

"How does it work?"

"There was a door in the back of the room. The illusionist covers himself with a large piece of black silk so the audience can't see him in the mirror and slips through the back door just after he walks inside. There's a speaker built into one of the walls to make it sound like he was inside all the time and a gimmick that hits the walls and sounds like he's pounding. Once the illusionist's outside he does a quick change behind the silk into an assistant's costume."

Sachs nodded. "That's it, all right. Could we get a short list of people who know the routine?"

"No, sorry—it's pretty common."

The Vanished Man . . .

Sachs was recalling that the killer had changed disguises quickly to become an older man, recalling, too, Balzac's lack of cooperation and the cold look in his eyes— almost sadistic—when he was talking to Kara. She asked, "I need to ask—where was he this morning?"

"Who?"

"Mr. Balzac."

"Here. I mean, in the building. He lives there, above the store. . . . Wait, you're not thinking he was involved?"

"These're questions we need to ask," Sachs said noncommittally. The young woman seemed more amused than upset by the inquiry, though. She gave a laugh. "Look, I know he's gruff and he has this . . . I guess you'd call it an edge, you know. A temper. But he'd never hurt anybody."

Sachs nodded but then asked, "Still, you know where he was at eight this morning?"

Kara nodded. "Yeah, he was at the store. He got in early because some friend of his is in town doing a show and needed to borrow some equipment. I called to tell him I'd be a little late."

Sachs nodded. Then a moment later asked, "Can you take a little time off work?"

"Me? Oh, no way." An embarrassed laugh. "I was lucky to sneak out now. There're a thousand things to do around the store. Then I've got three or four hours of rehearsing with David for a show I'm doing tomorrow. He doesn't let me rest the day before a performance. I—"

Sachs held the woman's crisp blue eyes.

"We're really afraid this person's going to kill someone else."

Kara's eyes swept the sticky mahogany bar.

"Please. Just for a few hours. Look over the evidence with us. Brainstorm."

"He won't let me. You don't know David."

"What I *know* is that I'm not letting anybody else get hurt if there's anyway I can stop it."

Kara finished her coffee and absently played with the cup. "Using our tricks to kill people," she whispered in a dismayed voice.

Sachs said nothing and let silence do the arguing for her.

Finally the young woman grimaced. "My mother's in a home. She's been in and out of the infirmary. Mr. Balzac knows that. I guess I could tell him I have to go check on her."

"We really could use your help."

"Oh-oh. The sick mother excuse. . . . God's gonna get me for this one."

Sachs glanced down again at Kara's perfect, black nails. "Hey, one thing: What happened to that quarter?"

"Look under your coffee cup," the girl replied.

Impossible. "No way."

Sachs lifted up the cup. There sat the coin.

The bewildered policewoman asked, "How'd you do that?"

Kara's answer was an enigmatic smile. She nodded at the cups. "Let's get a couple more to go." She picked up the coin. "Heads you buy, tails it's on me. Two out of three." She flipped it into the air.

Sachs nodded. "Deal."

The young woman caught it and glanced into her cupped palm. She looked up. "We said two out of three, right?"

Sachs nodded.

Kara opened her fingers. Inside were two dimes and a nickel. The dimes were heads up. No sign of the quarter. "Guess this means you're buying."

Chapter Eight

"Lincoln, meet Kara."

She'd been warned, Rhyme could see, but the young woman still blinked in surprise and glanced at him with the Look. The one he knew so well. Accompanied by the Smile.

It was the famous don't-look-at-his-body gaze, accompanied by the oh-you're-handicapped-I-never-noticed grin.

And Rhyme knew she'd be counting down the moments until she could get the hell out of his presence.

The spritely young woman walked farther into the parlor lab in Rhyme's town house. "Hi. Nice to meet you." The eyes remained rooted in his. At least she didn't start forward with that minuscule lean that told him she was stifling an offered handshake and then cringe in horror at the faux pas.

Okay, Kara. Don't worry. You can give the gimp your insights then get the hell out.

He offered her a superficial smile that matched hers crease for crease and said how pleased he was to meet her too.

Which on a professional level, at least, wasn't sardonic—Kara was, it turned out, the only magician lead they'd snared. None of the employees at the other shops in town had been any help—and everyone had alibis for the time of the killing.

She was introduced to Lon Sellitto and Mel Cooper. Thom nodded and did one of the things he was known for, whether Rhyme wanted him to or not: offered refreshments.

"We're not really in a church social mode here, Thom," Rhyme muttered.

Kara said no that was all right but Thom said no he was insisting.

"Maybe coffee?" she asked.

"Coming up."

"Black. Sugar. Maybe a couple sugars?"

"We really—" Rhyme began.

"For the whole room," the aide announced. "I'll make a pot. Get some bagels too."

"Bagels?" Sellitto asked.

"You could open a restaurant in your spare time," Rhyme snapped to the aide. "Get it out of your system."

"What's spare time?" came the trim blond man's fast quip. He headed for the kitchen.

"Officer Sachs," he continued to Kara, "told us that you had some information you thought might help."

"I hope so." Another tight perusal of Rhyme's face. The Look again. Closer this time. Oh, for Christ's sake, just say *something*. Ask me how it happened. Ask me if it hurts. Ask me what it's like to pee into a tube.

"Hey, what're we calling him?" Sellitto tapped the top of the evidence whiteboard. Until the identity of the unsub—for "unknown subject"—was learned, many law enforcers gave perps nicknames. "How 'bout the 'Magician'?"

"No, that sounds too tame," Rhyme said, looking at the pictures of the victim. "How's the 'Conjurer'?" Surprising himself by offering this decidedly right-brained suggestion.

"Works for me."

In handwriting far less elegant than Thom's the detective wrote the words on top of the chart.

The Conjurer . . .

"Now let's see if we can make him appear," Rhyme said.

Sachs said, "Tell them about the Vanished Man."

The young woman rubbed her hand over her boyish hair as she described an illusionist's trick that sounded almost identical to what the Conjurer had done at the music school.

She added the discouraging news, though, that most illusionists would know about it.

Rhyme asked, "Give us some idea about how he does the tricks. Techniques. So we'll know what to expect from him if he tries to target somebody else."

"You want me to tip the gaff, huh?"

"Tip the—?"

"Gaff," Kara said, then explained: "See, all magic tricks're made up of an effect and a method. The *effect* is what the audience sees. You know: the girl levitating, the coins falling through a solid tabletop. The *method* is the mechanism of how the magician does it—wires holding up the girl, palming the coins then dropping identical ones from a rig under the table."

Effect and method, Rhyme reflected. Kind of like what I do: the effect is catching a perp when it seems impossible. The method is the science and logic that let us do it.

Kara continued, "Tipping the gaff means giving away the method of a trick. Like I just did—explaining how the Vanished Man worked. It's a sensitive thing—Mr. Balzac, my mentor, he's always hounding magicians who tip the gaff in public and give away other people's methods."

Thom carted a tray into the room. He poured coffee for those who wanted some. Kara dumped sugar into hers and sipped it fast, even though to Rhyme it seemed scalding hot. He glanced at the Macallan eighteen-year-old single malt on a bookcase across the room. Thom noticed his eyes and said, "It's mid-morning. Don't even think about it."

Sellitto gave a similarly lustful gaze toward the bagels. He allowed himself only half. Without cream cheese. He looked pained with every bite.

They went over each item of evidence with Kara, who studied it carefully and delivered the discouraging news that there were hundreds of sources for most of the items. The rope was a color-changing rope trick, sold in F.A.O. Schwarz as well as magic stores throughout the country. The knot was one Houdini used in his routines when he planned to cut the cord to escape; it was virtually impossible for a bound performer to untie.

"Even without the cuffs," Kara said softly, "that girl never had a chance of getting away."

"Is *that* rare? The knot?"

She explained that, no, anyone with a basic knowledge of Houdini's routines would know it.

The castor oil in the makeup, Kara continued, meant that he was using very realistic and durable theatrical cosmetics, and the latex was, as Rhyme had suspected, probably from the fake finger cups, which were also popular magician's tools. The alginate, Kara suggested, wouldn't be from dental work but was used to make molds for latex casting, probably for the finger cups or the bald cap he'd worn in his janitor disguise.

The disappearing ink was more of a novelty, though some illusionists occasionally used it in their shows.

Only a few things were unique, she explained: the circuit board (which was a "gimmick," she said, a prop the audience can't see), for instance. But he'd made that himself. The Darby handcuffs were rare. Rhyme ordered someone to check out the escapology museum in New Orleans that Kara had mentioned. Sachs suggested they take the responding officers, Franciscovich and Ausonio, up on their offer to help. This was the sort of assignment that'd be perfect for a couple of eager young officers. Rhyme agreed and Sellitto arranged it through the head of the Patrol Services Division.

"How about his escape?" Sellitto said. "What's the deal where he changed into janitor clothes so fast."

"'Protean magic' it's called," Kara said. "Quick change. It's one of the things I've been studying for years. I just use it as part of my routines but there're some people, it's all they do. It can be amazing. I saw Arturo Brachetti a few years ago. He could do three or four dozen changes in one show—some of them in under three seconds."

"Three seconds?"

"Yeah. And see, true quick-change artists don't just change clothes. They're actors too. They walk differently, hold themselves differently, speak differently. He'll prepare everything ahead of time. The clothes are breakaway—they're held together with snaps or Velcro. Most of quick change is really quick *strip.* And they're made of silk or nylon, real thin, so we can wear layers of them. I sometimes wear five costumes under my top outfit."

"Silk?" Rhyme asked. "We found gray silk fibers," he explained. "The officers on the scene reported that the janitor was wearing a gray uniform. The fibers were abraded—sort of buffed to a matte finish."

Kara nodded. "So they'd look like cotton or linen, not shiny. We also use collapsible hats and suitcases, shoe coverings, telescoping umbrellas, all kinds of props that we hide on our bodies. Wigs, of course."

She continued, "To alter a face the most important thing is the eyebrows. Change those and the face is sixty, seventy percent different. Then add some prostheses—we call them 'appliances': latex strips and pads you put on with spirit gum. Quick-change performers study the basic facial structures of different races and genders. A good protean artist knows the proportions of a woman's face versus a man's and can change genders in seconds. We study psychological reactions to faces and posture—so we can become beautiful or ugly or scary or sympathetic or needy. Whatever."

The magic esoterica was interesting but Rhyme wanted specific suggestions. "Is there anything concrete you can tell us that'll help *find* him?"

She shook her head. "I can't think of anything that might lead you to a particular store or other place. But I do have some general thoughts."

"Go ahead."

"Well, the fact he used the changing rope and finger cups tells me he's familiar with sleight of hand. That means he'll be good at picking pockets, hiding guns or knives or things like that. Getting people's keys and IDs. He also knows quick change and it's obvious what kind of problem *that'll* be for you. But more important—the Vanished Man routine, the fuses and squibs, the disappearing ink, the black silk, the flash cotton means he's a classically trained illusionist."

She explained the difference between a sleight-of-hand artist and a true illusionist, whose acts involved people and large objects.

"Why's that important for us?"

Kara nodded. "Because illusion is more than just physical technique. Illusionists study audience psychology and create whole routines to trick them—not just their eyes but their minds too. Their point isn't making you laugh because a quarter disappears; it's to make you believe in your heart that everything you see and believe is one way when in fact it's the opposite. There's one thing you'll have to keep in mind. Never forget it."

"What?" Rhyme asked.

"Misdirection. . . . Mr. Balzac says it's the heart and soul of illusion. You've heard the expression that the hand is quicker than the eye? Well, no, it's not. The eye is always quicker. So illusionists *trick* the eye into not noticing what the hand is doing."

"Like, you mean, diversion, distraction?" Sellitto asked.

"That's part of it. Misdirection is pointing

the audience's attention where you want it and away from where you *don't* want it. There're lots of rules he's been drumming into me—like, the audience doesn't notice the familiar but're drawn to novelty. They don't notice a series of similar things but focus on the one that's different. They ignore objects or people that stand still but they're drawn to movement. You want to make something invisible? Repeat it four or five times and pretty soon the audience is bored and their attention wanders. They can be staring right at your hands and not see what you're doing. That's when you zing 'em.

"Okay, now there're two kinds of misdirection he'll be using: first, *physical* misdirection. Watch." Kara stepped near Sachs and stared at her own right hand as she lifted it very slowly and pointed to the wall, squinting. Then she dropped her hand. "See, you looked at my arm and where I pointed. Perfectly natural reaction. So you probably didn't notice that my left hand's got Amelia's gun."

Sachs gave a faint jump as she glanced down and saw that, sure enough, Kara's fingers had lifted the Glock partway out of the holster.

"Careful there," Sachs said, reholstering the pistol.

"Now, look in that corner." Pointing with her right hand again. This time, though, Rhyme and the others in the room naturally looked at Kara's left hand.

"Caught my left hand, didn't you?" She laughed. "But you didn't notice my foot, pushing that white thing behind the table."

"A bedpan," Rhyme said acerbically, irritated that he'd been tricked again but feeling he'd scored a point or two by mentioning the indelicate nature of the object she'd moved.

"Really?" she asked, unfazed. "Well, it's not *just* a bedpan; it's also a misdirection. Because when you were looking at it just now, I got this with my *other* hand. Oh, here," she said. "Is this important?" She handed a canister of Mace back to Sachs.

The policewoman frowned, looked down at her utility belt to see if anything else was missing and replaced the cylinder.

"So, that's *physical* misdirection. That's pretty easy. The second kind of misdirection is *psychological.* This is harder. Audiences aren't stupid. They know you're going to try to trick them. I mean, that's why they've come to the show in the first place, right? So we try to reduce or eliminate the audience's suspicion. The most important thing in psychological misdirection is to act naturally. You behave and say things that're consistent with what the audience expects. But underneath the surface you're getting away with . . ." Her voice faded as she realized how close she'd come to using the word that described the death of the young student that morning.

Kara continued, "As soon as you do something in an unnatural way, the audience is on to you. Okay, I say I'm going to read your mind and I do this." Kara put her hands on Sachs's temples and closed her eyes for a moment.

She stepped away and handed Sachs back the earring she'd just plucked from the policewoman's left ear.

"I never felt a thing."

"But the audience'd know instantly how I did it—because touching someone while you're pretending to read minds, which most people don't believe in anyway, isn't natural. But if I say part of a trick is for me to whisper a word so that nobody else can hear." She leaned closer to Sachs's ear, with her right hand over her own mouth. "See, that's a natural gesture."

"You missed the other earring," Sachs said, laughing; she'd lifted a protective hand to her ear when Kara had stepped close.

"But I vanished your necklace. It's gone."

Even Rhyme couldn't help but be impressed—and amused, watching Sachs touch her neck and chest, smiling but troubled to keep losing accessories. Sellitto laughed like a little kid and Mel Cooper gave up on the evidence to watch the show. The policewoman looked around her for the jewelry and then at Kara, who offered her empty right hand. "Vanished," she repeated.

"But," Rhyme said suspiciously, "I *do* notice that your left hand's in a fist behind your back. Which is, by the way, a rather *unnatural* gesture. So I assume the necklace is there."

"Ah, you're good," Kara said. Then laughed. "But not at catching moves, I'm afraid." She opened her left hand and it too was empty.

Rhyme scowled.

"Keeping my left fist closed and out of sight? Well, that was the most important misdirection of all. I did that because I knew you'd spot it and it would focus your attention on my left hand. We call it 'forcing.' I *forced* you to think you'd figured out my method. And as soon as you did that your mind snapped shut and you stopped considering any other explanations for what had happened. And when you—and everybody else—were staring at my left hand that gave me the chance to slip the necklace into Amelia's pocket."

Sachs reached inside and pulled the chain out.

Cooper applauded. Rhyme gave a grudging but impressed grunt.

Kara nodded toward the evidence board. "So, that's what *he's* going to do, this killer. Misdirection. You'll think you've figured out what he's up to but that's part of his plan. Just like I did, he'll use your suspicions—and your intelligence—against you. In fact, he *needs* your suspicions and intelligence for his tricks to work. Mr. Balzac says that the best illusionists'll rig the trick so well that they'll point directly at their method, directly at what they're really going to do. But you won't believe them. You'll look in the opposite direction. When that happens,

you've had it. You've lost and they've won."
The reference to her mentor seemed to upset her and she glanced at the clock and offered a faint grimace. "I really have to get
back now. I've been away too long."

Sachs thanked her, and Sellitto said, "I'll
get a car to take you back to the store."

"Well, *near* the store. I don't want him to
know where I've been. . . . Oh, one thing
you might want to do? There's a circus in
town. The Cirque Fantastique. I know they
have a quick-change act. You might want to
check it out."

Sachs nodded. "They're setting up right
across the street in Central Park."

The park was often the site for large-scale
outdoor concerts and other shows during
the spring and summer. Rhyme and Sachs
had once "attended" a Paul Simon concert
by sitting in front of the criminalist's open
bedroom windows.

Rhyme scoffed. "Oh, *that's* who was rehearsing that god-awful music all night."

"You don't like the circus?" Sellitto asked.

"Of course I don't like the circus," he
snapped. "Who does? Bad food, clowns,
acrobats threatening to *die* in front of your
children. . . . But"—he turned to Kara—

"it's a good suggestion. Thanks. . . . Even though one of *us* should've thought of it before," he said caustically, looking over the others on the team.

Rhyme watched her sling an ugly black-and-white purse over her shoulder. Escaping from him, fleeing into the crip-free world, taking the Look and the Smile with her.

Don't worry. You can give the gimp your insights then get the hell out.

She paused and looked at the evidence board once more with a cloud in her striking blue eyes then started for the door.

"Wait," Rhyme said.

She turned.

"I'd like you to stay."

"What?"

"Work with us on the case. At least for today. You could go with Lon or Amelia to talk to the people at the circus. And there might be more magic evidence we uncover."

"Oh, no. I can't really. It was hard for me to get away now. I can't spend any more time."

Rhyme said, "We could use your help. We've just scratched the surface with this guy."

"You saw Mr. Balzac," she said to Sachs.

In nomine patri . . .

"You know, Linc," Sellitto said uneasily, "better not to have too many civilians on a case. There *are* regs on that."

"Didn't you use a psychic one time?" Rhyme asked dryly.

"*I* didn't fucking hire her. Somebody at HQ did."

"And then you had the dog tracker and—"

"You keep saying 'you.' No, *I* don't hire civilians. Except you. Which gets me into enough shit."

"Ah, you can never get into enough shit in police work, Lon." He glanced at Kara. "Please. It's very important."

The young woman hesitated. "You really think he's going to kill someone else?"

"Yes," he replied, "we do."

The girl finally nodded. "If I'm going to get fired, at least it'll be for a good cause." Then she laughed. "You know, Robert-Houdin did the same thing."

"Who's that?"

"A famous French illusionist and magician. He helped out the police too, well, the French army. Sometime, I don't know, in the 1800s, there were these Algerian extremists, the Marabouts. They were trying to get local tribes to rise up against the French and they kept saying they had magic powers. The French government sent him to Algeria to have a sort of magical duel. To show the tribes that the French had better magic—you know, more power. It worked. Robert-Houdin had tighter tricks than the Marabouts." Then she frowned. "Though I think they almost killed him."

"Don't worry," Sachs reassured her. "I'll make sure that doesn't happen to you."

Then Kara looked over the evidence chart. "You do this in all your cases? Write down all the clues and things you've learned?"

"That's right," Sachs confirmed.

"Here's an idea—most magicians specialize. Like the Conjurer doing both quick-change and large-scale illusion? That's unusual. Let's write down his techniques. That might help narrow down the number of suspects."

"Yeah," Sellitto said, "a profile. Good."

The young woman grimaced. "And I'll have to find somebody to replace me at the shop. Mr. Balzac was going to be out of the store with that friend of his. . . . Oh, man, he's not going to like this." She looked around the room. "There a phone I can use? You know, one of those special ones?"

"Special one?" Thom asked.

"Yeah, in private. So there's nobody around to hear you lie to your boss."

"Oh, *those* phones," the aide said, putting his arm around her shoulders and directing her toward the doorway. "The one *I* use for that's in the hall."

THE CONJURER

Music School Crime Scene

- Perp's description: Brown hair, fake beard, no distinguishing, medium build, medium height, age: fifties. Ring and little fingers of left hand fused together. Changed costume quickly to resemble old, bald janitor.

- No apparent motive.

- Victim: Svetlana Rasnikov.
  - Full-time music student.
  - Checking family, friends, students, coworkers for possible leads.
    - No boyfriends, no known enemies. Performed at children's birthday parties.

- Circuit board with speaker attached.
  - Sent to FBI lab, NYC.

- Digital recorder, probably containing perp's voice. All data destroyed.
  - Voice recorder is a "gimmick." Homemade.

- Used antique iron handcuffs to restrain victim.
  - Handcuffs are Darby irons. Scotland Yard. Checking with Houdini Museum in New Orleans for leads.

- Destroyed victim's watch at exactly 8:00 A.M.

- Cotton string holding chairs. Generic. Too many sources to trace.

- Squib for gunshot effect. Destroyed.
  - Too many sources to trace.

- Fuse. Generic.
  - Too many sources to trace.

- Responding officers reported flash in air. No trace material recovered.
  - Was from flash cotton or flash paper.
    - Too many sources to trace.

- Perp's shoes: size 10 Ecco.

- Silk fibers, dyed gray, processed to a matte finish.
  - From quick-change janitor's outfit.

- Unsub is possibly wearing brown wig.

- Red pignut hickory and Parmelia conspersa lichen, both found primarily in Central Park.

- Dirt impregnated with unusual mineral oil. Sent to FBI for analysis.

- Black silk, 72 x 48''. Used as camouflage. Not traceable.
  - Illusionists use this frequently.

- Wears caps to cover up prints.
  - Magician's finger cups.

- Traces of latex, castor oil, makeup.
  - Theatrical makeup.

- Traces of alginate.
  - Used in molding latex "appliances."

- Murder weapon: white silk-knit rope with black silk core.
  - Rope is a magic trick. Color changing. Not traceable.

- Unusual knot.
  - Sent to FBI and Maritime Museum—no information.
  - Knots are from Houdini routines, virtually impossible to untie.

- Used disappearing ink on sign-in register.

Profile as Illusionist

- Perp will use misdirection against victims and in eluding police.
  - Physical misdirection (for distraction).
  - Psychological (to eliminate suspicion).

- Escape at music school was similar to Vanished Man illusion routine. Too common to trace.

- Perp is primarily an illusionist.

- Talented at sleight of hand.

- Also knows protean (quick change) magic. Will use breakaway clothes, nylon and silk, bald cap, finger cups and other latex appliances. Could be any age, gender or race.

Chapter Nine

They sensed many smells as they walked: blooming lilacs, smoke from the pretzel vendors' carts and families barbecuing chicken and ribs, suntan lotion.

Sachs and Kara were making their way to the huge white tent of the Cirque Fantastique through the damp grass of Central Park.

Noticing two lovers kissing on a bench, Kara asked, "So, he's more than your boss?"

"Lincoln? That's right."

"I could tell. . . . How'd you meet?"

"A case. Serial kidnapper. A few years ago."

"Is it hard, him being that way?"

"No, it's not," Sachs replied simply, which was the complete truth.

"Can they do anything for him, the doctors?"

"There's some surgery he's been thinking about. It's risky, though, and it probably wouldn't do any good. He decided not to last year and hasn't mentioned it since. So the whole thing's been on hold for a while. He may change his mind at some point. But we'll see."

"You don't sound like you're in favor of it."

"I'm not. A lot of risk and not much gain. To me, it's a question of balancing risks. Let's say you want to bust a perp real bad, lots of paper on him, okay? Warrants, I mean. You know he's in a particular apartment. Well, do you go ahead and kick the door in even when you don't know if he's asleep or if he and his buddies have two MP5s pointed at the door? Or do you wait for backup and take the chance that he'll get away? Sometimes the risk is worth it, sometimes it's not. But if he wants to go ahead with the surgery I'm with him. That's the way we work."

Then Sachs explained that he'd been undergoing treatments that involved electronic stimulation of his muscles and a series of exercises that Thom and some physical therapists had been administering—the same exercises that the actor Christopher Reeve had been doing, with remarkable results. "Reeve's an amazing man," Sachs said. "Incredible determination. Lincoln's the same. He doesn't talk about it much but sometimes he just disappears and has Thom and the PTs work on his exercises. I don't hear from him for a few days."

"Another sort of vanished man, hm?" the young woman asked.

"Exactly," Sachs replied, smiling. They were silent for a moment and she wondered if Kara expected more about their relationship. Stories of perseverance over the obvious obstacles, some hint about the knobby details of life as a quad. People's reactions when they were out in public. Or even some hint about the nature of the intimacies. But if she was curious she didn't pursue it.

In fact, Sachs detected mostly envy. Kara continued, "I haven't had much luck lately in the man department."

"Not seeing anybody?"

"I'm not sure," Kara replied pensively. "Our last contact was French toast and mimosas. My place. Brunch in bed. Way romantic. He said he'd call me the next day."

"And no call."

"No call. Oh, and maybe I should add that the aforementioned brunch was three weeks ago."

"Have you called him?"

"I wouldn't do that," she said firmly. "It's in his court."

"Good for you." Pride and power were born joined at the hip, Sachs knew.

Kara laughed. "There's an old routine a magician named William Ellsworth Robinson did. It was way popular. It was called How to Get Rid of a Wife, or The Divorce Machine." A laugh. "That's my story. I can vanish boyfriends faster than anybody."

"Well, they're also pretty good at vanishing themselves, you know," Sachs offered.

"Most of the guys I'd meet working at my old job, the magazine, or the store're interested in two things. A one-night romp in the hay. Or else the opposite—wooing then settling down in the 'burbs. . . . You ever get wooed?"

"Sure," Sachs said. "It can be creepy. Depending on the wooer, of course."

"You got it, sister. So hay-romping or wooing and 'burb-settling . . . they're both a problem for me. I don't want either. Well, a romp now and then. Let's be realistic."

"What about men in the business?"

"Ah, so you noticed I excluded them from the romp/woo equation. Other performers . . . naw, I don't go there. Too many conflicts of interest. They also claim they like strong women but the truth is most of them don't want us in the business at all. The ratio of men to women is about a hundred to one. It's better now. Oh, you see some famous women illusionists. Princess Tenko, an Asian illusionist—she's brilliant. And there're a few others. But that's recent. Twenty, thirty years ago you never saw a woman as the star, only the assistant." A glance at Sachs. "Kind of like the police, huh?"

"It's not as bad as it used to be. Not my generation. The sixties and seventies— that's when women were breaking the ice. That was the hard time. But I've had my share. I was a portable before I moved to crime scene and—"

"A what?"

"A portable's a beat cop. If we ever worked Hell's Kitchen in Midtown they'd partner a woman with some experienced male cop. Sometimes I'd have a knuckle-dragger who hated being with a woman. Just hated it. He didn't say a word to me for the entire watch. Eight hours, walking up and down the streets, this guy not saying a word. We'd go ten-sixty-three for lunch and I'd be sitting there trying to be pleasant and he'd be two feet away, reading the sports section and sighing 'cause he had to waste his time with a woman." Memories came back to her. "I was working the Seven-five house—"

"The what?"

Sachs explained, "Precinct. We call them 'houses.' And most cops don't say Seventy-fifth. In numbers it's always Seven-five or Seventy-five. Like Macy's is on Three-four Street."

"Okay."

"Anyway, the usual supervisor was off and we had a temporary sergeant who was old school. So it's one of my first days at the Seven-five and I'm the only woman on this particular watch. I go to roll call in the assembly room and there're a dozen Kotex taped to the lectern."

"No!"

"Kid you not. The regular supervisor never

would've let anybody get away with that. But cops're like kids in a lot of ways. They push until an adult stops 'em."

"Not what you see in the movies."

"Movies're made in Hollywood. Not in the Seven-five."

"What'd you do? About the pads?"

"I walked up to the front row and asked the cop sitting right in front of the lectern if I could have his seat—which is where I was going to sit anyway. They were all laughing so hard I'm surprised some of them didn't pee their pants. Well, I sat down and just started to take notes about what the sergeant was telling us—you know, outstanding warrants and community relations things and street corners with known drug activity. And about two minutes later, no more laughter. The whole thing became embarrassing. Not for me. For them."

"You know who did it?"

"Sure."

"Did you report him?"

"No. See, that's the hardest part of being a woman cop. You have to work with these people. You need them behind you, watching your back. You can fight every step of the way. But if you have to do that you've already lost. The hardest part isn't having the balls to fight. It's knowing *when* to fight and when to just let it go."

Pride and power . . .

"Like us, I guess. My business. But if you're good, if you can bring in audiences, management'll hire you. It's a catch-22 though. You can't prove you'll draw crowds if they don't hire you, and they won't hire you if you can't bring in door receipts."

They walked closer to the massive, glowing tent and Sachs watched the young woman's eyes light up as she gazed at it.

"This the sort of place you'd like to work?"

"Oh, man, I'll say. This's my idea of heaven. Cirque Fantastique and doing TV specials." After a moment of silence as she gazed around her, she said, "Mr. Balzac has me learning all the old routines and that's important—you've got to know 'em cold. But"—a nod toward the tent—"this is the direction magic's going. David Copperfield, David Blaine . . . performance art, street magic. Sexy magic."

"You should audition here."

"Me? You're kidding," Kara replied. "I'm

nowhere near ready yet. Your act has to be perfect. You have to be the best."

"Better than a man, you mean?"

"No, better than *everybody,* men and women."

"Why?"

"For the audience," Kara explained. "Mr. Balzac's like a broken record: you owe it to the *audience.* Every breath you take on-stage is for your *audience.* Illusion can't be just okay. You can't just satisfy—you have to thrill. If one person in the audience catches your moves you've failed. If you hesitate just a moment too long and the effect is dull you've failed. If one person out there yawns or looks at his watch you've failed."

"You can't be at a hundred percent all the time, I'd think," Sachs offered.

"But you have to be," Kara said simply, sounding surprised anyone would feel different.

They arrived at the Cirque Fantastique, where rehearsals for the opening show tonight were under way. Dozens of performers were walking around, some in costumes, some in shorts and T-shirts or jeans.

"Oh, man. . . ." came a breathy voice. It

was Kara's. Her face was like a little girl's, eyes taking in the brilliant white canvas of the sweeping tent.

Sachs jumped at the sound of a loud crack above and behind her. She looked up and saw two huge banners, thirty or forty feet high, snapping in the wind, glowing in the sunlight. On one was painted the name CIRQUE FANTASTIQUE.

On the other was a huge drawing of a thin man in a black-and-white-checkered body-suit. He was holding his arms forward, palms up, inviting his audience inside. He wore a black, snub-nosed half-mask, the features grotesque. It was a troubling image. She thought immediately of the Conjurer, hidden by masks of disguise.

His motives and plans hidden too.

Kara noticed Sachs's gaze. "It's Arlecchino," she said. "In English, that's 'Harlequin.' You know commedia dell'arte?" she asked.

"No," Sachs said.

"Italian theater. It lasted from, I don't know, the fifteen hundreds for a couple of hundred years. The Cirque Fantastique uses it as a theme." She pointed to smaller banners on the sides of the tent that displayed other masks. With their hook noses or beaks, arching brows, high serpentine cheekbones, they appeared otherworldly and unsettling. Kara continued, "There were a dozen or so continuing characters that all the commedia dell'arte troupes used in their plays. They wore masks to show who they were playing."

"Comedy?" Sachs asked, lifting an eyebrow as she looked at a particularly demonic mask.

"We'd call them black comedies, I guess. Harlequin wasn't exactly a heroic figure. He had no morals at all. All he cared about was food and women. And he'd just appear and disappear, sneak up on you. Another one, Pulcinella, was way sadistic. He played really mean pranks on people, even his lovers. Then there was a doctor who'd poison people. The only voice of reason was this woman, Columbine." Kara added, "One of the things I like about commedia dell'arte was that her part was really played by a woman. Not like in England, where women weren't allowed to perform."

The banner snapped again. Harlequin's eyes seemed to stare off slightly behind them as if the Conjurer were easing up close, an echo of the search at the music school earlier.

No, we don't have a clue who or where he is . . .

She turned away to see a guard approaching, looking over her uniform. "Help you, Officer?"

Sachs asked to see the manager. The man explained that he was away but did they want to talk to an assistant?

Sachs said yes and a moment later a short, thin, harried woman—dark, gypsy-like—arrived.

"Yes, I can help you?" she asked in an indeterminate accent.

After introductions, Sachs said, "We're investigating a series of crimes in the area. We'd like to know if you have any illusionists or quick-change artists appearing in the show."

Concern blossomed in the woman's face. "We have that, yes, of course," she said. "Irina and Vlad Klodoya."

"Spell those please."

Kara was nodding as Sachs wrote down the names. "I know about them, sure. They were with the Circus of Moscow a few years ago."

"Right," confirmed the assistant.

"Have they been here all morning?"

"Yes. They rehearsed until about twenty minutes ago. Now it is they are shopping."

"You're sure this's the only time they've been away?"

"Yes. I supervise myself where everyone is."

"Anyone else?" Sachs asked. "Maybe somebody who's had training at illusion or magic? I mean, even if they're not performing."

"No, nobody. Those are only the two."

"Okay," Sachs said. "What we're going to do is have a couple of police officers parked outside. They should be here in about fifteen minutes. If you hear about anyone bothering your employees or the audience, acting suspicious, tell the officers right away." This had been Rhyme's suggestion.

"I will tell everyone, yes. But can you please to tell me what is this about?"

"A man with some illusionist experience was involved in a homicide earlier today. There's no connection to your show that we know of but we just want to be on the safe side."

They thanked the assistant, who offered a

troubled farewell, probably sorry that she'd asked the reason for the visit.

Outside, Sachs asked, "What's the story on those performers?"

"The Ukrainians?"

"Yeah. Do we trust 'em?"

"Husband and wife team. Have a couple of children who travel with them. They're two of the best quick-change artists in the world. I can't imagine they'd have anything to do with the killings." She laughed. "See *that's* who gets jobs at Cirque Fantastique—performers who've been pros since they were five or six."

Sachs called Rhyme's phone and got Thom. She gave him the Ukrainian performers' names and what she'd learned. "Have Mel or somebody run them through NCIC and the State Department."

"Will do."

She disconnected the call and they started out of the park, walking west toward a slash of livid clouds, like striations of bruise, in the otherwise brilliant sky.

Another loud snap behind her—the banners again, flapping in the breeze, as the playful Harlequin continued to beckon passersby into his otherworldly kingdom.

• • •

Refreshed, Revered Audience?

Relaxed?

Good, because it's time now for our second routine.

You may not know the name P. T. Selbit, but if you've been to any magic shows at all or seen illusionists on television you're probably familiar with some of the tricks this Englishman made popular in the early 1900s.

Selbit began his career performing under his real name, Percy Thomas Tibbles, but he soon learned that such a mild name didn't suit a performer whose forte wasn't card tricks, vanishing doves or levitating children but sadomasochistic routines that shocked—and therefore, of course, drew—crowds throughout the world.

Selbit—yes, his stage name was the reverse of his surname—created the famous Living Pincushion, in which a girl was apparently skewered with eighty-four needle-sharp spikes. Another of his creations was the Fourth Dimension, a routine where audiences watched in horror as a young woman was seemingly crushed to death under a huge box. One of my favorites of Selbit's was a routine he introduced in 1922. The title says it all, Revered Audience: The Idol of Blood, or Destroying a Girl.

Today I'm delighted to present to you an updated variation of Selbit's most renowned illusion, one that he presented in dozens of countries and that he was invited to perform at the Royal Command Variety Performance in the London Hippodrome.

It's known as . . .

Ah, but no . . .

No, Revered Audience. I think I'll keep you in suspense and refrain for the moment from mentioning the name of the illusion. But I'll give you one clue: when Selbit was performing this routine he instructed his assistants to pour fake blood into the gutters in front of the theater to tantalize passersby and get them to buy tickets. Which, naturally, they did.

Enjoy our next routine.

I hope you will.

I know of one person who most certainly won't.

Chapter Ten

How much sleep? the young man wondered.

The play had ended at midnight then there'd been drinks at the White Horse until who knew when, home at three, on the phone for forty minutes with Bragg, no, maybe an hour. Then the ridiculous plumbing had started up its ridiculous banging at 8:30.

How many hours' sleep was that then?

The math eluded Tony Calvert and he decided that it was probably better not to know too much about the extent of his exhaustion. At least he was working on Broadway and not doing advertising shoots, where you started work sometimes at—heaven help us—6:00 A.M. His afternoon call at the Gielgud Theater tidily made up for the fact that he had to work Saturdays and Sundays.

He surveyed the tools of his trade and decided he needed some more tattoo concealer since chisel-chin boy was standing in today and the ladies from Teaneck and Garden City might wonder about the credibility of a leading man who lusted after the ingenue starlet when his ample biceps said "Love Forever Robert."

Calvert closed the big yellow makeup case and glanced in the mirror by the door. He looked better than he felt, he had to admit. His complexion still retained a bit of the tan from the glorious March trip down to St. Thomas. And his trim build belied the dumpy sluggishness churning in his belly. (God's sake, keep it to four beers. Okay? *Hello,* can we live with that?) His eyes, though: yep, pretty red. But that's easily taken care of. A stylist knows hundreds of ways to make the old look young, the plain look beautiful and the weary look alert. He attacked with eyedrops and then followed through with the coup de grâce—a swipe or two with an under-eye touch-up stick.

Calvert pulled on his leather jacket, locked the door and started down the hallway of his East Village apartment building, quiet now, a few minutes before noon. Most of the people in the building, he guessed, were outside, enjoying the first truly nice spring weekend this year or were still sleeping off their own debaucheries.

He used the back exit, as he always did, which deposited him in the alleyway behind the building. Starting for the sidewalk, forty feet away, he noticed something: motion down one of the culs-de-sac leading off the alley.

He stopped and squinted into the dimness. An animal. Jesus, was that a rat?

But no—it was a cat, apparently injured. He looked around but the alleyway was completely deserted, no sign of its owner.

Oh, the poor thing!

Calvert wasn't a pet person but he'd sat for a neighbor's Norwich terrier last year and remembered the man telling him that, just in case, Bilbo's vet was around the corner on St. Marks. He'd take the cat in on the way to the subway. Maybe his sister'd want it. She adopted children. Why not cats?

Lingering in alleys wasn't the best idea in this neighborhood but Calvert saw that he was still completely alone. He moved slowly over the cobblestones so he wouldn't spook the animal. It was lying on its side, meowing faintly.

Could he pick it up? Would it try to scratch him? He remembered something in *Prevention* about cat-scratch fever. But the animal looked too weak to hurt him.

"Hey, what's the matter, fella?" he asked in a soothing voice. "You hurt?"

Crouching down, he set his makeup case on the cobblestones and reached out carefully in case the cat took a swipe at him. He touched it but then drew his hand back in shock. The animal was ice-cold and emaciated—he could feel stiff bones beneath the skin. Had it just died? But, no, the leg was still moving. And it uttered another faint meow.

He touched it again. And, wait, those weren't *bones* under the skin. They were rods, and inside its body was a metal box.

What the fuck was this?

Was he on *Candid Camera*? Or was some asshole just ragging him?

Then he glanced up and saw someone ten feet away. Calvert gasped and reared back. A man was crouching—

But, no, he realized. It was his *own* image,

reflected in a full-length mirror sitting in the corner at the end of the dark alley. Calvert saw his face, shocked, eyes wide, frozen for a moment. He started to relax and laughed. But then he frowned, watching himself slowly falling forward—as the mirror pivoted to the cobblestones and shattered.

The bearded, middle-aged man hiding behind it charged forward, raising a large piece of pipe.

"No! Help me!" the young man cried, scrabbling away. "My God, my God!"

The pipe swung down in a fierce arc directly toward his head.

But Calvert grabbed the makeup case fast and thrust it toward the attacker, deflecting the blow. He struggled to his feet and began to run. The assailant started after him but slipped on the slick cobblestones and went down hard on one knee.

"Take the wallet! Take it!" He pulled his billfold from his pocket and flung it behind him. But the man ignored it and rose, continuing after him. He was between Calvert and the street; the only escape was back into the building.

Oh, Jesus, Jesus, Lord. . . .

"Help me, help me, help me!"

Keys! he thought. Get them now! Fishing them out of his jeans as he gave a brief glance behind him. The man was only thirty feet or so away. If I don't get the door unlocked on the first try, that's it . . . I'm dead.

Calvert didn't even slow down. He slammed hard into the metal door and, a miracle, slid the key home instantly, turning it fast. The latch opened, he pulled the key out and leaped through the doorway, slamming the steel door shut behind him. It locked automatically.

Heart pounding fiercely, gasping in fear, he rested only for a moment. Thinking, mugger? Gay-basher? Druggie? Didn't matter, he thought. I'm not letting the prick get away. He ran up the hall to his apartment. This door too he opened fast. He leaped inside, swinging it shut after him and locking it.

Hurrying into the kitchen, he seized the phone and dialed 911. A moment later a woman's voice said, "Police and fire emergency."

"A man! A man just attacked me! He's outside."

"Are you injured?"

"No, but you have to send the police!" he shouted. "Hurry!"

"Is he there with you?"

"No, he didn't get in. I locked the doors. But he could still be in the alley! You have to hurry!"

What was that? Calvert wondered. He felt a sudden breeze against his face. The sensation was familiar and he realized that it was the feeling of cross ventilation when someone opened the front door to his apartment.

The 911 operator asked, "Hello, sir, are you there? Can you—"

Calvert spun toward the door and cried out, seeing the bearded man with the pipe, standing only a few feet from him, calmly unplugging the phone line from the wall. The doors! How did he get through the locks?

Calvert backed away as far as he could—against the refrigerator; there was nowhere else to go.

"What?" he whispered, noting the scars on the man's neck, his deformed left hand. "What do you want?"

The assailant ignored him for a moment and looked around—first at the kitchen table then at the large wooden coffee table in the living room. Something about the sight of it seemed to please him. He turned back and when he brought the pipe down on Calvert's raised arms the swing seemed almost like an afterthought.

They rolled up, silent.

Two RMPs, two officers in each.

The sergeant climbed out of the first squad car before it'd braked to a stop. Only six minutes had elapsed since the 911 call came in. Even though the call had been cut off, Central knew which building and apartment it had been placed from, thanks to caller-ID technology.

Six minutes. . . . If they were lucky they'd find the vic alive and well. If they were less lucky, at least the doer'd still be in the apartment, shopping through the vic's valuables.

He called in on his Motorola. "Sergeant Four Five Three One to Central. I'm ten-eighty-four on the scene of that assault on Nine Street, K."

"Roger, Four Five Three One. EMS bus en route. Injuries, K?"

"Don't know yet. Out."

"Roger, Four Five. Out."

He sent one of his men around to the back to cover the service door and the rear windows and told another to stay in the front. The third officer trotted with the sergeant toward the lobby.

If they were lucky the perp'd jump out a window and break an ankle. The sergeant wasn't in any mood to run assholes to ground on this fine day.

This was Alphabet City, its name courtesy of the north-south avenues here—A, B, C how fast I can cook some smack and shoot up. It was improving slowly but was still one of the most dangerous neighborhoods in Manhattan. Both cops had their weapons drawn by the time they approached the door.

If they were lucky he'd be armed only with a knife. Or something like what that cluck-head gone on crack had threatened him with last week: a chopstick and garbage can lid for a shield.

Well, they got one break at least—they didn't have to find somebody to let them through the security door. An elderly woman, listing against the weight of a shopping bag that sprouted a huge pineapple, was on her way out. Blinking in surprise, she held the door open for the two cops and they hurried inside, answering her question about their presence with a non-committal, "Nothing to be concerned about, ma'am."

If we're lucky . . .

Apartment 1J was on the ground floor toward the back. The sergeant positioned himself to the left of the door. The other officer, opposite, glanced at him and nodded. The sergeant rapped hard with his big knuckles. "Police. Open the door. Open it now!"

No response from inside.

"Police!"

He tried the knob. More luck. It was unlocked. The sergeant shoved the door open and both men stood back, waiting. Finally the sergeant peeked 'round the corner.

"Oh, Christ on earth," he whispered when he saw what was in the center of the living room.

The word "luck" vanished from his thoughts entirely.

The secret to successful protean magic—quick change—is making distinct but sim-

ple changes to your appearance and demeanor while simultaneously distracting
your audience with misdirection.

And no change was more distinctive than
turning yourself into a seventy-five-year-old
bag woman.

Malerick had known the police would arrive quickly. So after the brief performance
in Tony Calvert's apartment he did a fast
change into one of his escape outfits: a
high-necked blue dress and a white wig. He
pulled his elasticized jeans above the hem-
line of the dress, revealing opaque support
hose. The beard came off and he applied a
heavy base of eccentric-lady rouge. He
painted on excessive eyebrow liner. Several
dozen strokes with a thin sienna pencil gave
him septuagenarian wrinkles. A change of
shoes.

As for the misdirection, he'd found a
shopping bag and filled the bottom with
newspaper—along with the pipe and the
other weapon he'd used for his routine—
and added a large fresh pineapple from
Calvert's kitchen. If he met anyone as he left
the building they might glance at him but
they'd focus on the sizable pineapple,

which is just what happened as he politely held the door open for the arriving officers.

Now, a quarter mile from the building, still dressed as the woman, he stopped and leaned against the wall of a building as if he were catching his breath. Then he eased into a dim alley. With one tug the dress, held together by tiny Velcro dots, came off. This garment and the wig went under a foot-wide elastic band he wore around his stomach, which compressed the items and made them invisible under his shirt.

He tugged his pants cuffs down, took makeup removal pads from a Baggie in his pocket and wiped his face until the rouge, wrinkles and eyebrow pencil were gone, checking to make sure with a small pocket mirror. The pads he dropped into the shopping bag with the pineapple, which he in turn placed in a green garbage bag. He found a car illegally parked, picked the lock to the trunk and tossed the bag inside. The police would never think to search the trunks of parked cars and, anyway, the odds were that the car would be towed before the owner returned.

Back on the street, heading for one of the West Side subways.

And what did you think of our second act, Revered Audience?

He himself thought it had gone well, considering that because he'd slipped on the damn cobblestones the performer had gotten away and managed to close and lock two doors.

But by the time Malerick had gotten to the back door of Calvert's building he had his picking tools in hand.

Malerick had studied the fine art of lock-picking for years. It was one of the first skills his mentor had taught him. A picker uses two tools: a tension wrench, which is inserted into the lock and twisted to keep pressure on the locking pins inside, and the pick itself, which pushes each pin out of the way so the lock can be turned to the open position.

It can be time-consuming to push aside the pins one at a time, though, so Malerick had mastered a very difficult technique called "scrubbing," in which you move the pick back and forth quickly, brushing the pins out of the way. Scrubbing only works when the lock picker senses exactly the right combination of torque on the cylinder and pressure on the pins. Using tools that were only a few inches long, it had taken Malerick less than thirty seconds to scrub open the locks in both the back door and the apartment door of Calvert's place.

Does that seem impossible, Revered Audience?

But that's the job of illusionists, you know: rendering the impossible real.

Pausing outside the subway he bought a *New York Times* and flipped through it as he studied passersby. Again, it seemed that no one had followed him. He trotted down the stairs to catch the train. A truly cautious performer might have waited a bit longer to be absolutely sure he wasn't being tailed. But Malerick didn't have much time. The next routine would be a difficult one—he'd set quite major challenges for himself—and he had to make some preparations.

He didn't dare risk disappointing his audience.

Chapter Eleven

"It's bad, Rhyme."

Amelia Sachs was speaking into the stalk mike as she stood in the doorway of apartment 1J, in the heart of Alphabet City.

Earlier that morning Lon Sellitto had ordered all dispatchers at Central to call him immediately with news of any homicide in New York City. When a report came in about this particular killing they concluded that it was the work of the Conjurer: the mysterious way the killer had gained access to the man's apartment was one clue. The clincher, though, was that he'd smashed the victim's wristwatch—just as he'd done with the student's at the first killing that morning.

One thing that was different was the cause of death. Which had prompted Sachs's comment to Rhyme. While Sellitto gave commands to the detectives and patrol officers in the hall Sachs studied the unfortunate vic—a young man named Anthony Calvert. He lay on his back in the middle of the coffee table in the living room, spread-eagled, hands and feet tied to the legs of the table. His abdomen had been sawn completely through down to his spine.

Sachs now described the injury to Rhyme.

"Well," said the criminalist unemotionally. "Consistent."

"Consistent?"

"I'd say he's keeping with the magic theme. Ropes in the first killing. Cutting someone in half now." His voice rose as he called across the room, presumably to Kara. "That's a magic trick, right? Cutting somebody in half?" A pause and then he was addressing Sachs again. "She said it's a classic illusionist trick."

He was right, she realized; she'd been shocked at the sight and hadn't made the connection between the two killings.

An illusionist trick . . .

Though grotesque mutilation described it better.

Keep detached, she told herself. A sergeant would be detached.

But then a thought occurred to her. "Rhyme, you think . . ."

"What?"

"You think he was alive when the perp started cutting? His hands're tied to the table legs, spread-eagle."

"Oh, you mean maybe he left something for us, some clue about the killer's identity? Good."

"No," she said softly. "Thinking about the pain."

"Oh. That."

Oh. That . . .

"Blood work'll tell."

Then she noticed a major blunt-object trauma to Calvert's temple. That wound hadn't bled much, which suggested that his heart had stopped beating soon after the skull had been crushed.

"No, Rhyme, looks like the cutting was postmortem."

She vaguely heard the criminalist's voice talking to his aide, telling Thom to write this on the evidence chart. He was saying something else but she wasn't paying any attention. The sight of the victim gripped her hard and wouldn't let go. But this was as she wanted it. Yes, she could give up the dead—the way all crime scene cops had to do—and in a moment she would. But death, she felt, deserved a moment of stillness. Sachs did this not out of any sense of spirituality, though, or abstract respect for the dead; no, it was for herself, so that her heart would resist hardening to stone, a process that happened all too frequently in this calling.

She realized that Rhyme was talking to her. "What?" she asked.

"I was wondering, any weapons?"

"No sign of them. But I haven't searched yet."

A sergeant and a uniformed officer joined Sellitto in the doorway. "Been talking to the neighbors," one of them said. Nodding toward the body then doing a double take. She guessed he hadn't seen the carnage up close yet. "Vic was a nice, quiet guy. Everybody liked him. Gay but not into rough trade or anything. Hadn't been seeing anybody for a while."

Sachs nodded then said into her mike, "Doesn't sound like he knew the killer, Rhyme."

"We didn't think that was likely now, did we?" the criminalist said. "The Conjurer's got a different agenda—whatever the hell it is."

"What line of work?" she asked the officers.

"Makeup artist and stylist for one of the theaters on Broadway. We found his case in the alley. You know, hair spray, makeup, brushes."

Sachs wondered if Calvert had ever been hired by commercial photographers and, if so, if he'd worked on her when she'd been with the Chantelle modeling agency on Madison Avenue. Unlike many photographers and the ad agency account people, makeup artists treated models as if they were human beings. An account exec might offer, "All right, let's get her painted and see what she looks like," and the makeup artist would mutter, "Excuse me, I didn't know she was a picket fence."

An Asian-American detective from the Ninth Precinct, which covered this part of town, walked up to the doorway, hanging up his cell phone. "How 'bout this one, huh?" he asked breezily.

"How 'bout it," Sellitto muttered. "Any

idea how he got away? The vic called nine-one-one himself. Your respondings must've got to the scene in ten minutes."

"Six," the detective said.

A sergeant said, "We rolled up silent and covered all the doors and windows. When we got inside, the body was still warm. I'm talking ninety-eight point six. We did a door-to-door but no sign of the doer."

"Wits?"

The sergeant nodded. "The only person in the hall when we got here was this old lady. She was the one let us in. When she gets back we'll talk to her. Maybe she got a look at him."

"She left?" Sellitto asked.

"Yeah."

Rhyme had heard. "You know who it was, don't you?"

"Goddamn," the policewoman snapped.

The detective said, "No, it's okay. We left cards under everybody's door. She'll call us back."

"No, she won't," Sachs said, sighing. "That was the doer."

"Her?" the sergeant asked, his voice high. He laughed.

"She wasn't a *her*," Sachs explained. "She only looked like an old lady."

"Hey, Officer," Sellitto said, "let's not get too paranoid. The guy can't do a sex-change operation or anything."

"Yes, he can. Remember what Kara told us. It was her, Lieutenant. Want to bet?"

In her ear Rhyme's voice said, "I'm not taking odds on *that* one, Sachs."

The sergeant said defensively, "She was, like, seventy years old or something. And carrying a big bag of groceries. A pineapple—"

"Look," she said and pointed to the kitchen counter, on which were two spiky leaves. Next to them was a little card on a rubber band, courtesy of Dole, offering tasty recipes for fresh pineapple.

Hell. They'd *had* him—he was inches away from them.

"And," Rhyme continued, "he probably had the murder weapon in the grocery bag."

She repeated this to the increasingly sullen detective from the Nine.

"You didn't see her face, right?" she asked the sergeant.

"Not really. Just glanced at her. It was like, you know, all made up. Covered with, what's that stuff? My grandmother used to wear it?"

"Rouge?" Sachs asked.

"Yeah. And painted-on eyebrows. . . . Well, we'll find her now. She . . . *he* can't've got that far."

Rhyme said, "He's changed clothes again, Sachs. Probably dumped them nearby."

She said to the Asian detective, "He's wearing something else now. But the sergeant here can give you a description of the clothes. You should send a detail to check out the Dumpsters and the alleyways around here."

The detective frowned coolly and looked Sachs up and down. A cautionary glance from Sellitto reminded her that an important part of *becoming* sergeant was not acting like one until you actually were. He then authorized the search and the detective picked up his radio and called it in.

Sachs suited up in the Tyvek overalls and walked the grid in the hall and the alleyway (where she found the strangest bit of evidence she'd ever come across: a toy black cat). She then ran the gruesome scene in the young man's apartment, processed the body and assembled the evidence.

She was heading for her car when Sellitto stopped her.

"Hey, hold on, Officer." He hung up his phone, on which he'd apparently just had a difficult conversation, to judge from his scowl. "I've gotta meet with the captain and dep com about the Conjurer case. But I need you to do something for me. We're going to add somebody to the team. I want you to pick him up."

"Sure. But why somebody else?"

"'Cause we've had two bodies in four hours and there're no fucking suspects," he snapped. "And that means the brass aren't happy. And here's your first lesson about being a sergeant—when the brass ain't happy, *you* ain't happy."

The Bridge of Sighs.

This was the aerial walkway connecting the two soaring towers of the Manhattan Detention Center on Centre Street in downtown Manhattan.

The Bridge of Sighs—the route walked by the grandest Mafiosos with a hundred hired kills to their names. Walked by terrified young men who'd done nothing more than take a Sammy Sosa baseball bat to the asshole who'd knocked up their sister or cousin. By edgy cluckheads who'd killed a tourist for forty-two dollars 'cause I needed the crack, needed the rock, needed it, man, I *needed* it. . . .

Amelia Sachs crossed the bridge now, on her way to detention—technically the Bernard B. Kerik Complex but still known informally as the Tombs, a nickname inherited from the original city jail located across the street. Here, high above the governmental 'hood of the city, Sachs gave her name to a guard, surrendered her Glock (she'd left her unofficial weapon—a switchblade—in the Camaro) and entered the secure lobby on the other side of a noisy, electric door. It groaned shut.

A few minutes later the man she was here to pick up came out of a nearby prisoner interview room. Trim, in his late thirties, with thinning brown hair and a faint grin molded into his easygoing face. He wore a black sportscoat over a blue dress shirt and jeans.

"Amelia, hey there," came the drawl. "So

I can hitch a ride with you up to Lincoln's place?"

"Hi, Rol. You bet."

Detective Roland Bell unbuttoned his jacket and she caught a glimpse of his belt. He, too, in accordance with regs, was weaponless but she noticed *two* empty holsters on Bell's midriff. She remembered when they worked together they often compared stories of "driving nails," a southernism for shooting—one of his hobbies and for Sachs a competitive sport.

Two men who'd also been in the prisoner interview room joined them. One was in a suit, a detective she'd met before. Crew cut Luis Martinez, a quiet man with fast, careful eyes.

The second man wore Saturday business clothes: khaki slacks and a black Izod shirt, under a faded windbreaker. He was introduced to Sachs as Charles Grady though Sachs knew him by sight; the assistant district attorney was a celebrity among New York law enforcers. The lean, middle-aged Harvard Law grad had remained in the D.A.'s office long after most prosecutors had fled to more lucrative pastures. "Pit bull" and "tenacious" were just two of the many clichés the press regularly applied to him. He was likened favorably to Rudolph Giuliani; unlike the former mayor, however, Grady had no political aspirations. He was content to stay in the prosecutor's office and pursue his passion, which he described simply as "putting bad guys in jail."

And which he happened to be damn good at; his conviction record was one of the best in the history of the city.

Bell was here thanks to Grady's current case. The state was prosecuting a forty-five-year-old insurance agent who lived in a small rural town in upstate New York. Andrew Constable was known less for writing home-owner's policies, though, than for his local militia group, the Patriot Assembly. He was charged with conspiracy to commit murder and hate crimes and the case had been moved down here on a change of venue motion.

As the trial date approached, Grady had begun to get death threats. Then a few days ago the prosecutor had received a call from the office of Fred Dellray, an FBI agent who often worked with Rhyme and Sellitto. Dellray was currently in parts unknown on a classified anti-terrorist assignment but fellow agents had learned that a serious attempt on Grady's life might be imminent. Thursday night or early Friday morning Grady's office had been burglarized. At that point the decision was made to call Roland Bell.

The soft-spoken North Carolina native's official assignment was working Homicide and other major crimes with Lon Sellitto. But he also headed up an unofficial division of NYPD detectives known as SWAT, which wasn't the same famous acronym that every viewer of *Cops* knows; this version stood for the "Saving the Witness's Ass Team."

Bell had, as he expressed it, "this sorta knack for keeping people alive other people want dead."

The result was that in addition to his regular investigation caseload with Sellitto and Rhyme, Bell ended up doing double duty running the protection detail.

But now Grady's bodyguards were in place and the brass downtown—the *unhappy* brass—had decided to gear up the effort to nail the Conjurer. More muscle was needed on the Sellitto-Rhyme team and Bell was a logical choice.

"So that was Andrew Constable," Grady

said to Bell, with a nod through the greasy window into the interview room.

Sachs stepped to the window and saw a slim, rather distinguished-looking prisoner in an orange jumpsuit, sitting at a table, his head down, nodding slowly.

"He what you expected?" Grady continued.

"Don't reckon'," Bell drawled. "Was thinkin' he'd be more hill country. More of a blueprint bigot, you know what I mean? But that fella, he's fair mannerable. Fact is, Charles, I have to say, he didn't *feel* guilty."

"Sure doesn't." Grady grimaced. "Gonna be hard to get a conviction." Then a wry laugh. "But that's what they pay me the big bucks for." Grady's salary was less than that of a first-year associate at a Wall Street law firm.

Bell asked, "Anything more about the break-in at your office? The preliminary crime scene report ready yet? I need to see it."

"It's being expedited. We'll make sure you get a copy."

Bell said, "We got another situation needs looking into. I'll leave my fellows and girls with you and your family. But I'll be a phone call away."

"Thanks, Detective," Grady said. He then added, "My daughter says hi. We've got to get her together with your boys. And meet that lady friend of yours. Where's she live again?"

"Lucy's down in North Carolina."

"She's police too, right?"

"Yep, acting head of the sheriff's department. Metropolis of Tanner's Corner."

Luis Martinez noticed Grady start for the door and he was instantly at the prosecutor's side. "You just want to wait here for a minute, Charles?" The bodyguard left the secure area and retrieved his pistol from the guard who oversaw the lockbox behind the desk and looked over the hallway and bridge carefully.

It was then that a soft voice sounded behind them.

"Hello, miss."

Sachs detected in the words a particular lilt, formed by a history of service labor and contact with the public. She turned and saw Andrew Constable standing next to a huge guard. The prisoner was quite tall, his posture completely erect. His salt-and-pepper hair was wavy and thick. His short, round lawyer stood next to him.

He continued, "Are you part of the team looking out for Mr. Grady?"

"Andrew," his lawyer cautioned.

The prisoner nodded. But kept his eyebrow raised as he looked at Sachs.

"It's not my case," she said to him dismissively.

"Ah, no? Was just going to tell you what I told Detective Bell. I honestly don't know anything about those threats against Mr. Grady." He turned to Bell, who gazed back at the suspect. The Tarheel cop could sometimes look bashful and reserved but that was never the case when confronting a suspect. A cool glare was his response now.

"You have to do your job. I understand that. But believe me, I wouldn't hurt Mr. Grady. One of the things that made this country great is playing fair." A laugh. "I'll beat him at trial. Which I *will* do—thanks to my brilliant young friend here." A nod toward his lawyer. Then a look of curiosity at Bell. "One thing I wanted to mention, Detective. I was wondering if you might have some interest in what my Patriots've been doing up in Canton Falls."

"Me?"

"Oh, I don't mean that crazy conspiracy nonsense. I mean what we're really about."

The prisoner's lawyer said, "Come on, Andrew. Better to keep quiet."

"Just conversing here, Joe." A glance at Bell. "How 'bout it?"

"How d'you mean, sir?" Bell asked stiffly.

The expected allusion to racism and the detective's southern roots didn't rear its head. He said, "States' rights, working folk, local government versus federal. You should go to our website, Detective." He laughed. "People expect swastikas. They get Thomas Jefferson and George Mason." When Bell said nothing a thick silence filled the close air around them. The prisoner shook his head then he laughed and looked abashed. "Lord, sorry me. . . . Sometimes I just can't stop myself—all this ridiculous preaching. Get a few people around me and look what happens—I outstay my welcome."

The guard said, "Lessgo."

"All right then," the prisoner responded. A nod to Sachs, one to Bell. He shuffled down the hall to the faint clink of the shackles on his legs. His lawyer nodded to the prosecutor—two adversaries who respected and yet were wary of each other—and left the secure area.

A moment later Grady, Bell and Sachs followed, and joined Martinez.

The policewoman said, "Doesn't seem like a monster. What're the charges exactly?"

Grady said, "Some ATF folk working undercover on a weapons sting upstate found out about this plot we think Constable was behind. Some of his people were going to lure state troopers to remote areas of the county on fake nine-one-one calls. If any of them were black they were going to kidnap them, strip them naked and lynch 'em. Oh, there was some suggestion of castration too."

Sachs, who'd dealt with plenty of terrible crimes in her years on the force, blinked in shock at this horrific news. "Are you serious?"

Grady nodded. "And that was just the start of it. It seems the lynchings were all part of a grand plan. They were hoping that if they murdered enough troopers and the media televised the hangings, the blacks'd rise up in some kind of revolt. That'd give the whites around the country the chance to retaliate and wipe them out. They were hoping the Latinos and Asians would join the blacks, and the white revolution could take them out too."

"In this day and age?"

"You'd be surprised."

Bell nodded to Luis. "He's in your care now. Stay close."

"You bet," the detective responded. Grady and the slim bodyguard left the detention lobby while Sachs and Bell retrieved their weapons from the check-in desk. As they returned to the courthouse portion of the Criminal Courts building, walking over the Bridge of Sighs, Sachs told Bell about the Conjurer and his victims.

Bell winced, hearing about Anthony Calvert's gruesome death. "Motive?"

"Don't know."

"Pattern?"

"Ditto."

"What's the perp look like?" Bell asked.

"Little dicey on that part too."

"Nothin' at *all*?"

"We think he's a white male, medium build."

"So nobody's got a look at him, huh?"

"Actually a lot of people have. Except the first time they did, he was a dark-haired, bearded male in his fifties. Next time he was a bald janitor in his sixties. Then he was a woman in her seventies."

Bell waited for her to laugh, signifying that this was a joke. When she remained grim-faced he asked, "This for no foolin'?"

"'Fraid it is, Roland."

"I'm good," Bell said, shaking his head and tapping the automatic pistol on his right hip. "But I need a target."

Now there's a prayer for you, thought Amelia Sachs.

Chapter Twelve

The evidence from the second scene had arrived and Mel Cooper was arranging the bags and vials on examining tables in Rhyme's parlor.

Sellitto had just returned from a tense meeting at the Big Building about the Conjurer case. The deputy commissioner and the mayor wanted details on the progress of a case about which there were few details and had been no progress.

Rhyme had heard back about the Ukrainian illusionists with the Cirque Fantastique and learned that they had no record. The two police officers stationed at the tent had also been checking around the circus and reported no leads or suspicious activity.

A moment later Sachs strode into the room, accompanied by the even-keeled

Roland Bell. When Sellitto had been ordered to add another detective to the team Rhyme had immediately suggested Bell; he liked the idea of a streetwise cop, who was a crack shot, backing up Sachs in the field.

Greetings and introductions all around. Bell hadn't been told about Kara and she answered his querying glance with: "I'm like him." A nod toward Rhyme. "Sort of a consultant."

Bell said, "Nice to meetcha." And blinked to see her absently rolling three coins back and forth over her knuckles simultaneously.

As Sachs went to work on the evidence with Cooper, Rhyme asked, "Who was he, the vic?"

"Name was Anthony Calvert. Thirty-two. Unmarried. Well, no partner, in his case."

"Any connection with the student at the music school?"

"Doesn't seem to be," Sellitto answered. "Bedding and Saul've checked it out."

"What was his job?" Cooper asked.

"Makeup stylist on Broadway."

And the first one was a musician and music student, Rhyme reflected. One straight female, one gay male victim. Lived and worked in different neighborhoods. What could link the killings? He asked, "Any feel-good stuff?"

But since the first crime hadn't been sexual in nature Rhyme wasn't surprised when Sachs said, "Nope. Not unless he takes his memories home to bed with him. . . . And he gets off on this." She stepped to the whiteboard and taped up the digital photos of the body.

Rhyme wheeled closer and studied the gruesome images.

"Sick fuck." Sellitto offered this lethargic observation.

"And the weapon was?" Roland Bell asked.

"Looks like a crosscut saw," Cooper said, examining some close-ups of the wounds.

Bell, who'd seen his share of carnage as a cop both in North Carolina and New York, shook his head. "Well, now that's a tough shell."

As Rhyme continued to study the pictures he was suddenly aware of an odd noise, an erratic hissing from nearby. He turned to see Kara behind him. The sound was her frantic breath. She was looking at the pictures of Calvert's body. She ran her hand compulsively over her short hair as she stared, transfixed, at the photos, tear-filled eyes wide in shock. Her jaw trembled. She turned away from the board.

"Are you—?" Sachs began.

Kara held up a hand, closed her eyes, breathing hard.

Rhyme knew then, seeing the pain in her face, that this was it for her. She'd reached the end. His life—crime scene work—entailed this type of horror; her world didn't. The risks and dangers in her profession were, of course, illusory and it was too much to expect civilians to confront this revulsion voluntarily. This was a true shame because they needed her help desperately. But, seeing the horror in her face, he knew they couldn't subject her to any more of this violence. He wondered if she was going to be sick.

Sachs started toward her but stopped when Rhyme shook his head—his message: he knew they were losing the girl and they had to let her go.

Except that he was wrong.

Kara took another deep breath—like a high diver about to plunge off the board—and turned back to the pictures, a determined look in her eyes. She'd just been steeling herself to confront the photos again.

She studied them closely and finally nodded. "P. T. Selbit," she said, wiping her blue eyes.

"That's a person?" From Sachs.

Kara nodded. "Mr. Balzac used to do some of his routines. He was an illusionist who lived a hundred years ago. He did that routine. It's called Sawing a Woman in Half. This's the same, tied down, spread-eagle. The saw. The only difference is he picked a *man* for the performance." She blinked at the benign word. "I mean, the *murder.*"

Again Rhyme asked, "Would only a limited number of people know it?"

"Nope. It was a famous trick, even more famous than the Vanished Man. Anybody with the slightest knowledge of magic history'd be aware of it."

He had expected this discouraging answer but said, "Put it on the profile anyway, Thom." Then to Sachs: "Okay, tell us what happened at Calvert's."

"Looks like the vic left through his building's back entrance on his way to work—like he always did, the neighbors said. He walked past an alley and saw that." She pointed to the black toy cat in a plastic bag. "A toy cat."

Kara looked it over. "It's an automaton. Like a robot. We'd call it a feke."

"A—?"

"F-E-K-E. A prop that the audience is supposed to think is real. Like a fake knife with a disappearing blade or a coffee cup with a hidden reservoir in it."

She pushed a switch and suddenly it started to move, giving off a realistic-sounding meow. "The vic must've seen the cat and walked over to it, maybe thought it was hurt," Sachs continued. "That's how the Conjurer got him into the cul-de-sac."

"Source?" Rhyme asked Cooper.

"Sing-Lu Manufacturing in Hong Kong. I checked the website. The toy's available in hundreds of stores around the country."

Rhyme sighed. "Too common to trace" was the theme of the case, it seemed.

Sachs continued, "So Calvert walked to the cat, crouched down to check it out. The perp was hiding somewhere and—"

"The mirror," Rhyme interrupted. A glance at Kara, who was nodding. "Illusionists do a lot with mirrors. You aim them just right and you can vanish whatever or whoever's behind them completely."

Rhyme recalled the name of her store was Smoke & Mirrors.

"But something went wrong and the vic got away," Sellitto continued. "Now, this is the crazy part. We checked the nine-one-one tape. Calvert got back inside and into his apartment then called emergency. He told them the attacker was outside the building and the doors were locked. But then the line went dead. Somehow the Conjurer got inside."

"Maybe the window—Sachs, did you search the fire escape?"

"No. The window on the escape was locked from the inside."

"Still should've searched it," Rhyme said shortly.

"He didn't get in that way. There wasn't time."

"Well, then he must've had the vic's keys," the criminalist said.

"There were no latents on them," Sachs countered. "Only the vic's."

"He must have," Rhyme insisted.

"No," Kara said. "He picked the lock."

"Impossible," Rhyme said. "Or maybe

he'd gotten in before and had a mold made of the key. Sachs, you should go back and check out if he had—"

"He picked the lock," the young woman said adamantly. "I guarantee it."

Rhyme shook his head. "In sixty seconds he got through two doors? He couldn't possibly."

Kara sighed. "I'm sorry, but, yeah, in sixty seconds he got through two doors. And it might've taken him less than that."

"Well, let's assume he didn't," Rhyme said dismissively. "Now—"

The young woman snapped, "Let's assume he *did.* Look, we can't skip over this. It tells us something else about him—something important: that locked doors don't even slow him up."

Rhyme glanced at Sellitto, who said, "I gotta say, working Larceny I busted a dozen burglars and none of 'em could get through locks that fast."

"Mr. Balzac has me practicing lock picking ten hours a week," Kara said. "I don't have my kit with me but if I did I could open your front door in thirty seconds, the deadbolt in sixty. And I don't know how to scrub a lock. If the Conjurer does he could cut that time in half. Now, I know you like all this, like, evidence stuff. But you're wasting your time to have Amelia go search for something that isn't there."

"You sure?" Sellitto asked.

"If you don't trust my opinion, then why'd you want my help?"

Sachs glanced at Rhyme. He grudgingly accepted Kara's assessment with a stony nod (though privately he was pleased that the woman had shown some grit; it made up a lot for the Look and the Smile). He said to Thom, "Okay, put down on the chart that our boy's a master lock picker too."

Sachs continued, "No sign of whatever the Conjurer used to knock him out. Blunt-object trauma. Looks like a pipe probably. But he took that with him too."

The report from Latents came in. Eighty-nine separate prints from areas of the crime scene near the victim and the places the Conjurer most likely touched. But Rhyme noticed immediately that some of the prints looked odd and, on closer examination, he could see that they were from the finger cups. He didn't bother to scan the others.

Turning to the trace Sachs had collected at the scene, they found minuscule amounts of the same mineral oil they'd recovered at the music school that morning and more of the latex, makeup and alginate.

Detective Kuan from the Ninth Precinct called and reported that a search of the Dumpsters around Calvert's building had turned up no sign of the man's quick-change outfit or the murder weapons. Rhyme thanked him and told him to keep at it. The man said he would but with such fake enthusiasm that Rhyme knew the search had already ended.

The criminalist asked Sachs, "You said he smashed Calvert's watch?"

"Yep. At noon exactly. A few seconds after."

"And the other victim was at eight. He's on a timetable, looks like. And probably has somebody else lined up for four this afternoon."

Less than three hours from now.

Cooper continued, "No luck with the mirror. No manufacturer—that must've been on the frame and he scraped it off. A few real prints but they're covered up by his finger cup smudges so I'd guess that they're from the clerk where he bought it or the manufacturer. I'll send 'em through AFIS anyway."

208 / Jeffery Deaver

"Got some shoes," Sachs said, lifting a bag out of a cardboard box.

"His?"

"Probably. They're the same Ecco brand we found at the music school—same size, too."

"He left 'em behind. Why?" Sellitto wondered.

Rhyme suggested, "Probably thought that we knew he was wearing Eccos at the first scene and was worried the respondings'd noticed them on an elderly woman."

Examining the shoes, Mel Cooper said, "We've got some good trace in the indentation in front of the heel and between the upper and sole." He opened a bag and scraped the material out. "Horn o' plenty," the tech said absently and bent over the dirt.

It was hardly a cornucopia but for forensic purposes the residue was as big as a mountain and might reveal a wealth of information. "Scope it, Mel," Rhyme ordered. "Let's see what we've got."

The workhorse of tools in a forensic lab is the microscope and although there've been many refinements over the years the instrument isn't any different in theory from the tiny brass-plate microscope that Antonie van Leeuwenhoek invented in the Netherlands in the 1500s.

In addition to an ancient scanning electron microscope, which he rarely needed, Rhyme had two other microscopes in his homegrown laboratory. One was a compound Leitz Orthoplan, an older model but one he swore by. It was trinocular—two eyepieces for the operator and a camera tube in the middle.

The second—which Cooper was preparing to use now—was a stereo microscope, which the tech had used to examine the fibers from the first scene. These instruments have relatively low magnification and are used for examining three-dimensional objects like insects and plant materials.

The image popped onto the computer screen for Rhyme and the others to see.

First-year criminalistics students invariably click immediately on a microscope's highest power to examine evidence. But in reality the best magnification for forensic purposes is usually quite low. Cooper began at 4× and then went up to 30×.

"Ah, focus, focus," Rhyme called.

Cooper adjusted the high-ratio screw of

the objective so that the image of the material came into perfect clarity.

"Okay, let's walk through it," Rhyme said.

The tech moved the stage, with imperceptible twists of the controls connected to the stage. As he did, hundreds of shapes scrolled past on the screen, some black, some red or green, some translucent. Rhyme felt, as he always did when looking through the eyepiece of a microscope, that he was a voyeur, examining a world that had no idea it was being spied upon.

And a world that could be very revealing.

"Hairs," Rhyme said, studying a long strand. "Animal." He could tell this by the number of scales.

"What kind?" Sachs asked.

"Dog, I'd say," Cooper offered. Rhyme concurred. The tech went on-line and a moment later was running the images through an NYPD database of animal hair. "Got two breeds, no, three. Looks like a medium-length-coat breed of some kind. German shepherd or malinois. And hairs from two longer-haired breeds. English sheepdog, briard."

Cooper brought the screen to a stop.

They were looking at a mass of brownish grains and sticks and tubes.

"What's that long stuff?" Sellitto asked.

"Fibers?" Sachs suggested.

Rhyme glanced at it. "Dried grass, I'd say, or some kind of vegetation. But I don't recognize that other material. GC it, Mel."

Soon the chromatograph/spectrometer had spit out its data. On the monitor a chart appeared, giving the results from the analysis: bile pigments, stercobilin, urobilin, indole, nitrates, skatole, mercaptans, hydrogen sulfide.

"Ah."

"Ah?" Sellitto asked. "What's 'ah'?"

"Command, microscope one," Rhyme commanded. The image reappeared on the computer screen and he replied to the detective, "It's obvious—dead bacterial matter, partially digested fiber and grass. It's shit. Oh, excuse me for being indelicate," he said sarcastically. "It's *doggy* do. Our perp stepped where he should not have."

This was encouraging; the hairs and fecal matter were good class evidence and, if they found similar trace on a suspect, at a particular location or in a car there'd be a strong presumption that he was, or had contact with, the Conjurer.

The fingerprint report on the shards of mirror in the alley came in from the AFIS system. It was negative, to no one's surprise.

"What else from the scene?" Rhyme asked.

"Zip," Sachs said. "That's it."

Rhyme was scanning the evidence charts when the doorbell rang and Thom went to answer it. A moment later he returned, accompanied by a uniformed officer. He stood timidly in the doorway, as many young law enforcers did when they entered the den of the legendary Lincoln Rhyme. "I'm looking for Detective Bell. I was told he was here?"

"That's me," Bell said.

"Crime scene report. From the break-in at Charles Grady's office."

"Thanks, son." The detective took the envelope and nodded to the young man, who, with a brief, intimidated glance at Lincoln Rhyme, turned and left.

Reading the contents, Bell shrugged. "Not my expertise. Hey, Lincoln, any chance you could take a look at it?"

"Sure, Roland," Rhyme said. "Pull the staples out and mount it in the turning frame there. Thom'll do it. What's the story? This about the Andrew Constable case?"

"Is." He told Rhyme about the break-in at Charles Grady's office. When the aide was finished mounting the report Rhyme drove into position. He read the first page carefully. Then said, "Command, turn page." He continued reading.

The break-in had been accomplished by simply shattering the corner of the glass window in the door to the hall and unlatching it from the inside (the door between the secretary's outer office and prosecutor's interior office was double-locked and made of thick wood; it had defeated the burglar).

The CS searchers, Rhyme noted, had found something interesting—on and around the secretary's desk were a number of fibers. The report indicated only their color—mostly white, some black and a single red one—but nothing else about them. They also found two tiny flecks of gold foil.

The CS team had learned that the break-in had occurred after the cleaning service had finished with the office so the fibers probably had not been left by Grady's secretary or anyone legitimately in her office during the day. Most likely they'd come from the intruder.

Rhyme came to the last page. "That's *it?*" he asked.

"Reckon so," Bell responded.

A grunt from the criminalist. "Command, telephone. Call Peretti comma Vincent."

Rhyme had hired Peretti as a crime scene cop some years ago and he'd proved talented at forensics. What he'd truly excelled at, though, was the far more esoteric art of police department politics, which, unlike Rhyme, he preferred to the work of actually running crime scenes. He was now head of the NYPD's Investigation and Resource Division, which oversaw the crime scene unit.

When Rhyme was finally put through, the man asked, "Lincoln, how are you?"

"Fine, Vince. I—"

"You're on this Conjurer case, right? How's it going?"

"It's going. Listen, I'm calling about something else. I'm here with Roland Bell. I've got the report on the Grady office break-in—"

"Oh, the Andrew Constable thing. Those threats against Grady. Right. What can I do?"

"I'm looking at the report now. But it's just the preliminary. I need some more information. Crime Scene found some fibers. I need to know the exact composition of each one, length, diameter, color temperature, dyes used and amount of wear."

"Hold on. I'll get a pen." A moment later: "Go ahead."

"I also need electrostatics of all the footprints and photos of their patterns on the floor. And I want to know everything that was on the secretary's desk, credenza and bookshelves. Everything on any surface, in any drawer, on the wall. And its exact location."

"Everything the perp touched? Okay, I guess. We'll—"

"No, Vince. Everything that was in the office. *Everything.* Paper clips, pictures of the secretary's children. Mold in the top drawer. I don't care whether he touched it or not."

Huffy now, Peretti said, "I'll make sure somebody does it."

He didn't see why Peretti didn't do it himself, which is what Rhyme would have done, even as head of IRD, to make sure the job got done immediately.

But in his present role as consultant he

had only limited clout. "Sooner is better. . . . Thanks, Vince."

"Don't mention it," the man said coolly.

They hung up. Rhyme said to Bell, "Not much else I can do, Roland, until we get that information."

A glance at the break-in report. Fibers and backwoods militiamen . . . Mysteries. But at the moment they'd have to remain somebody else's. Rhyme had his own enigmas to unravel and not much time in which to do so: the notations on the evidence chart about the broken watches reminded him that they had less than three hours to stop the Conjurer before he found his next victim.

THE CONJURER

Music School Crime Scene

- Perp's description: Brown hair, fake beard, no distinguishing, medium build, medium height, age: fifties. Ring and little fingers of left hand fused together. Changed costume quickly to resemble old, bald janitor.

- No apparent motive.

- Victim: Svetlana Rasnikov.
  - Full-time music student.

- Checking family, friends, students, coworkers for possible leads.
  - No boyfriends, no known enemies. Performed at children's birthday parties.

- Circuit board with speaker attached.
  - Sent to FBI lab, NYC.
    - Digital recorder, probably containing perp's voice. All data destroyed.
  - Voice recorder is a "gimmick." Homemade.

- Used antique iron handcuffs to restrain victim.
  - Handcuffs are Darby irons. Scotland Yard. Checking with Houdini Museum in New Orleans for leads.

- Destroyed victim's watch at exactly 8:00 A.M.

- Cotton string holding chairs. Generic. Too many sources to trace.

- Squib for gunshot effect. Destroyed.
  - Too many sources to trace.

- Fuse. Generic.
  - Too many sources to trace.

- Responding officers reported flash in air. No trace material recovered.
  - Was from flash cotton or flash paper.
    - Too many sources to trace.

- Perp's shoes: size 10 Ecco.

- Silk fibers, dyed gray, processed to a matte finish.
  - From quick-change janitor's outfit.

- Unsub is possibly wearing brown wig.

- Red pignut hickory and Parmelia conspersa lichen, both found primarily in Central Park.

- Dirt impregnated with unusual mineral oil. Sent to FBI for analysis.

- Black silk, 72 x 48". Used as camouflage. Not traceable.
  - Illusionists use this frequently.

- Wears caps to cover up prints.
  - Magician's finger cups.

- Traces of latex, castor oil, makeup.
  - Theatrical makeup.

- Traces of alginate.
  - Used in molding latex "appliances."

- Murder weapon: white silk-knit rope with black silk core.
  - Rope is a magic trick. Color changing. Not traceable.

- Unusual knot.
  - Sent to FBI and Maritime Museum—no information.
  - Knots are from Houdini routines, virtually impossible to untie.

- Used disappearing ink on sign-in register.

East Village Crime Scene

- Victim Two: Tony Calvert.
  - Makeup artist, theater company.
  - No known enemies.
  - No apparent connection with first victim.

- No apparent motive.

- Cause of death:
  - Blunt-object trauma to head followed by postmortem dismemberment with crosscut saw.

- Perp escaped portraying woman in her 70s. Checking vicinity for discarded costume and other evidence.
  - Nothing recovered.

- Watch smashed at 12:00 exactly.
  - Pattern? Next victim presumably at 4:00 P.M.

- Perp hid behind mirror. Not traceable. Fingerprints sent to FBI.
  - No matches.

- Used cat toy ("feke") to lure victim into alley. Toy is untraceable.

- Additional mineral oil found, same as at first scene. Awaiting FBI report.

- Additional latex and makeup from finger cups.

- Additional alginate.

- Ecco shoes left behind.

- Dog hairs found in shoes, from three different breeds of dog. Manure too.

Profile as Illusionist

- Perp will use misdirection against victims and in eluding police.
  - Physical misdirection (for distraction).
  - Psychological (to eliminate suspicion).

- Escape at music school was similar to Vanished Man illusion routine. Too common to trace.

- Perp is primarily an illusionist.

- Talented at sleight of hand.

- Also knows protean (quick change) magic. Will use breakaway clothes, nylon and silk, bald cap, finger cups and other latex appliances. Could be any age, gender or race.

- Calvert's death = Selbit's Cutting a Woman in Half routine.

- Proficient at lock picking (possibly lock "scrubbing").

Chapter Thirteen

In 1900 Manhattan's horse population was over 100,000 and, space being at a premium on the island even in those days, many animals were housed in high-rises—at least that's what their second- and third-story quarters would have been considered at the time.

One such elevated stable can still be found in the borough, the well-known Hammerstead Riding Academy on the Upper West Side. Still in its original structure, built in 1885, the academy features hundreds of stalls above the ground-level arena, which is the site for both private riding lessons and shows. A large, busy stable like this seems an anomaly in a city like Manhattan in the twenty-first century until you consider that Central Park's six miles of well-tended bridle paths are only a few blocks away.

Ninety horses reside in the academy, some privately owned and some for rent, and one of these latter variety was now being led down a steep ramp from his stall by a groom, a redheaded teenage girl, to a waiting rider.

Cheryl Marston felt the same thrill she did every Saturday at this time of day when she saw the tall, feisty horse with the mottled rump of an Appaloosa.

"Hey, Donny Boy," she called, her pet name for the animal, whose real name was Don Juan di Middleburg. A ladies' man, she often said. A joke but true enough: under a male rider the animal would shy and whinny and resist from the git-go. But with Marston he was putty.

"See you in an hour," she told the groom, swinging up onto Donny Boy, gripping the supple reins, feeling his astonishing muscles beneath her.

A touch to the ribs and they were on their way. Out onto Eighty-sixth Street, moving east slowly toward Central Park, the shod feet clopping loudly on the asphalt, drawing everyone's attention, as they examined both the gorgeous animal and, high atop him, the thin-faced, serious woman dressed in jodhpurs, a red jacket and black velvet helmet, out of which dangled a long blonde French braid.

Crossing into Central Park itself, Marston glanced south and saw in the distance the office building in Midtown where she spent fifty hours a week practicing corporate law. There were a thousand thoughts that might have overwhelmed her now about the job, projects that were "front-burnered," as one of her partners said with irritating frequency. But none of these thoughts intruded at the moment. Nothing could. She was invulnerable to everything when she sat here, on one of God's most magnificent creations, feeling the sun-warmed, loam-scented air on her face as Donny Boy trotted along the dark path, surrounded by early jonquils and forsythia and lilacs.

The first beautiful day this spring.

For a half hour she circled the reservoir slowly, lost in the rapture of that unique connection between two different, complementary animals, each powerful and smart in its own way. She enjoyed a brief canter and then slowed to post in a trot as they came to the sharper turns in the deserted northern part of the park, near Harlem.

Completely at peace.

Until the worst happened.

She wasn't sure exactly how it occurred. She'd slowed to make the turn through a narrow gap between two stands of bushes when a pigeon flew directly into Donny Boy's face. Whinnying, he skidded to a stop so fast that Marston was nearly thrown off. Then he reared and she almost went backward over his rump.

She grabbed his mane and the front edge of the saddle to keep from falling eight feet to the rocky ground. "Whoa, Donny," she cried, trying to pat his neck. "Donny Boy— it's all right. Whoa!"

Still, he kept rearing, crazed. Had the collision with the bird hurt his eyes? Her concern for the horse, though, was mixed with her own fear. Sharp rocks jutted from the ground on either side of them. If Donny Boy kept rearing he could lose his balance on the uneven ground and go down hard— possibly with her under him. Nearly all of the serious injuries among her fellow riders weren't from tumbling off a horse but were from being caught between the animal and the ground when it fell.

"Donny!" she called breathlessly. But he reared again and held the position, dancing in panic on his hind legs and edging toward the rocks.

"Jesus," Marston gasped. "No, no . . ."

She knew then she was going to lose him. His feet were clattering on the stones and she felt the huge muscles quivering in his own panic as he sensed his balance go. He whinnied loudly.

Knowing she'd crush her leg in a dozen places. Maybe her chest too.

Almost tasting the pain. Feeling *his* pain too.

"Oh, Donny . . ."

Then, from nowhere, a man in a jogging suit stepped from the bushes. Wide-eyed, he looked at the horse. He jumped forward, grabbing bit and bridle.

"No, get back!" Marston shouted. "He's out of control!"

He'd get kicked in the head!

"Get out of the . . ."

But . . . what was happening?

The man was looking not at her but directly into the brown eyes of the horse.

Speaking words she couldn't hear. Miraculously the Appaloosa was calming. The rearing stopped. Donny Boy dropped forward onto all four hooves. He was fidgety and he still trembled—just like her own heart—but the worst seemed to be over. The man pulled the horse's head down, close to his and he said a few more words.

Finally he stepped back, gave the horse an approving once-over and then glanced up at her. "Are you all right?" he asked.

"I think so." Marston inhaled deeply, touching her chest. "I just . . . It was all so fast."

"What happened?"

"A bird spooked him. Flew into his face. It might've hit him in the eyes."

A close examination. "Looks okay to me. You might want to have a vet look at him. But I don't see any cuts."

"What'd you do?" she asked. "Are you . . . ?"

"A horse whisperer?" he replied, laughing, glancing away from her shyly. He seemed more comfortable looking into the horse's eyes. "Not hardly. But I ride a lot. I have this calming effect, I guess."

"I thought he was going down."

He gave her a tentative smile. "Wish I could think of something to say that'd calm *you* down."

"What's good for my horse is good for me. I don't know how to thank you."

Another rider approached and the bearded man led Donny Boy off the path to let the chestnut by.

He was examining the horse closely. "What's his name?"

"Don Juan."

"You rent from Hammerstead? Or is he yours?"

"Hammerstead. But I feel like he's mine. I ride him every week."

"I rent there too sometimes. What a beautiful animal."

Calm now, Marston examined him more closely. He was a handsome man in his early fifties. He had a trim beard and thick eyebrows that met above the bridge of his nose. On his neck—and chest too—she could see what looked like bad scarring and his left hand was deformed. Though none of that mattered to her, considering his most important trait: he liked horses. Cheryl Marston, divorced for the last four of her thirty-eight years, realized that they were both sizing each other up.

He gave a faint laugh and looked away. "I was . . ." His voice faded and he filled the silence by patting Donny Boy's rippled shoulder.

Marston lifted an eyebrow. "What's that?" she encouraged.

"Well, since you're about to ride off into the sunset and I may never see you again . . ." He tromped on the shyness and continued boldly, "I was just wondering if it'd be out of line to ask if you want to get some coffee."

"Not out of line at all," she responded, pleased by his straightforward attitude. But she added, to let him know something about her, "I'm going to finish my hour. I've got about twenty minutes left. . . . Got to get back up on the horse, so to speak. How's that fit with your schedule?"

"Twenty minutes is perfect. I'll meet you at the stable."

"Good," Cheryl said. "Oh, I never asked: You ride English or Western?"

"Bareback mostly. I used to be a pro."

"Really? Where?"

"Believe it or not," he answered shyly, "I rode in the circus."

Chapter Fourteen

A faint ding resounded from Cooper's computer, indicating he'd received an email.

"A note from our friends on Ninth and Pennsylvania." He proceeded to decrypt the message from the FBI lab and a moment later he said, "The results from the oil. It's commercially available. Brand name Tack-Pure. Used to condition saddles, reins, leather feeding bags, equestrian-related products."

Horses . . .

Rhyme spun his Storm Arrow around and looked at the evidence board.

"No, no, no . . ."

"What's the matter?" Sachs asked.

"The manure on the Conjurer's shoes."

"What about it?"

"It's not from dogs. It's from *horses!* Look

at the vegetation. What the hell was I thinking of? Dogs're carnivores. They don't eat
grass and hay. . . . All right, let's think. The
dirt and the mold and the other evidence
placed him in Central Park. And the
hairs . . . You know that area, the dog knoll?
That's in the park too."

"It's right across the street," Sellitto
pointed out. "Where everybody walks their
dogs."

"Kara," he snapped, "does the Cirque
Fantastique have horses?"

"No," she said. "No animal acts at all."

"Okay, that lets the circus out. . . . What
else could he be up to? The dog knoll's right
next to the bridle path in the park, right? It's
a long shot but maybe he rides or's been
checking out riders. One of them could be a
target. Maybe not his next one but let's just
go on the assumption that it is—since it's
our only goddamn solid lead."

Sellitto said, "There's a stable someplace
around here, isn't there?"

"I've seen it nearby," Sachs said. "It's in
the eighties, I think."

"Find out," Rhyme called. "And get some
people over there."

Sachs glanced at the clock. It was 1:35 P.M.

"Well, we've got some time. Two and a half hours till the next victim."

"Good," Sellitto said. "I'll get surveillance teams set up in the park and around the stable. If they're in place by two-thirty that'll be plenty of time to spot him."

Then Rhyme noticed Kara frowning. "What is it?" he asked her.

"You know, I'm not sure you do have that much time."

"Why?"

"I was telling you about misdirection?"

"I remember."

"Well, there's also *time* misdirection. That's tricking the audience by making them think something's going to happen at one time when it really happens at another. Like, an illusionist'll repeat an act at regular intervals. The audience subconsciously comes to believe that whatever he's doing *has* to happen only at those times. But what the performer does then is shorten the time between the intervals. The audience isn't paying attention and they completely miss whatever he's doing. You can spot a time misdirection trick because the illusionist always lets the audience know what the interval is."

"Like breaking the watches?" Sachs asked.

"Exactly."

Rhyme asked, "So you don't think we have until four?"

Kara shrugged. "We might. Maybe he's planned to kill *three* people every four hours and then he'll murder the fourth victim only one hour later. I don't know."

"We don't know anything here," Rhyme said firmly. "What do you *think,* Kara? What would you do?"

She gave a troubled laugh, being asked to step into the mind of a killer. After a moment of hard debate she said, "He knows you've found the watches by now. He knows you're smart. He doesn't need to hammer it home anymore. If I were him I'd be going after the next victim before four. I'd be going after him right now."

"That's good enough for me," Rhyme said. "Forget surveillance and forget soft clothes. Lon, call Haumann and get ESU into the park. In a big way."

"It might scare him off, Linc—if he's in disguise and doing his own surveillance."

"I think we have to take that chance. Tell ESU we're looking for . . . who knows *what* the hell we're looking for? Give him a general description, as best you can."

Fifty-year-old killer, sixty-year-old janitor, seventy-year-old bag lady . . .

Cooper looked up from his computer. "Got the stable. Hammerstead Riding Academy."

Bell, Sellitto and Sachs started for the door. Kara said, "I want to go too."

"No," Rhyme said.

"There may be something I'll notice. Some sleight or a quick-change move by somebody in a crowd. I could spot it." A nod toward the other cops. "*They* might not."

"No. It's too dangerous. No civilians on a tactical operation. That's the rule."

"I don't care about the rules," the young woman said, leaning toward him defiantly. "I can help."

"Kara—"

But the young woman silenced him by glancing at the crime scene photos of Tony Calvert and Svetlana Rasnikov then turning back to Lincoln Rhyme with a cold expression in her eyes. In this simple gesture she reminded him that it was *he* who'd asked her here, *he* who'd brought her into his world and transformed her from an innocent into someone who could now look at these horrors without flinching.

"All right," Rhyme said. Then, nodding toward Sachs, he added, "But stay close to her."

She was cautious, Malerick observed, as befitted any woman who'd just been picked up by a man in Manhattan, even if that stranger was shy, friendly and able to calm rearing horses.

Still, Cheryl Marston was relaxing little by little, enjoying the tales of his times riding bareback with a circus, all of which were embellished considerably to keep her amused and to whittle down her defenses.

After the groom and the vet on call at Hammerstead had examined Donny Boy and declared him in good health Malerick and his next unwitting performer strolled from the stable to this restaurant, which was just off Riverside Drive.

The woman now chatted amiably with John (his persona for their date) about her life in the city, her early love of horses, the ones she'd owned or ridden, her hopes of buying a summer place in Middleburg, Virginia. He responded with occasional bits of equine lore—what he could deduce from her comments and what he knew from circuses and the world of illusion. Animals have always been an important part of the profession. Mesmerizing them, vanishing them, turning them into different species. An illusionist created a hugely popular routine in the 1800s—instantly transforming a chicken into a duck. (The method was simplicity itself: the duck made his entrance wearing a quick-change chicken costume.) Killing and resurrecting animals was popular in less politically correct times, though they were rarely actually harmed; after all, it's a rather inept illusionist who has to really kill an animal to create the illusion that it's dead. It tends to be expensive too.

For his routine in Central Park today to snare Cheryl Marston, Malerick had drawn on the routines of Howard Thurston, a popular illusionist in the early 1900s, who specialized in animal acts. The trick Malerick performed wouldn't've met with Thurston's approval, though; the famous illusionist had treated the animals in his act as if they were human assistants, if not family members.

Malerick had been less humane. He'd captured a pigeon by hand. He'd then turned it on its back and stroked the neck and sides slowly until it was hypnotized—a technique magicians have used for years to create the appearance of a dead bird. As Cheryl Marston approached on her horse, he'd flung the pigeon hard into the horse's face. Donny Boy's rearing in pain and fright had nothing to do with the bird, though, but was caused by an ultrasonic pitch generator, set to a frequency that stung the horse's ears. As Malerick stepped out of the bushes to "rescue" Cheryl he shut the generator off and by the time he grabbed the bridle the horse was calming.

Now, little by little, the equestrian was growing even less cautious as she learned how much they had in common.

Or *appeared* to.

This illusion was due to Malerick's use of mentalism, not one of his strongest skills but one that he was competent at. Mentalism has nothing to do with telepathically discerning someone's thoughts, of course. It's a combination of mechanical and psychological techniques to deduce facts. Malerick was now doing what the best mental-ists did—*body* reading, it was called, as opposed to mind reading. He was noting very subtle changes in Cheryl's poses and facial expressions and gestures in response to comments he made. Some told him he was straying from her thoughts, others that he was on the mark.

He mentioned, for instance, a friend who'd just been through a divorce and he could see easily that she had too—and she'd been on the receiving end. So, grimacing, he told her that he was divorced and that his wife'd had an affair and left him. It had devastated him but he was now recovering.

"*I* gave up a boat," she said, sourly, "just to get away from that son-of-a-bitch. A twenty-four-foot sailboat."

Malerick also used "Barnum statements" to make her think they had more in common than they did. The classic example was a mentalist sizing up his subject and offering gravely, "I sense you're often extroverted but at times you find yourself quite shy."

Which is interpreted as insightful but, of course, applies to nearly everybody on earth.

Neither the fictional John nor Cheryl had

children. Both had cats, divorced parents and a love of tennis. Look at all these coincidences! A match made in heaven. . . .

Almost time, he thought. Though he was in no hurry. Even if the police had some leads to what he was up to they'd be thinking he wouldn't kill anyone again until 4:00; it was now just after two.

You may think, Revered Audience, that the world of illusion never intersects the world of reality but that's not wholly true.

I think of John Mulholland, the renowned magician and editor of the magic magazine, The Sphinx. He abruptly announced his early retirement from magic and journalism in the nineteen fifties.

No one could figure out why. But then the rumors began—rumors that he'd started working for the American intelligence community to teach spies how to use magic techniques to deliver drugs in such subtle ways that even the most paranoid Communist didn't know he was being given a mickey.

What do you see in my hands, Revered Audience? Look closely at my fingers. Nothing, right? They seem empty. And yet, as you've probably guessed, they aren't. . . .

Now using one of Mulholland's smoother clandestine drugging techniques, Malerick picked up his spoon with his left hand. As he tapped it absently on the tabletop Cheryl glanced at it. A mere fraction of a second. But it gave Malerick enough time to empty a tiny capsule of tasteless powder into her coffee as he reached for the sugar with his other hand.

John Mulholland would've been proud.

After a few moments Malerick could see that the drug was having its effect; her eyes were slightly unfocused and she was weaving as she sat. She didn't sense anything was wrong, though. That was the good thing about flunitrazepam, the famous date-rape drug Rohypnol: you didn't know you'd been drugged. Not until the next morning. Which in Cheryl Marston's case wasn't going to be an issue.

He looked at her and smiled. "Hey, you want to see something fun?"

"Fun?" she asked drowsily. She blinked, smiling broadly.

He paid the check and then said to her. "I just bought a boat."

She laughed in delight. "A boat? I love boats. What kind?"

"Sailboat. Thirty-eight feet. My wife and I had one," Malerick added sadly. "She got it in the divorce."

"John, no, you're kidding me!" she said, laughing groggily. "My husband and I had one! He got *ours* in the divorce."

"Really?" He laughed and stood. "Hey, let's walk down to the river. You can see it from there."

"I'd love to." She rose unsteadily and took his arm.

He steered her through the doorway. The dosage seemed right. She was submissive but she wasn't going to pass out before he got her into the bushes next to the Hudson.

They headed toward Riverside Park. "You were talking about boats," she said drunkenly.

"That's right."

"My ex and I had one," she said.

"I know," Malerick said. "You told me."

"Oh, did I?" Cheryl laughed.

"Hold on," he said. "I have to get something."

He stopped at his car, a stolen Mazda, and took a heavy gym bag from the backseat, locked the car again. From inside the bag came a loud clank of metal. Cheryl glanced at it, began to speak but then seemed to forget what she was going to say.

"Let's go this way." Malerick led her to the end of the cross street, across a pedestrian bridge over the parkway and down into an overgrown, deserted strip of land on the riverbank.

He disengaged her arm from his and gripped her firmly around the back and under the arm. He felt her breast with his fingers as her head lolled against him.

"Look," she said, pointing unsteadily into the Hudson, where dozens of sailboats and cabin cruisers moved over the sparkling dark blue water.

Malerick said, "My boat's down there."

"I like boats."

"So do I," he said softly.

"Really?" she asked, laughing and adding in a whisper that, guess what, she and her ex-husband had had one. But she'd lost it in the divorce.

Chapter Fifteen

The riding academy was a slice of old New York.

Smelling powerful barn scent, Amelia Sachs looked through an archway into the interior of the woody old place at the horses and, atop them, riders—all of whom looked stately in their tan pants, black or red riding jackets, velvet helmets.

A half-dozen uniformeds from the nearby Twentieth Precinct stood in and outside the lobby. More officers were in the park, under the command of Lon Sellitto, deployed around the bridle path, looking for their elusive prey.

Sachs and Bell walked into the office and the detective flashed his gold shield to the woman behind the counter. She looked over his shoulder at the officers outside and asked uneasily, "Yes? Is there a problem?"

"Ma'am, do you use Tack-Pure to treat the saddles and leather?"

She glanced at an assistant, who nodded. "Yessir, we do. We use a lot of it."

Bell continued, "We found traces of some and of some horse manure at the scene of a homicide today. We think the suspect in that killing might work here or be stalking one of your employees or a rider."

"No! Who?"

"That's what we're not sure about, sorry to say. And we're not sure of the suspect's appearance either. All we know is he's average build. Around fifty years old. White. Might have a beard and brown hair but we aren't sure. Fingers on his left hand might be deformed. What we need is for you to talk to your employees, regular customers too if there're any hereabouts, and see if they've noticed anybody fitting that description. Or anybody who seems like they'd be a threat."

"Of course," she said uncertainly. "I'll do whatever I can. Sure."

Bell took several of the uniformed patrol officers and disappeared through an old doorway into the pungent sawdust-filled riding arena. "We'll do a search," he called back to Sachs.

The policewoman nodded and looked out the window, checking on Kara, who sat alone in Sellitto's unmarked car, parked at the curb next to Sachs's deep-yellow Camaro. The young woman wasn't happy being confined in the car but Sachs had been adamant about her staying out of danger.

Robert-Houdin had tighter tricks than the Marabouts. Though I think they almost killed him.

Don't worry. I'll make sure that doesn't happen to you.

Sachs glanced at the clock—2:00 P.M. She radioed in to Central and had the transmission patched into Rhyme's phone. A moment later the criminalist came on the line. "Sachs, Lon's teams haven't seen anything in Central Park. Any luck with you?"

"The manager's interviewing staff and riders here at the academy. Roland and his team are searching the stables." She then noticed the manager with a cluster of employees. There were assorted frowns and looks of concern on their faces. One girl, a round-faced redhead, suddenly raised her hand to her mouth in shock. She began to nod.

"Hold on, Rhyme. May have something."

The manager beckoned Sachs over and the teenager said, "I don't know if it's, like, anything important. But there's one thing?"

"What's your name?"

"Tracey?" she answered as if she were asking. "I'm a groom here?"

"Go ahead."

"Okay. What it is, is there's this rider who comes in every Saturday. Cheryl Marston."

Rhyme shouted into Sachs's ear, "At the same time? Ask her if she comes in at the same time every week."

Sachs relayed the question.

"Oh, yeah, she does," the girl said. "She's like, you know, clockwork. Been coming here for years."

The criminalist noted, "People with regular habits're easiest to target. Tell her to go on."

"And what about her, Tracey?"

"Today she comes back from a ride? About a half hour ago? And what it is is she hands off Don Juan to me, that's like her favorite horse, and she wants me and the vet to check him out careful because a bird flew into his face and spooked him. So, we're looking him over and she's telling me about this guy who came along and calmed Donny down. We tell her that Donny looks fine and she's going on about this guy, yadda, yadda, yadda, and how interesting he is and she's all excited 'cause she's going to have coffee with him and he might be a real horse whisperer. I saw him downstairs, waiting for her. And the thing is, I'm like, what's wrong with his hand? 'Cause he kinda hid it, you know. It looked like he only had three fingers."

"That's him!" Sachs said. "Do you know where they were going?"

She pointed west, away from the park. "I think that way. She didn't say where exactly."

"Get a description," Rhyme called.

The girl explained that he had a beard and his eyebrows were odd. "All kind of grown together."

To alter a face the most important thing is the eyebrows. Change those and the face is sixty, seventy percent different.

"Wearing?" she asked.

"A windbreaker, running shoes, jogging pants."

"Color?"

"The jacket and pants were dark. Blue or black. I didn't see his shirt."

Bell returned with his officers and muttered, "Not a burr on the dog."

"Got a lead here." She explained about the rider and the bearded man then asked the girl, "And you're pretty sure she didn't know this guy?"

"No way. Ms. Marston and me, we've known each other for a while and she told me she's like totally off dating. Doesn't trust men. Her ex, he cheated on her and then, in the divorce, he got the sailboat. She's still pissed about that."

The best illusionists, my friends, engage in a practice known as "routining." That means planning the order and the pacing of their acts carefully—to make the performances as intense as possible.

For our third act today we first saw our animal illusion, featuring wonder-horse Donny Boy, in Central Park. Then we slowed the pace with some classic sleight of hand, combined with a touch of mentalism.

And now we turn to escapism.

We'll see what is perhaps Harry Houdini's most famous escape. In this routine, which he developed himself, he was bound, hung by his heels and submerged in a narrow tank of water. He had only a few minutes to try to bend upward from the waist, release his ankles and open the locked top of the chamber before he drowned.

The tank was, of course, "prepared." The bars apparently intended to keep the glass from shattering were actually handholds that let him pull himself up to reach his ankles. The locks on his feet and the top of the tank itself had hidden latches that would instantly release his ankles and the lid.

Our re-creation of the famous escapist's popular feat, needless to say, doesn't offer such features. Our performer will be on her own. And I've added a few variations of my own. All for your entertainment, of course.

And now, courtesy of Mr. Houdini, the Water Torture Cell.

Now beardless and dressed in chinos and a white dress shirt over a white T-shirt, Malerick wrapped chains tightly around Cheryl Marston. Her ankles first then her chest and arms.

He paused and looked around again but

they remained hidden from view of the road and the river by thick bushes.

They were beside the Hudson River, next to a small stagnant pool of water, which at one time had apparently been a tiny inlet for dinghies. Landfill and debris had sealed it long ago and created this foul-smelling pond about ten feet in diameter. On one side was a rotting pier in the middle of which was a rusty crane that had been used for lifting boats out of the water. Malerick now swung a rope over the crane, caught the end and began tying it to the chains holding Cheryl's feet.

Escapists love chains. They look impressive, they have a wonderfully sadistic flavor to them and seem more formidable than silks and ropes. And they're heavy—just the thing to keep a bound performer under water.

"No, no, noooo," whispered the groggy woman.

He stroked her hair as he surveyed the chains. Simple and tight. Houdini wrote, "Strange as it may appear, I have found that the more spectacular the fastening to the eyes of the audience, the less difficult the escape really proves to be."

This was true, Malerick knew from experience. Dramatic-looking masses of thick ropes and chains wound around and around the illusionist were in fact easy to get out of. Fewer restraints and simpler fasteners were much harder. Like these, for instance.

"Noooooo," she whispered groggily. "It hurts. Please! . . . What are you—?"

Malerick pressed duct tape over her mouth. Then he braced himself, took a good grip and slowly pulled down on the rope, which in turn lifted the whimpering lawyer's feet and began dragging her slowly toward the brackish water.

On this glorious spring afternoon a busy crafts fair filled the large central square of West Side College between Seventy-ninth and Eightieth Streets, so dense with visitors it would be virtually impossible to spot the killer and his victim in the crowd.

On this glorious spring afternoon customers filled the scores of neighborhood restaurants and coffee shops, in any one of which the Conjurer might at this moment be suggesting to Cheryl Marston that she go for a drive with him or they stop at her apartment.

On this glorious spring afternoon fifty alleyways bisected the blocks here and offered, in their dim seclusion, a perfect killing ground.

Sachs, Bell and Kara jogged up and down the streets, looking through the crafts fair, the restaurants and the alleys. And every other place they could think to search.

They found nothing.

Until, desperate minutes later, a break.

The two cops and Kara walked into Ely's Coffee Shop near Riverside Drive and scanned the crowd. Sachs gripped Bell's arm, nodding toward the cash register. Next to it were a black velvet riding hat and a stained leather crop.

Sachs ran to the manager, a swarthy Middle Easterner. "Did a woman leave those here?"

"Yeah, ten minutes ago. She—"

"Was she with a man?"

"Yeah."

"Beard and a running suit?"

"That's them. She forgot the hat and that whip thing on the floor under the table."

"Do you know where they went?" Bell asked.

"What is happening? Is there—"

"Where?" Sachs insisted.

"Okay, I hear him say he going to show her his boat. But I hope he took her home."

"How do you mean?" Sachs asked.

"The woman, she was sick. I figure that why she forgot her stuff."

"Sick?"

"Couldn't walk steady, you know what I'm saying? Seem drunk but all they drank was coffee. And she was fine when they got here."

"He drugged her," Sachs muttered to Bell.

"Drugged her?" the manager asked. "Hey, what is story?"

She asked, "Which table were they at?"

He pointed to one where four women sat, talking and eating, and doing both quite loudly. "'Scuse me," Sachs said to them and gave the area a fast examination. She saw no obvious evidence on or beneath the table.

"We've gotta look for her," she said to Bell.

"If he said boat, let's go west. The Hudson."

Sachs nodded to where the Conjurer and Cheryl had sat. "That's a crime scene—don't wash it or sweep under it. And move them to a different table," she shouted, pointing to the four wide-eyed and momentarily silent women, and ran outside into the dazzling sunlight.

Chapter Sixteen

She saw her husband crying.

Tears of regret that he had to "end the marriage."

End *the* marriage.

Like taking out *the* trash.

Walking *the* dog.

It was our fucking *marriage*! It wasn't a *thing.*

But Roy didn't feel that way. Roy wanted a stubby assistant securities analyst instead of her and that was that.

Another gagging flood of hot slimy water shot up her nose.

Air, air, air. . . . Give me air!

Now Cheryl Marston saw her father and mother at Christmas, decades ago, coyly wheeling out the bicycle Santa had brought her from the North Pole. Look, honey, Santa even has a pink helmet for you to protect your pretty little noggin. . . .

"Ahhhhhh . . ."

Coughing and choking, gripped by constricting chains, Cheryl was hauled out of the opaque water of the greasy pond, upside down, spinning lazily, held by a rope looped over a metal crane jutting over the water.

Her skull throbbed as the blood settled in her head. "Stop, stop, stop!" she screamed silently. What was going on? She remembered Donny Boy rearing, somebody calming him, a nice man, coffee in a Greek restaurant, conversation, something about boats, then the world uncoiling in dizziness, silly laughter.

Then chains. The terrible water.

And now this man studying her with pleasant curiosity on his face as she died.

Who is he? Why is he doing this? *Why?*

Inertia spun her slowly in a circle and he could no longer see her pleading eyes, as the inverted, hazy line of New Jersey miles away across the Hudson came into view.

She revolved slowly back until she was looking at the brambles and lilacs. And *him.*

He in turn looked down at her, nodded,

then played out the rope, lowering her into the disgusting pond again.

Cheryl bent hard at the waist, trying desperately to keep away from the surface of the water, as if it were scalding hot. But her own weight, the weight of the chains pulled her down below the surface. Holding her breath, she shivered fiercely and shook her head, struggling vainly to pull free from the unbreakable metal.

Then Cheryl's husband was here again, in front of her, explaining, explaining, explaining why the divorce was the best thing that could've happened to her. Roy looked up, wiped away crocodile tears and said it was for the best. She'd be happier this way. Look, here was something for her. Roy opened a door and there was a shiny new Schwinn bike. Streamers on the handle grips, training wheels in the back and a helmet—a pink one—to protect her noggin.

Cheryl gave up. You win, you win. Take the goddamn boat, take your goddamn girlfriend. Just let me go, let me go in peace. She inhaled through her nose to let comforting death into her lungs.

• • •

"There!" Amelia Sachs cried.

She and Bell ran forward over the pedestrian walkway toward the thick cluster of bushes and trees on the edge of the Hudson River. A man stood on a rotting pier, which had apparently been a dock years ago before access to the river had been filled in. This area was overgrown, filled with trash and stank of stagnant water.

A man in chinos and a white shirt was holding a rope that arced over a small rusting crane. The other end disappeared below the surface.

"Hey," Bell called, "you!"

He had brown hair, yes, but the outfit was different. No beard, either. And his eyebrows didn't seem that thick. Sachs couldn't see if the fingers of his left hand were fused together.

Still, what did that mean?

The Conjurer could be a man, could be a woman.

The Conjurer could be invisible.

As they jogged closer he looked up in apparent relief. "Here!" he cried. "Help me! Over here! There's a woman in the water!"

Bell and Sachs left Kara beside the overpass and sprinted through the brush surrounding the brackish pond. "Don't trust him," she called breathlessly to Bell as they ran.

"I'm with you there, Amelia."

The man pulled harder and feet and then legs in tan slacks emerged, followed by a woman's body. She was wrapped in chains. Oh, the poor thing! Sachs thought. Please let her be alive.

They closed the distance fast, Bell calling on his handy-talkie for backup and medics. Several other people who were on the east side of the pedestrian bridge were gathering, alarmed at what was going on.

"Help me! I can't pull her up alone!" the rescuer called to Bell and Sachs. His voice was a gasp, out of breath from the effort. "This man, he tied her up and pushed her into the water. He tried to kill her!"

Sachs drew her weapon and trained it on the man.

"Hey, what're you doing?" he asked in shock. "I'm trying to save her!" He glanced down at a cell phone on his belt. "*I'm* the one called nine-one-one."

She still couldn't see his left hand; it was enclosed by his right.

"Keep your hands on that rope, sir," she said. "Keep 'em where I can see them."

"I didn't do anything!" He was wheezing—an odd sound. Maybe it wasn't exertion but asthma.

Staying clear of her line of fire, Bell grabbed the crane and swung it toward the muddy shore. When the woman was in arm's reach he tugged her toward him, as the man holding the rope let out slack until she was lying on the ground. She lay on the grass, limp and cyanotic. The detective pulled the tape off her mouth, unhooked the chains and began to give her CPR.

Sachs called to the dozen people gathered nearby, drawn by the commotion, "Is anybody a doctor?"

No one answered. She glanced back at the victim and saw her stirring. . . . Then she began choking and spitting out water. Yes! They'd gotten to her in time. In a minute she'd be able to confirm the man's identity. Then she looked past the scene and noticed a wad of shiny navy-blue cloth. She caught sight of a zipper and sleeve. It could be the jogging jacket he'd quick-changed out of.

The man's eyes followed hers and he saw it too.

Was there a reaction, a faint wince? She thought so but couldn't tell for sure.

"Sir," she called firmly, "until we get things sorted out here, I'm going to put some cuffs on you. I want your hands—"

Suddenly a man's panicked voice shouted, "Yo, lady, look out! That guy in the jogging suit—to yo right! He got a gun!"

People screamed and dropped to the ground and Sachs crouched, spinning to her right, squinting for a target. "Roland, look out!"

Bell too dropped to the ground, beside the woman, and looked in the same direction as Sachs, his Sig in his hand.

But Sachs saw nobody in a jogging suit.

Oh, no, she thought. No! Furious with herself, she understood what had happened—he'd mimicked the voice himself. Ventriloquism.

She turned back fast to see a brilliant fireball explode from the rescuer's hand. It hovered in the air, blinding her.

"Amelia!" Bell called. "I can't see anything! Where is he?"

"I don't—"

A fast series of gunshots sounded from where the Conjurer had been standing. The onlookers fled in panic as Sachs aimed at the sound of the shooting. Bell did too. They both squinted for targets but the killer was gone by the time her vision returned; she found herself aiming at a cloud of faint smoke—from more of the explosive squibs.

Then, to the east, she saw the Conjurer on the other side of the parkway. He started up the middle of the street but saw an RMP speeding his way, its lights and sirens frantic, and he leaped up the wide stairway that led to the college and vanished into the crafts fair, like a copperhead disappearing into tall grass.

Chapter Seventeen

They were everywhere. . . .

Dozens of police.

All searching for him.

Gasping from the sprint, his lungs stinging, the muscles in his side on fire, Malerick leaned against the cool limestone of one of the college's classroom buildings.

In front of him a fair spread out over the large plaza, which was jammed with people. He looked behind him, west, the direction he'd come from. Already the police had cut off that entrance. On the north and south sides of the square were tall concrete buildings. The windows were sealed and there were no doors. His only exit was east, on the other side of a football-field-size expanse of booths and dense crowds.

He made his way in that direction. But he didn't dare run.

Because illusionists know that fast attracts attention.

Slow makes you invisible.

He glanced at the goods for sale, nodded in pleasure at a guitarist's performance, laughed at a balloon-tying clown. He did what everyone else did.

Because unique attracts attention.

Similar makes you invisible.

Easing east. Wondering how the police had located him. Of course he'd expected they'd find the drowned body of the woman lawyer sometime today. But they'd moved too fast—it was as if they'd *anticipated* that he'd kidnap someone in that part of the city, maybe even at the riding academy itself. How?

Farther east.

Past the booths, past the concession stand, past a Dixieland band on a red, white and blue draped stage. Ahead of him was the exit—the east stairway leading from the square down to Broadway. Only another fifty feet to freedom, forty.

Thirty . . .

But then he saw flashing lights. They

seemed nearly as bright as the burst from the flash cotton he'd used to escape from the redheaded officer. The lights were atop four squad cars that squealed to a stop beside the stairway. A half-dozen uniformed officers jumped out. They scanned the stairs and remained with their cars. Meanwhile other officers, in plain clothes, were arriving. They now climbed the stairs and merged into the crowd, looking over the men at the fair.

Now surrounded, Malerick turned and headed back toward the center of the festival.

The plain-clothed officers were slowly moving westward. They were stopping men in their fifties who were clean shaven, wearing light shirts and tan slacks. Exactly like him.

But they were also stopping fifty-year-olds who were bearded and were wearing other clothes. Which meant they knew about his quick-change techniques.

Then he saw what he'd been dreading: The policewoman with the steely eyes and fiery red hair, who'd tried to arrest him at the pond, appeared at the top of the stairs at the west end of the fair. She plunged into the crowd.

Malerick turned aside, lowering his head and studying some very bad ceramic sculpture.

What to do? he thought desperately. He had one remaining quick-change outfit left, under what he now wore. But after that, there was no backup.

The redheaded officer spotted someone who was built and dressed similarly to him. She examined the man closely. Then she turned away and continued to scan the crowd.

The trim, brown-haired cop who'd been giving Cheryl Marston CPR now crested the stairs and joined the policewoman in the crowd. They conferred for a few moments. Another woman was with him—she didn't seem like a cop. She had brilliant blue eyes and short reddish-purple hair and was quite thin. She looked over the crowd and whispered something to the woman officer, who headed off in a different direction. The short-haired girl stayed with the male cop and they began to work their way through the crowd.

Malerick knew he'd be spotted sooner or

later. He had to get out of the fair now, before even more cops arrived. Walking to the row of Porta Potties, he stepped inside the fiberglass box and executed a change. In thirty seconds he stepped out again, politely holding the door open for a middle-aged woman, who hesitated and turned away, deciding to wait for a john whose prior user wasn't a ponytailed biker with a beer gut, wearing a Pennzoil cap, a greasy long-sleeved denim Harley-Davidson shirt and dirty black jeans.

He picked up a newspaper and rolled it up, gripping it in his left hand to obscure his fingers, then moved toward the east side of the fair again, checking out stained glass, mugs and bowls, handmade toys, crystals, CDs. One cop looked right at him but the glance was brief and he turned away.

Malerick now returned to the eastern edge of the fair.

The stairway that led down to Broadway was about thirty yards wide and the uniformed police had managed to close off much of it. They were now stopping all adult men and women who left the fair and asking for IDs.

He saw the detective and the purple-haired girl nearby, next to the concession stand. She was whispering to him. Had she noticed him?

Malerick was swept by a burst of uncontrollable fury. He'd planned the performance so carefully—every routine, every trick choreographed to lead up to tomorrow's finale. This weekend was supposed to be the most perfect illusion ever performed. And it was all crumbling around him. He thought of how disappointed his mentor would be. He thought of letting down his revered audience. . . . He found his hand, holding a small oil painting of the Statue of Liberty, beginning to shake.

This is not acceptable! he raged.

He put the picture down and turned.

But he stopped fast, giving a sharp gasp.

The red-haired policewoman stood only a few feet from him, looking away. He quickly turned his attention to a case of jewelry and asked the vendor, in a thick Brooklyn accent, how much a pair of earrings cost.

From the corner of his eye he could see the policewoman glance at him but she paid him no mind and a moment later made a call on her radio. "Five Eight Eight Five. Requesting a landline patch to Lincoln

Rhyme." A moment later: "We're at the fair, Rhyme. He *has* to be here. . . . He couldn't've gotten out before they sealed the exits. We'll find him. If we have to frisk everybody we'll find him."

Malerick eased into the crowd. What were his options?

Misdirection—that seemed to be the only answer. Something to distract the police and give him just five seconds to slip through the line and disappear among the pedestrians on Broadway.

But what would misdirect them long enough to let him escape?

He didn't have any more squibs to simulate gunshots. Set a booth on fire? But that wouldn't cause the sort of panic he now needed.

Anger and fear seized him again.

But then he heard his mentor's voice from years ago, after the boy had made a mistake onstage and nearly ruined one of the man's routines. The demonic, bearded illusionist had pulled the youngster aside after the performance. Close to tears, the boy had gazed down at the floor as the man asked, "What is illusion?"

"Science and logic" had been Malerick's

instant response. (The mentor had drummed a hundred answers like this one into his assistants' souls.)

"Science and logic, yes. If there's a mishap—because of you or your assistant or God Himself—you use science and logic to take charge instantly. Not one second should pass between the mistake and your reaction. Be bold. Read your audience. Turn disaster into applause."

Hearing those words in his mind now, Malerick grew calm. He tossed his biker braid and looked around, considering what to do.

Be bold. Read your audience.

Turn disaster into applause.

Sachs scanned the people near her again— a mother and father with two bored children, an elderly couple, a biker in a Harley shirt, two young European women bargaining with a vendor over some jewelry.

She noticed Bell across the square, near the food concession area. But where was Kara? The young woman was supposed to stay close to one of them. She started to wave to the detective but a cluster of people ambled between them and she lost sight of him. She walked in his direction and her head swiveled back and forth, scanning the crowd.

Feeling, she realized, as unsettled as at the music school that morning, despite the fact that the sky was clear and the sun bright, hardly the gothic setting of the first scene. *Spooky . . .*

She knew what the problem was.

Wire.

When you walked a beat, either you had wire or you didn't. A cop expression, "having wire" meant you were connected to your neighborhood. It was more than a question of knowing the people and the geography of your beat; it was knowing what kind of energy drove them, what kind of perps you could expect, how dangerous they were, how they'd come at their vics—and at you.

If you didn't have wire in a 'hood you had no business walking a beat there.

With the Conjurer, Sachs now understood, she didn't have wire at all. He could be on the number 9 train right now, headed downtown. Or he could be three feet away from her. She just didn't know.

In fact, just then, someone passed close behind her. She felt a breath or wafting of cloth on her neck. She spun around fast, shivering in fear—hand on the butt of her gun, remembering how easily Kara had distracted her as she'd lifted Sachs's weapon from its holster.

A half-dozen people were nearby but no one seemed to have stirred the air behind her.

Or had they?

A man was walking away, limping. He couldn't be the Conjurer.

Or could he?

The Conjurer can become somebody else in seconds, remember?

Around her: an elderly couple, the ponytailed biker, three teenagers, a huge man wearing a ConEd uniform. She was at sea, frustrated and scared for herself and for everyone around her.

No wire . . .

It was then that a woman's scream filled the air.

A voice called, "There! Look! God, somebody's hurt."

Sachs drew her weapon and headed toward the cluster gathering nearby.

"Get a doctor!"

"What's wrong?"

"Oh, God, don't look, honey!"

A large crowd had formed near the eastern edge of the plaza, not far from the concession stand. They gazed down in horror at someone lying on the bricks at their feet.

Sachs lifted her Motorola to call for a medical team and pushed through the crowd. "Let me through, let me—"

She stopped inside the ring of onlookers and gasped.

"No," she whispered, shuddering in dismay at the sight.

Amelia Sachs was staring at the Conjurer's latest victim.

Kara lay on the ground, blood covering her purple blouse and the bricks around her. Her head was back and her still, dead eyes stared toward the azure sky.

Chapter Eighteen

Numb, Sachs lifted her hand to her mouth.

Oh, Lord, no . . .

Robert-Houdin had tighter tricks than the Marabouts. Though I think they almost killed him.

Don't worry. I'll make sure that doesn't happen to you. . . .

But she hadn't. She'd been so focused on the Conjurer that she'd neglected the girl.

No, no, Rhyme, some dead you can't give up. This tragedy would be with her forever.

But then she thought: There'll be time to mourn. There'll be time for recrimination and consequences. Right now, start thinking like a goddamn cop. The Conjurer's nearby. And he is *not* getting away. This is a crime scene and you know what to do.

Step one. Seal the escape routes.

Step two. Seal the scene.

Step three. Identify, protect and interview witnesses.

She turned to two fellow patrol officers to delegate some of these tasks. But as Sachs started to speak she heard a voice in her clattering radio. "RMP Four Seven to all available officers on that ten-twenty-four by the river. Suspect just broke through perimeter at the east side of the street fair. Is now on West End approaching Seven-eight Street, heading north on foot. . . . Wearing jeans, blue shirt with Harley-Davidson logo. Dark hair, braid, black base-ball cap. Can't see any weapons. . . . I'm losing him in the crowd. . . . All available portables and RMPs respond."

The biker! He'd ditched his business-man's clothes and quick-changed. He'd stabbed Kara to misdirect them and then slipped through the perimeter when the officers started toward the girl.

And I was three feet from him!

Other officers called in their acknowledg-ments and joined the chase though it seemed that the killer had a good head start. Sachs caught sight of Roland Bell, who was looking down at Kara, frowning as he pressed the headset of his Motorola closer to his ear, listening to the same transmission that Sachs was. They caught each other's eyes and he nodded in the direction of the pursuit. Sachs barked orders to a nearby patrolman to seal the scene of Kara's murder, call the medical examiner and find witnesses.

"But—" the balding young officer began to protest, none too happy, she guessed, to be taking orders from a peer his own age.

"No buts," she said, not in the mood for a pissing contest about weeks or days of seniority between them. "You can bitch to your supervisor about it later."

If he said anything else she didn't hear; ignoring the painful arthritis, she leaped down the stairs two at a time after Roland Bell and began pursuit of the man who'd killed their friend.

He's fast.

But I'm faster.

Six-year-vet Patrolman Lawrence Burke sprinted out of Riverside Park onto West End Avenue, only twenty feet behind the speeding perp, some biker asshole in a Harley shirt.

Running around pedestrians, broken field, exactly the way he used to do in high school, going after the receiver.

And just like back then, Legs Larry was closing in.

He'd been on his way to the Hudson River to help secure a 10–24 assault crime scene when he'd heard a further-to pursuit call and turned about-face to find himself staring at the perp—a scuzzy biker.

"Yo, you! Hold it!"

But the man hadn't stopped. He'd dodged past Burke and kept right on going north in a panic run. And so just like at the Woodrow Wilson High homecoming game when he'd sprinted seventy-two yards after Chris Broderick (managing to bring him down with a breathless wallop two feet shy of the end zone), Legs went into overdrive and started after the perp.

Burke didn't draw his weapon. Unless the perp you're after is armed and there's an immediate danger he's going to shoot you or a passerby you can't use deadly force to stop him. And shooting *anybody* in the back looks very bad at the shooting incident inquiry, not to mention at promotion reviews and in the press.

"Hey, you fuck loser!" Burke gasped.

The biker turned east down a cross street, glancing back with wide eyes, seeing Legs steadily closing the distance.

The guy skidded to the left, down an alley. The cop took the turn even smoother than Mr. Harley and stayed right on the man's ass.

Some police departments issued nets or stun guns to stop fleeing felons but the NYPD wasn't so high-tech. Besides, it didn't matter, not in this case. Larry Burke had more skills than running. Tackling, for instance.

From three feet away he launched himself into the air, remembering to aim high and use the guy's own body for padding when they went down.

"Jesus," the biker gasped as they crashed to the cobblestones and skidded into a pile of garbage.

"Goddamn!" Burke muttered, feeling skin flay off his elbow. "You motherfuck."

"I didn't do anything!" the biker gasped. "Why were you chasing me?"

"Shut up."

Burke cuffed him and because the guy was such a fuck-all runner he used a plastic restraint on his ankles too. Nice and tight. He examined his bloody elbow. "Damn, I lost skin. Ow, that hurts. You fuck."

"I didn't do anything. I was at that fair is all I was doing. I just—"

Spitting on the ground, Burke inhaled deeply a number of times. He gasped, "What part about *shut up*'re you having trouble with? I'm not gonna tell you again. . . . Fuck, that stings!"

He frisked the man carefully and found a wallet. There was no ID inside, only money. Curious. And he had no weapons or drugs either, which was pretty odd for a biker.

"You can threaten me all you want but I want a lawyer. I'm going to sue you! If you think I did something, you're way wrong, mister."

But then Burke tugged up the guy's shirt and T-shirt and blinked. His chest and abdomen were badly scarred. It was creepy to look at. But even stranger was a bag around his waist, like those belly packs he and the wife'd worn on their European vacation. Burke expected a stash, but no, all that the guy was hiding was a pair of jogging pants, a turtleneck, chinos, white shirt and a cell phone. And—this was really weird—makeup. A ton of wadded-up toilet paper too, stuffed in the pack, as if he was trying to make himself look fat.

Pretty weird . . .

Burke inhaled deeply again and got an unfortunate whiff of garbage and urine from the alley. He pushed the button on his Motorola. "Portable Five Two One Two to Central. . . . I've got the perp in that ten-two-four in custody, K."

"Injuries?"

"Negative."

Except for one fucking sore elbow.

"Location?"

"Block and a half east of West End, K. Hold on a minute. I'll get the cross street."

Burke walked to the mouth of the alley to look for the street sign and wait for his fellow cops to show up. It was only then that the adrenaline began to subside, leaving in its wake a tasty euphoria. Not a shot fired. One bad-ass loser belly down. . . . Godlovingdamn, it felt nice—almost as good as that game twelve years ago, bringing down Chris Broderick, who gave a girlie yelp as he slammed into the turf on the one-yard line, having covered the whole length of the field without a clue that Legs Larry had been right behind him all the way.

"Hey there, you okay?"

Bell touched Amelia Sachs on the arm. She was so shaken by Kara's death that she couldn't answer. She nodded, breathless with grief.

Ignoring the pain in her knees from the earlier jogging, Sachs and the detective continued quickly up West End toward where Patrolman Burke had radioed that he'd collared the killer.

Wondering if Kara had siblings. Oh, God, we'll have to tell her family.

No, not *we*.

I'll have to do it. This's my fault. *I* make that call.

Sick with the sorrow she hurried toward the alleyway. Bell glanced at her again, inhaling deeply to catch his breath.

But at least they'd caught the Conjurer.

Though she was, in her private heart, sorry she hadn't been the arresting officer. She wished she'd found herself alone in the alley facing the Conjurer, a gun in his hand.

She might've used the Glock before the Motorola and tapped his shoulder with a single round. In movies shoulder shots were just flesh wounds, inconveniences, and the heroes survived with nothing more than a sling. The truth, though, was that even a small bullet wound changed your life for a long, long time. Sometimes forever.

But the killer had been caught and she'd have to be satisfied with multiple murder convictions.

Don't worry, don't worry, don't worry . . .

Kara . . .

Sachs realized she didn't even know her real name.

It's my stage name but I use it most of the time. Better than the one my parents were kind enough to give me.

This small bit of missing information brought her close to tears.

She realized that Bell was saying something to her. "You, uhn, with us here, Amelia?"

A curt nod.

They turned the corner onto Eighty-eighth Street, where the patrolman had downed the perp. Both ends of the street were being sealed off by RMPs. Bell squinted up the block and noted an alleyway. "There," he said, pointing. He motioned several cops—both plainclothes detectives and uniformed patrol officers—to follow them.

"Okay, let's go wrap him up," Sachs muttered. "Man, I hope Grady goes for the needle."

They stopped and looked into the dim canyon. The alley was empty.

"Isn't this it?" Bell asked.

"He said Eight-eight, right?" Sachs asked. "A block and a half east of West End. I'm sure that was the call."

"Me too," a detective said.

"This's gotta be the place." She looked up and down the street. "No other alleys."

Three more officers joined them. "We get it wrong?" one asked, looking around. "This the place or not?"

Bell called on his Motorola, "Portable Five Two One Two, respond, K."

No answer.

"Portable Five Two, what street are you on, K?"

Sachs squinted down the alley. "Oh, no." Her heart sank.

Running forward, she found, resting on the cobblestones near a pile of garbage, a pair of handcuffs, open. Next to them was a plastic hog tie, which had been severed. Bell ran up beside her.

"He got out of the goddamn cuffs and cut the restraint." Sachs looked around.

"Well, where are they?" one of the uniformed officers asked.

"Where's Larry?" another one called.

"In pursuit?" somebody else offered. "Maybe he's out of reception area."

"Maybe," drawled Bell, the concern in his tone reflecting the fact that the workhorse Motorolas rarely malfunctioned and their reception in the city was better than most cell phones'.

Bell called in a 10–39, escaped suspect, with an officer missing or in pursuit. He asked the dispatcher if there'd been any transmissions from Burke but was told there'd been none. No third-party reports of shots fired in the vicinity either.

Sachs walked the length of the alley, looking for any clues that might suggest where the killer had gone or where the Conjurer might've dumped the patrol officer's body if he'd gotten control of Burke's gun and killed him. But neither she nor Bell found any sign of the officer or the perp. She returned to the cluster of cops at the mouth of the alley.

What a terrible day. Two dead this morning. Kara too.

And now a police officer was missing.

Her hand rose to the speaker/mike of her SP-50 handy-talkie and pulled it off her shoulder. Time to tell Rhyme. Oh, brother. Don't want to make this call. She called in to Central on the radio and asked for a patch. As she was waiting for the call to go through she felt a tug on her sleeve.

Sachs turned. As she inhaled a shocked breath the mike slipped from her hand and swung at her side, a pendulum.

Two people stood in front of her. One was the balding officer Sachs had been giving orders to at the fair ten minutes ago.

The other was Kara, wearing an NYPD windbreaker. Frowning, the young woman looked up and down the alley. She asked, "So where is he?"

Chapter Nineteen

"Are you all right?" Sachs stammered. "What . . . Wait, what happened?"

"All right? Yeah, I'm fine. . . ." Kara took in the woman's astonished gaze and said, "You mean you didn't know?"

The balding officer said to Sachs, "I tried to tell you. But you ran off before I had a chance."

"Tell me . . . ?" Sachs's voice stopped working. She was so stunned—and riddled with relief—that she couldn't speak.

"You thought I was really hurt?" Kara said. "Oh, God."

Bell walked up, nodding a greeting to Kara, who said, "Amelia didn't know."

"About?"

"Our plan. The fake stabbing."

The expression on Bell's face was pure

shock. "Lord, you thought she was really dead?"

The patrol officer repeated to Bell, "I tried to let her know. First, I couldn't find her and then, when I did, she just tells me to seal the scene and call the M.E. and takes off."

Kara explained, "Roland and I were talking? And we figured that the Conjurer was going to hurt somebody for real—maybe set a fire or shoot or stab somebody. You know, to misdirect us so he could get away. So we thought we'd make up our own misdirection."

"To flush that boy outta the brush," Bell added. "She got some catsup at the concession stand, squirted it on herself, screamed then fell down."

Kara opened the blue windbreaker to reveal the red stain on her purple tank top.

The detective continued, "Was worried a few folks at the fair'd be all tore up over it—"

Well, I'd guess . . .

"—but we were thinking that'd be better than somebody really getting clocked or stabbed by the Conjurer." Bell added proudly, "Was her idea. No foolin'."

"I'm getting a feel for how he thinks," the young woman said.

"Jesus." Sachs found herself trembling. "It was so real."

Bell nodded. "She does dead good."

Sachs gave her a hug then said sternly, "But from now on, stay close. Or keep me in the loop. I'm too young for heart attacks."

They waited a short while but no reports came in of suspects spotted in the area. Finally Bell said, "You search the scene here, Amelia. I'm going to go interview the victim. See if she can tell us anything. Meet you back at the fair."

A crime scene bus was parked on Eighty-Eighth Street. She walked to it and began to collect her equipment to run the scene. A voice clattered through her dangling speaker, startling her. She pulled her hands-free headset off her belt and plugged it in. "Five Eight Eight Five. Repeat, K."

"Sachs, what the hell's going on? I heard you had him and now he's gone?"

She told Rhyme what had happened, about flushing the Conjurer from the fair.

"Kara's idea? Playing dead? Hmm." The final sound—a grunt really—was a high compliment, coming from Lincoln Rhyme.

"But he's disappeared," Sachs added. "And we can't find that officer either. Maybe he's in pursuit. But we don't know. Roland's interviewing the woman we saved. See if she has any leads."

"Okay, well, run the scene, Sachs."

"Scenes plural," she corrected sourly. "The coffee shop, the pond and the alley here. Too damn many."

"Not too many at all," he replied. "Three times the chance to find some good evidence."

Rhyme had been right.

The three scenes had yielded a good amount of evidence.

They'd been difficult to work, though for an unusual reason: the Conjurer had been present at each one—his phantom, at least. Hovering nearby. Making her pause often to tap the grip of her Glock, turning around and making sure the killer hadn't materialized behind her.

Search well but watch your back.

She never actually saw anyone. But then Svetlana Rasnikov hadn't seen her killer shed the black camouflage and creep up behind her from the shadows.

Tony Calvert hadn't seen him hiding behind the mirror in the alley when he'd walked toward the fake cat.

And even Cheryl Marston hadn't truly *seen* the Conjurer though she'd sat and talked with him. She'd seen someone else entirely, never suspecting the terrible death he had planned for her.

Sachs walked the grids at the various locations, took digital photos and released the scenes to Latents and Photo. She then returned to the fair, where she met Roland Bell. He'd interviewed Cheryl Marston at the hospital. They of course couldn't rely on anything the killer had told her ("Pack of goddamn lies," Marston had summarized bitterly) but she remembered some details from before the drug reached its full effect. She gave a good description of him, including particulars about the scars. She also recalled that he'd stopped at a car. She remembered the make and the first few letters of the tag. This was good news. There are a hundred ways to trace a car to a perpetrator or witness. Lincoln Rhyme called cars "evidence generators."

DMV had reported that a car matching the description—a 2001 tan Mazda 626 had been stolen from the White Plains airport a week ago. Sellitto put out an emergency vehicle locator request to all law enforcement agencies in the metro area and sent officers to check the blocks around the site of the attack to see if they could find the car, though neither officer had much faith that it would still be there.

Bell was concluding his narrative about Cheryl Marston's harrowing ordeal when a patrol officer taking a radio call interrupted him.

"Detective Bell? What was that car again? The one the perp was driving?"

"Tan Mazda. Six two six. Tag's F-E-T two three seven."

"That's it," the officer said into his mike. Then to Bell and Sachs he added, "Just got a report—RMP spotted him on Central Park West. They went after him but—get this—he drove over the curb into the park itself. The RMP tried to follow but got stuck on the embankment."

"CPW and what?" Sachs asked.

"Around Nine-two."

"He probably bailed," Bell said.

"He *will* bail," Sachs said. "But he's going to get some distance first." She nodded to the evidence crates. "Get all this to Rhyme," she called and ten seconds later she was in the seat of her Camaro and had the big engine rattling. She snapped the race-car harness on and pulled the canvas straps snug.

"Amelia, wait!" Bell called. "ESU is on the way."

But the squeal of rubber and the cloud of blue smoke the Goodyears left behind were her only response to Bell's words.

Skidding onto Central Park West, heading north, Sachs concentrated on avoiding pedestrians, poky cars, bicyclists and Rollerbladers.

Baby strollers too. They were *everywhere.* Man, why weren't these kids home taking naps?

She pitched the blue flasher onto the dash and plugged it into the cigarette lighter outlet. The brilliant light began rotating and as she hurtled forward she found herself slapping the horn in time to the flash.

A streak of gray in front of her.

Shit. . . . As she braked hard to avoid the

U-turner the Camaro ended up a scant foot from the side of a car that was worth twice her annual income. Then she crunched the accelerator again and the General Motors horses responded instantly. She managed to keep the needle under fifty until the traffic thinned out, around Ninetieth Street, and then she went to the floor.

In a few seconds she hit seventy.

A clatter through the headset of her Motorola, which lay on the front passenger seat. She grabbed it with one hand and pulled it on.

"'Lo?" she called, dispensing with any pretense of requisite police radio codes.

"Amelia? Roland here," Bell called. He'd also given up on standard communication protocols.

"Go ahead."

"We've got cars on the way."

"Where is he?" she asked, shouting over the roar of the engine.

"Hold on. . . . Okay, he drove out of the park on Central Park North. Sideswiped a truck and kept going."

"Headed where?"

"That was . . . It was less'n a minute ago. He's going north."

"Got it."

Heading north in Harlem? Sachs considered. There were several routes out of the city from that area of town but she doubted that he'd take them; they all involved bridges and most were via controlled-access highways, where he'd easily be trapped.

More likely he'd abandon the sedan in a relatively quiet neighborhood and carjack a new one.

A new voice resounded in her headset. "Sachs, we've got him!"

"Where, Rhyme?"

He'd turned westbound on 125th Street, the criminalist explained. "Near Fifth Avenue."

"I'm just about at One-two-five and Adam Clayton Powell. I'll try to block him. But get me some backup," she called.

"We're on it, Sachs. Just how fast are you going?"

"I'm not really looking at the speedometer."

"Probably just as well. Keep your eyes on the road."

Sachs honked her way into the busy intersection at 125th Street. She parked crosswise, blocking the westbound lanes. She jumped out of her car, her Glock in her hand. Several cars were stopped in the eastbound lanes. Sachs shouted to the drivers, "Out! Police action. Get out of those cars and get under cover. The drivers—a delivery man and a woman in a McDonald's uniform—instantly did as they were told.

Now all the lanes of 125th Street were blocked.

"Everybody," she shouted. "Get under cover! Now!"

"Motherfuck."

"Yo."

She glanced to her right to see four gang-bangers leaning against a chain-link fence, staring with jaded interest at the Austrian gun, the Detroit car and the redhead they belonged to.

Most other people on the street had taken cover but these four teenagers stayed right where they were, looking casual as Sunday. Why move? It wasn't often that a Wesley Snipes movie came to their 'hood.

In the distance Sachs saw the Mazda weaving frantically through traffic as it sped west toward her impromptu roadblock. The Conjurer didn't notice the blockade until he was past the street that he could've taken to avoid her. He skidded to a halt. Behind him a garbage truck making a turn braked hard. The driver and the trash collectors saw what was happening and they bailed, leaving the truck to block him from the rear.

She glanced at the teens again. "Get down!" she called.

Sneering, they ignored her.

Sachs shrugged, leaned over the hood of the Camaro and centered the blade sight on the windshield.

So here he was at last, the Conjurer. She could see his face, his blue Harley shirt. Beneath a black cap his fake braid whipped back and forth as he looked desperately for some way to escape.

But there wasn't any.

"You! In the Mazda! Get out of the car and lie down on the ground!"

No response.

"Sachs?" Rhyme's voice came through the headset. "Can you—"

She ripped the unit off and centered the sight once more on the silhouette of the killer's head.

You have the gun to use, and you may as well use it. . . .

Hearing Detective Mary Shanley's words looping through her head, Sachs breathed deeply and kept the gun steady, a bit high, a bit to the left, compensating for gravity and the pleasant April breeze.

When you shoot, nothing exists but you and the target, connected by an invisible cable, like the quiet energy of light. Your ability to hit your target depends exclusively on where this energy originates. If its source is your brain you may hit what you're aiming at. But if it's your heart you almost always will. The Conjurer's victims—Tony Calvert, Svetlana Rasnikov, Cheryl Marston, Officer Larry Burke—now seated this power solidly in the latter and she knew that she couldn't miss.

Come on, she thought, you son of a bitch. Put the goddamn car in drive. Try for me.

Come on!

Give me an excuse . . .

The car edged forward. Her finger slipped inside the trigger guard.

As if he sensed this the Conjurer braked.

"Come on," she found herself whispering.

Thinking about how to handle it. If he just tried to get away she'd take out the fan blades or a tire and try to capture him alive.

But if he drove toward her or aimed for the sidewalk, endangering someone else, then she'd drop him.

"Yo!" one of the teens on the sidewalk called.

"Shoot the motherfuck!"

"Cap his ass, bitch!"

You don't have to convince me, homes. Ready, willing and able . . .

She decided that if he drove ten feet toward her, at any kind of speed, she'd nail him. The engine of the Band-Aid-colored car revved and she saw—or imagined—that the vehicle shuddered.

Ten feet. That's all I'm asking.

Another growl of the engine. Do it! she pleaded silently.

And then Sachs saw a slow-moving mass of yellow ease behind the Mazda.

A school bus from Zion Prophetic Tabernacle Church, filled with children, pulled away from the curb into traffic, the driver unaware of what was happening. It stopped at an angle between the Mazda and the garbage truck.

No . . .

Even a direct hit might not stop the slug,

which could careen into the bus after it passed through its target.

Finger off the trigger, muzzle safely in the air, Sachs looked through the windshield of the Mazda. She could see the faint motion of the Conjurer's head as he glanced up and to his right, locating the bus in the rearview mirror.

He then looked back toward her and she had the impression that he smiled, deducing that she couldn't fire now.

The raw squeal of the Mazda's front tires filled the street as he floored the pedal and headed toward Sachs at twenty, forty, fifty miles an hour. He bore straight down on the policewoman and her Camaro, which was a far brighter yellow than the Bible school bus, whose presence had cast its blessing of holy protection over the Conjurer.

Chapter Twenty

As the Mazda headed straight at her, Sachs ran to the sidewalk to try for a cross-fire shot.

Lifting the Glock, she aimed at the dark form that was the Conjurer's head, leading him by three or four feet. But beyond him were dozens of store windows and apartments and people crouching on the sidewalk. There was simply no way to fire even a single round safely.

Her chorus didn't care.

"Yo, bitch, lessee you waste that motherfuck."

"Whatcho waitin' fo'?"

She lowered the gun, shoulders slumped as she watched the Mazda streak straight for the Camaro.

Oh, not the car. . . . No!

Thinking of when her father had bought her the '69 muscle car, a junker, and how together they'd rebuilt much of the engine and suspension, added a new transmission, and stripped it, to goose the horsepower skyward. This vehicle and a love of policing were his essential legacies to his daughter.

Thirty feet from the Camaro the Conjurer turned the wheel hard to the left, toward where Sachs crouched. She leaped aside and he turned the other way, back toward the Chevy. The Mazda skidded, cutting diagonally toward the sidewalk. At a glancing angle it slammed into the passenger door and right front fender of the Camaro, spinning it in a circle over two lanes onto the far sidewalk, where the four kids finally showed some energy and scattered.

Sachs dove out of the way and landed on her knees on the concrete, gasping at the pain in her arthritic joints. The Camaro came to rest a few feet from her, its rear end off the ground, jacked up by the battered orange metal trash basket it had rolled over.

The Mazda went over the far sidewalk then back into the street and turned right, heading north. Sachs climbed to her feet but didn't even bother to lift her gun in the direction of the beige car; there was no safe shot. A glance at the Camaro. The side was a mess, the front end too, but the torn fender wasn't binding on the tires. Yeah, she could probably catch him. She jumped in and fired up the engine. First gear. A roar. The tach shot up to 5000 and she popped the clutch.

But she didn't move an inch. What was the problem? Was the drive train cracked?

She glanced out the window and saw that the rear wheels—the drive wheels—were jacked up off the ground, thanks to the trash basket. She sighed in frustration, slammed the steering wheel with her palm. Damn! She saw the Mazda, three blocks away. The Conjurer wasn't escaping that fast; the collision had taken a toll on his car too. There was still a chance to catch him.

But not in a car up on goddamn blocks.

She'd have to—

The Camaro began to rock back and forth.

She looked in the rearview mirror and saw that three of the gangbangers had shed their combat jackets and were straining as they tried to shove the car off its perch. The fourth, bigger than the others, the leader of this crew, walked slowly up to the window. He leaned down, a gold tooth shining bright in the middle of his dark face. "Yo."

Sachs nodded and held his eye.

He looked back at his friends. "Yo, nig- gers, *push* the fuckin car! You makin' like you jerkin' off with it."

"Fuck you," came the winded reply.

He leaned down again. "Yo, lady, we gonna get you down. Whatcha gonna shoot that motherfuck with?"

"A Glock. Forty caliber."

He glanced at her holster. "Sweet. Be the twenty-three. The C?"

"No, the full size."

"That a good gun. I got myself a Smittie." He lifted his throwaway sweatshirt and, with a mix of defiance and pride, showed her the brushed silver handle of a Smith and Wes- son automatic. "But I'ma get me a Glock like yo's."

So, she reflected, an armed teenager. How would a sergeant handle this situa- tion?

The car bounced down off the trash can, rear wheels ready to roll.

Whatever a proper sergeant would say or do, she decided, didn't matter under the present circumstances. The way *she* handled it was to give him a solemn nod. "Thanks, homes." Then the woman with wire added ominously, "Don't shoot anybody and make me come lookin' for you. You got that?"

A wide gold grin.

Then, snap, into first gear and the gutsy tires burned wormholes into the asphalt. In a few seconds Amelia Sachs was doing sixty.

"Go, go, go," she muttered to herself, focused on the faint blur of tan in the distance. The Chevy wobbled like crazy but it drove more or less straight. Sachs struggled to get the Motorola headset on. She called Central to report the pursuit and redirect the backup along this route.

Accelerating fast, braking hard . . . the streets of crowded Harlem aren't made for high-speed pursuits. Still, the Conjurer was in the same traffic as she was—and he wasn't half the driver. Slowly she closed the gap. Then he turned toward a school yard, in which kids were playing half-court basketball and whacking softballs into fake outfields. The playground wasn't crowded; the gate was padlocked shut and anybody wishing to play here either had to squeeze through the gap like a contortionist or be willing to scale a twenty-foot chain-link fence.

The Conjurer, however, simply gunned the engine and went though the gate. The kids scattered and he narrowly missed some of them as he sped up again to take out a second gate on the far side.

Sachs hesitated but decided not to follow—not in an unstable car with youngsters around. She sped around the block, praying she'd pick him up on the other side, then skidded around the corner and stopped.

No sign of him.

She didn't see how he'd gotten away. He'd been out of sight for only ten seconds or so as she made the sweep around the playground and the school. And the only other escape route was a short dead-end street, terminating in a wall of bushes and small saplings. Beyond that, she could see the elevated Harlem River Drive, beyond which was just a scuzzy mud bank leading down to the river.

So, he got away. . . . And all I've got to show for the pursuit is five thousand bucks of bodywork. Man. . . .

Then a voice crackled. "All units in the vicinity of Frederick Douglass and One-five-three Street, be advised of a ten-five-four."

Car accident with probable injuries.

"Vehicle has gone into the Harlem River. Repeat, we have a vehicle in the water."

Could it be him? she wondered. "Crime Scene Five Eight Eight Five. Further to that ten-five-four. You have the make of the vehicle? K."

"Mazda or Toyota. Late model. Beige."

"Okay, Central, believe that's the subject vehicle of the Central Park pursuit. I'm ten-eight-four at the scene. Out."

"Roger, Five Eight Eight Five. Out."

Sachs sped her Camaro to the end of the cul-de-sac and parked on the sidewalk. She climbed out as an ambulance and Emergency Services Unit truck arrived and rocked slowly through the brush, which had been crushed by the speeding Mazda. She followed, walking carefully over the rubble. As they broke from the vegetation she saw a cluster of decrepit shanties and lean-tos. Dozens of homeless, mostly men. The place was muddy and filled with brush and garbage, dumped appliances, stripped, rusting cars.

Apparently the Conjurer, expecting to find a road on the other side of the bushes, had gone through the brush fast. She saw the panicked skid marks as he slid uncontrollably through the slick muck, careened off a shack, knocking it apart, then went off a rotting pier into the river.

Two ESU officers helped the residents of the shack out of the wreckage—they were unhurt—while others scanned the river for any sign of the driver. She radioed Rhyme and Sellitto and told them what had happened and asked the detective to call in a priority request for a crime scene rapid response bus.

"They get him, Amelia?" Sellitto asked. "Tell me they got him."

Looking at the slick of oil and gasoline on top of the choppy water, she said, "No sign."

Walking past a shattered toilet and a ripe-smelling trash bag, Sachs approached several men who were talking excitedly in Spanish among themselves. They held fishing rods; this was a popular place to use bloodworms or cut bait to catch stripers, bluefish and tommycod. They'd been drinking but were sober enough to give her a coherent account. The car had sped through the bushes fast and gone straight into the river. They'd all seen a man in the driver's seat and they were positive he hadn't jumped out.

Sachs talked briefly with Carlos and his friend, the two homeless men who lived in the now-demolished shack. They were both stoned and, since they'd been inside when the Mazda struck it, they hadn't seen anything that could help. Carlos was belligerent and seemed to feel the city owed him some compensation for his loss. Two other witnesses, ripping open trash bags for refundable bottles and cans at the time of the accident, reiterated the story of the fishermen.

More police cars were arriving, TV crews too, turning their cameras on what was left of the shack and on the police boat, off the stern of which two wet-suited divers were rolling backward into the water.

Now that the emergency activity had shifted to the river itself, the land-side operation became Amelia Sachs's. She had little crime scene equipment in the Camaro but she did have plenty of yellow tape, with which she now sealed off a large area of the riverbank. By the time she finished the RRV had arrived. Hooking up her headset, she called Central and was patched through to Rhyme once more.

"We've been following it, Sachs. The divers haven't found anything yet?"

"Don't think so."

"Did he bail out?"

"Not according to the witnesses. I'm going to run the scene here on the riverbank, Rhyme," she told him. "It'll be good luck."

"Luck?"

"Sure. I go to the trouble to run the scene. That means the divers'll be sure to find his body and a search'll be a waste of time."

"There'll still be an inquiry and—"

"It was a joke, Rhyme."

"Yeah, well, this par-*tic*-ular perp doesn't make me feel like laughing. Get going on the grid."

She carried one of the CS suitcases to the perimeter of the scene and was opening it when she heard an accented voice call out urgently, "My God, what happened? Is everyone all right?"

Near the TV crews a well-coiffed Latino in jeans and a sports jacket pushed forward through the crowd. He squinted in alarm at the damaged shack and then began to run toward it.

"Hey," Sachs called. He didn't hear her.

The man ducked under the yellow tape and made straight for the shack, tromping over the Mazda's tire treads and possibly obliterating anything that the Conjurer might have thrown from the car or had fallen out— maybe even destroying the killer's own footprints if he *had* bailed, despite what the fishermen believed they'd seen.

Suspicious of everyone now, she checked out his left hand and could see that the index and little finger weren't fused together. So he wasn't the Conjurer but who the hell is he? Sachs wondered. And what was he doing in *her* crime scene?

The man was now wading through the wreckage of the shack, grabbing planks and sheets of wood and corrugated metal, flinging them over his shoulder.

"Hey, you!" she called. "Get the hell out of there!"

He shouted over his shoulder, "There could be somebody inside!"

Angry now, she snapped, "This's a crime scene! You can't be in there."

"There could be somebody inside!" he repeated.

"No, no, no. Everybody's out. They're okay. Hey, you hearing me? . . . Excuse me, buddy. Are you *hearing* me?"

Whether he was or not apparently didn't matter, not to him. He continued to dig feverishly. What was his point? The man was dressed well and wearing a gold Rolex; crack-head Carlos was clearly not a relative.

Reciting to herself the famous cop's prayer—Lord, deliver us from concerned citizens—she gestured to two nearby patrol officers. "Get him out."

He was shouting, "We need more medics! There could be children inside."

Sachs disgustedly watched the officers' footprints adding to the slow erosion of her crime scene. They grabbed the intruder by the arms and pulled him to his feet. He yanked his arms away from the officers, haughtily called his name to Sachs as if he was some kind of mafioso that everybody should know and began to lecture her on the police's shameful treatment of the neglected Latino population here.

"Lady, do you have any idea—"

"Cuff him," she said. "Then get him the hell out of there." Deciding that the community relations part of the sergeant's handbook slogan took second place to criminal investigation in this case.

The officers ratcheted the cuffs on the red-faced man and he was led, fuming and cursing, out of the scene. "Want we should book him?" one officer called.

"Naw, just put him in time-out for a while," she shouted, drawing laughter from some of the onlookers. She watched him being deposited in the back of a squad car, yet another obstacle in the seemingly impossible search for an elusive killer.

Sachs then dressed in the Tyvek outfit and armed with camera and collection bags, and with rubber bands at last on her feet, she waded into the scene, starting with the remains of Carlos's destroyed mansion. She took her time and searched carefully. After this harrowing daylong pursuit Amelia Sachs was accepting nothing at face value. True, the Conjurer might be floating forty feet below the surface of the gray-brown water. But he could just as easily be crawling safely up the riverbank nearby.

She wouldn't even have been surprised to

find out that he was already miles away, dressed in a new disguise, stalking his next victim.

The Reverend Ralph Swensen had been in town for several days—his first visit to New York City—and he'd decided he could never get used to the place.

The thin man, somewhat balding, somewhat shy, ministered to souls in a town thousands of times smaller than and dozens of years removed from Manhattan.

Whereas at home he looked out the window of his church to see rolling acres of land where placid animals grazed, here he looked out the barred window of his cheap hotel room near Chinatown and saw a brick wall with a swirl of grainy spray paint that was part of an obscenity.

Whereas at home when he walked down the street of his town, people would say, "Hello, Reverend," or "Great sermon, Ralph," here they would say, "Gimme a dollar," or "I got AIDS," or simply "Suck me."

Still, Reverend Swensen was here only for a brief time so he supposed he could survive a little culture shock for a bit longer.

For the past several hours he'd been trying to read the ancient, crumbling Gideon Bible the hotel had provided. But finally he gave up. The Gospel according to St. Matthew, as compelling as that story was, couldn't compete with the sound of a gay hooker and his client banging away at each other and howling loudly in pain or pleasure or, most likely, both.

The reverend knew he should be honored to have been picked for this mission to New York but he felt like the Apostle Paul on one of *his* missionary quests among the nonbelievers in Greece and Asia Minor, greeted with only derision and scorn.

Ah, ah, ah, ah . . . Right there, right there . . . Oh, yeah, yeah, yeah, that's it that's it that's . . .

Okay, that *was* it. Even Paul hadn't had to put up with this level of depravity. The concert recital wasn't scheduled to start for several hours but Reverend Swensen decided to leave early. He brushed his hair, found his glasses and tossed the Bible, a map of the city and a sermon he was working on in his attaché case. He took the stairs to the lobby, where another prostitute was

314 / Jeffery Deaver

sitting. This one was—or appeared to be—a woman.

Our Father in heaven, full of grace . . .

A knot of tension in his gut, he hurried past, staring at the floor, anticipating a proposition. But she—or he, or whatever it was—merely smiled and said, "Beautiful weather, ain't it, Father?"

Reverend Swensen blinked and then smiled back. "Yes, it is," resisting the urge to add, "my child," which is something he'd never said in all his days as a minister. He settled for, "Have a nice day."

Outside, into the hard streets of the Lower East Side of New York City.

He paused on the sidewalk in front of the hotel as taxis shushed past, young Asians and Latinos hurried by purposefully, buses exhaled hot, metallic fumes and Chinese delivery boys on battered bicycles zipped over the sidewalk. It was all so very exhausting. Edgy and upset, the reverend decided that a walk to the school where the recital would be held would relax him. He'd consulted the map and knew it was a long way but he needed to do something to bleed off this mad anxiety. He'd do some window shopping, stop for dinner, work on his sermon.

As he oriented himself for the walk he sensed that he was being watched. He glanced to his left, into the alley next to the hotel. A man stood half hidden by a Dumpster, a lean, brown-haired man in overalls, holding a small toolkit. He was looking the priest up and down in a way that seemed purposeful. Then, as if he'd been caught, he turned and receded into the alley.

Reverend Swensen tightened his grip on the attaché case, wondering if he'd made a mistake not staying in the safety of his room—foul and noisy though it was—until it was time for the recital. Then he gave a faint laugh. Relax, he told himself. The man had been nothing more than a janitor or handyman, maybe an employee of the hotel itself, surprised to see a minister step out of the sleazy place.

Besides, he reflected as he started walking north, he *was* a man of the cloth, a calling that surely *had* to give him some degree of immunity, even here in this modern-day Sodom.

Chapter Twenty-one

Here one second, gone the next.

The red ball couldn't possibly get from Kara's outstretched right hand to the spot behind her ear.

But it did.

And after she'd plucked it away and tossed the crimson sphere into the air it couldn't possibly have vanished and ended up inside in the fold of her left elbow.

But it did that too.

How? Rhyme wondered.

She and the criminalist were in the downstairs lab of his town house, waiting for Amelia Sachs and Roland Bell. As Mel Cooper was setting the evidence out on examination tables and a CD pumped jazz piano into the room Rhyme was being treated to his own sleight-of-hand show.

Kara stood in front of a window, wearing one of Sachs's black T-shirts from the closet upstairs. Thom was currently washing her tank top, removing the Heinz 57 bloodstain from her improvised illusion at the crafts fair.

"Where'd you get those?" Rhyme asked, nodding at the balls. He hadn't seen her take them out of her purse or pocket.

She said with a smile that she'd "materialized" them (another trick magicians enjoyed, Rhyme had wryly observed, was transforming intransitive verbs into transitive ones).

"Where do you live?" he asked.

"The Village."

Rhyme nodded at some memories. "When my wife and I were together most of our friends lived down there. And SoHo, TriBeCa."

"I don't get north of Twenty-third much," she said.

A laugh from the criminalist. "In my day Fourteenth was the start of the demilitarized zone."

"Our side's winning, looks like," she joked as the red balls appeared and disappeared, moved from one hand to the other, then cir-

culated in the air in an impromptu juggling act.

"Your accent?" he asked.

"I have an accent?" she asked.

"Intonation then, inflection . . . *tone.*"

"Ohio probably. Midwest."

"Me too," Rhyme told her. "Illinois."

"But I've been here since I was eighteen.
Went to school in Bronxville."

"Sarah Lawrence, drama," Rhyme deduced.

"English."

"And you liked it here and stayed."

"Well, I liked it once I got out of the 'burbs
and into the city. Then after my father died
my mother moved out here to be closer
to me."

Daughter of a widowed mother . . . like
Sachs, Rhyme reflected. He wondered if
Kara had the same problems with her
mother as Sachs'd had with hers. A peace
treaty had been negotiated in recent years
but in Sachs's youth her mother had been
tempestuous, moody, unpredictable. Rose
didn't understand why her husband wanted
to be nothing more than a cop and why her
daughter wanted to be anything other than
what her mother wanted her to be. This nat-

urally drove father and daughter into an alliance, which made matters worse. Sachs had told him that their refuge on bad days was the garage, where they found a comfortably predictable universe: when a carburetor didn't seat it was because a simple and just rule of the physical world had been broken—machine tolerances were off or a gasket had been cut wrong. Engines and suspensions and transmissions didn't subject you to melodramatic moods or cryptic diatribes and even at the worst they never blamed you for their own failings.

Rhyme had met Rose Sachs on several occasions and found her charming, chatty, eccentric and proud of her daughter. But the past, he knew, is nowhere as present as it is between parents and children.

"And how does it work out, her being nearby?" Rhyme asked skeptically.

"Sounds like the sitcom from hell, huh? But, nope, Mum's great, my mom. She's . . . hey, you know, a *mother.* They're just a certain way. They never outgrow that."

"Where does she live?"

"She's in a care facility, Upper East Side."

"Is she very sick?"

"Nothing serious. She'll be fine." Kara

absently rolled the balls over her knuckles and into her palm. "As soon as she's better we're going to England, just the two of us. London, Stratford, the Cotswolds. My parents and I went there once. It was our best vacation ever. This time I'm going to drive on the left-hand side of the road and drink warm beer. They wouldn't let me the last time. Of course, I was thirteen. You ever been there?"

"Sure. I used to work with Scotland Yard from time to time. And I'd lecture there. I haven't been back since . . . well, not for a few years."

"Magic and illusion were always more popular in England than here. There's so much history. I want to show Mum where Egyptian Hall was in London. That was the center of the universe for magicians a hundred years ago. Sort of like a pilgrimage for me, you know."

He glanced toward the door. No sign of Thom. "Do me a favor."

"Sure."

"I need some medicine."

Kara noticed some pill bottles against the wall.

"No, over on the bookcase."

"Ah, gotcha. Which one?" she asked.

"The one on the end. Macallan, eighteen years." He whispered, "And probably the quieter you poured it, the better."

"Hey, you're talking to the right person. Robert-Houdin said there were three skills you needed to master to be a successful illusionist. Dexterity, dexterity and dexterity." In a moment a healthy dose of the smokey whisky had been poured into his tumbler—indeed silently and almost invisibly. Thom could've been standing nearby and would never have noticed. She slipped the straw into the cup and fitted it into the holder on his chair.

"Help yourself," he said.

Kara shook her head and gestured toward the coffeepot—which she alone had nearly drained. "That's my poison."

Rhyme sipped the scotch. He tilted his head back and let the burn ease into the back of his mouth then disappear. Watching her hands, the improbable behavior of the red balls. Another long sip. "I like it."

"What?"

"This idea of illusion." Don't get fucking maudlin, he told himself. You get maudlin when you're drunk. But this self-insight didn't stop him from taking another sip of whisky and continuing, "Sometimes reality can be a bit hard to take, you know." Nor could he avoid an unfortunate look down at his motionless body.

Instantly he regretted the comment—and the glance—and he started to change the subject. But Kara didn't offer any canned sympathy. She said, "You know, I'm not sure there *is* much reality."

He frowned, not getting her meaning.

"Isn't most of our lives an illusion?" she continued.

"How's that?"

"Well, everything in the past is memory, right?"

"True."

"And everything in the future is imagination. Those're both illusions—memories are unreliable and we just speculate about the future. The only thing that's completely real is this one instant of the present—and that's constantly changing from imagination to a memory. So, see? Most of our life's illusory."

Rhyme laughed softly at this. A logician, a scientist, he wanted to poke a hole in her theory. But, he couldn't. She was right, he concluded. He spent much of his time with memories of the Before, prior to the accident, and of how his life had changed After.

And the future? Oh, yes, he often dwelt there. Unknown to almost everyone except Sachs and Thom he spent at least an hour most days exercising—working through manual range-of-motion exercises, doing aqua therapy at a nearby hospital or riding the Electrologic stimulation bicycle tucked away in a bedroom upstairs. This exercise regimen was partly to regain some nerve and motor functions, improve his stamina and prevent the adjunct health problems that can plague quads. But the main reason for his efforts was to keep his muscles in shape for the day when a cure was possible.

He applied Kara's theory to his profession too: working a case, he continually scanned his vast memory banks for knowledge about forensics and past crimes while he anticipated where a suspect might be and what he might do next.

Everything in the past is memory, everything in the future is imagination. . . .

"Since we've broken the ice," she said, adding sugar to her coffee, "I've got a confession."

Another sip. "Yes?"

"When I saw you for the first time I had this thought."

Oh, yes, he remembered. The Look. The famous escape-from-the-crip look. Served up with the Smile. The only thing worse than that was what now loomed: the ever-so-awkward *apology* for the Look and the Smile.

She hesitated, embarrassed. Then said, "I thought, what an amazing illusionist you'd be."

"Me?" a surprised Rhyme asked.

Kara nodded. "You're all about perception and reality. People'd look at you and see that you're handicapped. . . . Is that what you say?"

"The politically correct call it 'disabled.' I myself just say that I'm fucked."

Kara laughed and continued, "They see you can't move. They probably think you've got mental problems or you're slow. Right?"

This was true. People who didn't know him often spoke slower and louder, explained the obvious in simple terms. (To Thom's disgust, Rhyme would sometimes respond by muttering incoherently or feigning Tourette's syndrome and driving the horrified visitors out of the room.) "An audience'd have instant opinions about you and be convinced that you couldn't possibly be behind the illusions they were seeing. Half of them'd be obsessing with your condition. The other half wouldn't even look at you. That's when you'd hook 'em. . . . Anyway, there I was meeting you and you were in this wheelchair and'd obviously gone through a tough time. And I wasn't sympathetic, didn't ask how you were doing. I didn't even say, 'I'm sorry.' I was just thinking, damn, what a performer you'd be. That was pretty crass and I had a feeling you picked up on it."

This delighted him completely. He reassured her, "Believe me, I don't do well with sympathy or kid gloves. Crass scores a lot more points."

"Yeah?"

"Yep."

She lifted her coffee cup. "To the famous illusionist, the Immobilized Man."

"Sleight of hand'd be a bit of a problem," Rhyme pointed out.

Kara replied, "Like Mr. Balzac's always saying, sleight of *mind*'s the better skill."

Then they heard the front door open and the voices of Sachs and Sellitto speaking as they walked into the hallway. Rhyme lifted an eyebrow and leaned for the straw in the tumbler. He whispered, "Watch this. It's a routine I call Vanishing the Incriminating Evidence."

Lon Sellitto asked, "First of all, do we think he's dead? Sleepin' wit' da fishes?"

Sachs and Rhyme looked at each other and simultaneously said, "No."

The big detective said, "You know how rough that water is in the Harlem? Kids try and swim it and you never see 'em again."

"Bring me his corpse," Rhyme said, "and I'll believe it."

He was encouraged about one thing, though: that they'd had no reports of a homicide or disappearance. The near capture and the swim in the river had probably spooked the killer; maybe now that he knew the police were close on his trail he'd either give up the attacks or at least go to ground for a while, giving Rhyme and the team a chance to find where he was hiding out.

"What about Larry Burke?" Rhyme asked.

Sellitto shook his head. "We've got dozens of people out searching. Lot of volunteers too, officers and firemen off-duty, you know. The mayor's offering a reward.... But I gotta say, it's not looking good. I'm thinking he might be in the trunk of the Mazda."

"They haven't brought it up yet?"

"They haven't *found* it yet. Water's black as night and, with that current, a diver was telling me a car could drift a half mile before it hit the bottom."

"We have to figure," Rhyme pointed out, "that he's got Burke's weapon and radio. Lon, we should change the frequency so he can't hear what we're up to."

"Sure." The detective called downtown and had all transmissions about the Conjurer case changed to the citywide special-ops frequency.

"Let's get back to the evidence. What do we have, Sachs?"

"Nothing in the Greek restaurant," she said, grimacing. "I told the owner to preserve the scene but somehow it didn't translate. Or he didn't *want* it to translate. By the time we got back the staff had cleaned the table and mopped the floor."

"How 'bout the pond? Where you found him."

"We found some things there," Sachs said. "He blinded us with more of that flash cotton and then set off some squibs. We thought he was shooting at first."

Cooper looked over the burned residue. "Just like the others. Can't source it."

"All right," Rhyme sighed. "What else is there?"

"Chains. Two lengths."

He'd wrapped these around Cheryl Marston's chest, arms and ankles and secured them with snap clasps, like on the end of dog leashes. Cooper and Rhyme examined all of these items carefully. There were no manufacturers' markings on any of them. The story was the same with the rope and the duct tape he'd gagged her with.

The gym bag that the killer had collected from the car, presumably containing the chains and rope, was unbranded and had been made in China. Given enough manpower, it was sometimes possible to find a source for common items like this by canvassing discount stores and street vendors. But for a cheap, mass-produced bag a search of that magnitude was impossible.

Cooper inverted the bag above a porcelain examining tray and repeatedly tapped the bottom to dislodge whatever might be inside. A bit of white powder drifted out. The tech did a drug analysis and the substance turned out to be flunitrazepam.

"Date rape drug of choice," Sachs told Kara.

There were also tiny pellets of a sticky translucent material inside. It looked like a similar substance was lodged in the zipper and smeared on the handle. "I don't recognize it," Cooper said.

But Kara looked it over, smelled the substance and said, "Magician's adhesive wax. We use it to stick things together temporarily onstage. Maybe he had an open capsule of the drug stuck to the palm of his hand. When he reached over her drink or coffee he tipped it in."

"Sources for the wax are?" Rhyme asked cynically. "Let me guess—any magic supply store in the free world?"

Kara nodded. "Sorry."

Within the bag Cooper also found some tiny metallic shavings and a circular black mark—as if from some residue on the bottom of a small bottle of paint.

An examination through the microscope revealed the metal was probably brass and there were unique machining patterns on the metal. But any deductions were beyond Lincoln Rhyme. "Send some pictures down to our friends in the bureau." Cooper took the images, compressed them and sent them off via encrypted email to Washington.

The black stains turned out not to be paint but permanent ink. But the database couldn't identify what kind specifically; there were no markers to individuate it.

"What's that?" Rhyme asked, looking toward a plastic bag containing some navy-blue cloth.

"We were lucky there," Sachs said. "That's the windbreaker he was wearing when he picked up the Marston woman. He didn't get a chance to take it with him when he bolted."

"Individuate?" Rhyme asked, hoping that there might be some initials or laundry marks inside.

After a lengthy examination of the garment Cooper said, "Nope. And all the tags've been removed."

"But," Sachs said, "we found some things in the pockets."

The first item they examined was a press pass issued by one of the big cable-TV networks. The CTN reporter's name was Stanley Saferstein and the photo on the pass revealed a thin, brown-haired man with a beard. Sellitto called the network and spoke to the head of security. It turned out that Saferstein was one of their senior reporters and had worked the metro desk for years. His pass had been stolen last week—lifted during or after a press conference downtown. The reporter had never felt a thing as the thief had apparently cut the lanyard and pocketed the ID.

The Conjurer had snatched Saferstein's card, Rhyme assumed, because the reporter bore a slight resemblance: in his fifties, narrow-faced and dark-haired.

The stolen pass had been canceled, the security chief had explained, "but the guy could still flash it and get past a checkpoint. Guards and police don't check too close if they see our logo."

After they hung up, Rhyme said to Cooper, "Run 'Saferstein' through VICAP and NCIC."

"Sure. But why?"

"Just because," Rhyme answered.

He wasn't surprised when the results came back negative. He hadn't actually thought that the reporter had any connection with the Conjurer but with this particular perp Rhyme was taking no chances.

The jacket also contained a gray plastic hotel key card. Rhyme was delighted at this find. Even though there was no hotel name on it—just a picture of a key and an arrow to show the guest which end to insert in the lock—he assumed it would have codes in the magnetic strip to tell them which hotel and room it belonged to.

Cooper found the manufacturer's name in small type on the back of the card: APC INC., AKRON, OHIO. This, he found out from a search of a trademark database, stood for American Plastic Cards, a company that made hundreds of different identification and key cards.

In a few minutes the team was on the speakerphone with the president of APC himself—a shirtsleeve CEO, Rhyme imagined, who had no problem working on Saturday or picking up his own phone. Rhyme explained the situation to him, described the key and asked how many hotels in the New York City metro area it was sold to.

"Ah, that's the APC-42. It's our most popular model. We make them for all the big locking systems. Ilco, Saflok, Tesa, Ving, Sargent, all the others."

"Any suggestions on narrowing down which hotel it belongs to?"

"I'm afraid you'll just have to start calling hotels and see who uses gray APC-42s. We have that information here someplace but I wouldn't know how to dig it up myself. I'll try and track down my sales manager or his assistant. But it could be a day or two."

"Ouch," Sellitto said.

Yeah, ouch.

After they hung up, Rhyme decided he wasn't content to wait for APC so he had Sellitto send the key to Bedding and Saul with instructions to start canvassing hotels in Manhattan to find out who used the very fucking popular APC-42. He also ordered both the press pass and the key card fin-gerprinted—but the results were negative on this too. They revealed just smudges and two more of the finger-cup prints.

Roland Bell returned from the scenes on the West Side and Cooper briefed him on what the team had learned so far. They then returned to the evidence and found that the Conjurer's running jacket contained some-thing else: A restaurant check from a place called the Riverside Inn in Bedford Junction, New York. The bill revealed that four people had eaten lunch at table 12 on Saturday, April 6—two weeks ago. The meal consisted of turkey, meatloaf, a steak and one daily special. No one drank alcohol. It was soft drinks all around.

Sachs shook her head. "Where the hell's Bedford Junction?"

"Way upstate, I do believe," Mel Cooper said.

"There's a phone number on the receipt," Bell drawled. "Call 'em up. Ask Debby or Tanya, or whoever's the charmin' waitress if any regular foursome sits at"—he squinted at the receipt—"table twelve. Or at least if she remembers who ordered those things. Long shot, but who knows?"

"What's the number?" Sellitto asked.

Bell called it out.

It *was* a long shot—too long, as Rhyme had expected. The manager and the waitresses there had no idea who might've been in on that Saturday.

"It's a 'bustlin' spot,'" Sellitto reported, rolling his eyes. "That's a quote."

"I don't like it," Sachs said.

"What?"

"What's he doing having lunch with three other people?"

"Good point," Bell said. "You think he's working with somebody?"

Sellitto replied, "Naw, I doubt it. Pattern doers're almost always loners."

Kara disagreed. "I'm not sure. Close-in artists, parlor magicians—they work alone. But he's an illusionist, remember? They always work with other people. You've got volunteers from the audience. Then assistants onstage that the audience knows're working with the performer. And then there're confederates too. Those're people who're working for the illusionist but the audience *doesn't* know it. They might be disguised as stagehands, members of the audience, volunteers. In a good show you're never quite sure who's who."

Christ, Rhyme thought, this one perp was bad enough, with his skills at quick change, escape and illusionism. Working with assistants would make him a hundred times more dangerous.

"Mark it down, Thom," he barked. Then: "Let's look at what you found in the alley— where Burke collared him."

The first item was the officer's handcuffs.

"He got out of them in seconds. Had to've had a key," Sachs said. To the dismay of cops around the country most handcuffs can be opened with generic keys, available from law enforcement supply houses for a few dollars.

Rhyme wheeled over to the examination table and studied them carefully. "Turn them over. . . . Hold them up. . . . He *might've* used a key, true, but I see fresh scratches in the hole. I'd say it was picked. . . ."

"But Burke would've frisked him," Sachs pointed out. "Where'd he get a pick?"

Kara offered, "Could've been hidden anywhere. His hair, his mouth."

"Mouth?" Rhyme mused. "Hit the cuffs with the ALS, Mel."

Cooper donned goggles and shone an alternative light source on the cuffs. "Yep, we've got some tiny smears and dots around the keyhole." This meant, Rhyme explained to Kara, the presence of bodily fluid, saliva most likely.

"Houdini did that all the time. Sometimes he'd let somebody from the audience check his mouth out. Then just before he did the escape his wife'd kiss him—he said it was for luck but she was really passing a key from her mouth to his."

"But he'd be cuffed behind his back," Sellitto said. "How could he even reach his mouth?"

"Oh," Kara said with a laugh. "Any escapist can get cuffed hands in front of his body in three or four seconds."

Cooper tested the saliva traces. Some individuals secrete antibodies into all bodily fluids, which lets investigators determine blood type. The Conjurer, though, turned out not to be a secretor.

Sachs had also found a very tiny piece of serrated-edge metal.

"Yeah, it's his too," Kara said. "Another escapist tool. A razor saw. It's probably what he used to cut through those plastic bands on his ankles."

"Would that've been in his mouth too? Wouldn't it be too dangerous?"

"Oh, a lot of us hide needles and razor blades in our mouths as part of the acts. With practice it's pretty safe."

Examining the last of the trace from the alley scene, they found more bits of latex and traces of the makeup, identical to what they'd seen earlier. More Tack-Pure oil as well.

"At the riverside, Sachs, when he went into the river? You find anything?"

"Just skid marks in the mud." She pinned up the digital photos that Cooper had printed out from his computer. "Some helpful citizen managed to screw up the scene," she explained. "But I spent a half hour going through the muck. I'm pretty sure he didn't drop any evidence or bail out."

Sellitto asked Bell, "What about the vic, the Marston woman? She have anything to say?"

The Tarheel detective gave a summary of his interview with her.

An attorney, Rhyme considered. Why pick her? What the hell was the Conjurer's pattern with the victims? Musician, makeup artist and attorney.

Bell added, "She's divorced. Husband's out in California. Wasn't the friendliest divorce in the world but I don't reckon he's involved. I had LAPD make some calls and he was accounted for today. And there's no NCIC or VICAP sheet on him."

Cheryl Marston had described the Conjurer as slim, strong, bearded, scars on neck and chest. "Oh, and she confirmed his fingers *were* deformed, like we'd thought. Fused together, she said. He was hush about the neighborhood he lives in and he picked the alias 'John.' Now there's a clever boy for you."

Useless, Rhyme assessed.

Bell then explained how he'd picked her up and what had happened afterward. Rhyme asked Kara, "Anything sound familiar?"

"He could've hypnotized a pigeon or gull, pitched it at the horse then used some kind of gimmick to keep the horse agitated."

"What kind of gimmick?" Rhyme asked. "You know any manufacturers?"

"No, that's probably homemade too. Magicians used to use electrodes or prods to get lions to roar on cue, things like that. But animal rights activists'd never let you get away with that now."

Bell continued, describing what had happened when Marston and the Conjurer had gone to have coffee.

"One thing she said that was odd: it was like he could read her mind." Bell described what Marston had told him about the Conjurer's knowing so much about her.

"Body reading," Kara said. "He'd say something and then watch her close, check out her reactions. That'd tell him a lot about her. Coming on to somebody like that's called 'selling them the medicine.' A really good mentalist can find out all kinds of things just by having an innocent conversation with you."

"Then when she was gettin' comfortable with him he drugged her and took her to the pond. Dunked her upside down."

"It was a variation of the Water Torture Cell routine," Kara explained. "Houdini. One of his most famous."

"And his escape from the pond?" Rhyme asked Sachs.

"At first I wasn't sure it was him—he'd done a quick change," she said. "His clothes were different and"—a glance at Kara—"his eyebrows too. I couldn't get a look at his hand, to see the fingers. But he distracted me, used ventriloquism. I was looking right at his face—I never saw his lips move."

Kara said, "I'll bet he picked words that didn't have any *b*'s or *m*'s or *p*'s. Probably no *f*'s or *v*'s either."

"You're right. I think it was something like,

'Yo, look out, on your right, that guy in the jogging suit's got a gun.' Perfect black dialect." She grimaced. "I looked away—the same direction he looked, like everybody else. Then he set off that flash cotton and I got blinded. He fired the squibs and I thought he was shooting. He got me cold."

Rhyme saw the disgust in her face. Amelia Sachs reserved her worst anger for herself.

Kara, though, said, "Don't take it too hard. Hearing's the easiest sensation to fool. We don't use sound illusions much in shows. They're cheap shots."

Sachs shrugged this reassurance off and continued, "While Roland and I were still blinded from the flash he took off and disappeared, slipped into the crafts fair." Another grimace. "And then I saw him fifteen minutes later—this biker, wearing a Harley shirt. I mean, for God's sake, he was right *there* in front of me."

"Man," Kara said, shaking her head, "his coins definitely don't talk."

"What's that?" Rhyme asked. "Coins?"

"Oh, an expression magicians use. Literally it means you can't hear any clinking when you do coin tricks but we use it in general when somebody's really good. We'd also say he's got 'tight tricks.'"

Walking to the whiteboard reserved for the magician profile, she picked up the marker and added to it, commenting, "So, he does close-in and mentalism and even ventriloquism. And animal tricks. We knew he does lock picking—from the second murder—but now we know he's an escapist too. What kind of magic *doesn't* he do?"

As Rhyme leaned his head back, watching her write, Thom brought a large envelope into the room.

He handed it to Bell. "For you."

"Whatsis?" the Tarheel detective asked, pulling the contents out and reading them. He nodded slowly as he read. "This's the report on the follow-up search at Grady's office. The one you asked Peretti to run. You mind taking a gander, Lincoln?"

The curt note on top read: *LR— As requested. —VP.*

Rhyme read through the details of the report, Thom flipping the page for him with every stern nod. The CS techs had completed a thorough inventory of the secretary's office and had identified and mapped out all the footprints in the room, exactly as

Rhyme had asked. He read this carefully several times, closing his eyes and picturing the scene.

Then he turned to the complete analysis of the fibers that'd been found. Most of the white ones were a polyester/rayon blend. Some were attached to a thick cotton fiber—also white. Most were dull and dirty. The black fibers were wool.

"Mel, what do we think about the black ones there?"

The tech scooted off his stool and examined the images. "Photo work isn't the best," he said. After a moment he concluded, "From some tight weave, twilled fabric."

"Gabardine?" Rhyme asked.

"Can't tell without a bigger sample to see the diagonal. But I'll go with gabardine."

Rhyme read down the page and learned that the single red fiber found in the office was satin. "Okay, okay," he mused, closing his eyes and digesting everything he'd read.

The criminalist asked Cooper, "What do you know about fabric and clothing, Mel?"

"Not a lot. But if I can quote you, Lincoln, the important question isn't 'What do you *know* about something?' It's 'Do you know where to *find out* about it?' And the answer to that is yes, I do."

THE CONJURER

Music School Crime Scene

- Perp's description: Brown hair, fake beard, no distinguishing, medium build, medium height, age: fifties. Ring and little fingers of left hand fused together. Changed costume quickly to resemble old, bald janitor.

- No apparent motive.

- Victim: Svetlana Rasnikov.
  - Full-time music student.
  - Checking family, friends, students, coworkers for possible leads.
    - No boyfriends, no known enemies. Performed at children's birthday parties.

- Circuit board with speaker attached.
  - Sent to FBI lab, NYC.
    - Digital recorder, probably containing perp's voice. All data destroyed.
  - Voice recorder is a "gimmick." Homemade.

- Used antique iron handcuffs to restrain victim.
  - Handcuffs are Darby irons. Scotland Yard. Checking with Houdini Museum in New Orleans for leads.

- Destroyed victim's watch at exactly 8:00 A.M.

- Cotton string holding chairs. Generic. Too many sources to trace.

- Squib for gunshot effect. Destroyed.
  - Too many sources to trace.

- Fuse. Generic.
  - Too many sources to trace.

- Responding officers reported flash in air. No trace material recovered.
  - Was from flash cotton or flash paper.
    - Too many sources to trace.

- Perp's shoes: size 10 Ecco.

- Silk fibers, dyed gray, processed to a matte finish.
  - From quick-change janitor's outfit.

- Unsub is possibly wearing brown wig.

- Red pignut hickory and Parmelia conspersa lichen, both found primarily in Central Park.

- Dirt impregnated with unusual mineral oil. Sent to FBI for analysis.
  - Tack-Pure oil for saddles and leather.

- Black silk, 72 x 48". Used as camouflage. Not traceable.
  - Illusionists use this frequently.

- Wears caps to cover up prints.
  - Magician's finger cups.

- Traces of latex, castor oil, makeup.
  - Theatrical makeup.

- Traces of alginate.
  - Used in molding latex "appliances."

- Murder weapon: white silk-knit rope with black silk core.
  - Rope is a magic trick. Color changing. Not traceable.

- Unusual knot.
  - Sent to FBI and Maritime Museum—no information.
  - Knots are from Houdini routines, virtually impossible to untie.

- Used disappearing ink on sign-in register.

East Village Crime Scene

- Victim Two: Tony Calvert.
  - Makeup artist, theater company.
  - No known enemies.
  - No apparent connection with first victim.

- No apparent motive.

- Cause of death:
  - Blunt-object trauma to head followed by postmortem dismemberment with crosscut saw.

- Perp escaped portraying woman in her 70s. Checking vicinity for discarded costume and other evidence.
  - Nothing recovered.

- Watch smashed at 12:00 exactly.
  - Pattern? Next victim presumably at 4:00 P.M.

- Perp hid behind mirror. Not traceable. Fingerprints sent to FBI.
  - No matches.

- Used cat toy ("feke") to lure victim into alley. Toy is untraceable.

- Additional mineral oil found, same as at first scene. Awaiting FBI report.
  - Tack-Pure oil for saddles and leather.

- Additional latex and makeup from finger cups.

- Additional alginate.

- Ecco shoes left behind.

- Dog hairs found in shoes, from three different breeds of dog. Manure too.
  - Manure from horses, not dogs.

Hudson River and Related Crime Scenes

- Victim: Cheryl Marston.
  - Attorney.
  - Divorced but husband not a suspect.

- No motive.

- Perp gave name as "John." Had scars on neck and chest. Deformed hand confirmed.

- Perp did quick change to unbearded businessman in chinos and dress shirt, then biker in denim Harley shirt.

- Car is in Harlem River. Perp presumably escaped.

- Duct tape gag. Can't be traced.

- Squibs, same as before. Can't be traced.

- Chains and snap fixtures, generic, not traceable.

- Rope, generic, not traceable.

- Additional makeup, latex and Tack-Pure.

- Gym bag, made in China, not traceable. Containing:
  - Traces of date rape drug flunitrazepam.
  - Adhesive magician's wax, not traceable.
  - Brass (?) shavings. Sent to FBI.
  - Permanent ink, black.

- Navy-blue windbreaker found, no initials or laundry marks. Containing:
  - Press pass for CTN cable network, issued to Stanley Saferstein. (He's not suspect—NCIC, VICAP search negative.)
  - Plastic hotel key card, American Plastic Cards, Akron, Ohio. Model APC-42, negative on prints.

- CEO is searching for sales records.
- Dets. Bedding and Saul canvassing hotels.
- Restaurant check from Riverside Inn, Bedford Junction, NY, indicating four people ate lunch, table 12, Saturday, two weeks prior. Turkey, meatloaf, steak, daily special. Soft drinks.

Staff doesn't know who diners were. (Accomplices?)

- Alley where Conjurer was arrested.
  - Picked the cuff locks.
  - Saliva (picks hidden in mouth).
  - No blood type determined.
  - Small razor saw for getting out of restraints (also hidden in mouth).

- No indication of Officer Burke's whereabouts.

- Harlem River scene:
  - No evidence, except skid marks in mud.

Profile as Illusionist

- Perp will use misdirection against victims and in eluding police.
  - Physical misdirection (for distraction).
  - Psychological (to eliminate suspicion).

- Escape at music school was similar to Vanished Man illusion routine. Too common to trace.

- Perp is primarily an illusionist.

- Talented at sleight of hand.

- Also knows protean (quick change) magic. Will use breakaway clothes, nylon and silk, bald cap, finger cups and other latex appliances. Could be any age, gender or race.

- Calvert's death = Selbit's Cutting a Woman in Half routine.

- Proficient at lock picking (possibly lock "scrubbing").

- Knows escapism techniques.

- Experience with animal illusions.

- Used mentalism to get information on victim.

- Used sleight of hand to drug her.

- Tried to kill third victim with Houdini escape. Water Torture Cell.

- Ventriloquism.

Chapter Twenty-two

Harry Houdini was renowned for his escapism but in fact there were many great escapists who preceded him and many who were his contemporaries.

What set Houdini apart from all the others was a simple addition to his act: the challenge. A major part of his show involved an invitation to anyone in the town where he was appearing to challenge Houdini to escape from a device or location that the challenger himself provided—maybe a local policeman's own handcuffs or a cell in the town lock-up.

It was this competitive, man-versus-man element of performing that made Houdini great. He thrived on these challenges.

And so do I, Malerick now thought, walking into his apartment after his escape from the Harlem River and a bit of reconnaissance work. But he was still badly shaken up by the events that afternoon. When he'd been performing regularly, before the fire, there was often an element of danger in the routines. Real danger. His mentor had beaten into him that if there was no risk how could you possibly hope to engage your audience? There was no sin worse to Malerick than boring those who'd come to be entertained by you. But what a series of challenges this particular act had turned out to be; the police were far better than he'd expected. How had they anticipated that he'd target the woman at the riding academy? And where he was going to drown her? Trapping him in the crafts fair then finding him in the Mazda, chasing him again—getting so close that he'd had to send the car into the river and get away in a very narrow escape. Challenges were one thing—but he was now feeling paranoid. He wanted to do more preparation for his next routine but he decided to stay in his apartment until the last minute.

Besides, there was something else that he needed to do now. Something for himself—not for his revered audience. He drew the shades of his apartment and placed a candle on the mantelpiece, next to a small inlaid wooden box. He struck a match and lit the candle. Then sat on the rough cloth of the cheap sofa. He controlled his breathing. Inhaled slowly, exhaled.

Slowly, slowly, slowly. . . .

Concentrating on the flame, drifting into a meditation.

Throughout its history the art of magic has been divided into two schools. First, there are the sleight-of-hand artists, the prestidigitators, the jugglers, the illusionists—people who entertain their audiences with dexterity and physical skill.

The second school of magic is far more controversial: the practice of the occult. Even in this scientific era some practitioners contend that they actually possess supernatural powers to read minds and move objects mentally, predict the future and communicate with spirits.

For thousands of years charlatan seers and mediums have grown rich claiming to be able to summon the spirits of the deceased for their distraught loved ones. Before the government began cracking down on such scams it was legitimate magicians who'd protect the gullible by publicly revealing the methods behind the supposedly occult effects. (Even today the brilliant magician James Randi spends much of his time debunking fakes.) Harry Houdini himself devoted much of his life and fortune to challenging fake mediums. Yet, ironically, one of the reasons he took up this cause was out of his desperate search for a legitimate medium who could contact the spirit of his mother, whose death he never completely recovered from.

Malerick now stared at the candle, the flame. Watching, *praying* for the spirit of his soul mate to appear and caress the yellow cone of illumination, to send him a sign. He used the candle for this medium of communication because it was fire that had taken his love away from him, fire that had changed Malerick's life forever.

Wait, did it flicker? Yes, maybe no. He couldn't tell.

Both schools of magic vied within him. As a talented illusionist, Malerick knew, of course, that his routines were nothing more than applied physics, chemistry and psychology. But still there was that one splinter of doubt in his mind that perhaps magic actually *did* hold the key to the supernatural: God as illusionist, vanishing our failing bodies then palming the souls of those we loved, transforming them and returning them to us, His sad and hopeful audience.

This was not unthinkable, Malerick told himself. He—

And then the candle flickered! Yes, he saw it.

The flame moved a millimeter closer to the inlaid box. Very possibly it was a sign that the soul of his dead beloved was hovering near, summoned not by mechanics but by the fiber of connection that magic might reveal if only he could stay receptive.

"Are you there?" he whispered. "Are you?"

Breathing so very slowly, afraid that his exhalation would reach the candle and make it shiver; Malerick wanted proof positive that he was not alone.

Finally the candle burned itself out and Malerick sat for a long time in his meditative state, watching gray smoke curl toward the ceiling then vanish.

A glance at his watch. He could wait no longer. He gathered his costumes and props, assembled them and dressed carefully. Applied his makeup.

The mirror told him that he was "in role."

He walked to the front lobby. A glance out the window. The street was empty.

Then outside into the spring evening for a routine that would be, yes, even more *challenging* than the prior ones.

Fire and illusion are soul mates.

Bursts of flash powder, candles, propane flames over which escape artists dangle . . .

Fire, Revered Audience, is the devil's toy and the devil has always been linked to magic. Fire illuminates and fire obscures, it destroys and it creates.

Fire transforms.

And it's at the heart of our next act, one I call The Charred Man.

The Neighborhood School just off Fifth Avenue in Greenwich Village is a quaint limestone building, as modest in appearance as in name. One would never suspect that the children of some of the richest and most politically connected families in New York City learn reading, 'riting, and 'rithmatic here.

It was known not only as a quality educational institution—if you can refer to an elementary school that way—but was also an important cultural venue in this part of the city.

The 8:00 P.M. Saturday music recitals, for instance.

To which Reverend Ralph Swensen was now making his way.

He'd survived his lengthy stroll through Chinatown and Little Italy to Greenwich Village without any harm other than your average accosting by your average panhandler, to which he was by now almost oblivious. He'd stopped at a small Italian restaurant for a plate of spaghetti (that and ravioli were the only dishes on the menu he recognized). And since the wife wasn't with him he ordered a glass of red wine. The food was wonderful and he remained in the restaurant for quite some time, sipping the forbidden drink and enjoying the sight of children playing in the streets of this boisterous ethnic neighborhood.

He'd paid the check, feeling somewhat guilty about using church funds for alcohol, then continued north, farther into the Village along a route that took him through a place called Washington Square. This appeared at first to be a miniature Sodom in its own right but when he plunged into the heart of the chaotic park the reverend found that the only sins were youngsters playing loud music and people drinking beer and wine out of containers in paper bags. Although he believed in a moral system that sent certain transgressors straight to hell (like noisy homosexual prostitutes who wouldn't let you get to sleep), the spiritual offenses he found here weren't the sort that'd guarantee a one-way ticket to the big furnace.

But partway through the park he began to grow uneasy. He thought again of the man who'd been spying on him, the one in overalls with the toolkit by the hotel. The reverend was sure he'd seen him a second time—in a store window reflection not long after he'd left the hotel. The same sense of being watched came over him now. He turned fast and looked back. Well, no workmen. But he did catch sight of a trim man in a dark sportscoat watching him. The man looked away casually and veered off toward a public rest room.

Paranoia?

Had to be. The man didn't look anything like the worker. But as the reverend left the square, walking north along Fifth Avenue, dodging the hundreds of strollers on the sidewalk, he sensed again that he was being followed. Another glance behind him. This time he saw a blond man, wearing thick glasses and dressed in a brown sportscoat and T-shirt, looking his way. Reverend Swensen also noticed that he was crossing to the same side of the street that he'd just crossed to.

But now he was *sure* he was paranoid. Three *different* men couldn't've been following him. Relax, he thought and continued north on Fifth Avenue toward the Neighborhood School, the street dense with people enjoying the beautiful spring evening.

Reverend Swensen arrived at the Neighborhood School at exactly 7 P.M., a half hour before the doors would open. He set down his briefcase and crossed his arms. Then he decided that, no, he should keep a hold on the attaché case and picked it up again. He lounged against a wrought-iron fence surrounding a garden next to the school, glancing uneasily in the direction he'd come.

No, no one. No workmen with toolkits. No men in sportscoats. He was—

"Excuse me, Father?"

Startled, he turned quickly and found himself looking at a big, swarthy man with a two-day growth of beard.

"Uhm, yes?"

"You here for the recital?" The man nodded toward the Neighborhood School.

"That's right," he answered, trying to keep his voice from quavering with uneasiness.

"What time's it start?"

"Eight. The doors open at seven-thirty."

"Thank you, Father."

"Not a problem."

The man smiled and walked away in the direction of the school. Reverend Swensen resumed his vigil, nervously squeezing the handle of his attaché case. A look at his watch. It read 7:15.

Then, finally, after an interminable five minutes, he saw what he'd been waiting for, what he'd traveled all these many miles for: the black Lincoln Town Car with the official government license plates. It eased to a stop a block from the Neighborhood School. The minister squinted in the dusk as he read the plate number. It was the right vehicle. . . . Thank you, Lord.

Two young men in dark suits got out the

front. They looked up and down the side-walk—including a glance at him—and were apparently satisfied that the street was safe.

One of them bent down and spoke through the open rear window.

The reverend knew whom he was speaking to: Assistant District Attorney Charles Grady, the man prosecuting the case against Andrew Constable. Grady was here with his wife for the recital that their daughter was participating in. It was the prosecutor, in fact, who was at the heart of his mission to Sodom this weekend. Like Paul, the Reverend Swensen had entered the world of the nonbelievers to show them the error of their ways and to bring them truth. He intended to do so in a somewhat more decisive way than the apostle, though: by murdering Charles Grady with the heavy pistol now resting in his briefcase, which he clutched to his chest as if it were the ark of the covenant itself.

Chapter Twenty-three

Sizing up the scene in front of him.

Carefully noting angles, escape routes, how many passersby were on the sidewalk, the amount of traffic on Fifth Avenue. He couldn't afford to fail. There was a lot riding on his success; he had a personal stake in making sure Charles Grady died.

Around midnight last Tuesday Jeddy Barnes, a local militiaman, had suddenly appeared at the door of the double-wide that served as Reverend Swensen's home and church. Barnes had reportedly been hiding out in a camper deep in the woods around Canton Falls after the state police raids against Andrew Constable's Patriot Assembly a few months ago.

"Make me some coffee," Barnes had

commanded, looking over the terrified reverend with his fierce fanatic's eyes.

Amid the staccato tap of rain on the metal roof, Barnes, a tough, scary loner with a gray crew cut and gaunt face, had leaned forward and said, "I need you to do something for me, Ralph."

"What's that?"

Barnes had stretched his feet out and looked at the plywood altar Reverend Swensen had made himself, thick with sloppy varnish. "There's a man out to get us. Persecuting us. He's one of them."

Swensen knew that by "them" Barnes was referring to an ill-defined alliance of federal and state government, the media, non-Christians, members of any organized political party and intellectuals—for starters. ("Us" meant everybody who wasn't in any of above categories, provided they were white.) The reverend wasn't quite as fanatical as Barnes and his tough militia buddies—who scared the soul out of him—but he certainly believed there was some truth to what they preached.

"We need to stop him."

"Who is it?"

"A prosecutor in New York City."

"Oh, the one going after Andrew?"

"That's him. Charles Grady."

"What'm I supposed to do?" Reverend Swensen had asked, envisioning a letter-writing campaign or a fiery sermon.

"Kill him," Barnes had said simply.

"What?"

"I want you to go to New York and kill him."

"Oh, Lord. Well, I can't do that." Trying to put on a firm front although his hands were shaking so bad he spilled his coffee on a hymnal. "For one thing, what good'll it do? It won't help Andrew any. Hell, they'll know he was behind it and they'll make it even harder—"

"Constable's not part of this. He's out of the equation. There're bigger issues here. We need to make a statement. You know, do what all those assholes in Washington're always saying in their press conferences. 'Send a message.'"

"Well, just forget it, Jeddy. I can't do it. It's crazy."

"Oh, I think you can."

"But I'm a minister."

"You hunt every Sunday—that's murder, if you want to look at it one way. And you

were in Nam. You got scalps—if your stories're true."

"That was thirty years ago." Whispering
desperately, avoiding both the man's eyes
and the admission that, no, the war stories
weren't true. "I'm not killing anybody."

"I'll bet Clara Sampson'd like you to."
Stony silence for a moment. "Chickens're
coming back to roost, Ralph."

Lord, Lord, Lord . . .

Last year Jeddy Barnes had stopped
Wayne Sampson from going to the police
after the dairy farmer had found the minister
with Sampson's thirteen-year-old daughter
in the playground he'd built behind the
church. It occurred to him now that Barnes
had played mediator solely to get some
leverage on him. "Please, look—"

"Clara wrote a nice letter, which I happen
to have. D'I mention I asked her to do that
last year? Anyway, she went and described
your private parts in more detail than I personally wanna read about but I'm sure a
jury'd appreciate it."

"You can't do this. No, no, no . . ."

"Don't wanta argue the matter with you,
Ralph. Here's the situation. If you *don't*
agree then come next month you'll be doin'

the same thing to niggers in prison that you had Clara Sampson doin' to you. Now, what's it gonna be?"

"Shit."

"I'll take that as a yes. Now, lemme walk you through what we have planned."

And Barnes had given him a gun, the address of a hotel and the location of Grady's office then shipped him off to New York City.

When he'd first arrived, a few days ago, Reverend Swensen had spent several days doing recon work. He'd gone into the state government building late Thursday afternoon and, with his slightly baffled demeanor and wearing his minister's garb, had wandered the halls unchallenged until he found a broom closet in a deserted corridor, where he hid until midnight. Then he'd broken into Grady's secretary's office and found out that the prosecutor and his family would be attending the recital at the Neighborhood School tonight; his daughter was one of the young performers.

Now, armed and edgy with cat nerves, the reverend stood fidgeting in front of the school and watching Grady's bodyguards talking with the prosecutor in the backseat. The plan was to kill Grady and his guards with the silenced pistol then drop to the ground himself, screaming in panic that a man had just driven by and was shooting from a car. The minister should be able to escape in the confusion.

Should be . . .

He now tried to say a prayer but, even though Charles Grady was a tool of the devil, asking help from the Lord our God to kill an unarmed white Christian bothered Reverend Swensen considerably. So he settled for a silent Bible recitation.

I saw another angel come down from heaven, having great power; and the earth was lit up by his glory. . . .

Reverend Swensen rocked on his feet, thinking that he couldn't bear to wait any longer. Cat-nerves, cat-nerves . . . He wanted to get back to his sheep, his farmland, his church, his ever-popular sermons.

Clara Sampson too, who was nearly fifteen now and for all intents and purposes fair game.

And the angel cried mightily with a strong voice, saying, Babylon the great is fallen and is become the habitation of devils, and the hold of every foul spirit. . . .

He considered the matter of Grady's family. The prosecutor's wife hadn't done anything wrong. Being married to a sinner wasn't the same as being a sinner yourself or choosing to work for one. No, he'd spare Mrs. Grady.

Unless she noticed that he was the one shooting.

As for the daughter Barnes had told him about, Chrissy. . . . He wondered how old she was and what she looked like.

And the fruits that thy soul lusted after are departed from thee, and all things which were dainty and goodly are departed from thee, and thou shalt find them no more at all. . . .

Now, he thought. Do it. Go, go, go.

And a mighty angel took up a stone like a great millstone, and cast it into the sea, saying, Thus with violence shall that great city Babylon be thrown down, and shall be found no more at all. . . .

Thinking, the stone of retribution *I've* got, Grady, is a well-built Swiss gun and the messenger isn't an angel from Heaven but a representative of all right-thinking people in America.

He started forward.

The bodyguards were still looking away.

Opening the attaché case, he took out the Rand McNally and the heavy gun. Hiding the weapon inside the colorful map, he strolled casually toward the car. Grady's bodyguards were now standing together on the sidewalk, with their backs to him. One reached down to open the door for the prosecutor.

Twenty feet away . . .

Reverend Swensen thought to Grady, God have mercy on your—

And then the angel's millstone landed squarely on his shoulders.

"On the ground, on the ground, now, now now now!"

A half-dozen men and women, a hundred demons, grabbed Reverend Swensen's arms and flung him hard to the sidewalk. "Don't move don't move don't move don't move!"

One grabbed the gun, one snatched away the briefcase, one pressed the reverend's neck down into the sidewalk like the weight of the city's sin. His face scraped against the concrete and pain shot through his wrists and shoulder sockets as handcuffs were ratcheted on him and his pockets turned inside out.

Crushed to the concrete Reverend Swensen saw Grady's car door open and three policemen leap out, wearing helmets and bulletproof vests.

"Stay down, head down down down!"

Jesus our Lord in Heaven. . . .

He watched a man's feet walk closer to him. In contrast to the fierceness of the other officers this man was quite polite. In a southern-accented voice he said, "Now, sir, we're going to roll you over and then I'm going to read you your rights. And you let me know if you understand 'em."

Several cops turned him over and pulled him to his feet.

The reverend started in shock.

The man speaking was the one in the dark sportscoat he'd thought was following him in Washington Square. Next to him was the blond man in glasses who'd apparently taken over the surveillance. The third, the swarthy man who'd asked about the time the concert began, stood nearby.

"Sir, my name's Detective Bell. And I'm going to read those rights now. You ready? Good. Here we go."

• • •

Bell looked over the contents of Swensen's attaché case.

Extra ammunition for the H&K pistol. A yellow pad inscribed with what looked to be a very bad sermon scrawled on it. A guidebook, *New York on Fifty Dollars a Day.* There was also a beat-up Gideon Bible stamped with the name and address: THE ADELPHI HOTEL, 232 BOWERY, NEW YORK, NEW YORK.

Hmmm, Bell thought wryly, looks like we can add a count of Bible larceny to the charges.

He found nothing, though, that suggested a direct connection between this attempt on Grady's life and Andrew Constable. Discouraged, he handed off the evidence to be logged in and called Rhyme to tell him that the impromptu operation by the Saving Asses team had been successful.

Back at Rhyme's an hour earlier the criminalist had continued to pore over the revised crime scene report while Mel Cooper had researched the fibers the CS team had found in Grady's office. Finally Rhyme had made some troubling deductions. The analysis of the footprints in the office revealed that the intruder had stood for some minutes in one spot—the right front corner of the secretary's desk. The inventory of the office showed only one item in this portion of the desk: the woman's daily calendar. And the only entry for this weekend was Chrissy Grady's recital at the Neighborhood School.

Which meant that the person who broke in undoubtedly noted this. As for the attacker himself, Rhyme had ventured that he might be disguised as a minister or priest. With the help of an FBI database Cooper managed to trace the black fibers and dye to a cloth manufacturer in Minnesota, which—Cooper and Rhyme learned from its website—specialized in black gabardine for clerical-clothing makers. Rhyme also noted that several of the white fibers CS had found were polyester bonded with starched cotton, which suggested a white lightweight shirt with a stiff clerical collar attached.

The single red satin fiber was the sort that could've come from a ribbon bookmark in an old book, as could the gold leaf. A Bible, for instance. Rhyme had run a case years ago in which a smuggler had hidden drugs in a hollowed-out Bible; that CS search team had found similar trace in the man's office.

Bell had ordered Grady and his family not to attend their daughter's recital. In their place a team of ESU troopers would drive to the school in Grady's city car. Teams stationed themselves north of the school on Fifth Avenue, on cross streets west at Sixth Avenue and east at University Place and south in Washington Square Park.

Sure enough, Bell, who'd taken the park, had spotted a minister walking nervously toward the school. Bell had started to tail him but was spotted so he'd peeled off. Another SWAT officer picked up and tracked him to the school. A third detective from Bell's SWAT group approached and asked about the concert, checking visually for signs of weapons, but not finding any obvious ones—and hence having no probable cause to detain and search him.

But the suspect remained under close surveillance and as soon as he was seen pulling the gun from his attaché case and starting for the decoys he was taken down.

Expecting a fake priest, they'd been surprised to find that they'd caught a real one, which the contents of Swensen's wallet confirmed—despite the contrary testimony of the embarrassingly bad sermon. Bell nodded at the H&K automatic. "Pretty big gun for a priest," he said.

"I'm a minister."

"Meant to say."

"Ordained."

"Good for you. Now I'm wondering: I read you those rights. You want to waive your right to remain silent? Tell you, sir, you bow up to what you just did and things'll go a lot easier for you. Tell us who wanted you to kill Mr. Grady."

"God."

"Hmm," Bell said. "Okay. How 'bout anybody else?"

"That's all I'm saying to you or to anybody. That's my answer. God."

"Well, all right, let's getcha downtown now and see if He's inclined to throw bail for you."

Chapter Twenty-four

They call that music?

A thud of a drum and then the raw sound of a brass instrument rehearsing short passages penetrated Rhyme's parlor. It was coming from the Cirque Fantastique, across the street in the park. The notes were jarring and the tone gaudy and brash. He tried to ignore it and returned to his phone conversation with Charles Grady, who was thanking him for his efforts in collaring the minister who'd come to town to kill him.

Bell had just interrogated Constable, down at the Detention Center. The prisoner said he knew Swensen but had drummed him out of the Patriot Assembly over a year ago because of an "unhealthy interest" in the daughters of some parishioners. Constable had had nothing to do with the man

after that and he'd fallen in with some backwoods militiamen, according to local gossip. The prisoner adamantly denied that he
knew anything about the attempted killing.

Still, Grady had arranged to have delivered to Rhyme a box of evidence from the
crime scene at the Neighborhood School
and one from the Reverend Swensen's hotel room. Rhyme had looked through it
quickly but found no obvious connection to
Constable. He explained this to Grady and
added, "We need to get it to some forensic
people upstate, in—what's the town?"

"Canton Falls."

"They can do some soil or trace compar-
isons. There might be something linking
Swensen to Constable but I don't have any
samples from up there."

"Thanks for checking, Lincoln. I'll have
somebody get it up there ASAP."

"If you want me to write an expert's opinion on the results I'd be happy to," the criminalist said then had to repeat the offer; the
last half was drowned out by a particularly
raucous horn solo.

Hell, yes, I *could* write better music than
that, he thought.

Thom called time-out and took Rhyme's

blood pressure. He found the results high. "I don't like it," he said.

"Well, for the record, *I* don't like a *lot* of things," Rhyme responded petulantly, frustrated with their slow progress with the case: a tech at the FBI lab in D.C. had called and said that it would be morning before they'd have any report on the bits of metal found in the Conjurer's bag. Bedding and Saul had called more than fifty hotels in Manhattan, but had found none that used APC key cards that matched the one found in the Conjurer's running jacket. Sellitto had also called the relief watch outside the Cirque Fantastique—fresh officers had replaced the two who'd been there since that morning—and they'd reported nothing suspicious.

And, most troubling of all, there'd been no luck in finding Larry Burke, the missing patrol officer who'd collared the Conjurer near the crafts fair. Dozens of officers were searching the West Side but had turned up no witnesses or evidence as to where he might be. One encouraging note, though: his body wasn't in the stolen Mazda. The car hadn't yet been raised but a diver who'd braved the currents reported that there were no bodies inside the car itself or the trunk.

"Where's the food?" Sellitto asked, looking out the window. Sachs and Kara had gone up the street to pick up some takeout from a nearby Cuban restaurant (the young illusionist was less excited about dinner than the prospect of her first Cuban coffee, which Thom described as "one-half espresso, one-half condensed milk, and one-half sugar," the concept of which, despite the impossible proportions, had instantly intrigued her).

The bulky detective turned to Rhyme and Thom and asked, "You ever have those Cubano sandwiches? They're the best."

But neither the food nor the case meant anything to the aide. "Time for bed."

"It's nine thirty-eight," Rhyme pointed out. "Practically afternoon. So it's not. Time. For. Bed." He managed to make his singsong voice sound both juvenile and threatening at the same time. "We have a fucking killer on the loose who keeps changing his mind about how often he wants to kill people. Every four hours, every two hours." A glance at the clock. "And he might just now be perpetrating his nine thirty-eight killing. I appreciate that you don't like *it.* But I have work to do."

"No, you don't. If you don't want to call it a night, all right. But we're going upstairs to take care of some things and then you're taking a nap for a couple of hours."

"Ha. You're just hoping I'll fall asleep till morning. Well, I won't. I'll stay awake all night."

The aide rolled his eyes. He announced in a firm voice, "Lincoln'll be upstairs for a few hours."

"How'd you like to be out of work," Rhyme snapped.

"How'd *you* like to be in a coma?" Thom shot back.

"This is fucking crip abuse," he muttered. But he was giving in. He understood the danger. When a quad sits too long in one position or is constricted in the extremities or, as Rhyme loved to put it so indelicately in front of strangers, needs to piss or shit and hasn't for a while—there was a risk of autonomic dysreflexia, a soaring of the blood pressure that could result in a stroke, leading to more paralysis or death. Dysreflexia's rare but it'll send you to the hospital, or a grave, pretty damn fast, and so Rhyme acquiesced to a trip upstairs for the personal business and then a rest. It was moments like this—disruptions of "normal" life—that infuriated him most about his disability. Infuriated and, though he refused to let on, deeply depressed him.

In the bedroom upstairs Thom took care of the necessary bodily details. "Okay. Two hours' rest. Get some sleep."

"One hour," Rhyme grumbled.

The aide was going to argue but then he glanced at Rhyme's face and, while he probably saw anger and don't-fuck-with-me eyes, which wouldn't have affected him one bit, he observed too the criminalist's heartfelt concern for the next victims on the Conjurer's list. Thom conceded, "One hour. *If* you sleep."

"An hour it is," Rhyme said. Then added wryly, "And I'll have the sweetest of dreams. . . . A drink *would* help, you know."

The aide tugged at the subtle purple tie—a gesture of weakening that Rhyme seized on like a shark lapping a molecule of blood. "Just one," the criminalist said.

"All right." He poured a little ancient Macallan into one of Rhyme's tumblers and arranged the straw next to his mouth.

The criminalist sipped long. "Ah, heaven . . ." Then he glanced at the empty glass. "Someday I'll teach you how to pour a real drink."

"I'll be back in an hour," Thom said.

"Command, alarm clock," Rhyme said sternly. On the flat-screen monitor a clock face appeared and he orally set the alarm to sound in one hour.

"I would've gotten you up," the aide said.

"Ah, well, just in case you were *occupied* and somehow forgot," Rhyme said coyly, "now I'll be sure to be awake, won't I?"

The aide left, closing the door behind him, and Rhyme's eyes slipped to the window, where the peregrine falcons perched, lording over the city, their heads turning in that odd way of theirs—both jerky and elegant at the same time. Then one—the female, the better hunter—glanced quickly at him, blinking her narrow slits of eyes, as if she'd just sensed his gaze. A cock of her head. Then she returned to her examination of the hubbub of the circus in Central Park.

Rhyme closed his eyes though his mind was speeding through the evidence, trying to figure out what the clues might mean: the brass, the hotel key, the press pass, the ink.

Mysteriouser and mysteriouser. . . . Finally his eyes sprang open. This was absurd. He wasn't the least bit tired. He wanted to get the hell back downstairs and return to work. Sleeping was out of the question.

He felt a breeze tickle his cheek and was angrier yet at Thom—for leaving the air-conditioning on. When a quad's nose runs, there goddamn well better be somebody nearby to wipe it. He summoned up the climate control panel on the monitor, thinking about telling Thom that he would've gotten to sleep except that the room was too cold. But one look at the screen told him that the air conditioner was off.

What had the breeze been?

The door was still closed.

There! He felt it again, a definite waft of air on his other cheek, his right one. He turned his head quickly. Was it from the windows? No, they too were closed. Well, it was prob-ably—

But then he noticed the door.

Oh, no, he thought, chilled to his heart. The door to his bedroom had a bolt on it— a latch that could be closed only by some-one in his room. Not from the outside.

It was locked.

Another breath on his skin. Hot, this time. Very close. He heard a faint wheeze too.

"Where are you?" Rhyme whispered.

He gasped as a hand appeared suddenly in front of his face, two fingers deformed, fused together. The hand held a razor blade, the sharp edge aimed toward Rhyme's eyes.

"If you call for help," said the Conjurer in a breathy whisper, "if you make a noise, I'll blind you. Understood?"

Lincoln Rhyme nodded.

Chapter Twenty-five

The blade in the Conjurer's hand vanished.

He didn't put it away, didn't hide it. One moment the metal rectangle was in his fingers, aimed at Rhyme's face; the next, it was gone.

The man—brown-haired, beardless, wearing a policeman's uniform—walked around the room, examining the books, the CDs, the posters. He seemed to nod approvingly at something. He studied one curious decoration: a small red shrine, inside of which was a likeness of the Chinese god of war and of police detectives, Guan Di. The Conjurer seemed to think nothing of the incongruity of such an item in the bedroom of a forensic scientist.

He returned to Rhyme.

"Well," the man said in his throaty whisper, looking over the Flexicair bed. "You're not what I expected."

"The car," Rhyme said. "In the river? How?"

"Oh, that?" he said dismissively. "The Submerged Car trick? I was never *in* the car. I got out in the bushes at the end of that street. A simple trick: a closed window—so the witnesses would see mostly glare—and my hat on the headrest. It was my audience's *imagination* that saw me. Houdini was never even in some of the trunks and barrels he pretended to escape from."

"So they weren't skid marks from braking," Rhyme said. "They were skid marks from *accelerating* tires." He was angry that he'd missed this. "You put a brick on the accelerator."

"A brick wouldn't've looked natural when the divers found the car; I wedged it down with a shoe." The Conjurer looked Rhyme over closely and asked in a wheezing voice, "But you never believed I was dead." Not a question.

"How did you get into the room without me hearing you?"

"I was here first. I slipped upstairs ten minutes ago. I was downstairs too in your war room, or whatever you call it. Nobody noticed me."

"You brought that evidence in?" Rhyme recalled being vaguely aware of two patrolmen carting in boxes of the evidence collected outside the Neighborhood School and the Reverend Swensen's hotel room.

"That's right. I was waiting on the sidewalk. This cop came up with a couple of boxes. I said hello and offered to help. Nobody ever stops you if you're in a uniform and you seem to have a purpose."

"And you've been hiding up here—covered up with a piece of silk that was the color of the walls."

"You caught on to that trick, did you?"

Rhyme frowned, looking at the man's uniform. It seemed genuine, not a costume. But contrary to regulations there was no nameplate on the breast. His heart suddenly sank. He knew where it had come from. "You killed him, Larry Burke. . . . You killed him and stole his clothes."

The Conjurer glanced down at the uniform and shrugged. "Reverse. Stole the uniform first," came the whispery, disembodied voice. "Convinced him that I wanted him naked to give me a chance to escape. He saved me the effort of stripping him afterward. *Then* I shot him."

Repulsed, Rhyme reflected that he'd considered the danger that the Conjurer had taken Burke's radio and his weapon. It hadn't occurred to him, though, that he'd use the man's uniform as a quick-change costume to attack his pursuers. He asked in a whisper, "Where's his body?"

"On the West Side."

"Where?"

"Keep that to myself, I think. Somebody'll find him in a day or two. Sniff him out. The weather's warm."

"You son-of-a-bitch," the criminalist snapped. He might be civilian now but in his heart Lincoln Rhyme would always be a cop. And there is no bond closer than that between fellow police officers.

The weather's warm. . . .

But he struggled to remain calm and asked casually, "How did you find me?"

"At the crafts fair. I got close to your partner. That redheaded policewoman. Very close. As close as I was to you just now. I breathed on her neck too—I'm not sure which I enjoyed more. . . . Anyway I heard her talking to you on her radio. She mentioned your name. Then it just took a little research to find you. You've been in the papers, you know. You're famous."

"Famous? A freak like me?"

"Apparently."

Rhyme shook his head and said slowly, "I'm old news. The chain of command passed me by a long time ago."

The word "command" zipped from Rhyme's lips through the microphone mounted to the headboard into the voice recognition software in his computer. "Command" was the latch word that told the computer to be prepared for instructions. A window opened up on the monitor, which he could see but the Conjurer could not. *Instruction?* it asked silently.

"Chain of command?" the Conjurer asked. "What do you mean?"

"I used to be in charge of the department. Now, sometimes the young officers, they won't even return my telephone call."

The computer seized the last two words of the sentence. Its response: *Whom would you like to call?*

Rhyme sighed. "I'll tell you a story: I needed to get in touch with an officer the other day. A lieutenant. Lon Sellitto."

The computer reported: *Dialing Lon Sellitto.*

"And I told him—"

A sudden frown from the Conjurer.

He stepped forward quickly, swinging the monitor away from Rhyme's face and looking it over. The killer grimaced, ripped the phone lines from the wall and unplugged the computer. With a faint pop it went silent.

As the man hovered a few feet from him Rhyme pressed his head into the pillows, expecting the terrible razor blade to appear. But the Conjurer stepped back, breathing hard with his asthmatic wheeze. He seemed more impressed than angered by what the criminalist had tried.

"You know what that was, don't you?" he asked, smiling coldly. "Pure illusionism. You distracted me with patter and then did some classic verbal misdirection. Ruse, we call it. That was good. What you were saying was very natural—until you mentioned the name. It was the *name* ruined it. See, telling me that *wasn't* natural. It made me suspicious. But up until then you were good."

The Immobilized Man . . .

He continued, "I'm good too, though."

The Conjurer reached forward with an open, empty palm. Rhyme cringed as the fingers passed close to his eyes. He felt a brush against his ear. When the Conjurer's hand appeared a second later there were *four* double-sided razor blades gripped between his fingers. He closed his hand into a fist and the four blades became a single one, now held once more between his thumb and index finger.

No, please. . . . Worse than the pain, Rhyme feared the horror of being deprived of yet another of his senses. The killer eased the edge close to Rhyme's eye, moved it back and forth.

Then the killer smiled and stepped back. He glanced across the room into the shadows on the far wall. "Now, Revered Audience, let's begin our routine with some prestidigitation. I'll be assisted by a fellow performer here." These words were spoken in an eerie, theatrical tone.

The man's hand rose and he displayed the glistening razor blade. In a smooth gesture the Conjurer pulled out the waistband of Rhyme's sweatpants and underwear and tossed the blade like a frisbee toward his naked groin.

The criminalist winced.

"What he must be thinking . . ." the Conjurer said to his imaginary audience. "Knowing that a razor blade is against his skin, perhaps cutting *into* his skin, his genitals, a vein or an artery. And he doesn't feel a thing!"

Rhyme stared at the front of his pants, waiting for blood to appear.

Then the Conjurer smiled. "But maybe the blade's not there. . . . Maybe it's someplace else. Maybe here." He reached into his own mouth and pulled the small rectangle of steel out. He held it up. Then frowned. "Wait." He removed another blade from his mouth. Then more. He now had the four blades back in his hand. He fanned them like cards then tossed them into the air above Rhyme, who gasped and cringed, waiting for them to hit him. But . . . nothing. They'd vanished.

In his neck and temple Rhyme felt his heart pounding, harder now, sweat trickling down his forehead and temple. Rhyme glanced at the alarm clock. It seemed like hours had passed. But Thom had left only fifteen minutes ago.

Rhyme asked, "Why are you doing this?

Those people you killed? What was the point?"

"They weren't *all* killed," he pointed out angrily. "You ruined my performance with the equestrian by the Hudson River."

"Well, *attacked* then. Why?"

"It was nothing personal," he said and broke into a coughing spell.

"Not personal?" Rhyme spat out, incredulous.

"Let's say it was more what they represented than who they were."

"What does that mean? 'Represented'? Explain."

The Conjurer whispered, "No. I don't think I will." He walked slowly around Rhyme's bed, breathing hard. "Do you know what goes through the mind of the audience during a performance? Part of them hopes that the illusionist *isn't* going to escape in time, that he'll drown, he'll fall on the spikes, burn up, get crushed to death. There's a trick called the Burning Mirror. My favorite. It starts out with a vain illusionist looking in a mirror. He sees a beautiful woman on the other side of the glass. She beckons to him and finally he gives in to temptation and steps through. We see they've changed places. The woman's now on the front side of the mirror. But there's a puff of smoke and she does a quick change and becomes Satan.

"Now the illusionist is trapped in hell, chained to the floor. Flames begin shooting up from the floor around him. A wall of fire moves closer. Just as he's about to be engulfed by flames he gets out of the chains and leaps through the fire at the back of the mirror to safety. The devil runs toward the illusionist, flies into the air and vanishes. The illusionist shatters the mirror with a hammer. Then he walks across the stage, pauses and snaps his fingers. There's a flash of light and, you've probably guessed, he becomes the devil. . . . The audience loves it. . . . But I know that part of everyone's mind is rooting for the fire to win and the performer to die." He paused. "And, of course, that *does* happen from time to time."

"Who *are* you?" Rhyme whispered, despairing now.

"Me?" The Conjurer leaned forward and passionately rasped, "I'm the Wizard of the North. I'm the greatest illusionist who ever was. I'm Houdini. I'm the man who can escape from the burning mirror. From handcuffs, chains, locked rooms, shackles, ropes, *anything. . . .*" He eyed Rhyme closely. "Except . . . except you. I was afraid that you were the one thing I *couldn't* escape from. You're too good. I had to stop you before tomorrow afternoon. . . ."

"Why? What's happening tomorrow afternoon?"

The Conjurer didn't answer. He looked into the gloom. "Now, Revered Audience, our main act—the Charred Man. Look at our performer here—no chains, no handcuffs, no ropes. Yet he can't possibly escape. This is even harder than the world's first escape routine: St. Peter. Thrown in a cell, shackled, guarded. And yet he escaped. Of course, *he* had an important confederate. God. Our performer tonight, however, is on his own."

A small gray object appeared in the Conjurer's hand and he leaned forward fast, before Rhyme could turn his head. The killer slapped a piece of duct tape over his mouth.

He then shut out all the lights in the room except a small night-light. He returned to Rhyme's bed, held an index finger up and flicked his thumb against it. A three-inch point of flame rose from the digit.

The Conjurer wagged the finger back and forth. "Sweating, I can see." He held the flame close to Rhyme's face. "Fire. . . . Isn't it fascinating? It's probably the most compelling image in illusionism. Fire's the perfect misdirection. Everyone watches flame. They never take their eyes off it onstage. I could do anything with my other hand and you'd never notice. For instance . . ."

The bottle of Rhyme's scotch appeared in the man's grip. He held the flame under the bottle for a long moment. Then the killer took a sip of liquor and held the flaming finger in front of his lips, looking directly at Rhyme, who cringed. But the Conjurer smiled, turned aside and blew the flaming spray toward the ceiling, stepping back slightly as the stream of fire vanished into the darkness of the ceiling.

Rhyme's eyes flickered to the wall in the corner of the room.

The Conjurer laughed. "Smoke detector? I got that earlier. The battery's gone." He blew another flaming stream toward the ceiling and set the bottle down.

Suddenly a white handkerchief appeared.

He wafted it under Rhyme's nose. It was soaked in gasoline. The astringent smell burned Rhyme's eyes and nose. The Conjurer coiled the handkerchief into a short rope and, ripping open Rhyme's pajama top, draped it around his neck like a scarf.

The man walked toward the door, silently opened the deadbolt and then the door, looked out.

Rhyme's nose detected another scent mixed with the gasoline. What was it? A rich, smoky scent. . . . Oh, the scotch. The killer must've left the bottle open.

Except that the smell soon overtook the gasoline's aroma. It was overpowering. There was scotch everywhere. And Rhyme understood with dismay what the man was doing. He'd poured a stream of liquor from the door to the bed, like a fuse. The Conjurer flicked his finger and a white fireball flew from his hand into the pool of single malt.

The liquor ignited and blue flames raced along the floor. Soon they'd set fire to a stack of magazines and a cardboard box next to the bed. One of the rattan chairs too.

Soon the fire would climb up the bedclothes and begin devouring his body, which he wouldn't feel, and then his face and head, which he horribly would. He turned to the Conjurer but the man was gone, the door closed. Smoke began to sting Rhyme's eyes and fill his nose. The fire crawled closer, igniting boxes and books and posters, melting CDs.

Soon the blue and yellow flames began lapping at the blankets at the foot of Lincoln Rhyme's bed.

Chapter Twenty-six

A diligent NYPD officer, perhaps hearing an odd noise, perhaps seeing an unlocked door, stepped into a West Side alleyway. Fifteen seconds later another man emerged, dressed in a lightweight maroon turtleneck, tight jeans, baseball cap.

No longer in the role of Officer Larry Burke, Malerick began walking purposefully up Broadway. Glancing at his face, noting the flirtatious way *he* glanced around him—a cruisin' look—you'd suspect that he was a man on the prowl, heading for some West Side bar to defibrillate his ego and his genitalia, both in arrest lately as he approached middle age.

He paused at a basement cocktail lounge, glanced inside. He decided this would be a good place in which to hide out temporarily until it was time to return briefly to Lincoln Rhyme's and see how much damage the fire had done.

He found a stool at the far end of the bar, near the kitchen, and ordered a Sprite and a turkey sandwich. Looking around: the arcade games with their electronic soundtracks, a dusty jukebox, the room smoky and dark, smelling of sweat and perfume and disinfectant, the liquor-induced brays of laughter and hum of pointless conversation. All of which transported him back to his youth in the city built from sand.

Las Vegas is a mirror surrounded by glaring lights; stare at it for hours but all you'll ever truly see is yourself, with your pocks, squinty wrinkles, vanity, greed, desperation. It's a dusty, hard place where the cheery illumination of the Strip fades fast just a block or two from the neon and doesn't penetrate to the rest of the city: the trailers, sagging bungalows, sandy strip malls, pawnshops selling engagement rings, suit jackets, prosthetic arms—whatever can be transformed into quarters or silver dollars.

And, everywhere, the dusty, endless, beige desert.

This was the world that Malerick was born into.

Father a blackjack dealer and mother a restaurant hostess (until her growing weight put her behind the scenes in a cash room), they were two of the army of Vegas service people treated like ants by casino management and guests alike. Two of the army who spent their lives so inundated with money that they could smell the ink, perfume and sweat on the bills, but who were forever aware that this astonishing flood was destined to pause in their fingers for only the briefest of moments.

Like many Vegas children left on their own by parents working long and irregular shifts—and like children living in bitter homes everywhere—their son had gravitated to a place where he found some comfort.

And that place for him was the Strip.

I was explaining, Revered Audience, about misdirection—how we illusionists distract you by drawing attention away from our method with motion, color, light, surprise, noise. Well, misdirection is more than a technique of magic; it's an aspect of life too. We're all desperately drawn toward flash and glitz and away from boredom, from routine, from bickering families, from hot, motionless hours on the edge of the desert, from sneering teens who chase you down because you're skinny and timid and then pound you with fists as hard as scorpions' shells. . . .

The Strip was his refuge.

The magic shops specifically. Of which there were many; Las Vegas is known among performers around the world as the Capital of Magic. The boy found that these shops were more than just retail outlets; they were places where aspiring, performing and retired magicians hung out to share stories and tricks and to gossip.

It was in one of these that the boy learned something important about himself. He might be skinny and timid and a slow runner but he was miraculously dexterous. The magicians here would show him palms and pinches and drops and conceals and he'd pick them up instantly. One of these clerks lifted an eyebrow and said about the thirteen-year-old, "A born prestidigitator."

The boy frowned, never having heard the word.

"A French magician made it up in the

eighteen hundreds," the man explained. "'Presti—' As in presto, fast. 'Digit.' As in finger. Prestidigitation—fast fingers. Sleight of hand."

So maybe, he slowly came to believe, he was someone more than odd man out in the family, something more than knuckle bait at the playground.

Every day he'd leave school at 3:10 and head directly to his favorite store, where he'd hang out and sop up method. At home he practiced constantly. One of the shop managers would hire him occasionally to put on demonstrations and brief shows for customers in the Magic Cavern in the back of the store.

He could still picture clearly his initial performance. From that day on Young Houdini—his first stage name—would talk, or bully, his way up onto stage at any opportunity. What a joy it was to mesmerize his audience, delight them, sell them the medicine, trick them. To scare them too. He liked to scare them.

Finally he got busted—by his mother. The woman eventually realized that the boy hardly spent any time at home and raided his room to learn why. "I found this money," she snapped, rising from her dinner and waddling into the kitchen one evening to confront him as he walked in the back door. "Explain."

"It's from Abracadabra."

"Who's *that?*"

"The store? By the Tropicana. I was telling you about it—"

"You stay off the Strip."

"Mom, it's just a store. That magic store."

"Where you been? Drinking? Let me smell your breath."

"Mom, no." Backing away, repulsed by the massive woman in the pasta-sauce-stained top, her own breath horrific.

"They catch you in a casino, I could lose my job. Your father could lose his."

"I was just at the store. I do a little show. People give me tips sometimes."

"That's too much for tip money. I never got tips like that when I was a hostess."

"I'm good," the boy said.

"So was I. . . . Show? What kind of show?"

"Magic." He was frustrated. He'd told her this months before. "Watch." He did a card trick for her.

"That was good," she said, nodding. "But for lying to me I'm keeping this money."

"I didn't lie!"

"You didn't tell me what you're doing. That's the same as lying."

"Mom, that's mine."

"You lie, you pay."

With some effort she stuffed the money into a jeans pocket sealed closed by her belly. Then she hesitated. "Okay, here's ten back. If you tell me something."

"Tell you . . . ?"

"Tell me something. You ever seen your father with Tiffany Loam?"

"I don't know. . . . Who's that?"

"You know. Don't pretend you don't. That waitress from the Sands was over here with her husband a couple months ago for dinner. She was in that yellow blouse."

"I—"

"Did you see them? Driving out to the desert yesterday?"

"I didn't see them."

She examined him closely and decided he was telling the truth. "If you *do* see them you let me know."

And she left him for her spaghetti, coagulating on a TV tray in the living room.

"My money, Mom!"

"Shut up. It's the Daily Double."

One day, performing a small show in Abracadabra, the boy was surprised to notice a slim, unsmiling man enter the store. As he walked toward the Magic Cavern all the magicians and clerks in the store fell silent. He was a famous illusionist and was appearing at the Tropicana. He was known for his temper and his dark, scary illusions.

After the show the illusionist gestured the boy over and nodded at the handwritten sign on stage. "You call yourself 'Young Houdini'?"

"Yeah."

"You think you're worthy of that name?"

"I don't know. I just liked it."

"Do some more." Nodding at a velvet table.

The boy did, nervous now, as the legend watched his moves.

A nod, which seemed to be an approving nod. That a fourteen-year-old boy would receive a compliment like this stunned the magicians in the room to silence.

"You want a lesson?"

The boy nodded, thrilled.

"Let me have the coins."

He held his open palm to offer the coins. The illusionist looked down, frowning. "Where are they?"

His hand was empty. The illusionist, laughing harshly at the boy's bewildered expression, had already dipped them; the quarters were in his own hands. The boy was astonished; he hadn't felt a thing.

"Now I'll hold this one up in the air. . . ."

The boy looked up but suddenly some instinct said, Close your fingers now! He's going to put the coins back. Embarrass him in front of a roomful of magicians. Grab his hand!

Suddenly, without looking down, the illusionist froze and whispered, "Are you *sure* you want to do it?"

The boy blinked in surprise. "I—"

"Think twice." A glance down at the boy's hand.

Young Houdini looked at his palm, which was tensed to catch the great illusionist's. He saw to his shock that the man *had* placed something there, but not the coins: five double-sided razor blades. If he'd closed his fingers as he'd planned, Young Houdini would've needed a dozen stitches.

"Let me see your hands," he said, taking

the blades out of them and vanishing them instantly.

Young Houdini held his palms up and the man touched them, stroked them with his thumbs. It felt to the boy that there was an electric current running between them.

"You've got the hands to be great," he whispered for the boy alone to hear. "You've got the drive and I *know* you've got the cruelty. . . . But you don't have the vision. Not yet." A blade appeared again and the man used it to slice through a piece of paper, which began to bleed. He crumpled the paper and then opened it up. There was no slash and no blood. He handed it to the boy, who noticed that on the inside was an address, written in red ink.

As the small audience of onlookers cheered and clapped with genuine admiration, or jealousy, the illusionist whispered, "Come see me," leaning forward, his lips brushing Young Houdini's ear. "You have a lot to learn. And I have a lot to teach."

The boy kept the illusionist's address but he couldn't work up the courage to go see him. Then, at his fifteenth birthday party, his mother changed the course of his life forever by flying into a tirade and flinging a

408 / Jeffery Deaver

platter of fettuccine at her husband over some recently received intelligence about the notorious Mrs. Loam. Bottles flew, collectibles shattered, police arrived.

The boy decided he'd had enough. The next day he went to visit the illusionist, who agreed to be his mentor. The timing was perfect. In two days the man was starting an extensive tour of the United States. He needed an assistant. Young Houdini cleaned out his secret bank account and did just what his namesake had done: he ran away from home to work as a magician. There was one major difference between them, however; unlike Harry Houdini, who'd left home only to make money to help his impoverished family and who was soon reunited with them, young Malerick would never see any member of his again.

"Hey, how you doing?"

The woman's husky voice woke him out of these durable memories as he sat at the bar of the Upper West Side tavern. A regular here, he guessed. Fiftyish trying unsuccessfully for the illusion of ten years younger, she'd picked this hunting ground based largely on the dim lighting. She scooted onto a stool next to his and was leaning forward, flying a flag of cleavage.

"Sorry?"

"Just asked how you're doing. Don't think I've seen you in here."

"Just in town for a day or two."

"Ah," she said drunkenly. "Say, I need a light." Conveying the irritating impression that he should consider it a privilege to light her cigarette.

"Oh, sure," he said.

He clicked a lighter and held it up. *This* flame flickered madly, he observed, as she wrapped her red, bony fingers around his to guide the lighter to her lips.

"Thanks." She shot a narrow stream of smoke toward the ceiling. When she looked back Malerick had paid the bill and was pushing away from the bar.

She frowned.

"I have to go." He smiled and said, "Oh, here, you can keep that."

He handed her the small metal lighter. She took it and blinked. Her frown deepened. It was her own lighter, which he'd dipped from her purse when she'd leaned toward him.

Malerick whispered coldly, "Guess you didn't need one after all."

Leaving her at the bar, two tears leading the mascara down her cheeks, he thought that of all the sadistic illusions he'd perpetrated, and had planned for, this weekend— the blood, the cut flesh, the fire—this one would perhaps be the most satisfying.

She heard the sirens when they were two blocks away from Rhyme's.

Amelia Sachs's mind did one of those funny jogs: hearing the urgent electronic catcall from some emergency vehicle, thinking the sound seemed to be coming from the direction of his town house.

Of course it wasn't, she decided.

Too much of a coincidence.

But then, the flashing lights, blue and red, *were* on Central Park West, where his place was located.

Come on, girl, she reassured herself, it's your imagination, stoked by the memory of the eerie harlequin on the banner in front of the Cirque Fantastique tent in the park, the masked performers, the horror of the Conjurer's murders. They were making her paranoid.

Spooky . . .

Forget it.

Shifting the large shopping bag containing garlicky Cuban food from one hand to the other, she and Kara continued down the busy sidewalk, talking about parents, about careers, about the Cirque Fantastique. About men too.

Bang, bang . . .

The young woman sipped her double Cuban coffee, to which, she said, she'd become addicted at first taste. Not only was it half the price of Starbucks', Kara pointed out, but it was twice as strong. "I'm not sure about the math but I think that makes it four times as good," the young woman said. "I'll tell you, I love finds like this. It's the little things in life, don't you think?"

But Sachs had lost the thread of the conversation. Another ambulance sped by. She sent a silent prayer that it keep going past Rhyme's.

It didn't. The vehicle braked to a fast stop at the corner next to his building.

"No," she whispered.

"What's going on?" Kara wondered. "An accident?"

Heart pounding, Sachs dropped the bags of food and began sprinting toward the building.

"Oh, Lincoln . . ."

Kara started after her, spilled hot coffee on her hand and dropped the cup. She kept up the pace beside the policewoman. "What's going on?"

As she turned the corner Sachs counted a half-dozen fire trucks and ambulances.

At first she'd suspected he'd had an attack of dysreflexia. But this had clearly been a fire. She looked up to the second story and gasped in shock. Smoke was drifting out of Rhyme's bedroom window.

Jesus, no!

Sachs ducked under the police line and ran toward the cluster of firefighters in the doorway. She leaped up the front stairs, her arthritis momentarily forgotten. Then she was through the door, nearly slipping on the marble floor. The hallway and the lab seemed intact but a faint haze of smoke filled the downstairs hallway.

Two firemen were walking slowly down

the stairs. It seemed their faces were filled with resignation.

"Lincoln!" she cried.

And started for the stairs.

"No, Amelia!" Lon Sellitto's gruff voice cut through the hallway.

She turned, panicked, thinking that he wanted to stop her from seeing his burned corpse. If the Conjurer had taken Lincoln away from her he was going to die. Nothing in the world would stop her.

"Lon!"

He motioned her off the stairs and embraced her. "He's not up there, Amelia."

"Is—"

"No, no, it's okay. He's all right. Thom brought him down to the guest room in the back. This floor."

"Thank God," Kara said. She looked around in dismay at more firefighters coming down the stairs, large men and women swollen even larger by their uniforms and equipment.

Thom, grim-faced, joined them from the back of the hall. "He's all right, Amelia. No burns, some smoke inhalation. Blood pressure's high. But he's on his meds. It'll be okay."

"What happened?" she asked the detective.

"The Conjurer," Sellitto muttered. He sighed. "He killed Larry Burke. Stole his uniform. That's how he got in. Somehow he snuck up to Rhyme's room. He set a fire around his bed. We didn't even know it down here; somebody saw the smoke from the street and called nine-one-one. And Dispatch called me. Thom and Mel and I got most of it out before the trucks got here."

She asked Sellitto, "I don't suppose we got him, the Conjurer?"

A bitter laugh. "Whatta you think? He vanished. Thin air."

Following the accident that left him paralyzed, after Rhyme had graduated from the stage of grief that called for him to spend months willing his legs to work again, he gave up on the impossible and turned his considerable focus and strength of will to a more reasonable goal.

Breathing on his own.

A C4 quad like Rhyme—his neck broken at the fourth vertebra from the base of the skull—is on the borderline of needing a ventilator. The nerves that lead from the brain down to the diaphragm muscles may or may not be functioning. In Rhyme's case his lungs appeared at first not to be pumping properly and he was put on a machine, a hose implanted in his chest. Rhyme hated the device, with its mechanical gasping and the odd sensation of not feeling the need to breathe even though he knew he himself wasn't. (The machine also had the nasty habit of occasionally stopping cold.)

But then his lungs began working spontaneously and he was freed from the bionic device. The doctors said the improvement was due to his body's natural post-trauma stabilizing. But Rhyme knew the real answer. He'd done it himself. With willpower. Sucking air into his lungs—meager breaths at first, yes, but *his* own breaths all the same—was one of the greatest accomplishments of his life. He was now working hard at those exercises that might lead to increased sensation throughout his body and even movement of his limbs; but however successful he was with these he didn't think his sense of pride would match what he'd felt when he was taken off the ventilator for the first time.

Tonight, lying in his small guest room, he recalled seeing the clouds of smoke flowing from the cloth and paper and plastic burning all around him in his room. In his panic he thought less about burning to death and more about the terrible smoke working into his lungs like metal splinters and taking away the sole victory he'd won in the war against his disability. It was as if the Conjurer had picked his single most vulnerable spot to attack.

When Thom, Sellitto and Cooper burst into the room his first thought was not about the fire extinguishers the two cops held but the green oxygen tank the aide wielded. He'd thought, Save my lungs!

Before the flames were out Thom had the oxygen mask over his face and he hungrily inhaled the sweet gas. They got him downstairs and both EMS and Rhyme's own SCI doctor had examined him, cleaning and dressing a few small burns and looking carefully for razor cuts (there were none; nor were any blades found in his pajamas). The spinal cord specialist declared that his lungs were all right, though Thom should rotate him more frequently than normal to keep them clear.

It was only then that Rhyme began to calm. But he was still very anxious. The killer had done something far more cruel than causing him physical injury. The attack had reminded Rhyme how precarious his life was and how uncertain his future.

He hated this feeling, this terrible helplessness and vulnerability.

"Lincoln!" Sachs walked fast into the room, sat on the old Clinitron bed and dropped to his chest, hugged him hard. He lowered his head against her hair. She was crying. He'd seen tears in her eyes perhaps twice since he'd known her.

"No first names," he whispered. "Bad luck, remember. And we've had enough of that today."

"You're okay?"

"Yes, I'm fine," he said in a whisper, stung by the illogical fear that if he spoke louder the particles of smoke would somehow puncture and deflate his lungs. "The birds?" he asked, praying that nothing had happened to the peregrine falcons. He wouldn't have minded if they moved to a different building. But it would have devastated him if they'd been injured or killed.

"Thom said they're fine. They're on the other sill."

She held him for a moment then Thom appeared in the doorway. "I need to rotate you."

The policewoman hugged him once more then stood back as Thom stepped close to the bed.

"Search the scene," Rhyme told her. "There's got to be something that he's left behind. There was that handkerchief he put around my neck. And he had some razor blades."

Sachs said she would and left the room. Thom took over and began expertly to clear his lungs.

Twenty minutes later Sachs returned. She stripped off the Tyvek suit and carefully folded and replaced it in the crime scene suitcase.

"Didn't find much," she reported. "Got that handkerchief and a couple of footprints. He's wearing a new pair of Eccos. But I didn't find any blades. And anything else he might've dropped got vaporized. Oh, and there was a bottle of scotch too. But I assume it's yours."

"Yes, it is," Rhyme whispered. Normally

he would've made a joke—something about the severity of the punishment for using eighteen-year-old single malt as an arson accelerant. But he couldn't bring himself to be humorous.

He knew there wouldn't be much evidence. Because of the extensive destruction in a fire the clues in most suspicious-origin fire scenes usually reveal only where and how the fire started. But they already knew that. Still, he thought there must be more.

"What about the duct tape? Thom pulled it off and dropped it."

"No duct tape."

"Look behind the head of the bed. The Conjurer was standing there. He might've—"

"I did look."

"Well, search again. You missed things. You must have."

"No," she said simply.

"What?"

"Forget the crime scene. It's toast—so to speak."

"We need to move this goddamn case forward."

"We're going to, Rhyme. I'm going to interview the witness."

"There was a witness?" he grumbled. "Nobody told me there was a witness."

"Well, there was."

She stepped to the doorway, called down the hall for Lon Sellitto to join them. He ambled inside, sniffing his jacket and wrinkling his nose. "A two-hundred-forty-fucking-dollar suit. History. Shit. What, Officer?"

"I'm going to interview the witness, Lieutenant. You have your tape recorder?"

"Sure." He took it out of his pocket and handed it to her. "There's a wit?"

Rhyme said, "Forget witnesses, Sachs. You know how unreliable they are. Stick with the evidence."

"No, we'll get something good. I'll make sure we do."

A glance at the doorway. "Well, who the hell is it?"

"You," she said, pulling a chair close to the bed.

Chapter Twenty-seven

"Me? Ridiculous."

"No. Not ridiculous."

"Forget it. Walk the grid again. You missed things. You searched way too fast. If you were a rookie—"

"I'm not a rookie. I know how to search a scene fast and I know when it's time to stop searching and go on to more productive things." She examined Sellitto's small recorder, checked the tape, and clicked it on.

"This is NYPD Patrol Officer Amelia Sachs, Badge Five Eight Eight Five, interviewing Lincoln Rhyme, witness in a ten-twenty-four assault and ten-twenty-nine arson at three-four-five Central Park West. The date is Saturday, April twentieth." She set the recorder on the table near Rhyme.

422 / Jeffery Deaver

Who glanced at the unit as if it were a snake.

"Now," she said. "Description."

"I told Lon—"

"Tell *me.*"

A sarcastic look at the ceiling. "He was medium-built, male, approximately fifty to fifty-five years of age, wearing a police officer's uniform. No beard this time. Scar tissue and discoloration on his neck and on his chest."

"His blouse was open? You could see his chest?"

"Excuse me," he said with bright sarcasm. "Scar tissue at the base of his neck *presumably* continuing down to his chest. Little and ring fingers of his left hand were fused together. He had . . . *appeared* to have brown eyes."

"Good, Rhyme," she said. "We didn't have his eye color before."

"And we may not now if he's wearing contacts," he snapped, feeling he'd scored a point here. "I could probably remember better with something to help." He looked toward Thom.

"Something to help?"

"I assume you have an unincinerated bottle of Macallan somewhere in the kitchen."

"Later," Sachs said. "Let's keep a clear head."

"But—"

Worrying her scalp with a nail, she continued, "Now. I want to go through everything that happened. What did he say?"

"I can't remember very much," he said impatiently. "It was mostly crazy ramblings. And I was hardly in the mood to pay attention."

"Maybe they sounded crazy to you. But I'll bet there was something we could use."

"Sachs," he said sardonically, "do you think I might've been a little spooked and confused? I mean, just a little *distracted* maybe?"

She touched his shoulder, a place where he could feel the contact. "I know you don't trust witnesses. But sometimes they do see things. . . . This's *my* specialty, Rhyme."

Amelia Sachs, the people cop.

"I'll walk you through it. Just like you walk me through the grid. We'll find something important."

She rose, walked to the door and called, "Kara?"

Yes, he distrusted witnesses, even those who had good vantage points and weren't part of the action itself. Anyone involved in the actual crime—especially a victim of violence—was totally unreliable. Even now, thinking about the killer's visit, all Rhyme could see was a random series of incidents—the Conjurer behind him, standing over him, lighting the fire. The razor blades. The smell of the scotch, the boiling smoke. He didn't even have a sense of the chronology of the killer's visit.

Memory, as Kara had said, is only an illusion.

A moment later the young woman appeared. "Are you all right, Lincoln?"

"Fine," he muttered.

Sachs was explaining that she wanted Kara to listen; she might recognize something the killer had said that could be helpful to them. The policewoman sat down again and pulled her chair close. "Let's go back there, Rhyme. Tell us what happened. Just in general terms."

He hesitated, glanced at the tape recorder. Then he began to recount the events as he remembered them. The Conjurer appearing, admitting he'd stolen the uniform then killed the officer, telling Rhyme about the officer's body.

The weather's warm . . .

He then said, "It was like he was pretending he was performing a show and I was a fellow performer." Hearing the man's odd rambling in his mind, Rhyme said, "I *do* remember one thing. He's got asthma. Or at least he sounded winded. He was gasping for breath a lot, whispering."

"Good," Sachs said. "I'd forgotten he sounded that way at the pond after the Marston assault. What else did he say?"

Rhyme looked at the dark ceiling of the small guest room. Shaking his head. "That's about it. He was either burning me or threatening to slice me up. . . . Oh, did you find any razor blades when you searched the room?"

"No."

"Well, there. This's what I'm talking about—evidence. I know he threw a blade in my sweatpants. The doctors didn't find it. It must've fallen out. See, *that's* the sort of thing you should be looking for."

"It was probably never in your pants," Kara said. "I know the illusion. He palmed the blade."

"Well, my point is that you don't tend to listen to people real close when they're torturing you."

"Come on, Rhyme, go on back there. It's earlier this evening. Kara and I're getting dinner. You've been looking over evidence. Thom's brought you upstairs. You were tired, right?"

"No," the criminalist said, "I *wasn't* tired. But he brought me up there anyway."

"Imagine you weren't too happy about that."

"No, I wasn't."

"So you're up in the room."

Picturing the lights, the silhouette of the birds. Thom, closing the door.

"It's quiet—" Sachs began.

"No, it's not quiet at all. There's that goddamn circus across the street. Anyway, I set the alarm—"

"For what time?"

"I don't know. An hour. What difference does it make?"

"One detail can give birth to two others."

A scowl. "Where'd that come from, a fortune cookie?"

She smiled. "Made it up. But it sounds

good, don't you think? Use it in the new edition of your book."

"I don't write books about witnesses," Rhyme said. "I write them about evidence." Feeling victorious again with this comeback.

"Now, how do you tell he's here at first? Did you hear anything?"

"No, I felt a draft. I thought it was the air-conditioning at first. But it was him. He was blowing on my neck and cheek."

"Just to—Why?"

"To scare me, I guess. It worked, by the way." Rhyme closed his eyes. Then he nodded as a few memories came back. "I tried to call Lon on the phone. But he"—a glance at Kara. "He caught my move. He threatened to kill me—no, he threatened to *blind* me—if I tried to call for help. I thought he was going to. But—it was odd—he seemed impressed. He complimented me on my misdirection. . . ." His voice faded as his memory trailed off into dimness.

"How did he get in?"

"He walked in with the officer who brought the evidence from the Grady hit."

"Shit," Sellitto said. "From now on we

check IDs—everybody who walks through the friggin' door. I mean, *everybody.*"

"He's talking about misdirection," Sachs continued. "He's complimented you. What else is he saying?"

"I don't know," Rhyme muttered. "Nothing."

"Nothing at all?" she asked, her voice a whisper.

"I. Don't. Know." Lincoln Rhyme was furious. At Sachs because she was pushing him. Because she wouldn't let him have a drink to numb the terror.

Furious mostly at himself for disappointing her.

But she had to understand how hard it was for him to go back there—to the flames, to the smoke that slipped into his nose and threatened his precious lungs—

Wait. Smoke . . .

Lincoln Rhyme said, "Fire."

"Fire?"

"I think that was what he talked about the most. He was obsessed with it. There was an illusion he mentioned. The . . . right, the Burning Mirror. That was it. Flames all over the stage, I think. The illusionist has to escape from them. He turns into the devil. Or somebody turns into the devil."

Both Rhyme and Sachs glanced at Kara, who was nodding. "I've heard of it. But it's rare. Takes a lot of setup and it's pretty dangerous. Most theaters owners won't let performers do it nowadays."

"He kept going on about fire. How it's the one thing you can't fake onstage. How audiences see fire and they secretly hope maybe the illusionist'll get burned. Wait. I remember something else. He—"

"Go on, Rhyme, you're on a roll."

"Don't interrupt me," he snapped. "I told you he was acting as if he were giving a performance? He seemed delusional. He kept looking at the blank wall and talking to somebody. It was like, 'My *something* audience.' I don't remember what he called them. He was manic."

"An imaginary audience."

"Right. Hold on. . . . I think it was 'respected audience.' Talking to them directly, 'My respected audience.'"

Sachs glanced at Kara, who shrugged. "We always talk to the audience. It's called patter. In the old days performers would say things like 'my esteemed audience,' or 'my dear ladies and gentlemen.' But everybody thinks that's hokey and pretentious. Patter's a lot less formal now."

"Let's keep going."

"I don't know, Sachs. I think I'm dry. Everything else is just a big blur."

"I'll bet there's more. It's like that one bit of evidence at the scene. It's there, it might be the key to the whole case. You just have to think a little differently to *find* it." She leaned closer to Rhyme. "Let's say this is your bedroom. You're in the Flexicair. Where was *he* standing?"

The criminalist nodded. "There. Near the foot of the bed, facing me. My left side, closest to the door."

"What was his pose?"

"Pose? I don't know."

"Try."

"I guess facing me. He kept moving his hands. Like he was speaking in public."

Sachs stood and took up a position. "Like this?"

"Closer."

She moved in.

"There."

Her standing in this pose did in fact bring back a memory. "One thing. . . . He was talking about the victims. He said killing them wasn't anything personal."

"Nothing personal."

"He killed . . . yes, I remember now. He killed them because of what they *represented.*"

Sachs was nodding, scribbling notes to supplement the tape recording. "Represented?" she mused. "What does that mean?"

"I didn't have any idea. One musician, one lawyer, one makeup artist. Different ages, sexes, professions, residences, no known connection to one other. What could they represent? Upper-middle-class lifestyles, urban dwellers, higher education. . . . Maybe one of those is the key—the rationalization for picking them. Who knows?"

Sachs was frowning. "There's something wrong."

"What?"

She finally said, "Something about what you're remembering."

"Well, it's not fucking verbatim. I didn't exactly have a stenographer handy."

"No, that's not what I mean." She considered for a minute. Then she nodded. "You're *characterizing* what he said. You're using *your* language, not his. 'Urban dwellers.' 'Rationalization.' I want *his* words."

"Well, I don't *remember* his words, Sachs. He said he didn't have anything personal against the victims. Period."

She shook her head. "No, I'll bet he didn't say that."

"What do you mean?"

"Murderers *never* think of the people they kill as 'victims.' It's impossible. They never humanize them. At least a pattern doer like the Conjurer wouldn't."

"That's hogwash from police academy psych 101, Sachs."

"No, it's the real world. *We* know they're victims but the perps always believe they deserve to die for one reason or another. Think about it. He didn't say 'victim,' did he?"

"Well, what difference does it make?"

"Because he said they were representative of something and we have to find out what. How did he refer to them?"

"I don't remember."

"Well, he didn't say 'victim.' I know that. Did he talk about any of them specifically? Svetlana, Tony. . . . How about Cheryl Marston? Did he call her the blonde woman? Did he say lawyer? Did he say the woman with big boobs? I guarantee he didn't say 'urban dweller.'"

Rhyme closed his eyes, tried to go back there. Finally he shook his head. "I don't—"

And then the word came to him.

"'Equestrian.'"

"What?"

"You're right. The word wasn't 'victim.' He called her 'the equestrian.'"

"Excellent!" she said.

Rhyme felt a burst of unreasonable pride. "How 'bout the others?"

"No, she was the only one he referred to." Rhyme was positive about this.

Sellitto said, "So he thinks of the vics as people doing a particular thing—that may or may not be their jobs."

"Right," Rhyme confirmed. "Playing music. Putting makeup on people. Riding horses."

"But whatta we *do* with that?" Sellitto asked.

And as Rhyme had said to her so often, when she posed this very same question about crime scene evidence, she replied, "We don't know yet, Detective. But it's a step closer to figuring him out." The policewoman then consulted the notes she'd been taking. "Okay, he did the razor-blade tricks, mentioned the Burning Mirror. He talked to his respected audience. He's obsessed with fire. He picked a makeup artist, a musician and a horseback rider to kill because of what they represent—whatever that is. Can you think of anything else?"

Eyes closed again. Trying hard.

But kept seeing the razor blades, the flames, smelling the smoke.

"Nope," he said, looking back at her. "I think that's it."

"Okay. Good, Rhyme."

And he recognized the tone in her voice.

He knew it because it was the tone he'd often use.

It meant she wasn't finished.

Sachs looked up from her notes and said slowly, "You know, you're always quoting Locard."

Rhyme nodded at the reference to the early French forensic detective and criminalist, who developed a principle that was later named for him. The rule held that at every crime scene there's always an exchange of evidence between the perpetrator and the victim or the locale itself, however minute.

"Well, I'm thinking there might be a *psychological* exchange too. Just like a physical one."

Rhyme laughed at the crazy idea. Locard was a scientist; he'd have balked at having his principle applied to something as slippery as the human psyche. "What're you getting at?"

She continued, "You weren't gagged the whole time, were you?"

"No, just at the end."

"So that means *you* communicated something too. You took part in an *exchange*."

"Me?"

"Didn't you? Didn't you say anything to *him*?"

"Sure. But so what? It's *his* words that're important."

"I'm thinking he might've said something in response to you."

Rhyme observed Sachs closely. A smudge of soot the shape of a quarter moon on her cheek, sweat just above her buoyant upper lip. She was sitting forward and, though her voice was calm, he could

436 / Jeffery Deaver

sense the tension of concentration in her pose. She wouldn't know it, of course, but she seemed to be feeling exactly the same emotions that he felt when he was guiding her through a crime scene miles away.

"Think about it, Rhyme," she said. "Imagine that you're alone with a perp. Not the Conjurer necessarily. Any perp. What would you say to him? What would you want to know?"

His reaction was to give a tired sigh that somehow managed to sound cynical. But, sure enough, her question jogged something in his mind. "I remember!" he said. "I asked him who he was."

"Good question. And he said?"

"He said he was a wizard. . . . No, not just *a* wizard but something specific." Rhyme squinted as he struggled to go back to that hard place. "It reminded me of *The Wizard of Oz.* . . . The Wicked Witch of the West." He frowned. Then he said, "Yeah, got it. He said he was the Wizard of the North. I'm sure that was it."

"Does that mean anything to you?" Sachs asked Kara.

"No."

"He said he could escape from anything.

Except, he didn't think that he'd be able to escape from us. Well, from me. He was worried we'd stop him. That's why he came here. He said he had to stop me before tomorrow afternoon. That's when he was going to start killing again."

"Wizard of the North," Sachs said, looking over her notes. "Now—"

Rhyme sighed. "I really think that's it, Sachs. The well. Is. Dry."

Sachs clicked the tape recorder off then leaned forward and with a tissue wiped the sweat off his forehead. "I figured. What I was going to say was now *I* need a drink. How 'bout it?"

"Only if *you* or Kara pour," Rhyme said to her. "Don't let him measure it." Nodding sourly toward Thom.

"Would you like something?" Thom asked Kara.

Rhyme said, "She'll want an Irish *coffee,* I'll bet. . . . Why doesn't Starbucks start selling *those?*"

Kara declined the liquor but put in an order for a straight Maxwell House or Folgers.

Sellitto asked about the likelihood of some food since his anticipated Cubano sandwich hadn't survived the trip back to the town house.

As the aide vanished into the kitchen Sachs handed Kara the notes she'd taken and asked if she'd write down anything she thought was relevant on the magician profile board. The young woman rose and went into the lab.

"That was good," Sellitto told Sachs, "that interviewing. I don't know any sergeants could've done it better."

She nodded an unsmiling acknowledgment but Rhyme could tell she was pleased at the compliment.

A few minutes later Mel Cooper walked into the doorway, his face smudged too. He held up a plastic bag. "This's all the evidence from the Mazda." The bag contained what seemed to be a four-page folio—a single folded sheet—of *The New York Times*. It was clear that Sachs hadn't run the scene; wet evidence should be stored in paper or fiber mesh containers, not plastic, which promotes molds that can quickly destroy it.

"That was *all* they found?" Rhyme asked.

"So far. They haven't been able to raise the car yet. Too dangerous."

Rhyme asked him, "Can you see the date?"

Cooper examined the soggy paper. "Two days ago."

"Then it has to be the Conjurer's," Rhyme noted. "The car was stolen before then. Why would somebody save just one sheet from a newspaper and not the whole section?" The question, as many of Rhyme's, was purely rhetorical and he didn't bother to let anyone else have a shot at it. "Because there's an article in it that was important to him. And therefore maybe important to *us.* Of course maybe he's a dirty old man and likes the Victoria's Secret ads. But even *that* might be helpful information. Can you read anything on it?"

"Nope. And I don't want to unfold it yet. Too wet."

"Okay, get it over to the document lab. If they can't open it at least they can image the headlines with infrared."

Cooper arranged for a messenger to take the sample to the NYPD crime lab in Queens and then called the head document examiner at home to expedite the analysis. He disappeared into the lab to transfer the newspaper to a better container for transport.

Thom arrived with the drinks—and a plate of sandwiches, which Sellitto promptly assaulted.

A few minutes later Kara returned and gratefully took the coffee mug from the aide. As she started pouring sugar in, she said to Sachs, "I was writing those things we found out about him on the board? And I got an idea. So I made a phone call. I think I found his real name."

"Whose?" Rhyme asked, sipping his heavenly scotch.

"Well, the Conjurer's."

The faint ring as Kara stirred the sugar into her coffee became the only sound in the otherwise dead-silent room.

Chapter Twenty-eight

"You've got his *name?*" Sellitto asked. "Who is he?"

"I think it's a man named Erick Weir."

"Spelled?" Rhyme asked.

"W-E-I-R." More sugar into the coffee. Then she continued. "He was a performer, an illusionist, a few years ago. I called Mr. Balzac—nobody knows the business like he does. And I gave him the profile and told him some of the things he'd said to Lincoln tonight. He got kind of weird—not to mention mad." A glance at Sachs. "The way he was this morning. He didn't want to help at first. But finally he calmed down and told me that it sounded like Weir."

"Why?" Sachs asked.

"Well, he'd be about the same age. Early fifties. And Weir was known for dangerous routines. Sleights with razor blades and knives. He's also one of the few people who's ever done the Burning Mirror. And remember I said illusionists always specialize? It's really unusual to find one performer who's good at so many different tricks—illusion and escape and protean and sleight, even ventriloquism and mentalism? Well, Weir did all of them. And he was an expert on Houdini. Some of what he's been doing this weekend are Houdini's routines or are based on them.

"Then that thing he also said—about being the wizard. There was a magician in the 1800s, John Henry Anderson. That's what he called himself—the Wizard of the North. He was real talented. But he had bad luck with fires. His show was nearly destroyed a couple of times. David told me that Weir was badly burned in a circus fire."

"The scars," Rhyme said. "The obsession with fire."

"And maybe his voice wasn't asthma," Sachs suggested. "The fire might've damaged his lungs or vocal cords."

"When was Weir's accident?" Sellitto asked.

"Three years ago. The circus tent he was

rehearsing in was destroyed and Weir's wife was killed. They'd just gotten married. Nobody else was badly hurt."

It was a good lead. "Mel!" Rhyme shouted, forgetting his concerns about imperiling his own lungs. *"Mel!"*

A moment later Cooper stepped into the room. "Feeling better, I hear."

"Lexis/Nexis search, VICAP, NCIC and state databases. Details on a Erick Weir. W-E-I-R. Performer, illusionist, magician. He may be our perp."

Kara added, "First name spelled E-R-I-C-K."

"You found his *name*?" the tech asked, impressed.

A nod toward Kara. "*She* found his name."

"My."

After a few minutes Cooper returned with a number of printouts. He riffled through them as he addressed the team. "Not much," he said. "It's like he kept everything about his life under wraps. Erick Albert Weir. Born Las Vegas, October 1950. Virtually no early history. Weir worked for various circuses, casinos and entertainment companies as an assistant then he went out on his own as an illusionist and quick-change artist. Married Marie Cosgrove three years ago. Just after that he was appearing in the Thomas Hasbro and The Keller Brothers circus in Cleveland. During a rehearsal a fire broke out. The tent was destroyed. He was badly burned—third degree—and his wife was killed. No mention of him after that."

"Track down Weir's family."

Sellitto said he would. Since Bedding and Saul were fully occupied the detective called some Homicide task force detectives in the Big Building and put them on the job.

"A few other things," Cooper said, flipping through the printouts. "A couple of years before the fire Weir was arrested and convicted of reckless endangerment in New Jersey. Served thirty days. A member of the audience was badly burned when something went wrong onstage. Then there were some civil lawsuits by managers for damage to theaters and injuries to employees and some suits by Weir for breach of contract. In one show the manager found out Weir was using a real gun and real bullets in an act. Weir wouldn't change the routine and so the manager fired him." More reading. Then the tech continued, "In one of the articles I found the names of two assistants who were working with him at the time of the fire. One's in Reno and one's in Las Vegas. I got their numbers from the Nevada State Police."

"It's earlier their time," Rhyme pointed out, glancing at the clock. "Dig up the speakerphone, Thom."

"No, after everything tonight you need some rest."

"Just two phone calls. Then beddy-bye. Promise."

The aide debated.

"Please and thank-you?"

Thom nodded and vanished. A moment later he returned with the phone, plugged it in, set the unit close to Rhyme on the bedside table. "Ten minutes and I'm pulling the main circuit breaker," the aide said with enough threat in his voice to make Rhyme believe he'd do it.

"Fair enough."

Sellitto finished his sandwich and dialed the number of the first assistant on Cooper's list. The recorded voice of Arthur Loesser's wife answered and told them that the family wasn't home but please leave a message. Sellitto did so then he dialed the other assistant.

John Keating answered on the first ring and Sellitto explained they were in the middle of an investigation and had some questions for him. A pause then a man's nervous voice rattled out of the tiny speaker. "Uhm, what's this about? This's the New York City police?"

"That's right."

"Okay. I guess it's okay."

Sellitto asked, "You used to work for a man named Erick Weir, didn't you?"

Silence for a moment. Then the man launched into a staccato reply. "Mr. Weir? Well, uh-huh. I did. Why?" The voice was edgy and high. He sounded as if he'd just had a dozen cups of coffee.

"Do you happen to know where he might be?"

"I mean, why are you asking me about him?"

"We'd like to talk to him as part of a criminal investigation."

"Oh, my God. . . . About what? What do you want to talk to him *about*?"

"We just have some general questions,"

Sellitto said. "Have you had any contact with him lately?"

There was a pause. This was the part where the nervous man would either spill all or run for the hills, Rhyme knew.

"Sir?" Sellitto asked.

"That's funny, okay. You asking me, I mean about *him.*" The words clattered like marbles on metal. "Here it is. I'll tell you. I hadn't heard from Mr. Weir for years. I thought he was dead. There was this fire in Ohio, the last job we were working. He got burned. Real bad. He disappeared and we all thought he was dead. But then maybe six or seven weeks ago he called."

"From where?" Rhyme asked.

"I don't know. He didn't say. I didn't ask. It doesn't occur to anyone to ask *where* somebody's calling from. Not the first thing. You just don't think about that. Do you ever ask that?"

Rhyme asked, "What did he want?"

"Okay, okay. He wanted to know if I still kept up with anybody at the circus where the fire happened. The Hasbro circus. But that was Ohio. It was three years ago. And Hasbro's not even in business anymore. After the fire the owner folded it and it became a different show. Why would I keep up with anybody there? Here I am in Reno. I said I didn't. And he got all ippity, you know."

Rhyme frowned again.

Sachs tried, "Angry?"

"Oh, hell-ooooh. Yeah, I'll say."

"Go on," Rhyme said, struggling against impatience. "Tell us what else he said."

"That was it. That was all. What I just told you. I mean, there were little things. Oh, he got his digs in like he always did. The claws. Just like old times. . . . You know what he did when he called?"

"What was that?" Rhyme encouraged.

"All he said was, 'It's Erick.' Not 'Hello.' Not 'Oh, John, how are you? Remember me?' No. 'It's Erick.' I hadn't talked to him since the fire. And what does he say? 'It's Erick.' All these years since I got away from him, working so hard to get away . . . and then it's like I haven't gotten away at all. I know I hadn't done anything wrong. And here he's making it sound like something's all my fault. It's like you take an order from a customer and then when you bring the food they claim it's not what they ordered. But everybody knows what happened—they changed their mind and they're making it sound like you got it wrong. Like it's your fault and *you're* the one who gets in trouble."

Sachs continued, "Can you tell us anything about him in general? Other friends, places he liked to go, hobbies."

"Sure," came the snappy voice. "All of the above: illusion."

"What?" Rhyme asked.

"That was his friends, places he liked to go to, hobbies. You get what I'm saying? There *was* nothing else. He was like totally absorbed in the profession."

Sachs tried again. "Well, what about his attitude toward people? His outlook? How he thought about things?"

A long pause. "Fifty minutes, twice a week for three years I've been trying to figure him out and I can't. For *three* years. And he still hurts me. I—" Keating broke into a harsh, eerie laugh. "You catch that? I said 'hurts.' I meant to say 'haunts.' He still *haunts* me. How's that for Freudian? I'll have something to share next Monday at nine A.M., won't I? He still haunts me and I don't have a clue what his fucking outlook is."

Rhyme could see everyone on the team was growing frustrated with the man's rambling. He said, "We heard his wife was killed in the fire. Do you know anything about her family?"

"Marie? No, they'd only gotten married a week or two before the fire. They were really in love. We thought she'd calm him down. Make him *haunt* us less. We were hoping that. But we never got to know her."

"Can you give us the names of anybody who might know something about him?"

"Art Loesser was first assistant. I was second. We were his boys. They called us 'Erick's boys.' Everybody did."

Rhyme said, "We have a call in to Loesser. Anyone else?"

"The only one I can think of is the manager of the Hasbro circus at the time. Edward Kadesky's his name. He's a producer in Chicago now, I think."

Sellitto got the spelling of the man's name. Then asked, "Did Weir ever call back?"

"No. But he didn't need to. Five minutes and he got the claws in. Hurting and haunting."

It's Erick . . .

"Look, I should go. I have to iron my uniform. I'm working the Sunday morning shift. It's a busy one."

After they hung up, Sachs walked to the speakerphone to hit the disconnect button. "Brother," she muttered.

"Needs more meds," Sellitto observed.

"Well, at least we've got a lead," Rhyme said. "Track down that Kadesky."

Mel Cooper disappeared for a few minutes and when he returned he had a printout of a database of theatrical companies. Kadesky Productions had its office on South Wells Street in the Windy City. Sellitto placed a call and, not surprisingly, being late Saturday night, got the answering service. He left a message.

Sellitto said, "Okay—Weir's messed up his assistant's life. He's unstable. He's injured people in the audience and now he's a pattern doer. But what's making him tick?"

Sachs looked up at this. "Let's give Terry a call."

Terry Dobyns was an NYPD psychologist. There were several on the force but Dobyns was the sole behavioral profiler, a skill he'd learned and honed at the FBI in Quantico, Virginia. Thanks to the press and popular

fiction the public hears a lot about psychological profiling and it can be valuable—but
only, Rhyme felt, in a limited type of crime.
Generally there's nothing mysterious about
the workings of a perp's mind. But in cases
were the motive is a mystery and his next
target is hard to anticipate, profiling can be
valuable. It helps investigators find inform-
ants or individuals who might know the suspect, anticipate his next move, set up decoys in appropriate neighborhoods, run
stakeouts and look for similar crimes in the
past.

Sellitto thumbed through an NYPD direc-
tory of phone numbers and placed a call to
Dobyns at home.

"Terry."

"Lon. You've got speakerphone echo. Let
me deduce that Lincoln's there too."

"Yep," Rhyme confirmed. He had a fond-
ness for Dobyns, the first person he saw
when he awakened after his spinal cord accident. Rhyme recalled that the man loved
touch football, opera and the mysteries of
the human mind in roughly the same degrees—and all passionately.

"Sorry it's late," Sellitto offered, not
sounding sorry at all. "But we need some

help with a multiple doer. We've got a name but not much else."

"This the one in the news? Killed the music student this morning? And that patrol officer too?"

"Right. He also killed a makeup artist and tried to kill a horseback rider. Because of what they and the student quote represented. Two straight women, one gay man. No sexual activities. We're at a loss. And he's told Lincoln that he's going to start up again tomorrow afternoon."

"He *told* Lincoln? Over the phone? A letter?"

"In person," Rhyme said.

"Hmm. That must've been quite a conversation."

"You don't know the half of it."

Sellitto and Rhyme gave the man a rundown on Weir's crimes and what they'd learned about him.

Dobyns asked a number of questions. Then he fell silent for a moment and finally said, "I see two forces at work in him. But they reinforce each other and lead to the same result. . . . Is he still performing?"

"No," Kara said. "He hasn't performed since the fire. Not that anybody's heard."

"Public performing," Dobyns said, "is such an intense experience, it's so compelling, that when it's denied someone who was successful the loss is profound. Actors and musicians—magicians too, I'd guess—tend to define themselves in terms of their careers. So the result is that the fire basically eradicated the man he had been."

The Vanished Man, Rhyme reflected.

"That in turn means he's now motivated not by ambition to succeed or to please his audience or a devotion to his craft but by anger. And that's aggravated by the second force: the fire deformed him and damaged his lungs. So as a public person he'd be particularly self-conscious of the deformities. They'd multiply the anger logarithmically. We could call it the Phantom of the Opera syndrome, I suppose. He'd see himself as a freak."

"So he wants to get even?"

"Yes, but not necessarily in a literal sense: fire quote murdered him—his old persona—and by murdering someone else he feels better; it reduces the anxiety that the anger builds up in him."

"Why these victims?"

"No way of knowing. 'What they repre-sented.' What did they do again?"

"Music student, makeup stylist and a lawyer though he referred to her as an equestrian."

"There's something about them that's tapped into his anger. I don't know what it could be—not yet, not without more data. The textbook answer is that each one of them devoted their lives to what Weir would consider 'crucible moments.' Important, life-changing times. Maybe his wife was a musician or they met at a concert. The makeup stylist—that could be a mother is-sue. For instance, the only happy times he might've had with her were as a young boy sitting in the bathroom and watching her put on makeup. The horses? Who knows? Maybe he and his father went horseback riding once and he enjoyed it. The happi-ness of moments like that was taken away from him by the fire and he's targeting people who remind him of those times. Or it could be the opposite; he has bad associa-tions with what the victims represent. You say his wife died during a rehearsal. Maybe there was music playing at the time."

"He'd go to all this trouble, staking them

out, making these elaborate plans to find them and kill them?" Rhyme asked. "This must've taken months."

"The mind *has* to scratch its itches," Dobyns said.

"One other thing, Terry. He also seemed to be talking to an imaginary audience. . . . Wait, I thought it was 'respected' audience. But I just remembered—it was 'revered.' Talking to them like they were really there. 'Now, Revered Audience, we're going to do this or that.'"

"'Revered,'" the psychologist said. "That's important. After his career and his loved one were taken away from him he shifted his reverence, his *love,* to an audience—an impersonal mass. People who prefer groups or crowds can be abusive, even dangerous, to individual human beings. Not only strangers but their partners, wives, children, family members too."

John Keating, Rhyme reflected, in fact sounded like a child who'd been abused by his father.

Dobyns continued, "And in Weir's case this frame of mind is even more dangerous because he's not talking to *real* audiences, only his imaginary one. This suggests to me that actual people have no value to him at all. He won't have any problem killing even in large numbers. This guy's going to be a tough one."

"Thanks, Terry."

"You get him in jar, let me know. I'd like to spend some time with him."

After they hung up Sellitto began, "Maybe we could—"

"Go to bed," Thom said.

"Huh?" the detective asked.

"And it's not a question of 'could.' It's a question of 'are.' You're going to bed, Lincoln. And everybody else is leaving. You look pale and tired. No cardiovascular or neuro events on my watch. If you'll recall, I wanted you to go to bed hours ago."

"All right, all right," Rhyme conceded. In fact, he was tired. And, though he wouldn't admit it to anyone, the fire had scared him badly.

The team departed for their respective homes. Kara found her jacket and as she put it on Rhyme observed that she was clearly upset.

"You okay?" Sachs asked her.

A dismissing shrug. "I had to tell Mr. Balzac why I needed to ask him about Weir.

He's totally pissed off. I've got to go pay penance."

"We'll write him a note," Sachs joked gently, "excusing you from class."

The girl smiled wanly.

Rhyme called out, "Hell with the note. If it wasn't for you we wouldn't have a clue who the perp was. Tell him to give me a call. I'll fix his clock."

Kara offered an anemic, "Thanks."

"You're not going to the store now, are you?" Sachs asked.

"Just for a little. Mr. Balzac is helpless with the details. I'll have to log in the receipts. And show him my routine for tomorrow."

Rhyme wasn't surprised that she was going to do what the man asked. He noted she'd said, *Mr.* Balzac. Sometimes he was "David." Not now. This echoed what they'd heard earlier: despite the Conjurer's coming close to destroying John Keating's life, the assistant had referred to the killer with the same respectful appellation. The power of mentors over their apprentices . . .

"Go on home," the policewoman persisted. "I mean, Jesus, you *did* get knifed to death today."

Another faint laugh, accompanied by a shrug. "I won't be there long." She paused in the doorway. "You know, I have that show in the afternoon. But I'll come back tomorrow morning if you want."

"We'd appreciate it," Rhyme said. "Though we'll try to nail Weir's ass before lunch so you won't have to stay long."

Thom walked her into the corridor and out the front door.

Sachs stepped into the doorway and inhaled the smoky air. "Phew," she exhaled. Then disappeared up the stairs. "I'm showering," she called.

Ten minutes later Rhyme heard her walk downstairs. But she didn't join him in the bedroom right away. From different parts of the house came thuds and creaks, muted words with Thom. Then finally she returned to the guest room. She was wearing her favorite pajamas—black T-shirt and silk boxers—but she had two accoutrements that were atypical of her sleep gear. Her Glock pistol and the long black tube of her issue flashlight.

She set them both on the bedside table.

"That guy gets into places too damn easy," she said, climbing into bed next to him. "I checked every square inch of the house, balanced chairs on all the doors and told Thom if he hears anything to give a shout—but to stay put. I'm in the mood to shoot somebody but I'd really rather it wasn't him."

II
METHOD

"A magical effect is like a seduction. Both are built through careful details planted in the mind of the subject."

—Sol Stein

Chapter Twenty-nine

Sunday morning passed in frustration as the search for Erick Weir stalled.

The team learned that after the fire in Ohio the illusionist had remained in the burn unit of a local hospital for several weeks and then left on his own, without officially checking out. There was a record that he sold his house in downtown Las Vegas not long after that but no public record of buying another. In that cash-fat city though, Rhyme supposed, one could easily buy a small place in the desert with a stack of greenbacks, no questions asked, no public filings involved.

The team managed to find Weir's late wife's mother. But Mrs. Cosgrove knew nothing of Weir's whereabouts. He'd never contacted them after the disaster to send his condolences about their daughter's death. She reported, though, that she wasn't surprised. Weir was a selfish, cruel man, she explained, who'd become obsessed with her young daughter and virtually hypnotized her into marrying him. None of the other Cosgrove relatives had had any contact with Weir.

Cooper compiled the remaining information from the computer searches on Weir but there wasn't much. No VICAP or NCIC reports. There were no other details on the man, and the officers tracking down Weir's family found only that both parents were deceased, that he was an only child and that no next of kin could be located.

Late in the morning Weir's other assistant, Art Loesser, returned their call from Las Vegas. The man wasn't surprised to learn that his former boss was wanted in connection with a crime and echoed what they'd learned already: that Weir was one of the world's greatest illusionists but that he took the profession far too seriously and was known for his dangerous illusions and hot temper. Loesser still had nightmares about being his apprentice.

I said "hurts." I meant to say "haunts." He still haunts *me.*

"All young assistants're influenced by their mentors," Loesser told the team via speakerphone. "But my therapist said that in Weir's case we were mesmerized by him."

So both of them are in therapy.

"He said being with Weir created a Stockholm syndrome relationship. You know what that is?"

Rhyme said he was familiar with the condition—where hostages form close bonds with, and even feel affection and love for, their kidnappers.

"When did you last see him?" Sachs asked. The assessment exercise over, she was in soft clothes today—jeans and a forest-green knit blouse.

"In the hospital, the burn unit. That was about three years ago. I'd go visit him regularly at first but all he'd talk about was getting even with anybody who'd ever hurt him or who didn't approve of his kind of magic. Then he disappeared and I never saw him after that."

But then, the former protégé explained, Weir had called out of the blue about two months ago. Around the same time, Rhyme reflected, he'd called his other assistant. Loesser's wife had taken the call. "He didn't leave a number and said he'd call back but he never did. Thank God. I'll tell you, I don't know that I could've handled it."

"Do you know where he was when he called?"

"No. I asked Kathy—I was afraid he was back in town—but she said he didn't say and the call came up 'out-of-area' on caller-ID."

"He didn't tell your wife what he might be calling about? Any clue where he might be?"

"She said he sounded odd, agitated. He was whispering, hard to understand. I remember that from after the fire. His lungs'd been damaged. Made him even scarier."

Tell me about it, Rhyme thought.

"He asked if we'd heard anything about Edward Kadesky—he was the producer of the Hasbro show when the fire happened. That was it."

Loesser couldn't provide any other helpful information and they hung up.

Thom let two policewomen into the lab. Sachs nodded a greeting and introduced them to Rhyme. Diane Franciscovich and Nancy Ausonio.

They were, he recalled, the respondings at the first murder and had been given the assignment of tracking down the antique handcuffs.

Franciscovich said, "We talked to all the dealers the director of the museum recommended." Beneath their crisp uniforms both the tall brunette and the shorter blonde looked exhausted. They'd taken their assignment seriously, it seemed, and probably hadn't gotten any sleep the night before.

"The handcuffs are Darbys, like you thought," Ausonio said. "They're pretty rare—and expensive. But we've got a list of twelve people who—"

"Oh, my God, look." Franciscovich was pointing to the evidence chart, where Thom had written:

- Perp's identity: Erick A. Weir.

Ausonio flipped through the sheets she held. "Erick Weir placed a mail order for a pair of the cuffs from Ridgeway Antique Weapons in Seattle last month."

"Address?" Rhyme asked excitedly.

"Post office box in Denver. We checked. But the lease lapsed. There're no records of a permanent address."

"And no record that Weir ever lived in Denver."

"Method of payment?" Sachs asked.

"Cash," was the simultaneous response from Ausonio and Rhyme, who added, "He's not going to make stupid mistakes. Nope. That trail's dead. But at least we've got a confirmation that this's our boy."

Rhyme thanked the officers and Sachs walked them to the door.

Another call came in on Rhyme's phone. The area code on the caller ID looked familiar but Rhyme couldn't place it. "Command, answer phone. . . . Hello?"

"Yessir. This's Lieutenant Lansing, State Police. I'm trying to reach Detective Roland Bell. I was given this number as his temporary command post."

"Hey, Harv," Bell called, walking closer to the speaker phone. "I'm here." He explained to Rhyme, "Our liaison on the Constable case up in Canton Falls."

Lansing continued, "We got the evidence you sent up here this morning. Our forensic boys're going through it. We had a couple of detectives go and talk to Swensen's wife—that minister you folks took down last night. She didn't say anything helpful and my boys didn't find anything in the trailer to connect him to Constable or anybody else in the Patriot Assembly."

"Nothin'?" Bell sighed. "Too bad. I figured him to be poke-easy careless."

"Maybe the Patriot boys got there first and scoured the place clean."

"That's more'n half likely. Man, I'm feeling we're due a little luck here. Okay, keep at it, Harv. Thanks."

"We'll let you know, we come up with anything else, Roland."

They hung up.

"This Constable case's full-up tough as this one." Nodding at the whiteboards.

Another knock on the front door.

Armed with a large coffee cup Kara walked into the room, looking more tired and haggard than the policewomen.

Sellitto was delivering a monologue about new techniques for weight loss when his Jenny Craig lecture was interrupted by yet another phone call.

"Lincoln?" the voice crackled through the speakerphone. "Bedding here. We think

we've narrowed the key down to three hotels. Reason it took so long—"

The voice of his partner, Saul, interrupted.
"Turns out that a lot of monthly and long-
term hotels use card keys too."

"Not to mention hourly rate places. But
that's a whole 'nother story."

"We had to check them all out. Anyway,
that's what we found. It's probably, I say,
probably, either the Chelsea Lodge, the
Beckman or the . . . what is it?"

"Or the Lanham Arms," his partner supplied.

"Right. They're the only ones using this
color Model 42. We're at the Beckman now.
Thirty-four and Fifth. We're about to start
trying it out."

"What do you mean trying it out?" Rhyme
called.

"How d'I put this?" Bedding or Saul wondered. "The keys work one way but not the
other."

"How's that?" Rhyme asked.

"See, only the lock unit on the hotel room
door can *read* a key. The machine at the
front desk that burns the room codes onto a
blank key can't read one that's already been
burned and tell you what room it is."

"Why not? That's crazy."

"Nobody ever needs to know that."

"Except us, of course, which is why we have to go from door to door and try them all."

"Shit," Rhyme snapped.

"Summarizes our feelings too," one of the detectives said.

Sellitto asked, "Okay. You need more people?"

"Nup. We can only do one door at a time. No other way to do it. And if there's a new guest in the room—"

"—this card'll be invalid. Which won't improve our moods any."

"Say, gentlemen?" Bell said into the phone.

"Hey there, Roland."

"We recognized the accent."

"You said the Lanham Arms. Where is that?"

"East Seventy-five. Near Lex."

"Something familiar 'bout the name. Can't quite place it." Bell was frowning, shaking his head.

"That's next on our list."

"After the Beckman."

"With its six hundred and eighty-two rooms. Better get to it."

They left the Twins to their arduous task.

Cooper's computer beeped and he read an incoming email. "FBI lab in Washington. . . . Finally got a report on the metal shavings in the Conjurer's gym bag. They say the markings suggest they're consistent with a clock mechanism."

"Well, it's *not* a clock," Rhyme said. "Obviously."

"How do you know?" Bell asked.

"It's a detonator," Sachs said solemnly.

"That's what I'd say," Rhyme confirmed.

"A gas bomb?" Cooper asked, nodding toward the handkerchief "souvenir" Weir had left last night, which had been soaked in gasoline.

"Likely."

"He's got a supply of gas and he's obsessed with fire. He's going to burn the next victim."

Just like what happened to him.

Fire quote murdered him—his old persona—and by murdering someone else he feels better; it reduces the anxiety that the anger builds up in him. . . .

Rhyme noticed the hour was approaching 12:00. Almost afternoon. . . . The next victim was going to die soon. But when, 12:01 or 4:00? A shudder of frustration and anger started at the base of his skull and vanished into his stony body. They had so little time.

Maybe no time at all.

But he could come to no conclusions based on the evidence they had. And the day dragged on, slow as an IV drip.

A fax arrived. Cooper read it. "From the document examiner in Queens. They opened up the newspaper that was in the Mazda. No notations anywhere and nothing was circled. Those're the headlines."

He taped it to the board.

ELECTRICAL BREAKDOWN
CLOSES POLICE STATION
FOR ALMOST 4 HOURS

NEW YORK IN RUNNING
FOR GOP CONVENTION

PARENTS PROTEST
POOR SECURITY AT
GIRLS' SCHOOL

MILITIA MURDER PLOT
TRIAL OPENS MONDAY

WEEKEND GALA AT MET
TO BENEFIT CHARITIES

SPRING ENTERTAINMENT
FOR KIDS YOUNG AND OLD

GOVERNOR, MAYOR MEET
ON NEW WEST SIDE PLAN

"One of those's significant," Rhyme said. But which one? Was the killer targeting the girls' school? The gala? Had he tested out a gimmick that disrupted the electricity at the police station? He felt all the more frustrated because they had some new evidence but its meaning remained elusive.

Sellitto's phone rang. As he took the call, everyone stared at him, anticipating another death.

The time was now 1:03.

Well into the afternoon, well into the killing time.

But apparently the news wasn't bad. The detective lifted an eyebrow in pleasant surprise and said into the receiver, "That's right. . . . Really? Well, that's not far away. Could you come over here?" He then gave Rhyme's address and hung up.

"Who?"

"Edward Kadesky. The manager of the circus in Ohio, the one where Weir was burned. He's in town. He got the message from his service in Chicago and he's coming over to talk to us."

THE CONJURER

Music School Crime Scene

- Perp's description: Brown hair, fake beard, no distinguishing, medium build, medium height, age: fifties. Ring and little fingers of left hand fused together. Changed costume quickly to resemble old, bald janitor.

- No apparent motive.

- Victim: Svetlana Rasnikov.
  - Full-time music student.
  - Checking family, friends, students, coworkers for possible leads.
    - No boyfriends, no known enemies. Performed at children's birthday parties.

- Circuit board with speaker attached.
  - Sent to FBI lab, NYC.

- Digital recorder, probably containing perp's voice. All data destroyed.
  - Voice recorder is a "gimmick." Homemade.

- Used antique iron handcuffs to restrain victim.
  - Handcuffs are Darby irons. Scotland Yard. Checking with Houdini Museum in New Orleans for leads.
    - Sold to Erick Weir last month. Sent to Denver P.O. box. No other leads.

- Destroyed victim's watch at exactly 8:00 A.M.

- Cotton string holding chairs. Generic. Too many sources to trace.

- Squib for gunshot effect. Destroyed.
  - Too many sources to trace.

- Fuse. Generic.
  - Too many sources to trace.

- Responding officers reported flash in air. No trace material recovered.
  - Was from flash cotton or flash paper.
    - Too many sources to trace.

- Perp's shoes: size 10 Ecco.

- Silk fibers, dyed gray, processed to a matte finish.
  - From quick-change janitor's outfit.

- Unsub is possibly wearing brown wig.

- Red pignut hickory and Parmelia conspersa lichen, both found primarily in Central Park.

- Dirt impregnated with unusual mineral oil. Sent to FBI for analysis.
  - Tack-Pure oil for saddles and leather.

- Black silk, 72 x 48''. Used as camouflage. Not traceable.
  - Illusionists use this frequently.

- Wears caps to cover up prints.
  - Magician's finger cups.

- Traces of latex, castor oil, makeup.
  - Theatrical makeup.

- Traces of alginate.
  - Used in molding latex "appliances."

- Murder weapon: white silk-knit rope with black silk core.
  - Rope is a magic trick. Color changing. Not traceable.

- Unusual knot.
  - Sent to FBI and Maritime Museum—no information.
  - Knots are from Houdini routines, virtually impossible to untie.

- Used disappearing ink on sign-in register.

East Village Crime Scene

- Victim Two: Tony Calvert.
  - Makeup artist, theater company.
  - No known enemies.
  - No apparent connection with first victim.

- No apparent motive.

- Cause of death:
  - Blunt-object trauma to head followed by postmortem dismemberment with crosscut saw.

- Perp escaped portraying woman in her 70s. Checking vicinity for discarded costume and other evidence.
  - Nothing recovered.

- Watch smashed at 12:00 exactly.
  - Pattern? Next victim presumably at 4:00 P.M.

- Perp hid behind mirror. Not traceable. Fingerprints sent to FBI.
  - No matches.

- Used cat toy ("feke") to lure victim into alley. Toy is untraceable.

- Additional mineral oil found, same as at first scene. Awaiting FBI report.
  - Tack-Pure oil for saddles and leather.

- Additional latex and makeup from finger cups.

- Additional alginate.

- Ecco shoes left behind.

- Dog hairs found in shoes, from three different breeds of dog. Manure too.
  - Manure from horses, not dogs.

Hudson River and Related Crime Scenes

- Victim: Cheryl Marston.
  - Attorney.
  - Divorced but husband not a suspect.

- No motive.

- Perp gave name as "John." Had scars on neck and chest. Deformed hand confirmed.

- Perp did quick change to unbearded businessman in chinos and dress shirt, then biker in denim Harley shirt.

- Car is in Harlem River.

- Duct tape gag. Can't be traced.

- Squibs, same as before. Can't be traced.

- Chains and snap fixtures, generic, not traceable.

- Rope, generic, not traceable.

- Additional makeup, latex and Tack-Pure.

- Gym bag, made in China, not traceable. Containing:
  - Traces of date rape drug flunitrazepam.
  - Adhesive magician's wax, not traceable.
  - Brass (?) shavings. Sent to FBI.
    - Consistent with clockwork mechanism, possible bomb timer.
  - Permanent ink, black.

- Navy-blue windbreaker found, no initials or laundry marks. Containing:
  - Press pass for CTN cable network, issued to Stanley Saferstein. (He's not suspect—NCIC, VICAP search negative.)
  - Plastic hotel key card, American Plastic Cards, Akron, Ohio. Model APC-42, negative on prints.
    - CEO is searching for sales records.
    - Dets. Bedding and Saul canvassing hotels.
      - Narrowed down to Chelsea Lodge, Beckman and Lanham Arms. Still checking.

- Restaurant check from Riverside Inn, Bedford Junction, NY, indicating four people ate lunch, table 12, Saturday, two weeks prior. Turkey, meatloaf, steak, daily special. Soft drinks. Staff doesn't know who diners were. (Accomplices?)

- Alley where Conjurer was arrested:
  - Picked the cuff locks.
  - Saliva (picks hidden in mouth).
  - No blood type determined.
  - Small razor saw for getting out of restraints (also hidden in mouth).

- No indication of Officer Burke's whereabouts.
  - Report body somewhere on Upper West Side.

- Harlem River scene:
  - No evidence on riverbank, except skid marks in mud.
  - Newspaper recovered from the car. Headlines:

ELECTRICAL BREAKDOWN
CLOSES POLICE STATION
FOR ALMOST 4 HOURS

NEW YORK IN RUNNING
FOR GOP CONVENTION

PARENTS PROTEST
POOR SECURITY AT
GIRLS' SCHOOL

MILITIA MURDER PLOT
TRIAL OPENS MONDAY

WEEKEND GALA AT MET
TO BENEFIT CHARITIES

SPRING ENTERTAINMENT
FOR KIDS YOUNG AND OLD

GOVERNOR, MAYOR MEET
ON NEW WEST SIDE PLAN

Lincoln Rhyme Crime Scene

- Victim: Lincoln Rhyme

- Perp's identity: Erick A. Weir.
  - LKA Las Vegas

- Burned in fire in Ohio, three years ago. Hasbro and Keller Brothers Circus. Disappeared after. Third-degree burns. Producer was Edward Kadesky.
- Conviction in New Jersey for reckless endangerment.
- Obsessed with fire.
- Manic. Referred to "Revered Audience."
- Performed dangerous tricks.
- Married to Marie Cosgrove, killed in fire.
  - He hasn't contacted her family since.
- Weir's parents dead, no next of kin.
- No VICAP or NCIC on Weir.
- Referred to himself as "Wizard of the North."
- Attacked Rhyme because he had to stop him before Sunday afternoon. (Next victim?)
- Eye color—brown.

- Psychological profile (per Terry Dobyns, NYPD): Revenge motivates him though he may not realize it. He wants to get even. Angry all the time. By killing he takes away some of the pain because of death of his wife, loss of ability to perform.

- Weir contacted assistants recently: John Keating and Arthur Loesser, in Nevada. Asking about the fire and people involved with it. Described Weir as crazed, overbearing, manic, dangerous, but brilliant.
  - Contacting former manager at time of fire, Edward Kadesky.

- Killed victims because of what they represented— possibly happy or traumatic moments before the fire.

- Gasoline-soaked handkerchief, not traceable.

- Ecco shoes, no trace.

Profile as Illusionist

- Perp will use misdirection against victims and in eluding police.
  - Physical misdirection (for distraction).
  - Psychological (to eliminate suspicion).

- Escape at music school was similar to Vanished Man illusion routine. Too common to trace.

- Perp is primarily an illusionist.

- Talented at sleight of hand.

- Also knows protean (quick change) magic. Will use breakaway clothes, nylon and silk, bald cap, finger cups and other latex appliances. Could be any age, gender or race.

- Calvert's death = Selbit's Cutting a Woman in Half Routine.

- Proficient at lock picking (possibly lock "scrubbing").

- Knows escapism techniques.

- Experience with animal illusions.

484 / Jeffery Deaver

- Used mentalism to get information on victim.

- Used sleight of hand to drug her.

- Tried to kill third victim with Houdini escape. Water Torture Cell.

- Ventriloquism.

- Razor blades.

- Familiar with Burning Mirror routine. Very dangerous, rarely performed now.

• • •

The man was stocky, of medium height. A silver beard and wavy hair to match.

Rhyme, now suspicious after Weir's visit last night, greeted Edward Kadesky then asked for identification.

"You don't mind," Sellitto continued, explaining that they'd recently had trouble with a perp masquerading as someone else.

Kadesky—a man not used to being unrecognized, let alone carded—was put out but he complied and offered Sellitto his Illinois driver's license. Mel Cooper took a subtle look at both the picture and the producer and then gave a nod to Rhyme. The tech had already gone on-line with Illinois DMV and gotten the license particulars and a picture of the man. All of which checked out.

"Your message said this was about Erick Weir?" Kadesky asked. His gaze was hawk-like and imperious.

"Right."

"So he's still alive?"

That the man would ask the question was a disappointment to Rhyme; it meant that Kadesky probably knew even less than they did.

Rhyme said, "Very much alive. He's a suspect in a series of homicides in town."

"No! Who did he kill?"

"Some local residents. A police officer too," Sellitto explained. "We were hoping you could give us some information that'd help find him."

"I haven't heard about him since just after the fire. Do you know about that?"

"A little," Sachs said. "Fill us in."

"He blamed me for it, you know. . . . It was three years ago. Weir and his assistants were doing the illusion and quick-change acts in our show. Oh, they were good. I mean, astonishing. But we'd been having complaints for months. From the staff *and* from the audience. Weir scared people. He was like a little dictator. And those assistants of his—we called them the Moonies. He had them indoctrinated. Illusion to him was like a religion. Sometimes people got hurt in rehearsal or during the show—even audience volunteers. And Weir couldn't've cared less. He thought magic worked best when there was some risk. He said magic should be a hot iron; it should brand your soul." The producer laughed grimly. "But we can't have that in the *entertainment* business, now, can we? So I talked to Sidney Keller—he was the owner—and we decided we had to fire him. One Sunday morning before the matinee I told the stage manager to let him go."

"That was the day of the fire?" Rhyme asked.

Kadesky nodded. "The manager found Weir rigging the stage with propane lines for an illusion of his. The Burning Mirror. He told him what we'd decided. But Weir lost it—he shoved the manager down the stairs and kept right on rigging the trick. I went down to the stage. He grabbed me. We weren't really fighting, just scuffling, but a propane line was loose. We fell into some metal chairs and, I guess, a spark ignited the gas. He was burned and his wife was killed. The whole tent was destroyed. We talked about suing him but he snuck out of the hospital and disappeared."

"We found a case in New Jersey. Reckless endangerment. Do you know if he was arrested anywhere else?" Rhyme asked.

"No idea." Kadesky shook his head. "I shouldn't've hired him. But if you'd ever seen his show, you'd understand. He was the best. The audiences may have been terrified, they may have been, well, abused, but they bought tickets to see him. And you should've heard the ovations." The producer looked at his watch. The time was 1:45. "You know, my show starts in fifteen minutes. . . . I think it'd be a good idea to get a few more police cars over there. With Weir around and everything that happened between us."

"Over where?" Rhyme asked.

"To my show." He nodded toward Central Park.

"That's *yours?* The Cirque Fantastique?"

"Right. I assumed you knew that. You had

the police car parked there. . . . You *do* know that Cirque Fantastique *is* the old Hasbro and Keller Brothers circus."

"What?" Sellitto asked.

Rhyme glanced at Kara, who was shaking her head. "Mr. Balzac never told me that when I called him last night."

"After the fire," Kadesky said, "we retooled. Cirque du Soleil was having so much success I recommended to Sid Keller that we do what they were. When we got the insurance money we started Fantastique."

"No, no, no, " Rhyme whispered, staring at the evidence charts.

"What, Linc?" Sellitto asked.

"*That's* what Weir's doing here," he announced. "Your show's his target. Cirque Fantastique."

"What?"

Scanning the evidence again. Applying facts to the premise.

Rhyme nodded. "Dogs!"

"What?" Sachs asked.

"Goddamn dogs! Look at the chart. Look at it! The animal hairs and Central Park dirt're from the dog knoll! Right outside the window." A fierce nod toward the front of his town house. "He wasn't checking out Cheryl Marston on the bridle path; he was checking out the *circus.* The newspaper, the one in his Mazda—look at that headline: 'Entertainment for Kids Young and Old.' Call up the paper—see if there's information about the circus in it. Thom—call Peter! Hurry."

The aide was good friends with a reporter for the *Times,* a young man who'd helped them occasionally in the past. He grabbed the phone and placed the call. Peter Hoddins worked the International desk but it took him less than a minute to find the answer. He relayed the information to Thom, who announced, "The circus was the feature of the story. All sorts of details—hours, acts, bios of the employees. Even a sidebar on security."

"Shit," Rhyme snapped. "He was doing his research. . . . And the press pass? That'd give him access to backstage." Rhyme was squinting as he looked at the evidence chart. "Yes! I get it now. The victims. What did they represent? Jobs in the circus. A makeup artist. A horseback rider. . . . And the first victim! Yes, she was a student but what was her *job?* Singing and entertaining kids—like a clown'd do."

"And the murder techniques themselves," Sachs pointed out. "They were all magic tricks."

"Yep. He's after your show. Terry Dobyns said his motive was ultimately revenge. Hell, he's planted a fuel bomb."

"My God," Kadesky said. "There're two thousand people there! And the show's starting in ten minutes."

At two in the *afternoon. . . .*

"The Sunday matinee," Rhyme added. "Just like in Ohio three years ago."

Sellitto grabbed his Motorola and called the officers stationed at the circus. There was no answer. The detective frowned and placed a call on Rhyme's speakerphone.

"Officer Koslowski here," the man answered a moment later.

Sellitto identified himself and barked, "Why isn't your radio on, Officer?"

"Radio? Well, we're off duty, Lieutenant."

"Off duty? You just went *on* duty."

"Well, Detective, we were told to stand down."

"You were *what?*"

"Some detective came by a half hour ago

and told us we weren't needed anymore. Said we could take the rest of the day off. I'm on my way to Rockaway Beach with my family. I can—"

"Describe him."

"Fifties. Beard, brown hair."

"Where'd he go?"

"No idea. Walked up to the car, flashed his shield and dismissed us."

Sellitto slammed the disconnect. "It's happening. . . . Oh, man, it's happening." He shouted to Sachs, "Call the Sixth, get the Bomb Squad there." Then he himself called Central and had Emergency Services and fire trucks sent to the circus.

Kadesky ran toward the door. "I'll evacuate the tent."

Bell said he was calling Emergency Medical Services and having burn teams established at Columbia Presbyterian.

"I want more soft-clothed in the park," Rhyme said. "A lot of them. I have a feeling the Conjurer's going to be there."

"Be there?" Sellitto asked.

"To watch the fire. He'll be close. I remember his eyes when he was looking at the flames in my room. He likes to watch fire. No, he wouldn't miss this for the world."

Chapter Thirty

He wasn't worried so much about the fire itself.

As Edward Kadesky sprinted the short distance from Lincoln Rhyme's apartment to the tent of the Cirque Fantastique he was thinking that with new codes and fire retardants, even the worst theater and circus tent fires proceed fairly slowly. No, the real danger is the panic, the tons of human muscles, the stampede that tramples and tears and crushes and suffocates. Bones broken, lungs burst, asphyxiation . . .

Saving people in a circus disaster means getting them out of the facility without panic. Traditionally, to alert the clowns and acrobats and other hands that a fire has broken out the ringmaster would send a subtle signal to the bandleader, who then launched into the energetic John Philip Sousa march, "Stars and Stripes Forever." The workers were supposed to take up emergency stations and calmly lead the audience through designated exits (those employees who didn't simply, of course, abandon ship themselves).

The tune had been replaced over the years by far more efficient procedures for the evacuation of a circus tent. But if a gas bomb detonated, spreading burning liquid everywhere?

The crowd would sprint to the exits and a thousand people would die in the crush.

Edward Kadesky ran into the tent and saw twenty-six hundred people eagerly awaiting the opening of his show.

His show.

That was what he thought. The show *he'd* created. Kadesky had been a hawker in sideshows, a curtain bitch at second-tier theaters in third-tier cities, a payroll manager and ticket seller in sweaty regional circuses. He'd struggled for years to bring to the public shows that transcended the tawdry side of the business, the carny aspect of circuses. He'd done it once, with the Hasbro and Keller Brothers show—which

Erick Weir had destroyed. Then he'd done it again with Cirque Fantastique, a world-renowned show that brought legitimacy, even prestige, to a profession that was so often disparaged by those who attended theater and opera, and ignored by those who watched E! and MTV.

Remembering the wave of searing heat from the Hasbro tent fire in Ohio. The flecks of ash like deadly, gray snow. The howl of the flames—the astonishing noise—as his show had lumbered to its death right in front of him.

There was one difference, though: three years ago the tent had been empty. Today thousands of men, women and children would be in the middle of the conflagration.

Kadesky's assistant, Katherine Tunney, a young brunette who'd risen high in the Disney theme park organization before coming to work with him, noticed his troubled gaze and instantly joined him. That was one of Katherine's big talents: sensing his thoughts almost telepathically. "What?" she whispered.

He told her what he'd learned from Lincoln Rhyme and the police. Her eyes began to sweep the circus tent, just like his, looking both for the bomb and at the victims.

"How do we handle it?" she asked tersely.

He considered this for a moment then gave her instructions. He added, "Then you leave. Get out."

"But are you staying? What are—?"

"Do it now," he said firmly. Then squeezed her hand. In a softer voice he added, "I'll meet you outside. It'll be okay."

She wanted to embrace him, he sensed. But his glance told her no. They were in view of most of the seats here; he didn't want anyone in the audience to think even for a moment that something was wrong. "Walk slowly. Keep smiling. We're performers before anything else, remember."

Katherine nodded and went first to the lighting man and then to the bandleader to deliver Kadesky's instructions. Finally she took up a position beside the main doorway.

Straightening his tie and buttoning his jacket, Kadesky glanced at the orchestra, nodded. A drum roll began.

Showtime, he thought.

As he strode, smiling broadly, into the middle of the ring the audience began to fall silent. He stopped in the direct center of the circle and the drum roll ceased. A moment later two fingers of white illumination targeted him. Though he'd told Katherine to have the lighting man hit him with the main spots he still gave a brief gasp, thinking for an instant that the brilliant lights were from the detonating gas bomb.

But his smile never wavered and he recovered instantly. He lifted a cordless microphone to his lips and began to speak. "Good afternoon, ladies and gentlemen, welcome to the Cirque Fantastique." Calm, pleasant, commanding. "We have a wonderful show for you today. And to begin I'm going to ask your indulgence. I'm afraid we're going to inconvenience you a bit but I think the effort will be well worth it. We have a special performance outside the tent. I apologize. . . . We tried to get the Plaza Hotel inside here but their management wouldn't let us. Something about the guests not agreeing."

A pause for the laughter.

"So I'm going to ask you to hold on to your ticket stubs and step outside into Central Park."

The crowd began murmuring, wondering what the act might be.

He smiled. "Find space anywhere nearby. If you can see the buildings on Central Park South you'll be able to watch the act just fine."

Laughter and excitement now in the seats. What could he mean? Were daredevils doing high-wire acts on the skyscrapers?

"Now, lower rows first, in an orderly manner, if you please. Use whatever exit is near you."

The houselights went up. He saw Katherine Tunney standing at the door, smiling and motioning people to leave. Please, he thought to her, get out. Leave!

The audience was chatting loudly as they rose—he could vaguely see them through the blinding lights. They were looking at their companions, wondering who should be the first to leave. Which way to go. Then they began to gather children, collecting purses and popcorn containers, checking for their ticket stubs.

Kadesky smiled as he watched them rise and amble toward the exits to safety. But he was thinking:

Chicago, Illinois, December 1903. At a

matinee performance of Eddie Foy's famous vaudeville routine at the Iroquois Theater a spotlight started a fire that quickly spread from the stage to the seats. The two thousand people inside raced to the exits, jamming them closed so completely that firemen couldn't get through the doors. More than six hundred in the audience died horrible deaths.

Hartford, Connecticut, July 1944. Another matinee. At the Ringling Brothers and Barnum & Bailey circus, just as the famous Wallenda family was starting its renowned high-wire act, a small fire started in the southeast side of the tent and soon devoured the canvas—which had been waterproofed with gasoline and paraffin. Within minutes more than one hundred fifty people had been burned, suffocated or crushed to death.

Chicago, Hartford, so many other cities too. Thousands of terrible deaths in theater and circus fires over the years. Was that going to happen here? Is that how the Cirque Fantastique, how *his* show would be remembered?

The tent was emptying smoothly. Yet, the price of avoiding panic was a slow exit.

There were still many people inside. And some, it seemed, remained in their seats, preferring to stay inside and miss the spectacle in the park. When most people had left he'd have to tell them what was really going on.

When was the bomb set to go off? Probably not right away. Weir would give the latecomers a chance to arrive and take their seats—to cause the most injuries. It was now 2:10. Maybe he'd set it for an even time: quarter past or 2:30.

And where was it?

He had no clue where one might leave a bomb so that it would do the most damage.

Glancing across the tent to the crowd massing at the front doorway he saw Katherine's silhouette—the woman's arm beckoning to him to leave.

But he was staying. He'd do whatever was necessary to evacuate the tent, including taking people by the hand and leading them to the door, pushing them out if he needed to and returning for more—even if the tent was falling in sheets of fire around him. He was going to be the last person out.

Smiling broadly, he shook his head to her and then lifted the microphone and continued to tell the audience what a delightful act awaited them outside. Suddenly loud music interrupted him. He glanced at the bandstand. The musicians had left—as Kadesky had ordered—but the bandleader stood over the computer console that controlled the prerecorded music they sometimes used. Their eyes met and Kadesky nodded in approval. The leader, a veteran of circus life, had put on a tape and turned the volume up. The tune was "The Stars and Stripes Forever."

Amelia Sachs pushed through the crowds exiting the Cirque Fantastique and ran into the center of the tent, where marching music was blaring loudly and Edward Kadesky was holding a microphone and enthusiastically urging everyone outside to see a special illusion—to avoid panic, she assumed.

Brilliant idea, she thought, picturing the horrific crush if this many people raced for the exits.

Sachs was the first officer to arrive—approaching sirens told her other rescue workers would be here soon—but she didn't wait for anyone else; she began the search immediately. She looked around, trying to decide the best place to leave a fuel bomb. To cause the most fatalities, she supposed, he'd plant it under some bleachers, near an exit.

The device—or devices—would be bulky. Unlike dynamite or plastic explosives, fuel bombs must be large to do significant damage. They could be hidden in a shipping container or a large cardboard box. Maybe in an oil drum. She noticed a plastic trash container—a big one, which would hold about fifty gallons, she guessed. It was just to the side of the main exit and dozens of people were walking slowly past it on their way outside. There were twenty or twenty-five such bins inside the tent. The dark green containers would be the perfect choice to hide bombs.

She ran to the one nearest her and paused at the drum. She was unable to see inside—the lid was in an inverted V-shape with a swinging door—but Sachs knew the door wouldn't be rigged to trigger the detonator; the brass told them he was using a timer. She took a small flashlight from her back pocket and shone it into the messy, foul-smelling interior. The bin was already more than half full of paper and food wrappers and empty cups; she couldn't see the bottom. She shifted the drum slightly; it was too light to hold even a gallon of gasoline.

Another glance around the tent. Still hundreds of people inside, heading slowly for the doors.

And dozens of other trash bins to check out. She started for the next one.

Then she stopped and squinted. Under the main bleachers and right near the south exit of the tent was an object about four feet square, covered by a black tarp. She thought immediately about Weir's trick of using a cloth to hide himself. Whatever was under the cloth was virtually invisible and was big enough to hold hundreds of gallons of gas.

A large crowd was within twenty feet of it.

Outside, sirens grew louder and then began to go silent as the emergency vehicles parked near the tent. Firemen and police officers began to enter. She flashed her shield to the one nearest her. "Bomb Squad here yet?"

"Should be five, six minutes."

She nodded and told them to carefully

check the trash drums then she started toward the tarp-covered box.

And then it happened.

Not the bomb itself. But the panic, which seemed to erupt as fast as a detonation.

Sachs wasn't sure what prompted it—the sight of the emergency vehicles outside and the firemen pushing their way inside probably made some patrons uneasy. Then Sachs heard a series of pops at the main doorway. She recognized the sound from yesterday: the snapping of the huge commedia dell'arte Harlequin banner in the wind. But the audience at that exit must've thought they were gunshots and turned back, panicked, looking for other exits. Suddenly the tent filled with a huge collective voice, like the inhalation of a breath in fear. A deep rustling, a roar.

Then the wave broke.

Screaming and crying out, people stampeded for the doors. Sachs was slammed from behind by the terrified mass. Her cheekbone struck the shoulder of a man in front of her, leaving her stunned. Screams rose, snatches of howls and shouts about fire, about bombs, about terrorists.

"Don't push!" she cried. But no one heard

her words. It would be impossible to stop the tide anyway. A thousand individuals had become a single entity. Some people tried to fend off its crushing body but in the surge from behind they were pressed into it and became part of the beast, which lurched desperately toward the glare of the opening.

Sachs wrenched her arm free from between two teenage boys, their ruddy faces long with fear. Her head was slammed forward and she glimpsed some tattered flesh on the tent floor. She gasped, thinking a child was being trampled. But no, it was a shredded balloon. A baby's bottle, a scrap of green cloth, popcorn, a souvenir Harlequin mask, a Discman were being ground apart under the massive weight of the feet. If anyone was to fall they'd die in seconds. Sachs herself felt no balance or control; it seemed she could tumble helplessly to the floor at any moment.

Then her feet were actually lifted off the floor, sandwiched between two sweating bodies—a big man in a bloody Izod shirt, holding a sobbing young boy above his head, and a woman who seemed to have passed out. The screams grew louder, children's and adults' mixed, and fueled the panic. Heat enveloped her and soon it was nearly impossible to breathe. The pressure on her chest threatened to crush her heart to silence. Claustrophobia—Amelia Sachs's one big fear—now wrapped its tight arms around her and she felt herself swallowed up by an unbearable sensation of confinement.

When you move they can't getcha . . .

But she wasn't moving anywhere. She was held tight by a suffocating mass of powerful, damp bodies, not even human now, a collection of muscles and sweat and fists and spit and feet pressing harder and harder into itself.

Please, no! Please, let me move! Let me get one hand free. Let me take one breath of air.

She thought she saw blood. She thought she saw torn flesh.

Maybe they were hers.

From terror as much as from the pain and the suffocation, Amelia Sachs felt herself start to black out.

No! Don't fall under their feet. Don't fall! Please!

She couldn't breathe. Not a cubic inch of air entered her lungs. Then she saw a knee inches from her face. It slammed into her cheek and stayed rooted there. She could smell dirty jeans, saw a scuffed boot in front of her eyes, inches away.

Please don't let me fall!

Then she realized that maybe she already had.

Chapter Thirty-one

Wearing a bellhop's uniform that closely matched those worn by the staff at the Lanham Arms Hotel, on the Upper East Side of Manhattan, Malerick walked along the fifteenth-floor hallway of the hotel. He carried a heavy room service tray on which was a domed plate cover and a vase containing a huge red tulip.

Everything about him was in harmony with his surroundings so as not to arouse suspicion. Malerick himself was the model of a deferential, pleasant bellhop. The averted eyes, the half smile, the unobtrusive walk, the spotless tray.

Only one thing set him apart from the other bellhops here at the Lanham: under the metal warming dome on the tray was not a plate of eggs Benedict or a club sandwich but a loaded Beretta automatic pistol, equipped with a sausage-thick sound suppressor, and a leather pouch of lock picking and other tools.

"Enjoying your stay?" he asked one couple.

Yes, they were, and they wished him a good afternoon.

He continued to nod and smile at the guests returning to their rooms after Sunday brunch or on their way to sightsee on this fine spring afternoon.

He passed a window, in which he could see a bit of green—a portion of Central Park. He wondered what sort of excitement was unfolding there at the moment, inside the white tent of the Cirque Fantastique— the place to which he'd spent the past few days directing the police with the clues he'd left at the sites of the murders.

Or *mis*directing them, he should say.

Misdirection and ruse were the keys to successful illusion and there was no one better at it than Malerick, the man of a million faces, the man who materialized like a struck match, who disappeared like a snuffed flame.

The man who vanished himself.

The police would be frantic, of course, looking for the gasoline bomb, which they believed would go off at any moment. But there was no bomb, no risk at all to the two thousand people at the Cirque Fantastique (no risk other than the possibility that some of them would be trampled to death in their mindless panic).

At the end of the hallway Malerick glanced behind him and observed that he was alone. Quickly he set the tray on the floor near a doorway and lifted the cover. He collected the black pistol and slipped it into a zippered pocket in his bellman's uniform. He opened the leather tool pouch, extracted a screwdriver and pocketed the pouch too.

Moving fast, he unscrewed the metal guard that allowed the window to open only a few inches (human beings *do* seem to take any opportunity to kill themselves, don't they? he reflected) and raised the window all the way. He carefully replaced the screwdriver in its spot in the leather pouch and zipped it away. His strong arms deftly boosted him onto the sill. He stepped carefully out on the ledge, 150 feet above the ground.

The ledge was twenty inches wide—he'd measured the same ledge from the window of the room he'd taken here a few days ago—and though he'd only done limited acrobatics in his life, he had the superb balance of all great illusionists. He moved along the limestone rim now as comfortably as if it were a sidewalk. After a stroll of only fifteen feet he came to the corner of the hotel and stopped, looking at the building next door to the Lanham Arms.

This, an apartment building on East Seventy-fifth Street, had no ledges but did have a fire escape, six feet away from where he now stood—overlooking an air shaft filled with the restless churning of air conditioners. Malerick took a brief running start and leaped over the bottomless gap, easily reaching the fire escape and vaulting over the railing.

He climbed up two flights and paused at a window on the seventeenth floor. A glance inside. The hallway was empty. He placed the gun and the tool kit on the window ledge then stripped off the fake bellhop's uniform in one fast peel, revealing beneath it a simple gray suit, white shirt and tie. The gun went into his belt and he used the tools again to open the window lock. He hopped inside.

Standing motionless, catching his breath. Malerick then started down the hallway toward the apartment he sought. Stopping at the door, he dropped to his knees and opened the tool kit again. Into the keyhole he inserted a tension bar and above it the lock pick. In three seconds he'd scrubbed the lock open. In five, the deadbolt. He pushed the door open only far enough to be able to see the hinges, which he sprayed with oil from a tiny canister, like breath spray, to keep them silent. A moment later he was inside the long, dark hallway of the apartment. Malerick eased the door shut.

He oriented himself, looking around the entryway.

On the wall were some mass-produced prints of Salvador Dalí's surreal landscapes, some family portraits and, most prominently, a clumsy watercolor of New York City painted by a child (the artist's signature was "Chrissy"). A cheap table sat near the door, its short leg lengthened with a folded yellow square of foolscap legal paper. A single ski, the binding broken, leaned forlornly in the corner of the hallway. The wallpaper was old and stained.

Malerick started down the corridor, toward the sound of the television in the living room, but he detoured momentarily, stepping into a small dark room that was dominated by an ebony Kawai baby grand piano. A book of music, instructions noted in the margin, sat open on the piano. The name "Chrissy" appeared here too— penned on the cover of the book. Malerick only had a rudimentary knowledge of music but as he flipped through the lesson book he observed that the pieces seemed quite difficult.

He decided that the girl might've been a bad artist but she was quite the talented young musician—this Christine Grady, the daughter of New York assistant district attorney Charles Grady.

The man whose apartment this was. The man Malerick was being paid one hundred thousand dollars to kill.

Amelia Sachs sat on the grass outside of the Cirque Fantastique tent, wincing from the pain throbbing around her right kidney.

She'd helped dozens of people away from the crush and had found a spot here to catch her breath.

Staring down at her from the huge black-and-white banner above her head was the masked Arlecchino, still rippling loudly in the wind. He'd seemed eerie yesterday; now, after the panic inside—which he'd caused—the image was repulsive and grotesque.

She had avoided being trampled to death; the knee and boot that'd clobbered her belonged to a man who'd scrabbled over the heads and shoulders of the audience to beat them out the door. Still, her back, ribs and face throbbed. She'd sat here for nearly fifteen minutes, faint and nauseated, partly from the crush, partly from the horrifying claustrophobia. She could generally tolerate small rooms, even elevators. Being completely restrained, unable to move, though, physically sickened her and racked her with panic.

Around her the injured were being treated. There'd been nothing serious, the EMS chief had reported to her—mostly sprains and cuts. A few dislocations and a broken arm.

Sachs and those around her had been spewed out the south exit of the tent. Once outside, she'd fallen to her knees on the grass, crawling away from the crowd. No longer trapped in an enclosed space with a potential bomb or an armed terrorist, the audience became better Samaritans and helped those who were woozy or hurt.

She'd flagged down an officer from the Bomb Squad and, looking at him upside down from her grassy bed, flashed her badge and told him about the tarp-covered object under the seats near the south door. He'd returned to his colleagues inside.

Then the brassy music from the tent had stopped and Edward Kadesky stepped outside.

Watching the Bomb Squad at work, some of the audience realized that there'd been a real threat and that Kadesky's quick thinking had saved them from a worse panic; they offered some impromptu applause, which he'd acknowledged modestly as he made the rounds, checking on his employees and the audience. Other circusgoers— injured and otherwise—were less generous and scowled and demanded to know what had happened and complained that he should have handled the evacuation better.

Meanwhile the Bomb Squad and a dozen firemen had scoured the tent and found no sign of a device. The tarp-covered box had turned out to be cartons of toilet paper. The search expanded to the trailers and supply trucks but the officers found nothing there either.

Sachs frowned. They'd been wrong? How could that be? she wondered. The evidence was so clear. It was Rhyme's way to make bold assumptions about evidence and sometimes, sure, he made mistakes. But in the case of the Conjurer it seemed that all the evidence had come together and pointed directly to the Cirque Fantastique as his target.

Had Rhyme heard that they'd found no bombs? she wondered. Rising unsteadily, she went off in search of someone's radio to borrow; her Motorola, now lying in pieces near the south door of the tent, had apparently been the sole fatality of the panic.

Stepping quietly out of the music room in Charles Grady's apartment, Malerick walked back into the darkened hallway and paused, listening to the voices from the living room and kitchen.

Wondering just how dangerous this would be.

He'd taken steps to make it less likely that Grady's bodyguards would panic and gun him down. At his lunch at the Riverside Inn in Bedford Junction two weeks ago, meeting with Jeddy Barnes and other militiamen from upstate New York, Malerick had laid out his plan. He'd decided it'd be best to have someone make an attempt on the prosecutor's life *before* Malerick's invasion of Grady's apartment today. The universal choice for a fall guy was some pervert of a minister from Canton Falls named Ralph Swensen. (Barnes had some leverage on the reverend but explained to Malerick that he hadn't fully trusted him. So after his escape from the Harlem River yesterday the illusionist had donned his janitor's costume and had followed the reverend from his fleabag hotel to Greenwich Village—just to make sure the loser didn't balk at the last minute.)

Malerick's plan called for Swensen's attempt to fail (the gun Barnes provided had a broken firing pin). Malerick had theorized that catching one assassin would lull Grady's guards into complacency and make them psychologically less likely to react violently when they saw a second killer.

Well, that was the theory, he reflected uneasily. Let's see if it holds up in practice.

Walking silently past more bad art, past more family portraits, past stacks of magazines—law reviews and *Vogues* and *The New Yorkers*—and scabby street-fair antiques the Gradys had bought intending to refinish but that sat as permanent testimonials to the proposition there just aren't enough hours in the day.

Malerick knew his way around the apartment; he'd been here once before briefly—disguised as a maintenance man—but that had been basic reconnaissance, learning the layout, the entrance and escape routes. He hadn't spent any time noticing the personal side of the family's life: the diplomas of Grady and his wife, who was also an attorney. Wedding photos. Snapshots of relatives and a gallery's worth of pictures of their blonde nine-year-old daughter.

Malerick recalled his meeting with Barnes and his associates over lunch. The militiamen had digressed into a cold debate about whether it made sense to kill Grady's wife and daughter too. According to Malerick's plan, sacrificing Swensen made sense. But what was the point, he'd wondered, of killing Grady's family? He'd posed this question to Barnes and the others between bites of very good roast turkey.

"Well now, Mr. Weir," Jeddy Barnes had said to Malerick. "That's a good question. I'd say you should kill 'em just because."

And Malerick had nodded, offering a thoughtful expression; he knew enough never to condescend to either an audience or fellow performers. "Well, I don't *mind* killing them," he'd explained. "But wouldn't it make more sense to leave them alive unless they're a risk—like a risk they could identify me? Or, say, the little girl goes for the phone to call the police? Probably there are *some* of your people who'd object to killing women and children."

"Well, it's your plan, Mr. Weir," Barnes had said. "We'll go with what you think." Though the idea of temperance seemed to leave him vaguely dissatisfied.

Now Malerick stopped outside Grady's living room and hung a fake NYPD badge around his neck, the one he'd flashed at the cops near the Cirque Fantastique when he'd sent them home for the day. He glanced in a flea-market mirror whose surface needed to be recoated.

Yes, he was in role, looking just like a detective here to protect a prosecutor against whom vicious death threats had been made.

A deep breath. No butterflies.

And now, Revered Audience, lights up, curtain up.

The real show is about to begin. . . .

Hands held naturally at his sides, Malerick turned the corner of the corridor and strode into the living room.

Chapter Thirty-two

"Hey, how's it going?" the man in the gray suit asked, startling Luis Martinez, the quiet, bulky detective working for Roland Bell.

The guard was sitting on the couch in front of the TV, a Sunday *New York Times* in his lap. "Man, surprised me." He nodded a greeting, glanced at the newcomer's badge and ID and then scanned his face. "You the relief?"

"That's right."

"How'd you get in? They give you a key?"

"Got one downtown." He was speaking in a throaty whisper, like he had a cold.

"Lucky you," Luis muttered. "We've gotta share one. Pain in the ass."

"Where's Mr. Grady?"

"In the kitchen. With his wife and Chrissy. How come you're early?"

"I dunno," the man replied. "I'm just the hired help. This's the time they told me."

"Story of our lives, huh?" Luis said. He frowned. "I don't think I know you."

"Name's Joe David," the man said. "Usually work over in Brooklyn."

Luis nodded. "Yeah, that's where I cut my teeth, the Seventy."

"This is my first rotation here. Bodyguard detail, I mean."

A loud commercial came on the TV.

"Sorry," Luis said. "I missed that. Your first rotation, you said?"

"Right."

The big detective said, "Okay, how 'bout your last too?" Luis dropped the newspaper and leaped up from the couch, drawing his Glock smoothly and pointing it at the man he knew was Erick Weir. Normally placid, Luis now shouted into his microphone, "He's *here*! He got in—in the living room!"

Two other officers who'd been waiting in the kitchen—Detective Bell and that fat lieutenant, Lon Sellitto—shoved through another doorway, both with astonished looks on their faces. They grabbed Weir's arms and pulled a silenced pistol from his belt.

"Down, now, now, now!" Sellitto shouted in a raw, edgy voice, his gun pressed into the man's face. And what an expression was on it! Luis thought. He'd seen a lot of surprised perps over the years. But this guy took the prize. He was gasping, couldn't speak. But Luis supposed he wasn't any more surprised than the cops were.

"Where the hell d'he come from?" Sellitto asked breathlessly. Bell only shook his head in dismay.

As Luis double-cuffed Weir roughly, Sellitto leaned close to the perp. "You alone? You got backup outside?"

"No."

"Don't bullshit us!"

"My arms, you're hurting my arms!" Weir gasped.

"Anybody else with you?"

"No, no, I swear."

Bell was calling the others on his handy-talkie. "Heaven help me—he got inside. . . . I don't know how."

Two uniformed officers assigned to the Saving the Witness's Ass Team hurried into the apartment from the hallway, where they'd been hiding near the elevator. "Looks like he jimmied the window on this floor," one of them said. "You know, the window at the fire escape."

Bell glanced at Weir and he understood. "The ledge from the Lanham? You jumped?"

Weir said nothing but that had to be the answer. They'd stationed officers in the alley between the Lanham and Grady's building and on the roofs of both structures too. But it had never occurred to them he'd walk along the ledge and leap over the air shaft.

Bell asked the officers, "And no sign of anybody else?"

"Nope. Looks like he was solo."

Sellitto donned latex gloves and patted him down. The search yielded burglary tools and various props and magic supplies. The oddest were the fake fingertips, glued on tightly. Sellitto pulled them off and deposited them in a plastic evidence bag. If the situation weren't so unnerving—that a hired killer had actually gotten into the apartment of the family they were protecting—the image of the ten finger pads in a bag would've been comical.

They looked over their prey as Sellitto continued to search him. Weir was muscular and in excellent shape, despite the fact

that the fire had caused some serious damage—the scarring was quite extensive.

"Any ID?" Bell asked.

Sellitto shook his head. "F.A.O. Schwarz."
Meaning low-quality fake NYPD badge and
ID card. Not much better than toys.

Weir glanced toward the kitchen, which
he could see was empty. He frowned.

"Oh, the Gradys aren't here," Bell said, as
if it were obvious.

The man closed his eyes and rested his
head on the threadbare carpet. "How? How
did you figure it out?"

Sellitto supplied an answer of sorts. "Well,
guess what? There's somebody who'd love
to answer that question for you. Come on,
we're going for a ride."

Looking over the shackled killer standing in
the doorway of the lab, Lincoln Rhyme said,
"Welcome back."

"But . . . the fire." Dismayed, the man
looked toward the stairway that led up to
the bedroom.

"Sorry we ruined your performance,"
Rhyme said coldly. "I guess you couldn't

quite escape from me after all, could you, Weir?"

He turned his gaze back to the criminalist and hissed, "That's not my name anymore."

"You changed it?"

Weir shook his head. "Not legally. But Weir's who I *used* to be. I go by something else now."

Rhyme recalled psychologist Terry Dobyns's observation that the fire had "murdered" Weir's old persona and he'd become somebody else.

The killer now looked over Rhyme's body. "You understand that, don't you? *You'd* like to forget the past and become somebody else too, I'd imagine."

"What *are* you calling yourself?"

"That's between me and my audience."

Ah, yes, his revered audience.

Double-handcuffed, looking bewildered and diminished, Weir wore a gray businessman's suit. The wig he'd worn last night was gone; his real hair was thick, long and dark blond. In the daylight Rhyme could better see the scarring above his collar; it looked quite severe.

"How'd you find me?" the man asked in his wheezing voice. "I led you to . . ."

"To the Cirque Fantastique? You did." When Rhyme had out-thought a perp his mood improved considerably and he was pleased to chat. "You mean you *misdirected* us there. See, I was looking over the evidence and I got to thinking that the whole case seemed a bit too easy."

"Easy?" He coughed briefly.

"In crime scene work there're two types of evidence. There're the clues that are inadvertently left by the perp and then there are *planted* clues, ones that are intentionally left to mislead us.

"After everyone ran off to look for gas bombs at the circus I got this sense that some of the clues had been planted. They seemed obvious—the shoes you left at the second victim's apartment had dog hairs and dirt and trace that led to Central Park. It occurred to me that a smart perp might've ground the dirt and hairs into the shoes and left them at the scene so we'd find them and think about the dog knoll next to the circus. And all the talk of fire when you came to see me last night." He glanced toward Kara. "Verbal misdirection, right, Kara?"

Weir's troubled eyes looked the young woman up and down.

"Yep," she said, pouring sugar in her coffee.

"But I tried to kill you," Weir wheezed. "If I'd told you those things to lead you off I'd need you to be alive."

Rhyme laughed. "You didn't try to kill me at all. You never intended to. You wanted to make it look that way to give what you told me credibility. The first thing you did after you set the fire in my bedroom was to run outside and call nine-one-one from a pay phone. I checked with dispatch. The man who called said he could see the flames from the phone kiosk. Except that it was around the corner. You can't see my room from there. Thom checked on that, by the way. Thank you, Thom," Rhyme called to the aide, who happened to be passing the doorway at that moment.

"*Nada*," came the harried reply.

Weir closed his eyes, shaking his head as he realized the depth of his mistake.

Rhyme squinted, staring at the evidence board. "All of the victims had jobs or inter-ests reflecting performers in the circus—the musician, makeup artist, horseback riding. And the murder techniques were magic tricks too. But if your motive really was to destroy Kadesky you would've led us *away* from Cirque Fantastique, not toward it. That meant you were leading us away from something else. What? I looked at the evidence again. At the third scene, by the river, we surprised you—you didn't have time to pick up your jacket with the press pass and hotel key card in the pocket, which meant that those couldn't've been planted clues. They had some legitimate connection to what you were really up to.

"The hotel card key was from one of three hotels—one of them was the Lanham Arms—Detective Bell thought it sounded familiar and checked his logbook. It turned out that he had coffee with Charles Grady in the lobby bar to talk about the security detail for his family a week ago. Roland told me that the Lanham was right next door to Grady's apartment. Then the press pass? I called the reporter you stole it from. He was covering the Andrew Constable trial and had interviewed Charles Grady several times. . . . We found some brass shavings and assumed the worst, that they were from a bomb timer. But they might've just come from a key or a tool."

Sachs took up the narrative. "Then *The*

New York Times page we found in your car in the river? It had an article about the circus, yes. But there was also an article about Constable's trial."

A nod toward the evidence board.

MILITIA MURDER PLOT
TRIAL OPENS MONDAY

Rhyme continued, "The restaurant check too. You should've thrown that out."

"What check?" Weir asked, frowning.

"Also in your jacket. From two Saturdays ago."

"But that weekend I was—" He stopped speaking abruptly.

"Out of town, you were going to say?" Sachs asked. "Yeah, we know. The check was from a restaurant in Bedford Junction."

"I don't know what you're talking about."

"A trooper in Canton Falls investigating the Patriot Assembly group called on my phone, asking for Roland," Rhyme said. "I recognized the area code from the caller-ID—it was the same as the number of the restaurant on the check."

Weir's eyes grew still and Rhyme continued, "Bedford Junction turns out to be the town next to Canton Falls, which's where Constable lives."

"Who's this Constable you keep talking about?" he asked quickly. But Rhyme could see telltale signs of recognition in his face.

Sellitto took over. "Was Barnes one of the people you had lunch with? Jeddy Barnes?"

"I don't know who you mean."

"You know the Patriot Assembly though?"

"Just what I've read about in the paper."

"We don't believe you," Sellitto said.

"Believe what you like," Weir snapped. Rhyme could see the fierce anger in the eyes, the anger that Dobyns had predicted. After a pause he asked, "How'd you find out my real name?"

No one answered but Weir's eyes settled on the latest additions about him on the evidence chart. His face grew dark as he gasped, "Somebody betrayed me, didn't they? They told you about the fire and Kadesky. Who was it?" A vicious smile as he glanced from Sachs to Kara and finally settled on Rhyme. "Was it John Keating? He told you that I called him, didn't he? Spineless shit. He never stood up to me. Art Loesser too, right? They're all fucking Judases. I'll remember them. I always remember the people who betray me." He had a coughing fit. When it ended Weir was looking across the room. "Kara. . . . Is that what he said your name is? And who are you?"

"I'm an illusionist," she said defiantly.

"One of us," Weir mocked, looking her up and down. "A girl illusionist. And you're, what? A consultant or something? Maybe after I'm released I'll come visit. Maybe I'll vanish you."

Sachs snapped, "Oh, you ain't getting released in this lifetime, Weir."

The Conjurer's gasping laugh was chilly. "Then how about when I escape? Walls are, after all, just an illusion."

"I don't think escape's much of an option either," Sellitto added.

Rhyme said, "Well, I answered your 'how,' Weir. Or whatever you're calling yourself. How 'bout if you answer my 'why'? We thought it was revenge against Kadesky. But then it turns out you're after Grady. What are you? Some kind of hit-man illusionist?"

"Revenge?" Weir asked, furious. "What the fuck good is revenge? Will it take the scars away and fix my lungs? Will it bring

my wife back? . . . You don't fucking understand! The only thing in my life, the only
thing that's *ever* meant anything to me is
performing. Illusion, magic. My mentor
groomed me for the profession all my life.
The fire took that away from me. I don't
have the strength to perform. My hand's deformed. My voice is ruined. Who'd come to
see me? I can't do the one thing that God
gave me talent for. If the only way I can perform is to break the law, then that's what
I'll do."

Phantom of the Opera syndrome . . .

He glanced at Rhyme's body again. "How
did *you* feel after your accident, thinking
you'd never be a cop again?"

Rhyme was silent. But the killer's words
hit home. How had he felt? The same anger
that fueled Erick Weir, yes. And, true, after
the accident the concepts of right and
wrong vanished completely. Why not be a
criminal? he'd thought in the madness of
fury and depression. I can find evidence
better than any human being on the face of
the earth. That means I can also manipulate
it. I could commit the perfect crime. . . .

In the end, of course, thanks to people
like Terry Dobyns and other doctors and fel-

low cops and his own soul, those thoughts had faded. But, yes, he did know exactly what Weir was talking about. Though even at the bleakest and angriest moments he never considered taking another life—except, of course, his own.

"So you sold your talents like a mercenary?"

Weir seemed to realize that he'd lost control for a moment and had said too much. He refused to say anything else.

Sachs's anger got the better of her and she stepped to the whiteboard and ripped down several pictures of the first two victims. Shoving them into Weir's face, she raged, "You killed these people just for diversion? That's all they meant to you."

Weir held her eye, blasé. Then he looked around and laughed. "You really think you can keep me in prison? Do you know that, for a challenge, Harry Houdini was stripped naked and put in death row in Washington D.C. He escaped from his cell so fast that he had time to open *all* the doors on the cellblock and switch the condemned prisoners to each other's cells—before the challenge panel got back from lunch."

Sellitto said, "Yeah, well that was a long

time ago. We're a little more sophisticated than that now." To Rhyme and Sachs he said, "I'll take him downtown, see if he wants to share a little more with us."

But as they started for the doorway Rhyme said, "Hold on." His eyes were on the evidence chart.

"What?" Sellitto asked.

"When he got away from Larry Burke after the crafts fair he slipped the cuffs."

"Right."

"We found saliva, remember? Take a look in his mouth. See if he's got a pick or key hidden there."

Weir said, "I don't. Really."

Sellitto pulled on the latex gloves that Mel Cooper offered. "Open up. You bite me and I'll vanish your balls. Got it? One bite, no balls."

"Understood." The Conjurer opened his mouth and Sellitto shined his flashlight into it, fished around a bit. "Nothing."

Rhyme said, "There's another place we ought to check too."

Sellitto grunted. "I'll make sure they do *that* downtown, Linc. Some things I do not do for the money they pay me."

As the detective led Weir toward the door

Kara said, "Wait. Check his teeth. Wiggle them. Especially the molars."

Weir stiffened as Sellitto approached. "You can't do that."

"Open up," the big detective snapped. "Oh, and the balls comment still applies."

The Conjurer sighed. "Right top molar. Right on my side, I mean."

Sellitto glanced at Rhyme then reached in and gently pulled. His hand emerged with a fake tooth. Inside was a small piece of bent metal. He dumped it on an examining board and replaced the tooth.

The detective said, "It's pretty small. He can actually use that?"

Kara examined it. "Oh, he could open a pair of regulation handcuffs in about four seconds with that."

"You're too much, Weir. Come on."

Rhyme thought of something. "Oh, Lon?" The detective glanced his way. "You have a feeling when he helped us find the pick in his tooth that might've been a little misdirection?"

Kara nodded. "You're right."

Weir looked disgusted as Sellitto searched again. This time the detective checked every tooth. He found a second lock pick in a similar fake tooth on the lower left jaw.

"I'm gonna make sure they put you some-place real special," the detective said omi-nously. He then called another officer into the room and had him shackle Weir's feet with two sets of cuffs.

"I can't walk this way," Weir complained in a wheeze.

"Baby steps," Sellitto said coldly. "Take baby steps."

Chapter Thirty-three

The man got the message at a diner on Route 244, which because he didn't have a phone in his trailer—didn't want one, didn't trust 'em—is where he took and made all his calls.

Sometimes a few days went by before he picked up the messages but because he was expecting an important call today he'd hurried—to the extent he ever hurried—to Elma's Diner right after Bible school.

Hobbs Wentworth was a bear-sized man with a thin red beard around his face and a fringe of curly hair, lighter than his beard. The word "career" was one that nobody in Canton Falls, New York, had ever associated with Hobbs, which wasn't to say that he didn't work like an ox. He'd give a man his money's worth, as long as the job was

out of doors, didn't require too much calcu-
lating and his employer was a white Christian.

Hobbs was married to a quiet, dusty
woman named Cindy, who spent most of
her time homeschooling, cooking, sewing
and visiting with women friends who did the
same. Hobbs himself spent most of *his*
time working and hunting and spending
evenings with men friends, drinking and arguing (though most of these "arguments"
should be called "agreements" since he and
his buddies were all extremely like-minded).
A lifelong resident of Canton Falls, he
liked it here. There was plenty of good hunting land, virtually none of it posted. People
were solid and good-natured and knew their
heads from their rumps ("like-minded" applied to almost everyone in Canton Falls).
Hobbs had lots of opportunities to do the
things he enjoyed. Like teaching Sunday
school, of all things. An eighth-grade graduate with a stolen mortarboard but no learning to show for it, Hobbs had never in the
Lord's universe thought anybody'd want
him to teach.

But he had a flair for kids' Sunday school,
it turned out. He didn't do prayer sessions

or counseling or any Jesus-Loves-Me-This-I-Know singing. . . . Nope, all he did was tell Bible stories to the youngsters. But he was an instant hit—thanks largely to his refusal to stick to the party line. For instance, in *his* account, instead of Jesus' feeding the crowds with two fish and five loaves, Hobbs reported how the Son of God went bow hunting and killed a deer from a hundred yards away and gutted and dressed it in the town square himself and he fed the people that way. (To illustrate the story Hobbs brought his compound Clearwater MX Flex to the classroom and, *chunk,* sent a tempered-tip arrow three inches into a cinderblock wall, to the delight of the kids.)

Having finished one of those classes now, he walked inside Elma's. The waitress walked up to him. "Hey, Hobbs. Pie?"

"Naw, make it a Vernors and a cheese omelette. Extra Kraft. Hey, d'I get a phone—"

Before he could finish she handed him a slip of paper. On it were the words: *Call me—JB.*

She asked, "That Jeddy? Sounded like him. Since the police've been 'round, those troopers, I mean, I ain't see him 't'all."

He ignored her question and said only,

"Hold that order for a minute." As he went to the pay phone, fishing hard for coins in his jeans, his mind went right back to a lunch he'd had two weeks ago at the Riverside Inn over in Bedford Junction. It'd been him and Frank Stemple and Jeddy Barnes from Canton Falls and a man named Erick Weir, who Barnes later took to calling Magic Man, because he was, of all things, a professional conjurer.

Barnes had puffed up Hobbs's day ten times by smiling and standing up when Hobbs arrived, saying to Weir, "Here, sir, meet the best shot we got in the county. Not to mention bow hunter. And a damn sharp operator too."

Hobbs had sat over the fancy food at the fancy restaurant, proud but nervous too (he'd never before even dreamed about eating at the Riverside), poking his fork into the daily special and listening as Barnes and Stemple told him how they'd met Weir. He was sort of like a mercenary soldier, which Hobbs knew all about, being a subscriber to *Soldier of Fortune*. Hobbs noticed the scars on the man's neck and the deformed fingers, wondering what kind of fight he'd been in that'd cause that kind of damage. Napalm, maybe.

Barnes had been reluctant to even meet with Weir at first, of course, thinking entrapment. But Magic Man had put him right at ease by telling them to watch the news on one particular day. The lead story was about the murder of a Mexican gardener—an illegal immigrant—working for a rich family in a town nearby. Weir brought Barnes the dead man's wallet. A trophy, like a buck's antlers.

Weir had been right up front. He'd told them that he'd picked the Mexican because of Barnes's views on immigrants but he personally didn't believe in their extreme causes—his interest was only in making money with his very special talents. Which suited everybody just fine. Over lunch, Magic Man Weir had laid out his plan about Charles Grady then he shook their hands and left. A few days ago Barnes and Stemple had shipped off the skippy, girl-lovin' Reverend Swensen to New York with instructions to kill Grady on Saturday night. And he'd bobbled the job as predicted.

Hobbs was supposed to "stay on call," Mr. Weir had said. "In case he was needed."

And apparently now he was. He punched

in the number of the cell phone Barnes used, the account in someone else's name, and heard an abrupt "Yeah?"

"S'me."

Because of the state police all over the county looking for Barnes they'd agreed to keep all conversations over the phone to a minimum.

Barnes said, "You gotta do what we talked about at lunch."

"Uh-huh. Go to the lake."

"Right."

"Go to the lake and take the fishing gear with me?" Hobbs said.

"That's right."

"Yessir. When?"

"Now. Right away."

"Then I will."

Barnes hung up abruptly and Hobbs changed his omelette to a coffee and a bacon and egg sandwich, extra Kraft, to go. When Jeddy Barnes said now, right away, now and right away was how you did whatever you were supposed to do.

When the food was ready he pushed outside, fired up his pickup and drove fast onto the highway. He had one stop to make—his trailer. Then he'd pick up the old junker

Dodge registered to somebody who didn't exist and speed down to the "lake," which didn't mean any kind of lake at all; it meant a particular place in New York City.

Just like the "fishing gear" he was supposed to take with him sure didn't mean a rod and reel either.

Back in the Tombs.

On one side of the floor-bolted table sat a grim-faced Joe Roth, Andrew Constable's pudgy lawyer.

Charles Grady was on the other side, flanked by *his* second, Roland Bell. Amelia Sachs stood; the pungent interview room, with its jaundiced, milky windows gave her a renewed sense of claustrophobia, which had been receding only slowly after the terrible panic at the Cirque Fantastique. She fidgeted and rocked her weight back and forth.

The door opened and Constable's guard led the prisoner into the room, recuffed his hands in front of him. Then he swung the door closed and returned to the corridor.

"It didn't work" was the first thing Grady said to him. A calm voice, oddly dispassionate, Sachs thought, considering that his family had nearly been wiped out.

"What didn't . . . ?" Constable began. "Is this about that fool Ralph Swensen?"

"No, this is about Erick Weir," Grady said.

"Who?" A frown that seemed genuine crossed the man's face.

The prosecutor went on to explain about the attempt on his family's life by the former illusionist turned professional killer.

"No, no, no. . . . I didn't have anything to do with Swensen. And I didn't have anything to do with *this*." The man looked helplessly at the scarred tabletop. There was some graffiti scraped in the gray paint beside his hands. It seemed to be an *A* then a *C* then a partial *K*. "I've told you all along, Charles, there're some people I've known in the past who've gone way overboard with things. They see you and the state as the enemies—working with the Jewish people and the African Americans or whoever— and they're twisting my words around and using me as an excuse to come after you." He said in a low voice, "I'll say it again. I promise you that I had nothing to do with this."

Roth said to the prosecutor, "Let's not

play games here, Charles. You're just fishing. If you've got something to connect my client to the break-in of your apartment, then—"

"Weir killed two individuals yesterday—and a police officer. That makes it capital murder."

Constable winced. His lawyer added bluntly, "Well, I'm sorry about that. But I notice you haven't charged my client. Because you don't have any evidence linking him to Weir, right?"

Grady ignored this and continued, "We're negotiating with Weir right now about turning state's evidence."

Constable turned his eyes to Sachs, looked her up and down. He seemed helpless and the gaze suggest that he was imploring her to help in some way. Perhaps she was supposed to provide the voice of female reason. But she remained silent, as did Bell. It wasn't their job to argue with suspects. The detective was here to keep an eye on Grady and see if he could learn more about the attempt on the D.A.'s life and possible future attacks. Sachs was here to see if she might learn more about Constable and his partners to help solidify the case against Weir.

Also, she'd been curious about this man—someone she'd been told was pure evil and yet who seemed to all appearances reasonable, understanding and genuinely troubled by the events of the past few days. Rhyme was content solely to look at the evidence; he had no patience for an examination of a perp's mind or soul. Sachs, though, was fascinated with questions of good and evil. Was she looking at an innocent man now or another Adolf Hitler?

Constable shook his head. "Look, it makes no sense for me to try and kill you. The state'd send in a replacement D.A. The trial'd go on, only I'd have a murder charge slapped on me. Why'd I want to do that? What possible reason would I have to kill you?"

"Because you're a bigot and a killer and—"

Constable interrupted heatedly, "Listen here. I've put up with a lot, sir. I was arrested, humiliated in front of my family. I've been abused here and in the press. And you know what my only crime is?" He leveled his gaze to Grady. "Asking hard questions."

"Andrew," Roth touched his arm. But, with a loud jangle, the prisoner pulled it away. He was indignant and wouldn't be stopped. "Right here in this room, right now, I'm going to commit the only crimes I've ever been guilty of. First offense: I'm asking if you don't agree that when government gets to be too big it loses touch with the people. That's when cops end up with the power to stick a mop handle up the rectum of a black prisoner in custody—an innocent prisoner, by the way."

"They were caught," Grady countered lethargically.

"Them going to jail's not going to give that poor man back his dignity, now, is it? And how many *don't* get caught? . . . Look at what's happened in Washington. They let terrorists walk right into our country, intent to kill us, and we don't dare offend 'em by keeping 'em out or forcing 'em to be finger-printed and carry ID cards. . . . How about another offense? Let me ask you, why don't we all just admit that there're differences between races and cultures? I've never said one race is better or worse than any other. But I do say you get grief if you go and try to mix them."

"We got rid of segregation some years ago," Bell drawled. "It is a crime, you know."

"Used to be a crime to sell liquor, Detective. Used to be a crime to work on Sunday. Used to be legal for ten-year-olds to work in factories. Then people wised up and changed those laws because they didn't reflect human nature."

He leaned forward and looked from Bell to Sachs. "My two police officer friends here. . . . Let me ask *you* a hard question. You get a report that a man might've committed a murder and he's black or Hispanic. You see him in an alley. Well, won't your finger be a little tighter on the trigger of your gun than if he's white? Or if he *is* a white man and looks like a smart man—if he has all his teeth and wears clothes that don't smell like yesterday's piss—well, then, are you going to be just a little slower to pull that trigger? Are you going to frisk him a little more gently?"

The prisoner sat back, shook his head. "Those're my crimes. That's it. Asking questions like those."

Grady said cynically, "Great material, Andrew. But before you play the persecution card, whatta you do with the fact that Erick

Weir had lunch with three other people at the Riverside Inn in Bedford Junction two weeks ago. Which is two clicks from the Patriot Assembly meeting hall in Canton Falls and about five from your house."

Constable blinked. "The Riverside Inn?" He looked out the window, which was so grimy it was impossible to tell if the sky was blue or polluted yellow or drizzly gray.

Grady's eyes narrowed. "What? You know something about that place?"

"I . . ." His lawyer touched his arm to silence him. They whispered to each other for a moment.

Grady couldn't resist pushing. "Do you know somebody who's a regular there?"

Constable glanced at Roth, who shook his head and the prisoner remained silent.

After a moment Grady asked, "How's your cell, Andrew?"

"My—"

"Your cell here in detention."

"Don't much care for it. As I suspect you know."

"It's worse in prison. And you'll have to go into solitary because the black crew in general pop would love to get—"

"Come on, Charles," Roth said wearily. "We don't need any of that."

The prosecutor said, "Well, Joe, I'm about at the end of the line here. All I've been hearing is I didn't do this, I didn't do that. That somebody's setting him up and using him. Well, if that's the case"—he now turned directly to Constable—"get off your ass and prove it to me. Show me you didn't have anything to do with trying to kill me and my family, *and* you get me the name of the people who did, then we'll talk."

Another whispered consultation between client and attorney.

Roth finally said, "My client's going to make some phone calls. Based on what we find he might be willing to consider cooperating."

"That's not good enough. Give me some names now."

Troubled, Constable said directly to Grady, "That's the way it's got to be. I need to be certain about this."

"Afraid you'll have to turn in some friends?" the prosecutor asked coolly. "Well, you say you like to ask hard questions. Let me ask *you* one: What kind of friends are they if they're willing to send

you to prison for the rest of your life?"
Grady stood up. "If I don't hear from you by
nine tonight we go to trial tomorrow as
planned."

Chapter Thirty-four

It wasn't much of a stage.

When David Balzac had retired from the illusionist circuit ten years ago and had bought Smoke & Mirrors he'd torn out the back half of the store to put in the small theater. Balzac didn't have a cabaret license so he couldn't charge admission but he'd still hold shows here—every Sunday afternoon and Thursday night—so that his students could get up onstage and experience what performing was really like.

And what a difference it was.

Kara knew that practicing at home and performing onstage were night and day. Something inexplicable happened when you got up in front of people. Impossible tricks that you continually flubbed at home went perfectly, owing to some mysterious spiritual adrenaline that took over your hands and proclaimed, "Thou shalt not fuck this one up."

Conversely, in a performance you might blow a trick that was second nature, like a one-coin French drop, a maneuver so simple that you'd never even think to have an out prepared in case it went south.

A high, wide black curtain separated the theater from the business end of the store. It rippled occasionally in the breeze as the front door opened and closed with a faint Roadrunner meep-meep from the electric-eye alert on the jamb.

Now approaching 4:00 P.M. on Sunday, people were entering the theater and finding seats—always beginning at the back (in magic and illusion performances *nobody* wants to sit in the front row; you never knew when you might get "volunteered" to be embarrassed up onstage).

Standing behind a backdrop curtain, Kara looked at the stage. The flat black walls were scuffed and streaked and the bowed oak floor was covered with dozens of bits of masking tape, from performers' blocking out their moves during rehearsal. For a backdrop, only a ratty burgundy shawl. And the entire platform was tiny: ten by twelve feet.

Still, to Kara it was Carnegie Hall or the MGM Grand itself and she was prepared to give her audience everything she had.

Like vaudevillians or parlor magicians, most illusionists simply string together a series of routines. The performers might pace the tricks carefully, building up to a thrilling finale, but that approach, Kara felt, was like watching fireworks—each burst more or less spectacular, but on the whole emotionally unsatisfying because there was no theme or continuity to the explosions. An illusionist's act should tell a story, all the tricks linked together, one leading to the next with one or more of the earlier tricks returning at the end to give the audience that delightful one-two punch that left them, she hoped, breathless.

More people were entering the theater now. She wondered if there'd be many here today, though it didn't really make any difference to her. She loved the story about Robert-Houdin, who walked out onstage one night to find three people in the theater. He presented the same show as if the house were full—except the finale was slightly different; he invited the audience to his home for dinner afterward.

She was confident of her routine—Mr. Balzac had her practice, even for these small shows, for weeks. And now, during the last few minutes before curtain time, she didn't think about her tricks but gazed at the audience, enjoying this momentary peace of mind. She supposed she had no right to feel this comfortable. There were a lot of reasons why she shouldn't be so content: her mother's worsening condition. The growing money problems. Her slow progress in Mr. Balzac's eyes. The brunch-in-bed guy who'd left three weeks ago today, promising he'd call her. Definitely. I promise.

But the Vanished Boyfriend trick, like Evaporating Money and the Wasting Mother, couldn't touch her here.

Not when she was onstage.

Nothing mattered to her except the challenge of materializing a certain look in the faces of the audience. Kara could see it so clearly: the mouth faintly smiling, the eyes opening wide with surprise, the eyebrows narrowing, asking the most compelling question in every illusionist show: How do they *do* that?

In close-in magic there are sleight-of-hand gestures known as takes and puts. You create the effect of transforming an object from one thing to another by subtly *taking* away the original and *putting* a second in its place, though the effect the audience sees is of one object becoming something else. And that's exactly what Kara's philosophy of performing was: taking her audience's sadness or boredom or anger and putting in its place happiness, fascination, serenity—transforming them into people with exhilaration in their hearts, however momentary that might be.

Just about starting time. She peeked out through the curtain again.

Most of the chairs were filled, she was surprised to see. On nice days like this, the attendance was usually quite small. She was pleased when Jaynene from the nursing home arrived, her huge figure blocking the back doorway momentarily. Several other nurses from Stuyvesant Manor were with her. They walked farther inside and found seats. A few of Kara's other friends too, from the magazine and her apartment building on Greenwich Street.

Then just after 4:00 the back curtain opened wide and one final member of the audience entered—someone she never in a million years would have expected to come see her show.

"It's accessible," Lincoln Rhyme commented wryly, driving his glossy Storm Arrow to a spot halfway down the aisle in Smoke & Mirrors and parking. "No ADA suits today."

An hour ago he'd surprised Sachs and Thom by suggesting they drive down to the store in his van—the ramp-equipped Rollx—to see Kara's performance.

Then he'd added, "Though it's a shame to waste a beautiful spring afternoon indoors."

When they'd stared at him—even before the accident he'd rarely spent a beautiful spring afternoon outside—he'd said, "I'm kidding. Could you get the van please, Thom."

"A 'please' no less," the aide had said.

As he looked around the shabby theater he noticed a heavyset black woman glance at him. She rose slowly and joined them, sitting next to Sachs, shaking her hand and nodding to Rhyme. She asked him if they were the police officers Kara'd told her about. He said yes and introductions were made.

Her name turned out to be Jaynene and she was a nurse working at the aging care facility where Kara's mother lived.

The woman glanced knowingly at Rhyme, who'd cast her a wry look at this description, and said, "Whoops. D'I really say that? Meant to say 'old folks home.'"

"I'm a graduate of a 'TIMC,'" the criminalist said.

The woman furrowed her brow and finally shook her head. "That's a new one on me."

Thom said, "Traumatic Incident Mitigation Center."

Rhyme said, "I called it the Gimp Inn."

"But he's deliberately provocative," Thom added.

"I've worked spinal units. We always liked the patients best who gave us crap. The quiet, cheerful ones scared us."

Because, Rhyme reflected, they were the ones who had friends slip a hundred Seconal into their drinks. Or who, if they had the use of a hand, poured water onto the pilot lights of their stoves and turned the gas up high.

A four-burner death, it was called.

Jaynene asked Rhyme, "You C4?"

"That's it."

"Off the ventilator. Good for you."

"Is Kara's mother here?" Sachs asked, looking around.

Jaynene frowned briefly and said, "Well, no."

"Does she ever come to see her?"

The woman said cautiously, "Her mother's not really involved with Kara's career."

Rhyme said, "Kara told me she's sick. Is she doing better?"

"A bit, yes," the woman said.

There was a story behind this, Rhyme sensed, but the woman's tone said that it wasn't for the nurse to go into confidential matters with strangers.

Then the lights dimmed and the crowd fell silent.

A white-haired man climbed up onstage. Despite the age and the signs of hard living—a drinker's nose and tobacco-stained beard—his eyes were keen, his posture erect and he floated to center stage with a performer's presence. He stood next to the only prop on the platform—a wooden cutout of a Roman column. The surroundings were shabby but the man wore a well-tailored suit, as if he had some rule that whenever you were up onstage you looked the best for your audience.

Ah, Rhyme deduced, the infamous mentor, David Balzac. He didn't identify himself but looked out over the audience for a moment, his eyes settling on Rhyme's for longer than most others'. Whatever he was thinking, though, remained hidden and he looked away. "Today, ladies and gentlemen, I'm pleased to present one of my most promising students. Kara has been studying with me for over a year now. She's going to treat you to some of the more esoteric illusions in the history of our profession—and some of my own as well as some of hers. Don't be surprised"—A demonic look that seemed directed at Rhyme himself—"or *shocked* at anything you see today. And now, ladies and gentlemen . . . I give you . . . Kara."

Rhyme had decided to pass this hour by being a scientist. He'd enjoy the challenge of spotting the methods of her illusions, noting how she did the tricks, how cards and coins were palmed and where her quick-change costumes were concealed. Kara was still several points ahead in this game of Catch the Moves, which she undoubtedly didn't know they were playing.

The young woman walked out onstage, wearing a tight black bodysuit with a cut-out in the shape of a crescent moon on her chest, under a shimmery, see-through drape, like a translucent Roman toga. He'd never thought of Kara as attractive, much less sexy, but the clinging outfit was very sensuous. She moved like a dancer, svelt and smooth. There was a long pause while she examined the audience slowly. It seemed that she looked at each person. The tension began to build. Finally: "Change," she said in a theatrical voice. "Change. . . . How it fascinates us. Alchemy—changing lead and tin into gold. . . ." She held up a silver coin. Closed it in her palm and opened it an instant later to reveal a gold coin, which she flung into the air; it turned into a shower of gold confetti.

Applause from the audience and murmurs of pleasure.

"Night . . ." The houselights suddenly dimmed to blackness and a moment later— no more than a few seconds—came back up. ". . . becoming day." Kara was now dressed in a similar, clinging outfit, except that it was golden and the cutout pattern on the front was a starburst. Rhyme had to laugh at the speed of the quick change. "Life . . ." A red rose appeared in her hand. ". . . becoming death . . ." She cupped the rose in her hands and it changed to a dried yellowish flower. ". . . becoming life." A bouquet of fresh flowers had somehow replaced the dead stalk. She tossed them to a delighted woman in the audience. Rhyme heard a surprised whisper: "They're real!"

Kara lowered her hands to her sides and looked out over the audience again with a serious expression on her face. "There's a book," she said, her voice filling the room. "A book written thousands of years ago by the Roman writer Ovid. The book is called *Metamorphoses.* Like 'metamorphosis'— when a caterpillar becomes a . . ." She opened her hand and a butterfly flew out and disappeared backstage.

Rhyme had taken four years of Latin. He recalled struggling to translate portions of

Ovid's book for class. He remembered that it was a series of fourteen or fifteen short myths in poetic form. What was Kara up to? Lecturing about classical literature to an audience of lawyer moms and kids thinking about their Xboxes and Nintendos (though he noticed that her tight costume held the attention of every teenage boy in the audience).

She continued, "*Metamorphoses.* . . . It's a book about change. About people becoming other people, animals, trees, inanimate objects. Some of Ovid's stories are tragic, some enthralling but all of them have one thing in common." A pause and then she said in a loud voice, "Magic!" With a burst of light and a cloud of smoke she vanished.

For the next forty minutes Kara captivated the audience with a series of illusions and sleight-of-hand tricks based on a few of the poems in the book. As for catching her moves, Rhyme gave up on that completely. True, he was lost in the drama of her stories. But even when he pulled himself back from her spell and concentrated on her hands he couldn't spot her method once. After a long ovation and an encore, during which she quick-changed into a tiny elderly woman and back again ("Young to old . . . old to young"), she left the stage. Five minutes later Kara emerged in jeans and a white blouse and stepped into the audience to say hello to friends.

A shop clerk laid out a table of jug wine, coffee and soda, cookies.

"No scotch?" Rhyme asked, looking over the cheap spread.

"Sorry, sir," the bearded young man replied.

Sachs, armed with wine, nodded at Kara, who joined them. "Hey, this is great. I never thought I'd see you guys here."

"What can I say?" Sachs offered. "Fantastic."

"Excellent," Rhyme said to her then turned back to the bar. "Maybe there's some whisky in the back, Thom."

Thom nodded at Rhyme and said to Kara, "Can you transform dispositions?" He took two glasses of Chardonnay, slipped a straw in one and held it out for his boss. "This or nothing, Lincoln."

He took a sip then said, "I liked the young-old ending. Didn't expect it. I was

worried you were going to become a butterfly at the end. Cliché, you know."

"You were *supposed* to be worried. With
me, expect the unexpected. Sleight of
mind, remember?"

"Kara," Sachs said, "you *have* to try out
for the Cirque Fantastique."

The woman laughed but said nothing.

"No, I'm serious—this was professional
quality," Sachs insisted.

Rhyme could tell that Kara didn't want to
pursue the issue. She said lightly, "I'm right
on schedule. There's no hurry. A lot of
people make the mistake of jumping too
fast."

"Let's get some food," Thom suggested.
"I'm starving. Jaynene, you come too."

The large woman said she'd love to and
suggested a new place near the Jefferson
Market at Sixth and Tenth.

Kara demurred, though, saying that she
had to stay and work on some of the routines she'd slipped up on during the performance.

"Girl, no way," the nurse said, frowning.
"You gotta work?"

"It'll only be a couple of hours. That friend
of Mr. Balzac's doing some private show

tonight and he's going to close up the store early to go watch it." Kara hugged Sachs and said goodbye. They exchanged phone numbers, each promising they'd be in touch. Rhyme thanked her again for her help in the Weir case. "We couldn't've caught him without you."

"We'll come see you in Las Vegas," Thom called.

Rhyme started to pilot the Storm Arrow toward the front of the store. As he did he glanced to his left and saw Balzac's still eyes watching him from the back room. The illusionist then turned to Kara as she joined him. Immediately, in his presence, she was a very different woman, timid and self-conscious.

Metamorphosis, Rhyme thought, and he watched Balzac slowly push the door closed, shutting out the rest of the world from the sorcerer and his apprentice.

Chapter Thirty-five

"I'm gonna say it again. You can have a lawyer, you want one."

"I understand that," Erick Weir muttered in his breathy whisper.

They were in Lon Sellitto's office at One Police Plaza. It was a small room, mostly gray, decorated with—as the detective himself might've put it in a report—"one infant picture, one male child picture, one adult female picture, one scenic lake picture of indeterminate locale, one plant—dead."

Sellitto had interviewed hundreds of suspects in this office. The only difference between them and the present suspect was that Weir was double-shackled to the gray chair across the desk. And an armed patrol officer stood behind him.

"You understand?"

"I said I did," Weir announced.

And so the interview began.

Unlike Rhyme, who specialized in forensics, Detective First-Grade Lon Sellitto was a full-service cop. He was a detective in the real sense of the word. He "detected" the truth, using all the resources that the NYPD and fellow agencies had to offer, as well as his own street-smarts and tenacity. It was the best job in the world, he often said. The work called on you to be an actor, a politician, a chess player and sometimes a gunslinger and tackle.

And one of the best parts was the game of interrogation, getting suspects to confess or reveal the names of associates and the location of loot or victim's bodies.

But it was clear from the beginning that this prick wasn't giving up a dustball of information.

"Now, Erick, what do you know about the Patriot Assembly?"

"Like I said, only what I read about them," Weir replied, scratching his chin on his shoulder as best he could. "You want to undo these cuffs just for a minute?"

"No, I don't. You only *read* about the Assembly?"

"That's right." Weir coughed for a moment.

"Where?"

"*Time* magazine, I think."

"And you're educated, you speak good. I wouldn't guess you go along with their philosophy."

"Of course not." He wheezed, "They seem like rabid bigots to me."

"So if you don't believe in their politics then the only reason to kill Charles Grady for them is for money. Which you admitted at Rhyme's. So I'd like to know exactly who hired you."

"Oh, I wasn't going to kill him," the prisoner whispered. "You misunderstood me."

"What's to misunderstand? You broke into his apartment with a loaded weapon."

"Look, I like challenges. Seeing if I can break into places nobody else can. I'd never hurt anybody." This was delivered half to Sellitto and half to a battered video camera aimed at his face.

"Say, how was the meat loaf? Or did you have the roast turkey?"

"The what?"

"In Bedford Junction. At the Riverside Inn. I'd say you had the turkey, and Constable's boys had the meat loaf and the steak and the daily special. Which one did Jeddy have?"

"Who? Oh, that man you asked me about? Barnes. You're talking about that receipt, right?" Weir said, wheezing. "The truth is I just found that. I needed to write something down and I grabbed a scrap of paper."

The truth? Sellitto reflected. Right. "You just needed to write something down?"

Struggling for breath, Weir nodded.

"Where were you?" persisted an increasingly bored Lon Sellitto. "When you needed this paper?"

"I don't know. A Starbucks."

"Which one?"

Weir squinted. "Don't remember."

Criminals had started to cite Starbucks a lot lately when offering up alibis. Sellitto decided it was because there were so many of the coffee outlets and they all looked alike— criminals could credibly sound confused about which one they'd been in at a particular time.

"Why was it blank?" Sellitto continued.

"What was blank?"

"The back of the receipt. If you'd taken it

to write something down why *didn't* you write on it?"

"Oh. I don't think I could find a pen."

"They have pens at Starbucks. People charge things a lot there. They need pens to sign their credit card vouchers."

"The clerk was busy. I didn't want to bother her."

"What was it you wanted to write down?"

"Uhm," came the breathy wheeze, "movie show time."

"Where's Larry Burke's body?"

"Who?"

"The police officer who arrested you on Eighty-eighth Street. You told Lincoln Rhyme last night that you killed him and the body was on the West Side somewhere."

"I was just trying to make him think I was going to attack the circus, lead him off. Feeding him false information."

"And when you admitted killing the other victims? That was false information too?"

"Exactly. I didn't kill anybody. Somebody else did and tried to pin it on me."

Ah, the oldest defense in the book. The lamest. The most embarrassing.

Though one that, of course, did sometimes work, Sellitto knew—depending on the gullibility of the jury.

"Who wanted to frame you?"

"I don't know. But somebody who knows me, obviously."

"Because they'd have access to your clothes and fibers and hairs and things, to plant at the scenes."

"Exactly."

"Good. Then it'd be a short list. Give me some names."

Weir closed his eyes. "Nothing's coming to me." His head slumped. "It's really frustrating."

Sellitto couldn't've put it better himself.

A tedious half hour of this game passed. Finally the detective just gave up. He was angry, thinking that he'd be going home soon to his girlfriend and the dinner she was making—turkey, ironically, just like what'd been on the lunch menu at the Riverside Inn in Bedford Junction—but that Officer Larry Burke would never be returning to his wife. He dropped the façade of the friendly but persistent interrogator and muttered, "I want you out of my sight."

Sellitto and the other officers drove the prisoner two blocks to the Manhattan Detention Center for booking on murder, attempt, assault and arson charges. The detective warned the DOC officers about the man's skills at escaping and they assured him that Weir would be placed in Special Detention, a virtually escape-proof facility.

"Oh, Detective Sellitto," Weir called in a throaty whisper.

The detective turned.

"I swear to God I didn't do it," he gasped, his voice echoing with what sounded like genuine remorse. "Maybe after I get some rest I'll remember some things that'll help you find the real killer. I really *do* want to help."

Downstairs in the Tombs the two officers, both with a firm grip on the prisoner's arms, let him shuffle his way to the booking station.

Doesn't look so scary to me, Department of Corrections Officer Linda Welles thought. He was strong, she could tell, but not like some of the beasts they'd processed here, those kids from Alphabet City or Harlem with perfect bodies that even huge quantities of crack and smack and malt liquor couldn't soften.

No, she didn't quite know why they were making all this fuss about this skinny old guy, Weir, Erick A.

"Keep a hold on him, watch his hands all the time. Don't take the shackles off." That'd been Detective Sellitto's warning. But the suspect just looked sad and tired and was having trouble breathing. She wondered what had happened to his hands and neck, the scarring. A fire or hot oil. The thought of the pain made her shiver.

Welles remembered what he'd told Detective Sellitto at the intake door. *I really do want to help.* Weir had seemed like a schoolchild who'd disappointed his parents.

Despite Detective Sellitto's concerns the fingerprinting and mug shots went without incident and soon he was back in double cuffs and ankle shackles again. Welles and Hank Gersham, a large male DOC officer, took an arm each and then started down the long corridor to intake.

Welles had handled thousands of criminals here and thought she was immune to their pleas and their protests and tears. But there was something about Weir's sad promise to Detective Sellitto that moved her. Maybe he actually was innocent. He hardly seemed like a murderer.

He winced and Welles relaxed her viselike grip on his arm slightly.

A moment later the prisoner moaned and slumped against her. His face was contorted in pain.

"What?" Hank asked.

"Cramp," he gasped. "It hurts . . . oh, God." He gave a whispered scream. "The shackles!"

His left leg was straight out, quivering, hard as wood.

The guard asked her, "Undo him?"

Welles hesitated. Then said, "No." To Weir: "Let's go down, down on your side. I'll work it out." A runner, she knew how to handle cramps. It probably wasn't fake—he seemed in too much genuine agony and the muscle was rock hard.

"Oh, Jesus," Weir cried in pain. "The shackles!"

"We've gotta get 'em off," her partner said.

"No," Welles repeated firmly. "Get him on the floor. I'll take care of it."

They eased Weir down and Welles began to massage his stiff leg. Hank stood back and watched her at work. Then she happened to glance up. She noticed that Weir's cuffed hands, still behind his back, had slid to his side and that his slacks had been pulled down a few inches.

She looked closely. She saw that a Band-Aid had been peeled away from his hip and beneath it—what the hell *was* that? She realized it was a slit in the skin.

It was then that his palm hit her square in the nose, popping the cartilage. A burst of pain seared her face and took her breath away.

A key! He'd had a key or pick hidden in that little crevice of skin under the bandage.

Her partner reached out fast but Weir rose even faster and elbowed him in the throat. The man went down, gasping and clutching his neck, coughing and struggling for air. Weir clamped a hand on Welles's pistol and tried to pull it from her holster. She struggled to control it with both hands, using every ounce of strength. She tried to scream but the blood from her broken nose flowed down her throat and she began to choke.

Still gripping her gun, the prisoner reached down with his left hand and in what seemed like seconds unshackled his legs. Then with both hands he began in earnest to get the Glock away from her.

"Help me!" she cried, coughing blood. "Somebody, help!"

Weir managed to pull the weapon out of her holster but Welles, thinking of her children, kept a vise grip on his wrist. The muzzle swung around the empty corridor, past Hank, on his hands and knees, retching and struggling for breath.

"Help! Officer down! Help!" Welles cried.

There was motion from the end of the corridor as a door opened and someone came running. But the hallway seemed to be ten miles long and Weir was getting a better grip on the pistol. They rolled to the floor, his desperate eyes inches from hers, the muzzle of the gun turning slowly toward her. It ended up between them. Gasping, he tried to get his index finger to the trigger.

"No, please, no, no," she whimpered. The prisoner smiled cruelly as she stared at the black eye of the weapon, inches from her face, expecting it to fire at any instant.

Seeing her children, seeing the girl's father, her own mother. . . .

No fucking way, Welles thought, furious. She planted her foot against the wall and shoved hard. Weir went over backward and she fell on top of him.

The pistol went off with a stunning explosion, the huge kick of recoil jarring her wrist, the sound deafening her.

Blood spattered the wall.

No, no, no!

Please let Hank be okay! she prayed.

But Welles saw her partner struggling to his feet. He was unhurt. Then she realized that she wasn't fighting for the weapon. It was in her hand alone; Weir no longer had a grip on it. Quivering, she leaped to her feet and backed away from him.

Oh, my God . . .

The bullet had struck the prisoner directly in the side of the head, leaving a horrible wound. On the wall behind him was a spatter of blood, brain matter and bone. Weir lay on his back, glazed eyes staring at the ceiling. Blood was flowing down his temple to the floor.

Shaking, Welles wailed, "Fuck me, look what I did! Oh, fuck! Help him, somebody!"

As a dozen other officers converged on the scene, she turned to look at the guards but then saw them freeze and drop into defensive crouches.

Welles gasped. Was there some other perp behind her? She spun around and saw that the corridor was empty. She turned back to see the other officers were still crouching, holding up their hands in alarm. Shouting. Ears deafened from the shot, she couldn't understand what they were saying.

Finally she heard, "Jesus, your weapon, Linda! Holster it! Watch where you're pointing it!"

She realized in her panic that she'd been waving the Glock around—toward the ceiling, toward the floor, toward them—like a child with a toy gun.

She barked a manic laugh at her carelessness. As she holstered the pistol she felt something hard on her belt and pulled it off. She examined the splinter of bloody bone from Weir's skull. "Oh," she said, dropped it and laughed like her daughter during a tickle-fest. She spit on her hand then began wiping her palm on her pants. The scrubbing grew more and more frantic until the laughter suddenly stopped and she dropped to her knees, consumed with wrenching sobs.

Chapter Thirty-six

"You should've seen it, Mum. I think I wowed 'em."

Kara sat on the edge of the chair, cradling the tepid Starbucks cup in her hands, the warmth from the cardboard perfectly matching the temperature of human skin— the temperature of her mother's skin, for instance, still pink, still glowing.

"I had the whole stage to myself for forty-five minutes. How 'bout that?"

"You . . . ?"

This word was not part of an imaginary dialogue. The woman was awake and had asked the question in a firm voice.

You.

Though Kara had no idea what her mother meant.

It might mean: What was it you just said?

Or: Who are you? Why are you coming into my room and sitting down here as if we know each other?

Or: I heard the word "you" once but I don't know what it means and I'm too embarrassed to ask. It's important, I know, but I can't remember. You, you, you . . .

Then her mother looked out the window, at the clinging ivy, and said, "Everything turned out fine. We got through it just fine."

Kara knew it would only be frustrating to try to carry on a conversation with her when she was in this state of mind. None of her sentences would be related to any other. Sometimes she'd even forget her train of thought within a sentence and her voice would fade to a confused silence.

So Kara herself now just rambled on, talking about the *Metamorphoses* show she'd just done. And then, even more excitedly, she told her mother about helping the police catch a killer.

For a moment her mother's eyebrow arched in recognition and Kara's heart began to pound. She leaned forward.

"I found the tin. I never thought I'd see it again."

Head back in the pillow.

Kara's hands clenched into knotted fists. Her breath came fast. "It's me, Mum! Me! The Royal Kid. Can't you see me?"

"You?"

Goddamnit! Kara raged silently to the demon who'd possessed the poor woman and muffled her soul. Leave her alone! Give her back to me!

"Hi there." A woman's voice from the doorway startled Kara, who subtly lifted several tears off her cheek, as smoothly as executing a French drop, before she turned around.

"Hey," she said to Amelia Sachs. "You tracked me down."

"I'm a cop. That's what we do." She walked into the room, holding two Starbucks cups. She glanced at the container in Kara's hand. "Sorry. Redundant present."

Kara thumped the carton she was holding. Almost out. She took the second cup gratefully. "Caffeine'll never go to waste around me." She started sipping. "Thanks. You guys have fun?"

"Sure did. That woman's a scream. Jaynene. Thom's in love with her. And she actually made Lincoln laugh."

"She has that effect on people," Kara said. "A way good soul."

Amelia said, "Balzac dragged you away pretty fast at the end of the show. I just wanted to come by and thank you again. And to say that you should send us a bill for your time."

"I never thought about it. You introduced me to Cuban coffee. That's payment enough."

"No, invoice us something. Send it to me and I'll make sure it goes to the city."

"Playing G-woman," Kara said. "It'll be a story I'll tell my grandkids. . . . Hey, I'm free for the rest of the night—Mr. Balzac's off with his friend. I was going to see some people down in SoHo. You want to come?"

"Sure," the policewoman said. "We could—" She looked up, over Kara's shoulder. "Hello."

Kara glanced behind her and saw her mother, looking with curiosity at the policewoman, and sized up the gaze. "She's not really with us right now."

"It was during the summer," the elderly woman said. "June, I'm pretty sure." She closed her eyes and lay back.

"Is she okay?"

"Just a temporary thing. She'll come back soon. Her mind's a little funny sometimes." Kara stroked the old woman's arm then asked Sachs, "Your parents?"

"It'll sound familiar, I've got a feeling. Father's dead. My mother lives near me in Brooklyn. Little too close for comfort. But we've come to an . . . understanding."

Kara knew that understandings between mother and daughter were as complex as international treaties and she didn't ask Amelia to elaborate, not now. There'd be time for that in the future.

A piercing beep filled the room and both women reached for the pagers on their belts. Amelia won. "I shut my cell off when I got here. There was a sign in the lobby that said I couldn't use it. You mind?" She nodded toward the telephone on the table.

"No, go ahead."

She picked up the phone and dialed and Kara rose to straighten the blankets on her mother's bed. "Remember that bed-and-breakfast we stayed at in Warwick, Mum? Near the castle?"

Do you remember? Tell me you remember!

Amelia's voice: "Rhyme? Me."

Kara's unilateral conversation was interrupted a few seconds later, though, when she heard the officer's voice ask a sharp, "What? When?"

Turning to the policewoman, Kara frowned. Amelia was looking at her, shaking her head. "I'll get right down there. . . . I'm with her now. I'll tell her." She hung up.

"What's the matter?" Kara asked.

"Looks like I can't join you guys after all. We must've missed a lock pick or key. Weir got out of his cuffs at detention and went for somebody's gun. He was killed."

"Oh, my God."

Amelia walked to the doorway. "I've got to run the scene down there." She paused and glanced at Kara. "You know, I was worried about keeping him under guard during the trial. That man was just too slippery. But I guess sometimes there is justice. Oh, that bill? Whatever you were going to charge, double it."

"Constable's got some information," the man's voice came crisply through the phone.

"He's been playing detective, has he?" Charles Grady asked the lawyer wryly.

Wryly—but not sarcastically. The prose-cutor had nothing against Joseph Roth, who—though he represented scum—was a defense lawyer who managed to step around the slime trail left by his clients and who treated D.A.'s and cops with honesty and respect. Grady reciprocated.

"Yeah, he has. Made some calls up to Canton Falls and put the fear of God into a couple of the Patriot Assembly folks. They checked things out. Looks like some of the former members've gone rogue."

"Who is it? Barnes? Stemple?"

"We didn't go into it in depth. All I know is he's pretty upset. He kept saying, 'Judas, Judas, Judas.' Over and over."

Grady couldn't stir up much sympathy. You lie down with dogs. . . . He said to the lawyer, "He knows I'm not letting him off scot-free."

"He understands that, Charles."

"You know Weir's dead?"

"Yep. . . . I've got to tell you Andrew was happy to hear it. I really believe he didn't have anything to do with trying to hurt you, Charles."

Grady didn't have any use for opinions from defense counsel, even forthright ones like Roth. He asked, "And he's got solid information?"

"He does, yes."

Grady believed him. Roth was a man you simply could not fool; if he thought Constable was going to dime out some of his people then it was going to happen. How successful the resulting case would be was a different matter, of course. But if Constable gave relatively hard information and if the troopers did a halfway decent job with their investigation and arrest he was confident he could put the perps away. Grady would also make sure that Lincoln Rhyme oversaw the forensics.

Grady had mixed feelings about Weir's death. While he'd publicly express his concern at the man's shooting and promise to look into it officially, he was privately delighted that the fucker'd been disposed of. He was still shocked and infuriated that a killer had walked right into the apartment where his wife and daughter lived, willing to murder them too.

Grady looked at the glass of wine he so dearly wanted a sip of, but realized that a consequence of this phone call was that it precluded alcohol for the time being. The

Constable case was so important that he needed all his wits about him.

"He wants to meet you face-to-face," Roth said.

The wine was a Grgich Hills Cabernet Sauvignon. A 1997, no less. Great vineyard, great year.

Roth continued, "How soon can you get down to detention?"

"A half hour. I'll leave now."

Grady hung up and announced to his wife, "The good news is no trial."

Luis, the still-eyed bodyguard, said, "I'll go with you."

After Weir's death Lon Sellitto had cut back the protection team to one officer.

"No, you stay here with my family, Luis. I'd feel better."

His wife asked cautiously, "If that's the good news, honey, what's the bad news?"

"I have to miss dinner," the prosecutor said, tossing a handful of Goldfish crackers into his mouth and washing them down with a very large sip of very nice wine, thinking, hell with it, let's celebrate.

● ● ●

Sachs's war-torn yellow Camaro SS pulled to a stop outside 100 Centre Street. She tossed the NYPD placard onto the dash then climbed out. She nodded to a crime scene crew standing beside their RRV. "Where's the scene?"

"First floor in the back. The corridor to intake."

"Sealed?"

"Yep."

"Whose weapon?"

"Linda Welles'. DOC. She's pretty shook up. Asshole broke her nose."

Sachs grabbed one of the suitcases and, hooking it up to a wheelie luggage carrier, started for the front door of the Criminal Courts building. The other CS techs did the same and followed.

This scene'd be a grounder, of course. An accidental shooting involving an officer and a suspect who'd tried to escape? Pro forma. Still, the event was a homicide and required a complete crime scene report for the Shooting Incident Board and any subsequent investigation and lawsuits. Amelia Sachs would run the scene as carefully as any other.

A guard checked their IDs and led the

team through a maze of corridors into the basement. Finally they came to a yellow police line tape across a closed door. Here she found a detective talking to a uniformed officer, her nose stuffed with tissue and bandaged.

Sachs introduced herself and explained that she was going to be running the scene. The detective stepped aside and Sachs asked Linda Welles what had happened.

In a halting, nasal voice the guard explained that on the way from fingerprinting to intake the suspect had somehow undone his handcuffs. "It took him two, three seconds. All the cuffs. Just like that, they were open. He didn't get my key." She pointed to her blouse pocket, where presumably it resided. "He had a pick or key or something on his hip."

"His pocket?" Sachs asked, frowning. She remembered they'd searched him carefully.

"No, his *leg.* You'll see." She nodded toward the corridor where Weir's body lay. "There's a cut in his skin. Under a bandage. Everything happened so fast."

Sachs supposed that he'd cut himself to create a hiding space. A queasy thought.

"Then he grabbed my weapon and we were struggling for it. It just discharged. I didn't mean to pull the trigger. I didn't, really. But . . . I tried to keep control and I couldn't. It just discharged."

Control . . . Discharge. The words, official copspeak, were perhaps an attempt to insulate her from the guilt she'd be feeling. This had nothing to do with the fact that a killer was dead, or that her life had been endangered, or that a dozen other officers had been taken in by this man; no, it was that this woman had stumbled. Women in the NYPD set the bar high; the falls are always harder than for men.

"*We* collared and searched him at the takedown," Sachs said kindly. "And we missed the key too."

"Yeah," the officer muttered. "But it's still gonna come up."

At the shooting inquiry, she meant. And, yeah, it would.

Well, Sachs'd do a particularly thorough job on her report to give this officer as much support as possible.

Welles touched her nose gently. "Oh, that hurts." Tears were streaming from her eyes. "What're my kids going to say? They always ask me if I do anything dangerous. And I tell 'em no. Look at this. . . ."

Pulling on latex gloves, Sachs asked for the woman's Glock. She took it, dropped the clip and ejected the round in the chamber. Everything went into a plastic evidence bag.

Slipping into her sergeant mode, Sachs said, "You can take an LOA, you know."

Welles didn't even hear her. "It just discharged," the woman said in a hollow voice. "I didn't want it to. I didn't *want* to kill anybody."

"Linda?" Sachs said. "You can take an LOA. A week, ten days."

"I can?"

"Talk to your supervisor."

"Sure. Yeah. I could do that." Welles rose and wandered over to the medic treating her partner, who had a nasty bruise on his neck but who otherwise seemed all right.

The CS team set up shop outside the door to the corridor where the shooting had occurred, opening the suitcases and arranging evidence collection equipment, friction ridge supplies and video and still cameras. Sachs dressed in the white Tyvek suit and accessorized with rubber bands around her feet.

She fitted the microphone over her head and asked for a radio patch to Lincoln Rhyme's phone. Ripping down the police tape, she opened the door, thinking: A slit in the skin to hide lock picks and cuff keys? Of all the perps she and Lincoln had been up against, the Conjurer was—

"Oh, goddamn," she spat out.

"Hello to you too, Sachs," Rhyme said acerbically through her headset. "At least I think it's you. Hell of a lot of static."

"I don't believe it, Rhyme. The M.E. took the body before I could process it." Sachs was looking into the corridor, bloody but empty.

"What?" he snapped. "Who approved that?"

The rule in crime scene work was that emergency medical personnel could enter a scene to save an injured person but, in the case of homicide, the body had to remain untouched by everyone, including the tour doctor from the Medical Examiner's office, until it'd been processed by someone from forensics. This was fundamental police work and the career of whoever'd released the Conjurer's corpse was now in jeopardy.

"There a problem, Amelia?" one of the techs called from the doorway.

"Look," she said angrily, nodding into the corridor. "The M.E. got the body before we processed it. What happened?"

The crew cut young tech frowned. He glanced at his partner then said, "Uhm, well, the tour doc's outside. He was the guy we were talking to when you showed up. The one feeding the pigeons. He was waiting to move the body till we were finished."

"What's going on?" Rhyme growled. "I hear voices, Sachs."

To him she said, "There's a crew from the M.E.'s office outside, Rhyme. Sounds like they *haven't* picked up the body. What's—"

"Oh, Jesus Christ. No!"

The chill went straight to her soul. "Rhyme, you don't think—?"

He barked out, "What do you see, Sachs? What's the blood spatter look like?"

She ran to where the shooting had happened and studied the bloodstain on the wall. "Oh, no. It doesn't look normal for a gunshot, Rhyme."

"Brain matter, bone?"

"Gray matter, yeah. But it doesn't look right either. There is some bone. Not much, though, for a close-range shot."

"Do a presumptive blood test. That'll be dispositive."

She sped back to the doorway.

"What's going . . . ?" one of the techs asked but he fell silent as he watched her dig frantically through the suitcases.

Sachs grabbed the Kastle-Meyer catalytic blood kit then returned to the corridor and took a swab from the wall. She treated this with phenolphthalein and a moment later she had the answer. "I don't know what it is but it's definitely not blood." She glanced down at the ruddy smears on the floor. This, however, looked real. She tested a sample and it showed positive. Then she noticed a bloody razor knife blade in the corner. "Christ, Rhyme he faked the shooting. Cut himself somewhere to bleed for real and fool the guards."

"Call security."

Sachs yelled, "It's an escape—have the exits sealed!"

The detective jogged into the hallway and stared at the floor. Linda Welles joined him, her eyes wide. The momentary relief that she hadn't in fact been involved in a man's death faded fast as she realized the far-worse implications of what had happened. "No! He was there. His eyes were open. He looked dead." Her voice was high, frantic. "I mean, his head . . . it was all bloody. I could see . . . I could see the wound!"

You could see the *illusion* of a wound, Sachs thought bitterly.

The detective called out, "They've notified the guards at all the exits. But, Christ, this isn't a lock-down corridor. As soon as we closed the doors here he could've stood up and wandered anywhere. He's probably stealing a car right now or on the subway to Queens."

Amelia Sachs began giving orders. Whatever the detective's rank he was so shaken by the escape that he didn't question her authority. "Get an escape bulletin out now," she said. "All agencies in the metro area. Federal and state. Don't forget MTA. The name is Erick Weir. White male. Early fifties. You've got the mug shot."

"What's he wearing?" the detective asked Welles and her partner, who both struggled to remember. They gave a rough description.

Sachs was thinking, though, that it hardly mattered. He'd be in different clothing now. She gazed down the four tentacles of dim corridors she could see from here and observed silhouettes of dozens of people. Guards, janitors, cops . . .

Or maybe the Conjurer, disguised as one of them.

But for the moment she left the issue of pursuit in others' hands and turned back to her own area of expertise: the crime scene, whose search was supposed to be a brief formality but had now become a matter of life and death.

Chapter Thirty-seven

Making his way cautiously through the basement of the Manhattan Detention Center, Malerick was reflecting on his escape, offering silent patter to his revered audience.

Let me share with you a trick of the illusionist's trade.

To truly fool people it's not enough to misdirect them during the illusion. This is because when confronted with a phenomenon that defies logic the human brain continues to replay the scene afterward to try to understand what happened. We illusionists call this "reconstruction," and unless we set up our trick cleverly enough an intelligent, suspicious audience will be fooled only briefly and will figure out our method after the routine is over.

So how do we trick audiences like this?

We use the most implausible method we can—either one absurdly simple or over-whelmingly complex.

An example: one famous illusionist appears to push an entire peacock feather through a handkerchief. Audiences rarely can figure out what kind of sleight of hand he uses to make it seem that the feather actually penetrates the cloth. What's the method? It does penetrate the cloth. There's a hole in the handkerchief! The audience considers this method at first but then invariably decides that it's too simple for such a great performer. They'd rather think he's doing something far more elaborate.

Another: an illusionist met some friends for dinner at a restaurant and was asked to show them a few tricks. He declined at first but finally agreed. He took a spare table-cloth, held it up in front of a table of two lovers dining nearby and vanished the couple and their table in one second. The friends were astonished. How could he have done it? They never guessed that, supposing that he'd probably be invited to perform, the illusionist had arranged with the maître d' to have a prepared, collapsible table on hand and hired an actor and actress to play the couple. When he'd held up the cloth they'd disappeared on cue.

In reconstructing what they'd seen, the diners rejected the actual answer as too improbable for such an apparently impromptu performance.

And this is what occurred with the illusion you just witnessed, one I call the Shot Prisoner.

Reconstruction. Many illusionists forget about this psychological process. But Malerick never did. And he'd considered it carefully when planning his escape in the detention center. The officers escorting him down the corridor to the lockup believed they saw a prisoner slip his cuffs, grab a gun and end up shot dead right in front of them.

There was shock, there was dismay, there was horror.

But even at such peak moments the mind does what it must and before the smoke dissipated the officers were analyzing the events and considering options and courses of action. Like any audience they engaged in reconstruction and, knowing that Erick Weir was a skilled illusionist, undoubtedly wondered if the shooting had been faked.

But their ears had heard a real gun fire a real bullet.

Their eyes had seen a head explode under the impact and, a moment later, a limp body in the pose of death and blood, brain, bone and glazed eyes.

The reconstruction resulted in a conclusion that it was far too implausible for a man to go to such elaborate lengths to fake the shooting. So, confident he was dead, they'd left him alone, unshackled, in the corridor while they went off to make their frantic radio or phone calls.

And my method, Revered Audience?

As they'd walked down the corridor Malerick had peeled off the bandage on his hip and removed a universal handcuff key from a tiny slit in his skin. Once out of the cuffs he hit the woman guard in the face, the other in the throat and pulled her gun from her holster. A struggle . . . and finally he'd aimed the gun *behind* his head and pulled the trigger. At the same time he tapped the firing circuit of the tiny squib taped to a shaved portion of his scalp under his long hair, blowing up a small bladder of fake blood, bits of gray rubber and fragments of beef bone. To add to the credibility of the act he'd used a razor knife blade—hidden in his hip with the key—to cut his scalp, an area of the body that bleeds profusely but with little pain.

Then he'd lain like a discarded rag doll, breathing as shallowly as he could. His eyes remained open because he'd filled them with viscous eyedrops that produced a milky appearance and allowed him not to blink.

Fuck me, look what I did! Oh, fuck! Help him, somebody!

Ah, but Officer Welles, it was too late to help me.

I was dead as a roadside deer.

He headed now through winding corridors in the interconnected basements of the government buildings here until he came to the supply closet where he'd stashed his new disguise several days ago. Inside the small room he stripped and then hid the wound appliance, his old clothes and shoes behind some boxes. Donning his new outfit and applying some makeup, he was in role in less than ten seconds.

A glance out the door. The corridor was empty. He stepped outside and hurried for the stairway. It was nearly time for the finale.

"It was an out," Kara said.

The young woman had been whisked back to Rhyme's town house from Stuyvesant Manor a few moments ago.

"An out?" the criminalist asked. "What's that?"

"It means an alternative plan. All good illusionists have one or two backups for every routine. If you screw up or the audience catches your moves, you have an escape plan to save the trick. He must've figured there was a chance he'd get caught so he rigged an out to let him get away."

"How'd he do it?"

"Explosive squib behind a blood bladder hidden in his hair. The shot? It might've been a fake gun," she suggested. "Most catch-the-bullet tricks use fekes, phony guns. They have a second barrel. Or they're real guns, loaded with blanks. He might've switched guns with the officer taking him to his cell."

"I doubt it," Rhyme said, looking at Sellitto.

The rumpled cop agreed. "Yeah, I don't see how he could've switched a service piece. Or unloaded it and reloaded it with funny slugs."

Kara said, "Well, he could've just pretended to shoot himself. Played with the angle of sight."

"What about the eyes?" Rhyme asked. "The wits said his eyes were open. He never blinked. And they looked glazed."

"There're dozens of dead-man fekes and gimmicks. He might've used eyedrops that lubricate the surface. You can keep them open for ten or fifteen minutes. And there're self-lubricating contact lenses too. They have a glazed look, like you're a zombie."

Zombies and fake blood . . . Christ, what a mess. "How'd he get through the goddamn metal detector?"

"They weren't in the lockdown area yet," Sellitto explained. "That's what they were on their way to."

Rhyme sighed. Then he snapped, "Where the hell's the evidence?" Looking from the door to Mel Cooper, as if the slim technician could make the delivery from the detention center materialize on command. It turned out that there were *two* crime scenes downtown: one was the corridor where the phony shooting had occurred. The other scene was in the basement of the courthouse—a janitor's closet. One of the search teams had found the fake wound appliance, clothes and some other things hidden in a bag there.

Thom answered the ringing door chime and a moment later Roland Bell hurried into the laboratory. "Can't believe it," he said breathlessly, his hair a sweaty mop on his forehead. "It's confirmed? He's rabbited?"

"Sure has," Rhyme muttered darkly. "ESU's scouring the place. Amelia's down there too. But they haven't found any leads."

Bell drawled, "He might be heading for the hills but I'm thinking it's time to get Charles and his family into a safehouse until we find out what's what."

Sellitto said, "Absolutely."

The detective pulled out his cell phone and placed a call. "Luis? It's Roland. Listen here, Weir's escaped. . . . No, no, he wasn't dead at all. Faked it. I want Grady and his family in a safehouse till that boy's caught. I'm sending a . . . *What?*"

At the sound of this single, shocked word, everyone's attention swiveled to Bell. "Who's with him? . . . By himself? What're you telling me?"

Rhyme was looking at Bell's face, the dark, cryptic frown in the otherwise comfortingly lackadaisical visage. Once again, as had happened so often on this case, Rhyme had a sense that events that seemed unforeseeable but had in fact been planned a long time ago were beginning to unfold.

Bell turned to Sellitto. "Luis said you called and had the baby-sitting team stand down."

"Called who?"

"Called Grady's house. You told Luis to send everybody but him home."

"Why would I do that?" Sellitto asked. "Fuck, he did it again. Just like sending the guards at the circus home."

Bell said to the team, "It gets worse—Grady's on his way downtown by himself to meet with Constable about some plea bargain deal." Into the phone he said, "Keep the family together, Luis. And call the others on the team. Get 'em back right now. Don't let *anybody* into the apartment 'less you know 'em. I'll try and find Charles." He hung up and dialed another number. He listened into the receiver for a long moment. "No answer." He left a message: "Charles, this is Roland. Weir's escaped and we don't know where he'd be or what he's getting up to. As soon as you hear this, get next to an armed officer you know personally and then call me."

He gave his number and then made another call, to Bo Haumann, head of Emergency Services. He alerted him that Grady was on his way to the detention center, unprotected.

The man with two guns hung up and shook his head. "Missed this one by a mile." He stared at the evidence charts. "So, what *is* this boy up to?"

"One thing I know," Rhyme said. "He's not leaving town. He's enjoying this."

The only thing in my life, the only thing that's ever meant anything to me is performing. Illusion, magic. . . .

"Thank you, sir. Thank you."

The guard hesitated slightly at these gentle words as he ushered the man who'd spoken them—Andrew Constable—into the interview room atop the Tombs in lower Manhattan.

The prisoner smiled like a preacher thanking his parishioners for tithes.

The guard uncuffed Constable's hands from behind his back and then recuffed them in front.

"Is Mr. Roth here yet, sir?"

"Siddown, shutup."

"Sure thing." Constable sat.

"Shutup."

Did that too.

The guard left and, alone in the room, the prisoner gazed out the greasy window at the city. He was a country boy through and through but he still appreciated New York. He'd felt stunned and angry beyond words at September 11. If he and the Patriot Assembly had had their way, the incident never would have happened because the people who wished to do harm to the American way of life would have been rooted out and exposed.

Hard questions . . .

A moment later the heavy metal door

opened and the guard let Joseph Roth into the room.

"Hi, Joe. Grady's agreed to negotiate?"

"Yeah. Should be here in about ten minutes, I'd guess. He's going to need something substantive from you, though, Andrew."

"Oh, he'll get it." The man sighed. "And I've found out more since I talked to you last. I'll tell you, Joseph, I'm heartsick about what's happening up in Canton Falls. And it's been going on, right under my nose, for a year or so. That story Grady kept harping on—about killing those troopers? I thought it was nonsense. But, nope, there were some folk actually planning that."

"You have names?"

Constable said, "You bet I have names. Friends of mine. Good friends. Used to be, at least. That lunch at the Riverside Inn? Some of them *did* hire that man Weir to kill Grady. I've got names, dates, places, phone numbers. And there's more coming. There're a lot of Patriots're going to cooperate to the hilt. Don't worry."

"Good," Roth said, looking relieved. "Grady'll be tough to deal with at first.

That's his style. But I think things're going to work out."

"Thanks, Joe." Constable sized up his attorney. "I'm glad I hired you."

"I have to tell you, Andrew, I was a little surprised at first, you hiring a lawyer that was Jewish. You know, with what I heard about you."

"But then you got to know me."

"Then I got to know you."

"That reminds me, Joe, I've been meaning to ask. When's Passover?"

"What?"

"That holiday of yours. When is it?"

"About a month ago. Remember that night I left early?"

"Right." He nodded. "What's it mean, 'Passover'?"

"When the firstborn of the Egyptians were killed, God 'passed over' the Jews' houses. He spared their sons."

"Oh. I thought it meant like you passed over a border to safety or something. Like the Red Sea."

Roth laughed. "Yeah, that makes sense."

"Anyway. Sorry I didn't wish you a happy holiday."

"I appreciate that, Andrew." Then he

looked into the man's eyes. "If things work out the way I'm hoping they will, maybe you and your wife could come to our Seder next year. That's a dinner, a celebration. We have about fifteen people. They're not all Jewish. It's a good time."

"You can consider that invitation accepted." The men shook hands. "All the more incentive to get me out of here. So let's get to work. Tell me about the charges again and what you think we can get Grady to agree to." Constable stretched. Felt good to have his hands in front of him and the shackles off his ankles. He felt so good, in fact, that he actually found it amusing to hear his lawyer recite the laundry list of reasons why the people of the state of New York found him unfit for social relations. This monologue was interrupted, though, a moment later when the guard came to the door. He motioned Roth outside.

When he returned the lawyer looked troubled and said, "We're supposed to sit tight here for a bit. Weir's escaped."

"No! Is Grady safe?"

"I don't know. I assume he's got guards looking out for him."

The prisoner sighed in disgust. "You know

who's going to come off the heavy? Me, that's who. I've had it. I'm just sick and tired of this crap. I'm going to find out where Weir is and what he's up to."

"You? How?"

"I'll have everybody I can muster up in Canton Falls track down Jeddy Barnes. Maybe they can convince him to let us know where Weir is and what he's doing."

"Hold on, Andrew," Roth said uneasily. "Nothing illegal up there."

"No. I'll make sure of that."

"I'm sure Grady'll appreciate it."

"Between you and me, Joe, I don't give a rat's ass about Grady. This's for *me*. Giving 'em Weir and Jeddy's head on a platter—I do that and maybe at last everybody'll believe I'm on the up-and-up. Now let's make some phone calls and get to the bottom of this mess."

Chapter Thirty-eight

Hobbs Wentworth didn't get away from Canton Falls very often.

Dressed like a janitor, wheeling a cart containing push brooms, mops and his "fishing gear" (that is, his Colt AR-15 semi-automatic assault rifle), Hobbs Wentworth realized that life in the big city had changed quite a bit in the past twenty years, the last time he'd been here.

And he noted that everything he'd heard about the slow cancer eating away the white race was true.

Lord above our green pastures, look at this: there were more Japanese people or Chinese or something—who could tell?—than in Tokyo. And Hispanics *everywhere* in this part of New York City, like mosquitoes. And ragheads too, who he didn't see why they weren't simply rounded up and shot because of the Trade Towers. A woman in one of those Moslem outfits, all covered up, was crossing the street. He had a fast urge to kill her because she might know somebody who knew somebody who'd attacked his country.

And Indians and Pakistanis too, who should be sent back home because he couldn't understand what the fuck they were saying, not to mention they weren't Christians.

Hobbs was furious at what the government had done, opening up the borders and letting these animals inside, to gobble up the country and force decent people into little islands of safety—places like Canton Falls—which were getting smaller and smaller every day.

But God had winked at sharp-operator Hobbs Wentworth and given him the blessed role of freedom fighter. Because Jeddy Barnes and his friends knew that Hobbs had one other talent aside from teaching Bible stories to children. He killed people. And he did it very, very well. Sometimes his fishing gear was a Ka-Bar knife, sometimes a garrote, sometimes the sweet

Colt, sometimes the compound bow. His dozen or so missions over the past few years had gone perfectly. A spic in Massachusetts, a leftist politician in Albany, a nigger in Burlington, a baby-killing doc in Pennsylvania.

And now he was going to add a prosecutor to his list.

He pushed the cart through the nearly empty underground parking garage off Centre Street and paused at one of the doors, waiting. Looking apathetic about starting his night shift as a janitor. After a few minutes the door opened and he nodded pleasantly at the woman stepping out of the downstairs lobby, a middle-aged woman with a briefcase, wearing jeans and a white blouse. She smiled but pulled the door shut firmly behind her and said, sorry, she couldn't let him inside, he understood, with security being what it was.

He said, sure, he understood. And smiled back.

A minute later he dumped her twitching body into the cart and pulled her ID card lanyard over her head. He slid it through the electronic reader and the door clicked open.

He now took the elevator to the third floor,

rolling the cart in front of him, the woman's body obscured by wads of garbage bags. Hobbs found the office that Mr. Weir had decided would be the best one to use. It offered a good view of the street and, since it belonged to the Department of Highway Statistics, wasn't likely to have any emergencies that would require employees to be here on Sunday evening. The door was locked but the big man simply kicked his way inside (Mr. Weir had said there wasn't time to teach him how to pick locks).

Inside, Hobbs took his gun from the cart, mounted the 'scope and sighted on the street below. A perfect shooting blind. He couldn't miss.

Truth be told, though, he was uneasy.

It wasn't actually bagging Grady that troubled him; he could easily catch that trophy, no problem. It was getting away afterward that had him somewhat concerned. He liked his life in Canton Falls, liked telling his Bible stories to the children, liked hunting and fishing and sitting around with all his like-minded friends. Even Cindy was fun on some nights, given the right lighting and a bit of liquor.

But Magic Man Weir's plan had made provisions for his escape.

When Grady appeared Hobbs would shoot five rounds, one right after the other, at him through the sealed window. The first bullet would shatter the glass and might be deflected but the rest would kill the prosecutor. Then, Mr. Weir explained, Hobbs should push open a fire door—but not actually leave that way. It would "misdirect" the police into thinking that was his escape route. Instead he should return to the parking garage. He'd move the old Dodge in a handicapped spot and climb into the trunk. At some point—possibly that night but more likely tomorrow—the car'd be towed to the parking violations impound garage.

The towing crews were prohibited from opening either the locked doors or the trunk of cars they were towing and so they'd take the car to the garage, driving right past any barricades, without a clue that it contained a passenger. When it seemed safe Hobbs would pop the trunk from the inside and escape back to Canton Falls. There was plenty of water and food in the trunk and an empty jar if he had to pee.

It was a smart plan.

And, as a God-winked sharp operator, Hobbs would try his best to pull it off.

Sighting on random passersby to get a feel for the killing field, Hobbs reflected that Mr. Weir must put on some damn fine magic shows. He wondered if, after this was all over, he could get the man to come back to Canton Falls and put on a show for the Sunday school.

At the very least, Hobbs decided, he'd make up some stories about Jesus being a magician and using his tricks to make the Romans and heathens disappear.

Sweating.

Chills from the cold perspiration trickling down Amelia Sachs's sides and back.

Chills from fear too.

Search well . . .

She turned down another dim corridor of the Criminal Courts building, hand near her weapon.

. . . but watch your back.

Ah, you bet, Rhyme. Love to. But watch out for *who?* A lean-faced fifty-something who might be wearing a beard or might not? An elderly woman in a cafeteria worker's uniform? A workman, a DOC guard, a jani- tor cop medic cook fireman nurse? Any one of the dozens of people who were legiti- mately here on a Sunday.

Who, who, who?

Her radio clattered. It was Sellitto. "I'm on the third floor, Amelia. Nothing."

"I'm in the basement. I've seen a dozen people. All their IDs match but, hell, who knows if he's been planning this for weeks and planted a fake badge here."

"I'm going up to four."

They ended the transmission and she re- sumed the search. Down more corridors. Dozens of doors. All locked.

But of course simple locks like these meant nothing to him. He could open one in seconds and hide inside a dark storage room. He could get into a judge's cham- bers, hide until Monday. He could slip through one of the padlocked grates that led down to the utility tunnels, which in turn would give him access to half the buildings in downtown Manhattan, as well as the subway.

She turned a corner and plunged down another dark corridor. Testing knobs as she went, she found one door unlocked.

If he was inside the closet he would've heard her—the click of the knob, if not her footsteps—so there was nothing to do but go in fast. Shoving the door inward, flashlight up, ready to jump to her left if she saw a weapon turn her way (recalling that there's a tendency for a right-handed shooter to pull the gun to the left when panic firing, which sends the slug to the target's right).

Arthritic knees screaming at the partial crouch, she swung the halogen beam throughout the room. A few boxes and file cabinets. Nothing else. Though as she turned to leave she recalled that he'd hidden in shadows by using a simple black cloth. She looked around the room again more slowly, probing with the flashlight.

As she did she felt a touch on her neck.

A gasp and she spun around, bringing the gun up—aiming at the center of the dust-coated cobweb that had caressed her skin.

Back into the corridor.

More locked doors. More dead ends.

Footsteps approached. A man walked past her now, bald, in his sixties, dressed in a guard's uniform and wearing an appropriate ID badge. He nodded as he walked past. He was taller than Weir so she let him pass with no more than a glance.

But then she thought there might be a way for a quick-change artist to change his height.

Turning back, fast.

The man was gone; she saw only an empty corridor. Or an *apparently* empty corridor. She recalled again the silk the Conjurer had hidden beneath to kill Svetlana Rasnikov, the mirror to kill Tony Calvert. Her body a knot of tension, she unholstered her weapon and started toward where the guard—the *apparent* guard—had disappeared.

Where? Where was Weir?

Trotting along Centre Street, Roland Bell surveyed the landscape in front of him. Cars, trucks, hot dog vendors in front of their steaming metal carts, young people who'd been working at their perpetual-motion law firms or investment banks, others woozy from pitchers of beer at the South Street Seaport, dog walkers, shoppers, dozens of the Manhattanites who roam the streets on days beautiful and days gray simply because the city's energy draws them outside.

Where?

Bell thought much of life was like driving a nail—shooting, in his local vernacular. He'd been raised in the Albemarle Sound area of North Carolina, where guns were a necessity, not a fetish, and he'd been taught to respect them. Part of this involved concentration. Even simple shots—at a paper target, a rattlesnake or copperhead, a deer—could go wide and dangerous if you didn't stay focused on the target.

Well, life was just like that. And Bell knew that whatever was going on inside the Tombs right now, he had to remain focused on his single job: protecting Charles Grady.

Amelia Sachs called in and reported that she was checking out every human being she could find in the Criminal Courts building, of whatever age, race or size (she'd just tracked down and ID'd a bald guard, who was far taller than Weir and looked nothing like the killer but who had only passed muster because it turned out that he'd known her late father). She'd finished one wing of the basement and was about to start on another.

Teams under Sellitto and Bo Haumann were still searching upper floors of the building, and the oddest addition of all to the hunt was none other than Andrew Constable himself, who was tracking down leads to Weir in upstate New York. Now that'd be a kick, Bell thought—if the man accused of the attempted murder in the first place turned out to be the one who found out where the real suspect was.

Looking into the cars he jogged past, looking at trucks on the street, looking down alleyways, guns ready but not drawn. Bell had decided that it made the most sense for them to hit Grady here on the street, before he entered the building, where there was a better chance of escaping alive. He doubted that these people were suicidal—that didn't fit the profile. In the moment between the time Grady parked his car and stepped out until he walked into the massive doors of the grimy Criminal Courts building the killer would go for his shot. And an easy one it would be—there was virtually no cover here.

Where was Weir?

And, just as important, where was *Grady*?

His wife had said he'd taken the family

car, not the city one. Bell had put out an emergency vehicle locator for the prosecutor's Volvo but no one had spotted it.

Bell turned slowly, surveying the scene, revolving like a lighthouse. His eyes rose to the building across the street, a government office building, a new one, with dozens of windows facing Centre Street. Bell had been involved in a brief hostage-taking in the building and he knew that it was practically deserted now, on Sunday. A perfect place to hide and wait for Grady.

But then the street would be a good vantage point too—for a drive-by, say.

Where, where?

Roland Bell recalled a time he'd gone hunting with his daddy up in the Great Dismal Swamp in southern Virginia. They'd been charged by a wild boar and his father'd winged the animal. It had disappeared into the brush. The man had sighed and said, "We gotta go git him. Can't ever leave a wounded animal."

"But he tried to attack us," the boy had protested.

"Well now, son, we walked into his world. He didn't walk into ours. But that's neither here nor there. It's not a question of fairness. It's a question of we got to find him if it takes all day. Not humane to him and now he's twice as dangerous to anybody else comes along."

Looking around them at the impossible tangle of brush and reeds and swamp grass and loblolly, stretching for miles, young Roland said, "But he could be anywhere, Dad."

His father laughed grimly. "Oh, don't worry 'bout finding him. He'll find us. Keep your thumb on that safety, son. You may have to shoot fast. You comfortable with that?"

"Yessir, I am."

Bell now made another visual circuit of the vans, the alleyways nearby, the buildings next to and across the street from the courthouse.

Nothing.

No Charles Grady.

No Erick Weir, no sign of any of the killer's confederates.

Bell tapped the butt of his gun.

Don't worry 'bout finding him. He'll find us. . . .

Chapter Thirty-nine

"I'm doing a door-to-door, Rhyme. The last wing of the basement."

"Let ESU handle it." He found his head craning forward tensely as he spoke into the microphone.

"We need everybody," Sachs whispered. "It's a damn big building." She was in the Tombs now, working her way through the corridors. "Eerie too. Like the music school."

Mysteriouser and mysteriouser . . .

"Someday you oughta add a chapter to your book about running crime scenes in spooky locations," she joked out of nervousness. "Okay, I'm going silent now, Rhyme. I'll call you back."

Rhyme and Cooper returned to the evidence. In the corridor on the way to intake in the Tombs Sachs had recovered the blade from the razor knife and fragments of beef bone and gray sponge—to simulate skull and brain matter—as well as samples of the fake blood: sugar syrup with red food coloring. He'd used his jacket or shirt to wipe up as much of his real blood as he could from the floor and the cuffs but Sachs had run the scene as methodically as ever and she'd recovered enough of a sample for analysis. He'd taken with him the key or lock picks he'd used to undo the cuffs. There was no other helpful evidence in the corridor scene.

The janitor's closet downstairs where he'd done his quick change yielded more—a paper bag in which he'd hidden the bloody squib and bladder and what he'd been wearing when they'd collared him at Grady's: the gray suit, the white shirt he'd used to wipe up and a pair of Oxford businessman's shoes. Cooper had found substantial trace evidence on these items: additional latex and makeup, bits of magician's adhesive wax, streaks of ink similar to those they'd found earlier, thick nylon fibers and dried smears of more fake blood.

The fibers turned out to be charcoal-gray carpet. The phony blood was paint. The databases they had access to didn't give any information about either of these materials so he sent the chemical composition analysis and photos down to the FBI, with an urgent request for sourcing.

Then an idea occurred to Rhyme. "Kara," he called, seeing the girl sitting next to Mel Cooper, rolling a quarter over her fingers as she stared at the computer image of a fiber. "Can you help us out with one thing?"

"Sure."

"Could you go over to the Cirque Fantastique and find Kadesky? Tell him about the escape and see if there's anything else he can remember about Weir. Any illusions he particularly liked, characters or disguises he kept going back to, what sort of routines he repeated most often. . . . Anything that'll give us an idea of what he might look like."

"Maybe he's got some old clippings or pictures of Weir in costume," she suggested, slinging her black-and-white purse over her shoulder.

He told her that was a good idea and then returned to the evidence chart, which still stood as testimony to his earlier observation: the more they learned, the less they knew.

THE CONJURER

Music School Crime Scene

- Perp's description: Brown hair, fake beard, no distinguishing, medium build, medium height, age: fifties. Ring and little fingers of left hand fused together. Changed costume quickly to resemble old, bald janitor.

- No apparent motive.

- Victim: Svetlana Rasnikov.
  - Full-time music student.
  - Checking family, friends, students, coworkers for possible leads.
    - No boyfriends, no known enemies. Performed at children's birthday parties.

- Circuit board with speaker attached.
  - Sent to FBI lab, NYC.
    - Digital recorder, probably containing perp's voice. All data destroyed.
  - Voice recorder is a "gimmick." Homemade.

- Used antique iron handcuffs to restrain victim.
  - Handcuffs are Darby irons. Scotland Yard. Checking with Houdini Museum in New Orleans for leads.
    - Sold to Erick Weir last month. Sent to Denver P.O. box. No other leads.

- No motive.

- Perp gave name as "John." Had scars on neck and chest. Deformed hand confirmed.

- Perp did quick change to unbearded businessman in chinos and dress shirt, then biker in denim Harley shirt.

- Car is in Harlem River.

- Duct tape gag. Can't be traced.

- Squibs, same as before. Can't be traced.

- Chains and snap fixtures, generic, not traceable.

- Rope, generic, not traceable.

- Additional makeup, latex and Tack-Pure.

- Gym bag, made in China, not traceable. Containing:
  - Traces of date rape drug flunitrazepam.
  - Adhesive magician's wax, not traceable.
  - Brass (?) shavings. Sent to FBI.
    - Consistent with clockwork mechanism, possible bomb timer.
  - Permanent ink, black.

- Navy-blue windbreaker found, no initials or laundry marks. Containing:
  - Press pass for CTN cable network, issued to Stanley Saferstein. (He's not suspect—NCIC, VICAP search negative.)

- Destroyed victim's watch at exactly 8:00 A.M.

- Cotton string holding chairs. Generic. Too many sources to trace.

- Squib for gunshot effect. Destroyed.
  - Too many sources to trace.

- Fuse. Generic.
  - Too many sources to trace.

- Responding officers reported flash in air. No trace material recovered.
  - Was from flash cotton or flash paper.
    - Too many sources to trace.

- Perp's shoes: size 10 Ecco.

- Silk fibers, dyed gray, processed to a matte finish.
  - From quick-change janitor's outfit.

- Unsub is possibly wearing brown wig.

- Red pignut hickory and Parmelia conspersa lichen, both found primarily in Central Park.

- Dirt impregnated with unusual mineral oil. Sent to FBI for analysis.
  - Tack-Pure oil for saddles and leather.

- Black silk, 72 x 48". Used as camouflage. Not traceable.
  - Illusionists use this frequently.

- Wears caps to cover up prints.
  - Magician's finger cups.

- Traces of latex, castor oil, makeup.
  - Theatrical makeup.

- Traces of alginate.
  - Used in molding latex appliances.

- Murder weapon: white silk-knit rope with black silk core.
  - Rope is a magic trick. Color changing. Not traceable.

- Unusual knot.
  - Sent to FBI and Maritime Museum—no information.
  - Knots are from Houdini routines, virtually impossible to untie.

- Used disappearing ink on sign-in register.

East Village Crime Scene

- Victim Two: Tony Calvert.
  - Makeup artist, theater company.
  - No known enemies.
  - No apparent connection with first victim.

- No apparent motive.

- Cause of death:
  - Blunt-object trauma to head followed by postmortem dismemberment with crosscut saw.

- Perp escaped portraying woman in her 70s. Checking vicinity for discarded costume and other evidence.
  - Nothing recovered.

- Watch smashed at 12:00 exactly.
  - Pattern? Next victim presumably at 4:00 P.M.

- Perp hid behind mirror. Not traceable. Fingerprints sent to FBI.
  - No matches.

- Used cat toy ("feke") to lure victim into alley. Toy is untraceable.

- Additional mineral oil found, same as at first scene. Awaiting FBI report.
  - Tack-Pure oil for saddles and leather.

- Additional latex and makeup from finger cups.

- Additional alginate.

- Ecco shoes left behind.

- Dog hairs found in shoes, from three different breeds of dog. Manure too.
  - Manure from horses, not dogs.

Hudson River and Related Crime Scenes

- Victim: Cheryl Marston.
  - Attorney.
  - Divorced but husband not a suspect.

- Plastic hotel key card, American Plastic Cards, Akron, Ohio. Model APC-42, negative on prints.
  - CEO is searching for sales records.
  - Dets. Bedding and Saul canvassing hotels.
    - Narrowed down to Chelsea Lodge, Beckman and Lanham Arms.
    - Hotel is Lanham Arms.
- Restaurant check from Riverside Inn, Bedford Junction, NY, indicating four people ate lunch, table 12, Saturday, two weeks prior. Turkey, meatloaf, steak, daily special. Soft drinks. Staff doesn't know who diners were. (Accomplices?)
- Alley where Conjurer was arrested:
- Picked the cuff locks.
- Saliva (picks hidden in mouth).
- No blood type determined.
- Small razor saw for getting out of restraints (also hidden in mouth).

- No indication of Officer Burke's whereabouts.

- Report body somewhere on Upper West Side.

- Harlem River scene:
  - No evidence on riverbank, except skid marks in mud.
  - Newspaper recovered from the car. Headlines:

ELECTRICAL BREAKDOWN
CLOSES POLICE STATION
FOR ALMOST 4 HOURS

NEW YORK IN RUNNING
FOR GOP CONVENTION

PARENTS PROTEST
POOR SECURITY AT
GIRLS' SCHOOL

MILITIA MURDER PLOT
TRIAL OPENS MONDAY

WEEKEND GALA AT MET
TO BENEFIT CHARITIES

SPRING ENTERTAINMENT
FOR KIDS YOUNG AND OLD

GOVERNOR, MAYOR MEET
ON NEW WEST SIDE PLAN

Lincoln Rhyme Crime Scene

- Victim: Lincoln Rhyme.

- Perp's identity: Erick A. Weir.
  - LKA Las Vegas.
  - Burned in fire in Ohio, three years ago. Hasbro and Keller Brothers Circus. Disappeared after. Third-degree burns. Producer was Edward Kadesky.
  - Conviction in New Jersey for reckless endangerment.
  - Obsessed with fire.
  - Manic. Referred to "Revered Audience."
  - Performed dangerous tricks.
  - Married to Marie Cosgrove, killed in fire.
    - He hasn't contacted her family since.
  - Weir's parents dead, no next of kin.
  - No VICAP or NCIC on Weir.
  - Referred to himself as "Wizard of the North."

- Attacked Rhyme because he had to stop him before Sunday afternoon.
- Eye color—brown.

- Psychological profile (per Terry Dobyns, NYPD): Revenge motivates him though he may not realize it. He wants to get even. Angry all the time. By killing he takes away some of the pain because of death of his wife, loss of ability to perform.

- Weir contacted assistants recently: John Keating and Arthur Loesser, in Nevada. Asking about the fire and people involved with it. Described Weir as crazed, overbearing, manic, dangerous, but brilliant.

- Killed victims because of what they represented— possibly happy or traumatic moments before the fire.

- Gasoline-soaked handkerchief, not traceable.

- Ecco shoes, no trace.

Detention Center Escape Scenes

- Squibs and bladder from fake wound—homemade, no source.

- Artificial blood (sugar syrup + red food coloring), fragments of beef bone, gray sponge to simulate brain, real blood, razor knife blade.

- DOC officer's Glock.

- Handcuffs.

- Unsuccessful attempt to clean up blood.

- Additional bits of latex and makeup, as at prior scenes.

- Adhesive wax.

- Permanent ink, black, similar to that found earlier.

- Dried artificial blood (paint), sent to FBI.

- Carpet fibers, sent to FBI.

Profile as Illusionist

- Perp will use misdirection against victims and in eluding police.
  - Physical misdirection (for distraction).
  - Psychological (to eliminate suspicion).

- Escape at music school was similar to Vanished Man illusion routine. Too common to trace.

- Perp is primarily an illusionist.

- Talented at sleight of hand.

- Also knows protean (quick change) magic. Will use breakaway clothes, nylon and silk, bald cap, finger cups and other latex appliances. Could be any age, gender or race.

- Calvert's death = Selbit's Cutting a Woman in Half routine.

- Proficient at lock picking (possibly lock "scrubbing").

- Knows escapism techniques.

- Experience with animal illusions.

- Used mentalism to get information on victim.

- Used sleight of hand to drug her.

- Tried to kill third victim with Houdini escape. Water Torture Cell.

- Ventriloquism.

- Razor blades.

- Familiar with Burning Mirror routine. Very dangerous, rarely performed now.

● ● ●

The Cirque Fantastique was coming alive, an hour before that night's performance.

Kara walked past the banner of Arlecchino and noticed a police car, which Lincoln Rhyme had ordered to remain after the scare that afternoon. Feeling a camaraderie with them since she herself had been playing cop, she smiled and waved to the officers, who, though they didn't know her, waved back.

No one was taking tickets yet so Kara wandered inside and made her way backstage. She noticed a young man holding a clipboard. An employee pass sat high on his belt like Amelia's gun.

"Excuse me," she said.

"Yes?" he replied in a thick French or French-Canadian accent.

"I'm looking for Mr. Kadesky."

"He is not here. I am one of his assistants."

"Where is he?"

"Not here. Who are you?"

"I'm working with the police. Mr. Kadesky met with them earlier. They have some more questions for him."

The young man glanced at her chest, presumably, though not necessarily, looking for ID.

"Uh-huh. Ah. Police. Well, he's at dinner. He will be back soon."

"Do you know where he's eating?" she asked.

"No. You'll have to leave. You can't be back here."

"I only need to see him—"

"Do you have a ticket?"

"No, I—"

"Then you can't wait. You must leave. He never said anything about the police."

"Well, I really need to see him," she said firmly to the man with Gallic good looks and a chill demeanor.

"Really, you must go. You can wait outside for him."

"I might miss him."

"I'll have to call a guard," he threatened in his thick accent. "I will do that."

"I'll buy a ticket," she said.

"They're sold out. And even if you could buy one you could not be back here. I will walk you out."

He herded her out the main door, where the ticket-takers were now on duty. Outside she paused and pointed over his shoulder toward a trailer on which was a sign, BOX OFFICE. "That's where I could buy a ticket?"

A demi-sneer crossed his face. "That's what a box office is. But, as I said, there are no more tickets. You can call Mr. Kadesky's company if you need to ask him something."

After he'd gone, Kara waited a moment or

two, then turned the corner of the tent and proceeded to the stage entrance in back. She smiled at the security guard and he smiled back, giving only a cursory glance at her belt, where now sat the French-Canadian's employee pass, which she'd easily unhooked from his belt when she'd pointed and asked the foolish, but quite misdirecting, question about the box office.

Now, there's a rule for you, she reflected: Never fuck with somebody who knows sleight of hand.

Inside the backstage portion of the tent once again she hid the badge in her pocket and found a friendlier employee. The woman, Katherine Tunney, nodded sympathetically when Kara explained what she was doing there—that a former illusionist wanted for murder had been identified as someone Mr. Kadesky had worked with a long time ago. The woman had heard about the killings and she invited Kara to wait until the producer returned from dinner. Katherine gave Kara a pass to sit in one of the VIP boxes and then left on another errand, promising that she'd tell the guards to make sure Mr. Kadesky came to see her as soon as he returned.

On her way to the box seat her pager sounded, an urgent beeping.

She gasped when she saw the number, ran to a bank of temporary pay phones and, hand shaking, made the call.

"Stuyvesant Manor," the voice said.

"Jaynene Williams, please."

A huge wait.

" 'Lo?"

"It's me. Kara. Is Mom okay?"

"Oh, she's fine, girl. But I wanted to tell you—don't get your hopes up. It might be nothin'. But a few minutes ago she woke up and asked for you. She knows it's Sunday night and she remembered you coming by earlier."

"You mean, 'me,' the *real* me?"

"Yep, your real name. Then she gave this little frown and said, 'Unless all she goes by is that crazy stage name of hers, Kara.' "

My God. . . . Could she be back?

"And she knew me and she asked where you were. Said she wanted to tell you some-thing."

Kara's heart accelerated.

Tell me something . . .

"Better get over here soon, honey. Might

last. But it might not. You know how that goes."

"I'm in the middle of something, Jaynene. I'll get there as soon as I can."

They hung up and, frantic, Kara returned to her seat. The tension was unbearable. Right this instant her mother might be asking where her daughter was. Frowning and disappointed that the girl wasn't there.

Please, she prayed, looking again toward the doorway for Kadesky.

Nothing.

Wishing she could tap a hickory magic wand on the battered metal railing in front of her, point it at the doorway and materialize the producer.

Please, she thought again, aiming the imaginary wand toward the doorway. *Please . . .*

Nothing for a moment. Then several figures entered. None of them was Kadesky, though. They were just three women dressed in medieval costumes and wearing masks whose forlorn expressions were belied by the buoyant spring in the step of actors about to begin their evening's performance.

●　　●　　●

Roland Bell was standing in one of the canyons of downtown Manhattan: Centre Street between the grimy, towering Criminal Courts building, crowned by the Bridge of Sighs, and the nondescript office building across the street from it.

Still no sign of Charles Grady's Volvo.

The lighthouse rotation once again. Where, where, where?

A honk nearby, in the direction of the entrance to the bridge. A shout.

Bell turned and jogged a few steps toward the sounds, wondering: Misdirection?

But, no, it was just a traffic dispute.

He turned back, toward the entrance to the Criminal Courts building, and found himself looking right at Charles Grady, who was strolling casually up the street, a block away. The prosecutor was walking with his head down, lost in his thoughts. The detective sprinted toward the man, calling, "Charles! Get down! Weir's escaped!"

Grady paused, frowning.

"Down!" Bell called breathlessly.

The alarmed man crouched on the sidewalk, between two parked cars. "What happened?" he shouted. "My family!"

"I've got people with them," the detective said. Then, to the pedestrians: "Everybody! Police action here! Clear the street!"

People scattered instantly.

"My family!" Grady called desperately. "You're sure?"

"They're fine."

"But Weir—"

"Faked the shooting in detention. He's out and somewhere around here. I've got an armored van on its way."

Turning again, squinting, surveying the scenery.

Roland Bell finally reached Grady and stood over him, his back to the dark windows of the government office building across the street.

"Just stay right where you are, Charles," Bell said. "We'll get out of this fine." And pulled his handy-talkie off his belt.

What was *this*?

Hobbs Wentworth watched his target below him—the prosecutor—cowering on the sidewalk behind a man in a sportscoat, a cop obviously.

The crosshairs of Hobbs's 'scope poked

around the officer's back, searching unsuccessfully for an unprotected shot at Grady.

The prosecutor was low, the cop standing. It seemed to Hobbs that if he shot through the cop's lower back he'd probably hit Grady in the upper chest, since he was crouching. But the risk was that the shot would be deflected and Grady'd only be wounded and fall to safety behind a car.

Well, he had to do something pretty soon. The cop was talking on his radio. There'd be a hundred more of 'em here in a minute. Come on, sharp operator, he said to himself. Whatcha gonna do?

Below him the cop was still looking around, covering Grady, who squatted like a bitch retriever peeing.

All right. What he'd do was shoot the cop in the upper leg, the thigh. That way, most likely, the cop would fall backward, exposing the prosecutor. The Colt was semiauto so he could fire five shots in two seconds. Not perfect but it was the best Hobbs could think of.

He'd give the cop a moment or two longer to step aside or sway out of the way.

Both eyes open as the right one stared through the 'scope, painting the back of the

detective with the crosshairs and thinking
that when he got back to Canton Falls he'd
make up a Bible story about this. Jesus
would play his role and would be armed
with a kick-ass compound bow, about to
ambush a bunch of Roman soldiers, who'd
been torturing Christians. Julius Caesar
would be hiding behind one soldier and
thinking he was safe but Jesus would shoot
through the soldier and kill the son-of-a-
bitch.

Good story. The kids'd love it.

The cop was still huddled over the prosecutor.

Well, that's it, Hobbs thought, clicking off
the safety of the big Colt. No time left. Burn
in brimstone, Christ-killing Romans.

He centered the crosshairs on the back of
the cop's leg and began to apply slow pressure on the trigger, thinking that his only regret was that the officer was white, not
black.

But one thing Hobbs Wentworth'd
learned in life: you take your targets the way
you find 'em.

Chapter Forty

Roland Bell smelled the distinctive plastic/sweat/metal scent of the Motorola handy-talkie as he clutched it to his face.

"ESU Four, you 'bout ready, K?" he drawled into the mike.

"Roger that, K," one of them replied.

"Okay, now—"

Which is when the muffled cracks of multiple shots resounded through the canyon of the street.

Bell jumped.

"Gunshots!" Charles Grady cried. "I heard shots! Are you hit?"

"Just stay down," Bell said as he dropped into a crouch. He spun around, lifting his gun and squinting hard at the government office building across the street.

He was counting furiously.

"Got the location," he called into the radio. "I make it the third floor, fifth office from the north end of the building." Then Bell examined the glass. "Ouch."

"Say again, K?" one of the officers called.

"I said, 'Ouch.'"

"Uhm. Roger. Out."

Grady, lying on the sidewalk, said, "What's going on?" He started to get up.

"Sit tight there," the detective told him, standing up cautiously. Turning now from the window and scanning the sidewalk around him. There was a possibility that more shooters were nearby. A moment later an armored Emergency Services van pulled up and five seconds after that Bell and Grady were inside, squealing away from the attempted hit and taking the prosecutor back to the Upper East Side and his family.

Bell glanced behind him to see more ESU troopers streaming into the building across the street from the courthouse.

Don't worry. . . . He'll find us.

Well, he sure as hell had.

Bell had concluded that the best way to try to hit Grady would be from the office building across the street. It was most likely that the killer would break into one of the lower offices facing the sidewalk. The roof was unlikely because it was monitored by dozens of CCTV cameras. Bell had remained in the open as bait because of something he knew about this particular building from the hostage situation he'd run there: the windows, as in many of the newer government buildings here, couldn't be opened and were made from bomb-proof glass.

There'd been a small risk, he supposed, that the shooter would use armor-piercing rounds, which might penetrate the inch-thick glass. But Bell had recalled an expression he'd heard during a case a couple of years ago: "God don't give out certain."

He'd taken the chance of luring the sniper into shooting, in hopes that the bullet would spider the window and reveal the man's location.

And his idea had worked—though with a variation, as Bell had mentioned to the ESU team. *Ouch. . . .*

"ESU Four to Bell. It's Haumann. You were right, K."

"Go ahead, K."

The tactical commander continued, "We're inside. Scene is secure. Only what do they call those? The Darwin Awards? You know, where criminals do stupid things, K?"

"Roger that," Bell responded. "Where'd he hit himself, K?"

Bell had spotted the shooter's location not because of cracked glass but because of a large spatter of blood on the window. The ESU chief explained that the copper-jacketed slugs that the man had fired toward Bell had ricocheted off the glass, shattered and struck the shooter himself in a half-dozen places, most significantly his groin, where they apparently severed a large artery or vein. The man had bled out by the time the ESU team had made its way to the office.

"Tell me it's Weir, K," Bell said.

"Nup. Sorry. It's somebody named Hobbs Wentworth. Address, Canton Falls."

Bell scowled angrily. So Weir and maybe others working with him were still around. He asked, "Find anything that'll give us a clue what Weir's up to or where he might be?"

"Negative," said the raspy-voiced commander. "Only his ID. And, get this, a book of Bible stories for kids." There was a pause. "Hate to say it but we got another victim, Roland. He killed a woman to get into the building, looks like. . . . Okay, we're going to secure the place and keep looking for Weir. Out."

The detective shook his head and said to Grady, "No sign of him."

Except that, of course, that was the whole problem. Maybe they *had* found plenty of signs of Weir, maybe they'd even found Weir himself—in the form of another cop, a med tech, an ESU officer, a reporter, a soft-clothed detective, a passerby or homeless man—and they simply didn't know it.

Through the yellowing window in the interview room Andrew Constable could see the grim face of a large black guard peer in and look at him. The face disappeared as the man stepped away from the door.

Constable rose from the metal table and walked past his lawyer to the window. He looked outside and saw two guards in the hall, speaking gravely to each other.

All right then.

"What's that?" Joseph Roth asked his client.

"Nothing," Constable responded. "I didn't say anything."

"Oh, I thought you did."

"No."

Though he wondered if he had. Made some comment, uttered a prayer.

He returned to the table, where the lawyer looked up from a pad of yellow foolscap that contained a half dozen names and phone numbers, which Constable's associates in Canton Falls had just provided in response to their questions about what Weir might have planned, where he might be.

Roth looked uneasy. They'd just learned that a man with a rifle had made an attempt on Grady's life in front of the building a few minutes ago. But it hadn't been Weir, who was still unaccounted for. The lawyer said, "I'm worried that Grady'll be too spooked to deal with us. I think we should call him at home and tell him what we've found." Tapping the sheets. "Or at least give this stuff to that detective. What was his name? Bell, right?"

"That's it," Constable said.

Moving his pudgy finger over the sheet of names and numbers, Roth said, "You think anybody here'll know something specific about Weir? That's what they'll want, something specific."

Constable leaned forward and looked at the list. Then at his lawyer's watch. He shook his head slowly. "I doubt it," he said.

"You . . . You doubt it?"

"Yeah. See this first number?"

"Yeah."

"It's the dry cleaner on Harrison Street in Canton Falls. And the one below it's the IGA. The next one's the Baptist church. And those names?" the prisoner continued. "Ed Davis, Brett Samuels, Joe James Watkins?"

"Right," Roth said. "Jeddy Barnes' associates."

Constable gave a chuckle. "Gosh no. They're all made up."

"What?" Roth frowned.

Leaning close to his lawyer, the prisoner stared into the man's confused eyes. "I'm saying that those names and numbers're fake."

"I don't understand."

Constable whispered, "Of course you don't, you pathetic fucking Jew," and slammed his fists into the side of the shocked lawyer's face before Roth could raise his arms to protect himself.

Chapter Forty-one

Andrew Constable was a strong man, strong from hiking to remote hunting and fishing grounds, from dressing deer and sawing bones, from chopping wood.

Paunchy Joe Roth was no match for him. The lawyer tried to rise and call for help but Constable struck him hard in the throat. The man's shout became a gurgling sound.

The prisoner pulled him to the floor and began pummeling the bleeding man with his cuffed fists. In a moment Roth was unconscious, his face swollen like a melon. Constable dragged him back to the table and propped him up on it, his back to the door. If one of the guards happened to glance in again it would look as if he were reading the papers, head down. Constable bent down, pulled off one of the lawyer's shoes and socks and wiped the blood off the table as best he could and covered the rest with documents and pads of paper. He'd kill the lawyer later. For now, for a few minutes at least, he needed this innocent-looking tableau.

A few minutes—until he was free.

Freedom . . .

Which was the whole point of Erick Weir's plan.

Constable's best friend, Jeddy Barnes, the second in command of the Patriot Assembly, had hired Weir not to kill Grady but to break the prisoner out of the notoriously secure Manhattan Detention Center, transport him to freedom over the Bridge of Sighs and ultimately into the New England wilderness, where the Assembly could resume its mission to wage war against the impure, the unclean, the ignorant. To rid the land of blacks, gays, Jews, Hispanics, foreigners—the "Them" that Constable railed against in his weekly lectures at the Patriot Assembly and in the secret websites subscribed to by the thousands of right-thinking citizens around the country.

Constable now rose, walked to the door, looked out again. The guards had no clue about what had just happened inside the interview room.

It occurred to the prisoner that he ought to have a weapon of some kind and so he lifted a metal mechanical pencil from the lawyer's bloody shirt and then nestled the butt of the pencil in the wadded-up sock to protect his palm. The sharp point would make a fine stabbing implement.

Then he sat back, across from Roth, and waited, thinking about the plan created by Weir, or "Magic Man," as Barnes called him. It was a masterpiece, involving dozens of tricks of the illusionist's trade. Feint and double feint, careful timing, clever diversions. It began with Weir carefully planting the idea with the police that there was a conspiracy to kill Grady. The Reverend Ralph Swensen laid the groundwork for this by making one attempt on the prosecutor's life. The bungled killing would reinforce the cops' belief that there was a plot to kill the prosecutor and they'd stop looking for any other crimes—such as the planned jail break.

Weir himself would then intentionally get caught during a second attempt to kill Grady and be taken to detention.

Meanwhile, Constable was supposed to do some misdirection of his own. He'd disarm his captors by being the voice of reason, pleading his innocence and winning sympathy and luring Grady to the courthouse this evening by offering to incriminate Barnes and other conspirators. Constable would even try to help track down the illusionist, further disarming the police and giving him the chance to deliver a coded message about his exact location in the detention center, which Barnes would pass on to Weir.

When Grady arrived, Hobbs Wentworth would try to kill the prosecutor but whether he succeeded or not didn't matter; the important thing was that Hobbs would divert the police from the detention center. Then Weir—who was roaming free in the building after faking his own death—would sneak up here in disguise, kill the guards and break Constable out.

There was one more part to the plan—an aspect that Constable'd been looking forward to for weeks. Just before Weir arrived at the interview room, Jeddy Barnes had told him, Constable was "supposed to take care of your lawyer."

"What's that mean?"

"Weir said it's up to you. He just said you're supposed to take care of Roth so he's not in the way."

Now, watching the blood drip from the lawyer's eyes and mouth, he thought, Well, the Jew's took care of.

Constable was wondering how Weir would kill the guards, what kind of disguises he'd have with him, what their escape route would be, when—right on schedule—he heard the distinctive buzz of the outer door.

Ah, his chariot to freedom had arrived.

Constable dragged Roth off the bench and dumped him in the corner of the interview room. He thought about killing him now, stomping on his windpipe. But he supposed Weir had a gun with a silencer. Or a knife. He could use that.

Hearing the click of the key in the lock of the interview room.

The door swung open.

For a split second he thought: Amazing! Weir'd managed to turn himself into a woman.

But then he remembered her; this was the redheaded officer who'd been with Detective Bell yesterday.

"Injury here," she shouted as she glanced down at Roth. "Call EMS!"

Behind her one guard grabbed a phone and the other hit a red button on the wall, sending a klaxon alarm braying into the hallway.

What was going on? Constable didn't understand. Where was Weir?

He glanced back at the woman to see the pepper spray—the only permissible weapon in detention—in her hand. He thought fast and began moaning loud, holding his belly. "Somebody got in here! Another prisoner. He tried to kill us!" Hiding the sharp pencil, he clutched his bloody hands to his belly. "I'm hurt. I've been stabbed!"

A fast glance outside. Still no sign of the Magic Man.

The woman frowned and looked around the cell as Constable slumped to the floor. Thinking: When she gets closer he'd stab toward her face with the pencil. Maybe hit her eye. He could get the spray away, blast her in the mouth or eyes with it. Maybe hold the pencil to her back; the guards would think it was a gun and open the door for him. Weir had to be close—maybe he was just outside the security doors.

Come on, honey. A little closer. She might have a bulletproof vest on, he reminded himself; aim for her pretty face.

"Your lawyer?" she asked, leaning over Roth. "Is he stabbed too?"

"Yes! It was some black prisoner. He said I was a racist. He said he wanted to teach me a lesson." His head was down but he could sense her stepping closer. "Joe's hurt bad. We have to save him!"

Just a few more feet. . . .

Or if he is *a white man and looks like a smart man—if he has all his teeth and wears clothes that don't smell like yesterday's piss—well, then, are you going to be just a little slower to pull that trigger?*

Constable moaned.

He sensed her very close.

She said, "Let me see how badly you're hurt."

He gripped the pencil firmly. Got ready to spring. He looked up to find his target.

And saw the nozzle of the pepper spray, a foot away from his eyes.

She pushed the button and the stream shot him square in the face. A hundred hot needles pierced his mouth and nose and eyes.

Constable screamed as the policewoman ripped the pen out of his hand and kicked him onto his back.

"Why'd you do that?" he cried, rising up on one elbow. "Why?"

Her answer was to debate for a brief moment then hit him with a second stream of fiery spray.

Chapter Forty-two

Amelia Sachs put the pepper spray canister away.

The potential sergeant in her was a bit troubled by the gratuitous second blast into Constable's face.

But having noticed the fourteen-karat shiv half concealed in his hand, Sachs the street cop with wire thoroughly enjoyed hearing the vicious bigot squeal like a pig as she sprayed him again. She stepped aside as the two floor guards grabbed the prisoner and dragged him out.

"A doctor! Get me to a doctor. My eyes! I have a right to a doctor!"

"I keep tellin' yo t'shuddup." The guards dragged him down the hall. Constable lashed out with his feet. They stopped, shackled his ankles, and then pulled him around the corner.

Sachs and two more guards looked over Joseph Roth. He was breathing but unconscious and badly hurt. She decided it was best not to move him. Soon a city EMS team arrived and, after Sachs checked their IDs, went to work on the lawyer, clearing his airway and getting a neck brace around him then strapping him onto a backboard, which they placed on a gurney. They took him out of the secure area for the drive to the hospital.

Sachs stood back and surveyed the room and the lobby to make sure that Weir hadn't slipped in unnoticed. No, she was sure he hadn't. She then went outside and it was only when she got her Glock back from the officer at the desk that she began to feel more at ease. She called Rhyme to tell him what had happened. Then she added, "Constable was expecting him, Rhyme."

"Expecting Weir?"

"I think so. He was surprised when I opened the door. He tried to recover but I could tell he was waiting for somebody."

"So that's what Weir's up to—breaking Constable out?"

"That's what I think."

"Goddamn misdirection," he muttered. "He's had us focused on the plot to kill Grady. I never thought they'd be going for a breakout." Then he added, "Unless the *escape* is misdirection and Weir's job really *is* to kill Grady."

She considered this. "That'd work too."

"And no sign of Weir anywhere?"

"None."

"Okay, I'm still going over what you found at Detention, Sachs. Come on back and we'll look over it."

"I can't, Rhyme," she said, studying the hallway in which a dozen onlookers stood gazing at the excitement in the secure portion of the lobby. "He's got to be here someplace. I'm going to keep hunting."

Suzuki piano lessons for children involve working through a series of progressively more difficult music books containing a dozen or so pieces. When a student completes a book successfully the parents often throw a small party for friends, family and the music teacher, during which the student gives a short recital.

Christine Grady's *Suzuki Volume Three* party was scheduled for a week from tonight and she'd been practicing hard for her mini concert. She was now sitting in the yanno room of the family's apartment, finishing up Schumann's "The Wild Rider."

The yanno room was dark and small but Chrissy loved it here. It contained only a few chairs, shelves of sheet music and a beautiful, shiny baby grand piano—hence her nickname for the place.

With some effort she played the andante movement of Clementi's Sonatina in C and then rewarded herself by playing the Mozart Sonatina, one of her favorites. She didn't think her playing was all that good, though. She was distracted by the police in their apartment. The men and women were all very nice and talked cheerfully about *Star Wars* or *Harry Potter* or Xbox games with big smiles on their faces. But Chrissy knew they weren't really smiling at all; they were only doing it to make her feel comfortable. But all the fake grins really did was make her more scared.

Because, even though they didn't say it, the fact that the police were here meant that somebody was trying to hurt her daddy.

She wasn't worried about somebody trying to hurt her. What scared her was that some bad man would take her daddy away from her. She wished he'd stop doing the court job he had. Once, she'd worked up her courage and asked him. But he'd said to her, "How much do you like playing the yanno, honey?"

"Lots."

"Well, that's how much I like doing my job."

"Oh. Okay," she'd said. Even though it *wasn't* okay at all. Because playing music didn't make people hate you and want to kill you. She now squinted harder and concentrated. Flubbed a passage once and then tried again.

And now, she'd learned, they were going to have to go live someplace else for a while. Just a day or two, her mom'd said. But what if it was for longer than that? What if they had to cancel the Suzuki party? Upset, she gave up playing, closed the music book and started to put it in her book bag.

Hey, look at this!

Resting on the music stand was a York peppermint patty. Not a little one but a full sizer, the kind they sell at the checkout stands at Food Emporium. She wondered who'd left it. Her mother didn't like anybody to eat in the yanno room and Chrissy was never allowed to have candy or anything sticky when she was playing.

Maybe it'd been her daddy. She knew he felt bad for her because of all the policemen around and because she hadn't been able to go to her recital last night at the Neighborhood School.

That was it—this was a secret treat from her father.

Chrissy glanced behind her, through the crack in the door. She saw people walking back and forth. Heard the calm voice of that nice policeman from North Carolina, who had two boys she was going to meet someday. Her mother brought a suitcase out of the bedroom. She had her unhappy face on and was saying, "This is crazy. Why can't you find him? He's one man. There're hundreds of you. I don't understand it."

Chrissy sat back, opened up the foil covering and slowly ate the candy. When she was finished she carefully examined her fingers. Yep, there was chocolate on them. She'd go to the bathroom and wash them off. And while she was there she'd flush the wrapper down the toilet so her mother wouldn't find out. That was called "disposing of the evidence," which she'd learned from that *CSI* television program her parents wouldn't let her watch, even though she managed to, every once in a while.

Roland Bell had returned safely with Charles Grady to the apartment, where the family was now packing up to go to an NYPD safehouse in the Murray Hill area of town. He'd pulled the shades down and told the family to stay away from the windows. He could see that this fueled their uneasiness. But his job wasn't to coddle psyches. It was to keep a very clever killer from taking their lives.

His cell phone rang. It was Rhyme. "Everything secure there?" the criminalist asked.

"Tight as a bed baby," Bell replied.

"Constable's in a secure cell."

"And we know his guards, right?" Bell asked.

"Amelia said Weir might be good but he's not good enough to turn himself into two Shaquille O'Neal look-alikes."

"Got it. How's the lawyer?"

"Roth? He'll live. Was a bad beating though. I'm . . ." Rhyme stopped talking as someone else in the room began speaking. Bell believed he heard the soft voice of Mel Cooper.

He then resumed speaking to Bell. "I'm still going through what Amelia found at the scenes in the detention center. Don't have any specific leads yet. But we've got something else I wanted to mention. Bedding and Saul finally tracked down which room at the Lanham Arms the key card belonged to."

"Who was it registered to?"

"Fake name and address," Rhyme explained. "But the desk clerk said the guest fit Weir's description perfectly. CS didn't get much but they found a discarded syringe behind the dresser. We don't know whether Weir left it or not but I'm going on the assumption he did. Mel found traces of chocolate and sucrose on the needle."

"Sucrose—that's sugar?"

"Right. And arsenic in the barrel of the syringe."

Bell said, "So he injected poison into some sweets."

"Sounds like it. Ask the Gradys if anybody's sent them any candy lately." Bell relayed the question to the prosecutor and his wife and they shook their heads, dismayed to even hear the question.

"No, we don't keep candy in the house," the prosecutor's wife said.

The criminalist then asked Bell, "You said he surprised you by getting into Grady's apartment itself this afternoon."

"Yup. We thought we'd nail him in the lobby, the basement or the roof. We never expected him to get in the front door."

"After he broke in, where did he go?"

"He just showed up in the living room. Shook us all up."

"So he might've had time to leave some candy in the kitchen."

"No, couldn't've been in the kitchen," Bell explained. "Lon and I were in there."

"What other rooms could he have gotten into?"

Bell posed the question to Grady and his wife.

"What's going on, Roland?" the prosecutor asked.

"Lincoln just found some more evidence and's thinking that Weir might've tried to get some poison into your house. It looks like it was in some candy. We're not sure he did but—"

"Candy?" From a soft, high voice behind them.

Bell, the Gradys and two of the other cops on protection detail turned to see the prosecutor's daughter staring at the detective, eyes wide with fear.

"Chrissy?" her mother asked. "What is it?"

"Candy?" the girl whispered again.

A foil wrapper fell from her hand and she began to sob.

Hands sweating, Bell looked at the passersby on the sidewalk in front of Charles Grady's apartment.

Dozens of people.

Was one of them Weir?

Or somebody else from that goddamn Patriot Assembly?

The ambulance rolled up and two techs jumped out. But before they got through the front door the detective carefully examined their IDs.

"What's all this about?" one of them asked, offended.

Bell ignored him and checked out the cars on the street, the passersby, the windows in the buildings nearby. When it was safe he gave a whistle and Luis Martinez, the quiet bodyguard, hustled the girl out and into the ambulance, accompanied by her mother.

Chrissy wasn't showing symptoms of poisoning yet though she was pale and shook from fearful crying. The girl had eaten a peppermint patty that had mysteriously appeared in her piano room. This was beyond evil to Bell—hurting children and, though he'd been suckered in by Constable's smooth talk momentarily, this incident clarified the complete depravity of people like those in the Patriot Assembly.

Differences between cultures? Between races? No, sir. There's only one difference. There's good and decency on the one side and evil on the other.

If the girl died Bell would make it his personal quest to see that both Weir and Constable received the punishment that corresponded to what he'd done to Chrissy—lethal injection.

"Don't you worry, honey," he now said to

her as one of the medics took her blood pressure. "You're going to be just fine."

The response to this was the girl's silent sobbing. He glanced at Chrissy's mother, on whose face was a look of tenderness that couldn't quite hide a fury exponentially greater than Bell's.

The detective radioed to Central and was patched through to Emergency Services at the hospital they were careening toward at the moment. He said to the supervisor, "We're gonna be at the admission dock in two minutes. Now listen here—I want that area and a route to a poison control center cleared of people. I don't want a soul around 'less they're wearing a picture ID badge."

"Well, Detective, we can't do that," the woman said. "That's a very busy section of the hospital."

"I'm gonna be muley on this one, ma'am."

"You're going to be what?"

"Stubborn. There's an armed perpetrator who's after this little girl and her family. And if I do see anybody in our line of sight without a badge, they're gonna get handcuffed and in a pretty impatient way."

"This's an emergency room in a city hospital, Detective," the woman responded testily. "Do you know how many people I'm looking at right now?"

"No, ma'am, I do not. But imagine lookin' at every one of 'em on their bellies and hog-tied. Which is what they're gonna be if they're not gone by the time we get there. And, by the by, that's looking to be all of two minutes from right now."

Chapter Forty-three

"Cases change color."

Charles Grady sat hunched forward in an orange plastic chair in a room off the Urgent Care waiting area, staring at the green linoleum, scuffed by thousands of despairing feet.

"Criminal cases, I mean."

Roland Bell sat next to him. Luis's vigilant form filled one doorway and nearby, at the entrance to a busy hallway, was another of Bell's SWAT officers, Graham Wilson, a handsome, intense detective with keen, stern eyes and a talent for spotting people packing weapons as if he had X-ray vison.

Grady's wife had accompanied Chrissy into the ER itself, along with Luis and another protection team officer.

"I had a law school professor one time,"

Grady continued, still as wood. "He'd been a prosecutor and then a judge. He told us once in class that in all his years of practicing law he'd never seen a black-and-white case come through the door. They were all different shades of gray. There was pretty damn dark gray and there was damn light gray. But they were all gray."

Bell glanced up the corridor, toward the impromptu waiting room that the duty nurse had made for the injured skateboarders and bicyclists. As Bell had insisted, this portion of the hospital had been cleared.

"But then, once you got involved in the case yourself, it changed color. It became black and white. Whether you were prosecuting or defending, the gray disappeared. Your side was one hundred percent good. The other side was one hundred percent evil. Right or wrong. My professor said you have to guard against that. You have to keep reminding yourself that cases were really gray."

Bell noticed an orderly. The young Latino seemed harmless but the detective nodded to Wilson, who stopped him and checked his badge nonetheless. He gave an okay sign to Bell.

Chrissy'd been in an operating room for fifteen minutes. Why couldn't somebody come out and at least give them some progress?

Grady continued, "But you know, Roland, all these months since we found out about that conspiracy in Canton Falls I kept seeing the Constable case as black and white. I never once considered it gray. I went after him with everything I had." A sad laugh. He looked up the hall again, the grim smile fading. "Where the hell's that doctor?"

Lowered his head again.

"But maybe if I'd seen more gray, maybe if I hadn't gone after him so hard, if I'd compromised more, he might not've hired Weir. He might not've . . ." He nodded toward where his daughter was at the moment. He choked and cried silently for a moment.

Bell said, "I'm thinking your professor was wrong, Charles. At least about people like Constable. Anybody who'd do what he's done, well, there *is* no gray with people like that."

Grady wiped his face.

"Your boys, Roland. They ever been in the hospital?"

Visiting their mother toward the end was

the detective's first thought. But Bell didn't say anything about that. "Off and on. Nothing serious—fixin' up whatever a softball can do to a forehead or a little finger. Or a shortstop running you down *armed* with a softball."

"Well," Grady said, "it takes your breath away." Another look up the empty hall. "Takes it clean away."

A few minutes later the detective was aware of motion in the corridor. A doctor wearing green scrubs noticed Grady and walked slowly toward them. Bell could read nothing on his face.

"Charles," the detective said softly.

But, though his head was down, Grady was already watching the man's approach.

"Black and white," he whispered. "Lord." He rose to meet the doctor.

Gazing out the window at the evening sky, Lincoln Rhyme heard his phone ring.

"Command, answer phone."

Click.

"Yes?"

"Lincoln? It's Roland."

Mel Cooper turned gravely to look at him.

They knew Bell was at the hospital with Christine Grady and her family.

"What's the word?"

"She's all right."

Cooper closed his eyes momentarily and if ever a Protestant came close to blessing himself this was the moment. Rhyme too felt a surge of relief.

"No poison?"

"Nothing. It was just candy. Not a lick of toxin anywhere."

"So *that* was misdirection too," the criminalist mused.

"Seems to be."

"But what the hell does it *mean?*" Rhyme asked in a faint voice, the question directed not so much to Bell but to himself.

The detective offered, "For my money, Weir pointing us to Grady? I'm thinking that means he's still going to try something else to spring Constable from detention. He's in the courthouse somewhere."

"You on your way to the safehouse?"

"Yup. Whole family. We'll sit it out there till you catch this fella."

Till?

How about *if?*

They hung up and Rhyme turned from the

window and wheeled back to the evidence chart.

The hand is quicker than the eye.

Except that it's not.

What did master illusionist Erick Weir have in mind?

Feeling his neck muscles tense to the point of cramping, he gazed out the window as he considered the enigma they were facing:

Hobbs Wentworth, the hit man, was dead and Grady and his family were safe. Constable had clearly been preparing to escape from the interview room at the Tombs but there'd been no overt attempt by Weir to actually spring him. So it *appeared* that Weir's plans were falling apart.

But Rhyme couldn't accept that obvious conclusion. With the supposed attempt on Christine Grady he'd taken their attention away from downtown and Rhyme now leaned toward Bell's conclusion that there was soon going to be another attempt to rescue Constable.

Or there was something else going on— maybe an attempt to *kill* Constable to keep him from testifying.

The frustration seared him. Rhyme had

long ago accepted that with his condition he would never physically capture a perp. But the compensation was the sinewy strength of a clever mind. Sitting motionless in his chair or bed, he could at least outthink the criminals he pursued.

Except that with Erick Weir, the Conjurer, he couldn't. This was a man whose soul was devoted to deception.

Rhyme considered if there was anything else to be done to find answers to the impossible questions raised by the case.

Sachs, Sellitto and ESU were scouring the detention center and courts. Kara was at the Cirque Fantastique awaiting Kadesky. Thom was placing calls to Keating and Loesser, the killer's former assistants, to see if the man had contacted them in the past day or if they'd happened to remember something else that could be helpful. A Physical Evidence Response Team, on loan from the FBI, was searching the scene of the office building where Hobbs Wentworth had shot himself, and technicians in Washington were still analyzing the fiber and fake-blood paint found by Sachs at the detention center.

What else could Rhyme do to find out what Weir had in mind?

Only one thing.

He decided to try something he hadn't done for years.

Rhyme himself began to walk some grids. This search started at the bloody escape scene in the detention center and took him through winding corridors, lit with algae-green fluorescence. Around corners banged dull from years of careening supply carts and pallets. Into closets and furnace rooms. Trying to follow the footsteps—and discern the thoughts—of Erick Weir.

The walk was, of course, conducted with his eyes closed and took place exclusively in his mind. Still, it seemed appropriate that he should engage in a hot pursuit that was wholly imaginary when the prey he sought was a vanished man.

The stoplight changed to green and Malerick accelerated slowly.

He was thinking about Andrew Constable, a conjurer in his own right, to hear Jeddy Barnes tell it. Like a mentalist Constable could size up a man in seconds and assume a countenance that would put him instantly at ease. Speaking humorously, intelligently, with understanding. Taking rational, sympathetic positions.

Selling the medicine to the gullible.

Of which there were plenty, of course. You'd think that people would tip to the nonsense that groups like the Patriot Assembly spewed. But as the great impresario of Malerick's own art, P. T. Barnum, noted, there's a sucker born every minute.

As he picked his way through the Sunday evening traffic Malerick was amused to think of Constable's utter bewilderment at the moment. Part of the plan for the prisoner's escape required Constable to incapacitate his lawyer. Two weeks ago, in the restaurant in Bedford Junction, Jeddy Barnes had said to him, "Well, Mr. Weir, the thing is, Roth's Jewish. Andrew'll enjoy hurting him pretty good."

"Makes no difference to me," Malerick had replied. "He can kill him if he wants to. That won't affect my plan. I just want him taken care of. Out of the way."

Barnes had nodded. "Suspect that'll be good news to Mr. Constable."

He could imagine the growing dismay and

panic within Constable as he sat over the cooling body of his lawyer, waiting for Weir to arrive with guns and disguises to sneak him out of the building—an event that, of course, was never going to happen.

The jail door would open and a dozen guards would haul the man back to his cell. The trial would go on and Andrew Constable—as confused as Barnes and Wentworth and everyone else in his Neanderthal clan in upstate New York—would never know how they'd been used.

As he waited at another stoplight he wondered how the other misdirection of his was unfolding. The Poisoned Little Girl routine (melodramatic, Malerick had assessed, if not an outright cliché, but he'd learned from years of performing that audiences do much better with the obvious). Not the best misdirection in the world, of course; he wasn't sure they'd discover the syringe in the Lanham. Nor could he be certain the girl or anyone else would eat the candy. But Rhyme and his people were so good that he guessed there was a chance they would leap to the horrifying conclusion that this was another attempt on the life of the prosecutor and his family. Then they'd find there was no poison in the candy after all.

What would they make of that?

Was there *other* tainted candy?

Or was this misdirection—to lead them away from Manhattan Detention, where Malerick *might* be planning some other way to break Constable out?

In short, the police too would be floating in a soup of confusion, having no idea what was actually going on.

Well, what's been going on for the past two days, Revered Audience, is a sublime performance featuring the perfect combination of physical and psychological misdirection.

Physical—by directing the attention of the police toward both Charles Grady's apartment and the detention center.

Psychological—by shifting suspicion away from what Malerick was really doing and toward the very credible motive that Lincoln Rhyme proudly believed he'd figured out: the hired killing of Grady and the orchestration of Andrew Constable's escape. Once the police had deduced that, their minds stopped looking for any other explanation as to what he was really up to.

Which had absolutely nothing to do with the Constable case. All of the clues he'd left so obviously—the illusionist-trick attacks on the first three victims, who represented aspects of the circus, the shoe with the dog hairs and dirt ground into it leading to Central Park, the references to the fire in Ohio and the connection with the Cirque Fantastique . . . all of those had convinced the police that his intent couldn't really be revenge against Kadesky because that, as Lincoln Rhyme had told him, was too obvious. He *had* to be up to something else.

But he wasn't.

Now, dressed in a medical technician's uniform, he eased the ambulance he was driving through the service entrance of the tent housing the World Renowned Internationally Heralded Critically Acclaimed Cirque Fantastique.

He parked under the box seats scaffolding, climbed out and locked the door. None of the stagehands, police or the many security guards paid any attention to him or the ambulance. After the bomb scare earlier in the day, it was perfectly normal for an emergency vehicle to be parked here—perfectly *natural,* an illusionist would note.

Look, Revered Audience, here is your illusionist, center stage yet completely invisible.

He's the Vanished Man, present but unseen.

No one even glanced at the vehicle, which wasn't an ordinary ambulance at all, but a feke. In place of medical equipment it now held a dozen plastic drums containing a total of seven hundred gallons of gasoline, attached to a simple detonation device, which would soon spark the liquid to life, sending the deadly flood erupting into the bleachers, into the canvas, into the audience of more than two thousand people.

Among whom would be Edward Kadesky.

See, Mr. Rhyme, when we talked before? My words were just patter. Kadesky and the Cirque Fantastique destroyed my life and my love and I'm going to destroy him. Revenge *is* what this is all about.

Ignored by everyone, the illusionist now walked casually out of the tent and into Central Park. He'd change out of the medical worker's uniform and into a new disguise and would return under cover of night, becoming, for a change, a member of the audience himself and finding a good vantage spot to enjoy the finale of his show.

Chapter Forty-four

Families, clusters of friends, couples, children were slowly entering the tent, finding their seats, filling in the bleachers and box seats, slowly changing from individuals into that creature called an *audience,* the whole becoming very different from the parts.

Metamorphosis . . .

Kara turned away from the sight and stopped a security guard. "I've been waiting for a while. You have any idea when Mr. Kadesky'll be back? It's really important."

No, he didn't know and neither did the two other people she asked.

Another glance at her watch. She felt heartsick. An image came to her of her mother, lying in the Stuyvesant home, looking around the room, pierced with clarity and wondering where her daughter was.

Kara wanted to cry in frustration at being trapped here. Knowing that she *had* to stay, do what she could to stop Weir, yet wanting so desperately to be at her mother's side.

She turned back to the brightly lit interior of the huge circus tent. Performers waited in the wings, getting ready for the opening act, wearing their eerie commedia dell'arte masks. The kids in the audience were wearing the face gear too, overpriced souvenirs from the stands outside. Pug and hooked noses, beaks. They gazed around, mostly excited and giddy. But some were uneasy, she could see. The masks and otherworldly decorations probably made the circus seem to them like a scene from a horror movie. Kara loved performing for children but she knew that you had to be careful; their reality was different from adults' and an illusionist could easily destroy youngsters' shaky sense of comfort. She only did funny illusions in her young children's shows and would often gather the kids around her afterward and tip the gaff.

Looking at all the magic around her, feeling the excitement, the anticipation. . . . Her palms were sweating as if she herself were about to go on. Oh, what she wouldn't give to be standing in the prep tent right now. Content, confident, yet wired, feeling the accelerating heartbeat of anticipation as the clock ticked toward show time. There was no sensation like that in the world.

She laughed sadly to herself. Well, here she'd made it to Cirque Fantastique.

But as an errand girl.

She wondered now, *Am* I good enough? Despite what David Balzac said, sometimes she believed she was. At least as good as, say, Harry Houdini during his early shows— the only escapism at those had been the audience members who snuck out of the halls, bored or embarrassed to watch him flub simple sleights. Robert-Houdin was so uncomfortable in *his* initial performances that he ended up offering the audience clockwork automatons like a wind-up Turk who played chess.

But as she gazed backstage, at the hundreds of performers who'd been in the business since childhood, Balzac's firm voice looped through her mind: *Not yet, not yet, not yet . . .* She heard these words with both disappointment yet comfort. He was right, she decided with finality. He was the expert, she was the apprentice. She had to have confidence in him. A year or two. The wait would be worth it.

Besides, there was her mother. . . .

Who was maybe sitting up in bed right now, chatting with Jaynene, wondering where her daughter was—the daughter who'd abandoned her on the one night when she should've been there.

Kadesky's assistant, Katherine Tunney, appeared at the top of the stairs and gestured toward her.

Was Kadesky here? Please. . . .

But the woman said, "He just called. He had a radio interview after dinner and he's running late. He'll be here soon. That's his box in the front. Why don't you wait there?"

Kara nodded and, discouraged, walked to the seat Katherine indicated, sat down and gazed back at the tent. She saw that the magic transformation was finally complete; every seat was filled. The children, the men, the women were now an audience.

Thud.

Kara jumped as a loud, hollow drum resonated through the tent.

The lights went down, extinguished completely, plunging them into a darkness broken only by the red exit lights.

Thud.

The crowd was instantly silent.

Thud . . . thud . . . thud.

The drum beat sounded slowly. You could feel it in your chest.

Thud . . . thud. . . .

A brilliant spotlight shot into the center of the ring, illuminating the actor playing Arlecchino, dressed in his black-and-white-checkered bodysuit, wearing his matching half mask. Holding a long scepter high in the air, he looked around mischievously.

Thud.

He stepped forward and began to march around the ring as a procession of performers appeared behind him: other commedia dell'arte characters, as well as spirits, fairies, princesses and princes, wizards. Some walking, some dancing, some cartwheeling slowly as if under water, some on high stilts stepping more gracefully than most people stroll down the sidewalk, some riding in chariots or carts decorated with tulle and feathers and lace and tiny glowing lights.

Everyone moving in perfect time to the drum.

Thud . . . thud . . .

Faces masked, faces painted white or black or silver or gold, faces dotted with glitter. Hands juggling glowing balls, hands carrying orbs or flares or candles or lanterns, hands scattering confetti like glittering snow.

Solemn, regal, playful, grotesque.

Thud . . .

Both medieval and futuristic, the parade was hypnotic. And its message was unmistakable: whatever existed outside the tent was invalid here. You could forget everything you'd learned about life, about human nature, about the laws of physics themselves. Your heart was now beating not to its own rhythm but in time to the crisp drum, and your soul was no longer yours; it had been captured by this unearthly parade making its deliberate way into the world of illusion.

Chapter Forty-five

We come now to the finale of our show, Revered Audience.

It's time to present our most celebrated—and controversial—illusion. A variation on the infamous Burning Mirror.

During our show this weekend you've seen the performances of illusions created by such masters as Harry Houdini and P. T. Selbit and Howard Thurston. But not even they would attempt an act like the Burning Mirror.

Our performer, trapped in a likeness of hell, surrounded by flames that close in inexorably—and the only route for escape, a tiny doorway protected by a wall of fire.

Though, of course, the door might not be an escape route at all.

Maybe it's just an illusion.

I have to warn you, Revered Audience, that the most recent attempt to perform this trick resulted in tragedy.

I know, because I was there.

So, please, for your own sake, spend a moment looking around the tent and consider what you will do should disaster strike. . . .

But on reflection, no, it's too late for that. Perhaps the best you can hope for now is simply to pray.

Malerick had returned to Central Park and was standing under a tree about fifty yards from the glowing white tent of the Cirque Fantastique.

Bearded once more, he was dressed in a jogging suit and a high-necked knit shirt. Tufts of sweaty blond hair poked from underneath a Chase Manhattan 10K Run for the Cure cap. Faux sweat stains—out of a bottle—attested to his present persona: a minor financial executive at a major bank out for his Sunday-night run. He'd stopped for a breather and was absently looking at the circus tent.

Perfectly natural.

He found himself oddly calm. This serenity reminded him of that moment just after
the Hasbro circus fire in Ohio, before the full
implications of the disaster had become
clear. While by rights he should have been
screaming, he in fact found himself numb.
In an emotional coma. He felt the same at
this moment, listening to the music, the
bass notes amplified, it seemed, by the taut
canvas of the tent itself. The diffuse applause, laughter, gasps of astonishment.

In his years of performing he'd rarely gotten stage fright. When you knew your act
cold, when you'd rehearsed sufficiently,
what was there to be nervous about? This is
what he now experienced. Everything had
been so carefully planned that he knew his
show would unfold as intended.

Scanning the tent in its last few minutes
on earth, he saw two figures just outside the
large service doorway through which he'd
driven the ambulance not long before. A
man and a young woman. Speaking to each
other, ear close to mouth so they could con-
verse over the sound of the music.

Yes! One of them was Kadesky. He'd
been worried that the producer might not be

present at the time of the explosion. The other was Kara.

Kadesky pointed inside and together they walked in the direction he'd indicated. Malerick estimated that they had to be no more than ten feet from the ambulance.

A look at his watch. Almost time.

And now, my friends, my Revered Audience . . .

Exactly at nine P.M. a spume of fire shot from the doorway of the tent. A moment later the silhouette of the huge flames inside rolled across the glowing canvas of the tent as they consumed the bleachers, the audience, the decorations. The music stopped abruptly, replaced by screams, and coils of dark smoke began to pour from the top of the tent.

He leaned forward, mesmerized by the horror of the sight.

More smoke, more screams.

Struggling not to let an *unnatural* smile slide onto his face, he offered a prayer of thanks. There was no deity Malerick believed in but he sent these words of gratitude to the soul of Harry Houdini, his namesake and idol, and the patron saint of magicians.

Gasps and cries as those around him in this secluded part of the park ran forward to help or to gape. Malerick waited a few moments longer but he knew that soon hundreds of police would fill the park. Looking concerned, pulling out his cell phone to pretend to call the fire department, he eased toward the sidewalk. Still, he couldn't help pausing once more. He looked back to see, half obscured by smoke, the huge banners in front of the tent. On one of them masked Arlecchino reached outward, holding up his empty palms.

Look, Revered Audience, nothing in my hands.

Except that, like a sleight-of-hand artist, the character *was* holding something—something hidden from view in a perfect backhand finger conceal.

And only Malerick knew what it was.

The coy Harlequin was holding death.

III
TIPPING THE GAFF

SUNDAY, APRIL 21, TO THURSDAY, APRIL 25

"To be a great magician, one must be able to present an illusion in such a way that people are not only puzzled, but deeply moved."

—S. H. Sharp

Chapter Forty-six

Amelia Sachs's Camaro hit ninety on the West Side Highway, speeding toward Central Park.

Unlike the FDR Drive, which was a controlled-access expressway, the roadway here was dotted with stoplights and, at Fourteenth Street, it featured a jog that sent her misaligned Chevrolet into an alarming skid, resulting in a sparking kiss between sheet steel and concrete barriers.

So the killer had tricked them with yet another genius's touch. Neither Charles Grady's death nor Andrew Constable's escape was Weir's goal; they were the ultimate misdirections. The killer had been after what they'd rejected yesterday as being too obvious—the Cirque Fantastique.

As she'd been about to kick in one of the

few remaining hiding spots in the basement of the court and detention center, Glock high, Rhyme had called her and told her the situation. Lon Sellitto and Roland Bell were headed for the circus, Mel Cooper was jogging over there to help out. Bo Haumann and several ESU teams were on their way too. Everybody was needed and Rhyme wanted her uptown as fast as possible.

"I'm on my way," she'd said, clicking the phone off. She'd turned and begun to sprint out of the basement but paused, returned to the door she'd been standing at and kicked it in anyway.

Just in case.

It'd been completely empty, completely silent—except for the sound of the killer's derisive laughter in her imagination.

Five minutes later she was in her Camaro, pedal down.

The light at Twenty-third Street was against her but the cross traffic wasn't too bad so she went through it fast, relying on the steering wheel, rather than her brakes or the conscience of citizens to yield to her flashing blue light, to get her to the other side.

Once through it, a fast downshift, pedal to

the floor and the rattling engine sped her up to eighty. Her hand found her Motorola and she called Rhyme to tell him where she was and to ask what exactly he needed her to do.

Malerick wandered slowly out of the park, jostled by people running the opposite way, toward the fire.

"What's going on?"

"Jesus!"

"The police. . . . Did somebody call the police?"

"Do you hear screaming? Do you hear that?"

At the corner of Central Park West and a cross street he collided with a young Asian woman, staring in concern toward the park. She asked, "You know what happened?"

Malerick thought, Yes, indeed I do: the man and the circus that destroyed my life are dying. But he frowned and said to her gravely, "I don't know. But it seems pretty serious."

He continued west, beginning what would be a very circuitous, half hour journey back to his apartment, during which he'd execute several quick changes and make absolutely certain no one was following him.

His plans called for him to stay at his apartment tonight then in the morning leave for Europe, where after several months of training he'd resume performing—under his new name. Not a soul on earth, other than his revered audience, knew "Malerick" and that's who he'd be to the public from now on. He had one regret—that he wouldn't be able to perform his favorite routine, the Burning Mirror; far too many people associated that with him. In fact, he'd have to trim a lot of the material. He'd give up ventriloquism, mentalism, and many of the close-in routines he'd done. Having such a broad repertoire could—as had happened this weekend—tip the gaff as to his identity.

Malerick continued to Broadway, then doubled back toward his apartment. He continued to check the streets behind and around him. He saw no one following.

He stepped inside the lobby and paused, studied the street for a full five minutes.

An elderly man—Malerick recognized him as a neighbor from across the street—walking his poodle. A kid on Rollerblades. Two teenage girls with ice cream cones. No one else. The street was empty: tomorrow was Monday, a work- and schoolday. People were now home ironing clothes, helping their children with lessons . . . and glued to the TV watching CNN reporting on the terrible tragedy in Central Park.

He hurried to his apartment, doused all the lights.

And now the show closes, Revered Audience, as they always do.

But it is the nature of our art that what's old to today's audience will be fresh and inventive to those elsewhere, tomorrow and the day after.

Did you know, my friends, that curtain calls are not to thank the performer but are intended to give him a chance to thank his audience—those people who were kind enough to lend him their attention during his show.

So I applaud you now for gracing me with your presence during these modest performances. I hope I've given you excitement and joy. I hope I've brought wonder to your hearts as you joined me in this netherworld where life is transformed to death, death to life and the real to the unreal.

I bow to you, Revered Audience. . . .

He lit a candle and settled into the couch. He kept his eyes fixed on the flame. Tonight, he *knew* that it would shudder, that he would receive a message.

Staring, sitting forward, bathed in the contentment of vengeance completed, rocking back and forth hypnotically, breathing slowly.

The candle flickered. Yes!

Speak to me.

Flicker again. . . .

And indeed only a moment later it did.

But the shuddering wasn't a message from the supernatural spirit of a loved one long gone but solely from the gust of cool April evening air that filled the room when the half dozen police officers in riot gear broke the door in with a battering ram. They flung the gasping illusionist to the floor, where one of them—the red-haired policewoman he recalled from Lincoln Rhyme's apartment—seated a pistol against the back of his head and gave a steady recitation of his rights.

Chapter Forty-seven

Their arms trembling against the weight of both Lincoln Rhyme and his Storm Arrow wheelchair, two sweating ESU officers carried their burden up the stairs into the building and deposited the criminalist in the lobby. He then took over and maneuvered his chair into the Conjurer's apartment, where he parked next to Amelia Sachs.

While their fellow Emergency Service officers cleared the rooms, Rhyme watched as Bell and Sellitto carefully searched the astonished killer. Rhyme had suggested they borrow a doctor from the Medical Examiner's office to help in the search. He arrived a moment later and did as requested. It turned out to be a good idea; the M.D. found several slits cut into the man's skin—they looked like small scars but could be pulled open. Inside were tiny metal tools.

"X-ray him at the detention infirmary," Rhyme said. "Hell, wait, do an MRI. Every square inch."

When the Conjurer was triple cuffed and double shackled, two officers pulled the man into a sitting position on the floor. The criminalist was examining a bedroom in which was a huge collection of magician's props and tools. The masks, fake hands and latex appliances made the place eerie, sure, but Rhyme sensed mostly loneliness, seeing these objects stored here for the killer's horrific purposes when they were meant to be part of a show to entertain thousands of people.

"How?" the Conjurer whispered.

Rhyme noted the look of astonishment. Dismay too. The criminalist relished the sensation. All hunters will tell you that the actual search for their quarry is the best part of the game. But no hunter can be truly great unless he feels peak pleasure when he finally brings down his prey.

"How did you figure it out?" the man repeated in his asthmatic wheeze.

"That your point was to hit the circus?" Rhyme glanced at Sachs.

She said, "There wasn't a lot of evidence but it suggested—"

"'Suggested,' Sachs? I'd say it screamed."

"Suggested," she continued, unfazed by his interjection, "what you were really going to do. In the closet—the one in the basement of the Criminal Courts building—we found the bag with your change of clothes in it, the fake wound."

"You found the bag?"

She continued, "There was some dried red paint on the shoes and your suit. And carpet fibers."

"I thought the paint was fake blood." Rhyme shook his head, angry with himself. "It was *logical* to make that assumption but I should've considered other sources. It turned out that the FBI's paint database identified it as Jenkin Manufacturing automotive paint. The shade is an orange-red that's used exclusively for emergency vehicles. That particular formula is sold in small cans—for touch-ups. The fibers were automotive too—they were from heavy-duty commercial carpet installed in GMC ambulances up until eight years ago."

Sachs: "So Lincoln deduced that you'd bought or stolen an old ambulance recently and fixed it up. It might've been for an escape or for another attempt on Charles Grady's life. But then he remembered the bits of brass—what if they actually *were* from a timer, like we'd thought originally? And since you'd used gas on the handkerchief in Lincoln's apartment, well, that meant that, possibly, you were going to hide a gas bomb in a fake ambulance."

Rhyme offered, "Then I simply used logic—"

"He played a hunch is what he's sayin'," Bell chided.

"Hunches," Rhyme snapped, "are nonsense. Logic isn't. Logic is the backbone of science, and criminalistics is pure science."

Sellitto rolled his eyes at Bell.

But insubordination in the ranks wasn't going to dampen Rhyme's enthusiasm. "Logic, I was saying. Kara had told us about pointing your audience's attention toward where you *don't* want them to look."

The best illusionists'll rig the trick so well

that they'll point directly at their method, directly at what they're really going to do. But you won't believe them. You'll look in the opposite direction. When that happens, you've had it. You've lost and they've won.

"That's what you did. And I have to say it was a brilliant idea. Not a compliment I give very often, is it, Sachs? . . . You wanted revenge against Kadesky for the fire that ruined your life. And so you created a routine that'd let you do it and get away afterward—just like you'd create an illusion for the stage, with layers of misdirections." Rhyme squinted in consideration. He said, "The first misdirection: You 'forced'—Kara told us that's the word illusionists use, right?"

The killer said nothing.

"I'm sure that's what she said. First, you *forced* the thought on us that you were going to destroy the circus for revenge. But I didn't believe it—too obvious. And our suspicion led to misdirection two: you planted the newspaper article about Grady, the restaurant receipt, the press pass and the hotel key to make us conclude you were going to kill him. . . . Oh, the jogging jacket by the Hudson River? You *were* going to leave that at the scene intentionally, weren't you? That was planted evidence you wanted us to find."

The Conjurer nodded. "I was, yes. But it worked out better because your officers surprised me and it looked more *natural* for me to leave the jacket when I escaped."

"Now, at that point," the criminalist continued, "we think you're a hired assassin, using illusion to get close to Charles Grady and kill him. . . . We've figured you out. There go our suspicions. . . . To an *extent.*"

The Conjurer managed a faint smile. "'An extent,'" he wheezed. "See when you use misdirection to trick people—smart people—they continue to be suspicious."

"So you hit us with misdirection number three. To keep us focused away from the circus you made us think that you got arrested intentionally to get inside the detention center not to kill Grady but to break Constable out of jail. By then we'd forgotten completely about the circus and Kadesky. But in fact you didn't care a bit about either Constable or Grady."

"They were props, misdirections to fool you," he admitted.

"The Patriot Assembly, they're not going to be too happy about that," Sellitto muttered.

A nod at the shackles. "I'd say that's the least of my worries, wouldn't you?"

Knowing what he did about Constable and the others in the Assembly, Rhyme wasn't too sure.

Bell nodded at the Conjurer and asked Rhyme, "But why'd he go to the trouble to set up Constable and plan the fake escape?"

Sellitto answered, "Obviously—to, you know, misdirect us away from the circus so he'd have an easier time getting the bomb there."

"Actually, no, Lon," Rhyme said slowly. "There was another reason."

At these words, or perhaps at the cryptic tone in Rhyme's voice, the killer turned toward the criminalist, who could see caution in his eyes—real caution, if not fear—for the first time that night.

Gotcha, Rhyme thought.

He said, "See, there was a *fourth* misdirection."

"Four?" Sellitto said.

"That's right. . . . He's not Erick Weir," Rhyme announced with what even he had to admit was excessive dramatics.

Chapter Forty-eight

With a sigh, the killer eased back against a chair leg, eyes closing.

"Not Weir?" Sellitto asked.

"That," Rhyme continued, "was the whole point of what he did this weekend. He wanted revenge against Kadesky and the Hasbro circus—the Cirque Fantastique now. Well, it's easy to get revenge if you don't care about escaping. But"—a nod toward the Conjurer—"he wanted to get away, stay out of prison, keep performing. So he did an *identity* quick change. He became Erick Weir, got himself arrested this afternoon, fingerprinted and then escaped."

Sellitto nodded. "So after he killed Kadesky and burned down the circus everybody'd be looking for *Weir* and not for who he really is." A frown. "And who the hell *is* he?"

"Arthur Loesser, Weir's protégé."

The killer gasped softly as the last shred of anonymity—and hope for escape—vanished.

"But Loesser called us," Sellitto pointed out. "He was out west. In Nevada."

"No, he wasn't. I checked the phone records. The call came up 'No caller ID' on my phone because he placed it through a prepaid long distance account. He was calling from a pay phone on West Eighty-seventh Street. He doesn't have a wife. The message on his voice mail in Vegas was fake."

"Just like he called the other assistant, Keating, and pretended to be Weir, right?" Sellitto asked.

"Yep. Asking about the Ohio fire, sounding weird and threatening. To back up what we thought: that Weir was in New York to get revenge against Kadesky. He had to leave a trail that Weir'd resurfaced. Like ordering the Darby handcuffs in Weir's name. The gun he bought too."

Rhyme looked over the killer. "How's the

voice?" he asked sardonically. "The lungs feel better now?"

"You know they're fine," Loesser snapped. The whisper and wheezing were gone. There was no damage to his lungs. It was just another ruse to make them believe he was Weir.

Rhyme nodded toward the bedroom. "I saw some designs for promotional posters in there. I assume you drew them. The name on them was 'Malerick.' That's you now, right?"

The killer nodded. "What I told you before is true—I hated my old name, I hate anything about me from before the fire. It was too hard to be reminded of those times. Malerick's how I think of myself now. . . . How did you catch on?"

"After they sealed the corridor in detention you used your shirt and wiped the floor and the cuffs," Rhyme explained. "But when I thought about that I couldn't figure out why. To clean up the blood? That didn't make sense. No, the only answer I could come up with was that you wanted to get rid of your fingerprints. But you'd just *been* printed; why would you be worried about leaving them in the corridor?" Rhyme gave a shrug, suggesting that the answer was painfully obvious. "Because your real prints were different from the ones on the card that'd just been rolled and filed."

"How the fuck d'he manage that?" Sellitto asked.

"Amelia found traces of fresh ink at the scene. That was from his being printed tonight. The trace wasn't important in itself but what was significant was that it matched the ink we found in his gym bag at the Marston assault. That meant he'd come in contact with fingerprint ink *before* today. I guessed that he stole a blank fingerprint card and printed it at home with the real Erick Weir's prints. He used that adhesive wax to hide it in his jacket lining tonight— we were looking for weapons and keys, not pieces of cardboard—and then after they rolled his prints he distracted the technicians and swapped the cards. Probably flushed the new one or threw it out."

Loesser grimaced in anger, a confirmation of Rhyme's deduction.

"DOC sent over the card they had on file and Mel processed it. The rolled prints *were* Weir's but the latents were Loesser's. He was in the AFIS database from when he was arrested with Weir on those reckless endangerment charges in New Jersey. We checked the DOC officer's Glock too. She took that with her and he didn't get a chance to wipe it down. Those prints came back a match for Loesser too. Oh, and we got a partial from the razor knife blade." Rhyme glanced at the small bandage on Loesser's temple. "You forgot to take that with you."

"I couldn't *find* it," the killer snapped. "I didn't have time to look."

"But," Sellitto pointed out to Rhyme, "he'd be younger than Weir."

"He *is* younger than Weir." He nodded toward Loesser's face. "The wrinkles're just latex appliances. Like the scars—they're all fake. Weir was born in 1950. Loesser's twenty years younger so he had to age." Then he muttered, "Oh, I missed that one. Should've thought better. Those bits of latex covered with makeup that Amelia found at the scenes? I assumed they were from those finger pads he was wearing. But that wouldn't make sense. Nobody'd wear makeup on his fingers. It would come off. No, it was from the other appliances."

Rhyme examined the killer's cheeks and brow. "The latex must be uncomfortable."

"You get used to it."

"Sachs, let's see what he really looks like."

With some difficulty she peeled off the beard and patches of wrinkles around his eyes and chin. The resulting face was blotchy from the adhesive but, yes, he was clearly much younger. The structure of his face was different too. He didn't look much at all like the man he'd been.

"Not like those masks in *Mission Impossible* hm? Put 'em on, pull 'em off."

"No, real appliances aren't like that at all."

"The fingers too." Rhyme nodded at the killer's left hand.

To make the fusing of the fingers credible they'd been bound together with a bandage then covered in thick latex. As a result the two digits were wrinkled, limp and virtually white but, of course, they were otherwise normal. Sachs examined them. "I was just asking Rhyme why you didn't uncover them at the street fair—since we were looking for a man with a deformed left hand." But the two digits had their own appearance of deformity and would've given him away.

Rhyme looked the killer over and said, "Pretty close to a perfect crime: a perp who made certain that we charged somebody else. We'd know Weir was guilty, we'd have positive ID. But then he'd disappear. Loesser would go on with his life and the escapee—Weir—would be gone forever. The Vanished Man."

And even though Loesser had picked the victims yesterday to misdirect the police, not out of any deep psychological urge, nonetheless Terry Dobyns's ultimate diagnosis fit perfectly—seeking revenge for the fire that had destroyed a loved one. The difference was that the tragedy hadn't been Weir's loss of his career and the death of his wife; it had been *Loesser's* loss of his mentor, Weir himself.

"But there's one problem," Sellitto pointed out. "All he did by swapping the print cards was make sure we'd go after the real Weir. Why would he do that to his mentor?"

Rhyme said, "Why do you think I made those strapping young officers carry me up the stairs into this extremely *in*accessible place, Lon?" He looked around the room. "I wanted to walk the grid myself—oh, excuse me, I should say *roll* the grid." He now wheeled through the room expertly, using the touchpad controller. He stopped by the fireplace and glanced up. "I think I've found our perp, Lon." He looked up at the mantel, on which sat an inlaid box and a candle. "That's Erick Weir, right? His ashes."

Loesser said softly, "That's right. He knew he didn't have much time left. He wanted to get out of the burn unit in Ohio and go back to his house in Vegas before he died. I snuck him out one night and drove him home. He lived another few weeks after we got there. I bribed a night-shift operator at a mortuary to cremate him."

"And the fingerprints?" Rhyme asked. "You rolled his prints after he died? Had stamps made so you could do the fake fingerprint card?"

A nod.

"So you've been planning this for years?"

Passionately Loesser said, "Yes! His death—it's like a burn that doesn't stop hurting."

Bell asked, "You risked all of this for revenge? For your boss?"

"Boss? He was more than my *boss*," Loesser spat out madly. "You don't understand. I think about my father a couple times a year—and he's still alive. I think about Mr. Weir every hour of the day. Ever since he came into the shop in Vegas where I was performing. . . . Young Houdini, that was me. . . . I was fourteen then. What a day that was! He told me he was going to give me the vision to be great. On my fifteenth birthday I ran away from home to travel with him." His voice wavered for a moment and fell silent. He continued, "Mr. Weir may've beat me and screamed at me and made my life hell sometimes but he saw what was inside me. He cared for me. He taught me how to be an illusionist. . . ." A cloud filled the man's face. "And then he was taken away from me. Because of Kadesky. He and that fucking *business* of his killed Mr. Weir. . . . And me too. Arthur Loesser died in that fire." He looked at the box and on his face there was an expression of sorrow and hope and such odd love that Rhyme felt a chill crawl down his neck until it disappeared into his numb body.

Loesser looked back to Rhyme and gave a cold laugh. "Well, you may've caught me. But Mr. Weir and I won. You didn't stop us in time. The circus is gone, Kadesky's gone.

And if he isn't dead himself, his career's over."

"Ah, yes, the Cirque Fantastique, the fire." Rhyme shook his head gravely. Then he added, "Still . . ."

Loesser frowned, sweeping the room with his eyes, trying to nab Rhyme's meaning. "What? What're you saying?"

"Think back a little. Earlier tonight. You're in Central Park, watching the flames, the smoke, the destruction, listening to the screams. . . . You figure you better leave—we'll be looking for you soon. You're on your way back here. Someone—a young woman, an *Asian* woman in a jogging suit—bumps into you. You exchange a few words about what's going on. You go your separate ways."

"What the hell're you talking about?" Loesser snapped.

"Check the back of your watchband," Rhyme said.

With a clink of the cuffs he turned his wrist over. On the band was a small black disk. Sachs peeled it off. "GPS tracker. We used that to follow you here. Weren't you a little surprised that we just showed up aknockin' on your door?"

"But who—? Wait! It was that illusionist, that girl! Kara! I didn't recognize her."

Rhyme said wryly, "Well, that *is* the whole point of illusion now, isn't it? We spotted you in the park but we were afraid you'd get away. You *do* have a tendency to do that, you know. And we assumed you'd take a complicated route back to where you were staying. So I asked Kara to do a little disguise of her own. She's good, that woman. Hardly recognized her myself. When she bumped into you she taped the sensor to your watch."

Sachs continued, "We might've been able to take you down on the street but you've been just a little too good at escaping. Anyway, we wanted to find your hidey-hole."

"But that means you knew *before* the fire!"

"Oh," Rhyme said dismissively, "your ambulance? The Bomb Squad found it and rendered safe in about sixty seconds. They drove it off and replaced it with another one so you wouldn't think we'd caught on. We knew you'd want to watch the fire. We got as many undercover officers as we could into the park, looking for a male about your build who'd watch the fire but then who'd leave not long after it started. A couple of them saw you and we had Kara nail you with the chip. And presto—" Rhyme smiled at his choice of word. "Here we are."

"But the fire . . . I *saw* it!"

Rhyme said to Sachs, "See what I keep saying about evidence versus witnesses? He *saw* the fire; therefore it *had* to be real." To Loesser he said, "But it *wasn't* real now, was it?"

Sachs said, "What you saw was smoke from a couple of National Guard smoke grenades we mounted on the top of the tent with a crane. The flames? From a propane burner at the stage door where the ambulance was. Then they backlit a couple more burners in the ring and projected the shadows of the flames onto the side of the tent."

"I heard screams," Loesser whispered.

"Oh, that was Kara's idea. She thought we could have Kadesky tell the audience they were taking an intermission from the show so a movie studio could shoot a scene in the tent—about a fire in a circus. He had everybody start screaming on cue. They loved it. They got to be extras."

"No," the Conjurer whispered. "It was—"

"—an illusion," Rhyme said to him. "It was all an illusion."

Some sleight of mind from the Immobilized Man.

"I better run the scene here," Sachs said, nodding around the room, and frowning.

"Sure, sure, Sachs. What *was* I thinking of? Here we are sitting around chatting and contaminating a crime scene."

With multiple cuffs and shackles binding him and an officer on either side, the killer was led out the door, far less cocky than the last time he'd been led down to detention.

As two ESU officers were about to schlepp Rhyme outside once more, Lon Sellitto's phone rang. He took the call. "She's right here. . . ." A glance at Sachs. "You want to talk to her . . . ?" Then he shook his head at her and continued to listen, looking grave. "Okay, I'll tell her." He hung up.

"That was Marlow," he said to Sachs.

The head of Patrol Services. What was up? the criminalist wondered, seeing the troubled look on Sellitto's face.

The rumpled detective continued, speaking to Sachs, "He wants you downtown tomorrow at ten A.M. It's about your promo-

732 / Jeffery Deaver

tion." Sellitto then frowned. "There was something else he wanted me to tell you, something about your score on the test. What was it?" He shook his head, stared at the ceiling. Clearly troubled. "What was it?"

Sachs looked on impassively, though Rhyme observed a fingernail make a brief assault on the cuticle of her thumb.

Then the detective snapped his fingers. "Oh, yeah, now I remember. He said you got the third highest score in the history of the department." A frown filled his face and he looked at Rhyme. "You know what this means, don'tcha? Christ have mercy—now there'll be no living with her."

Jogging, breathless.

The corridor was a mile long.

Kara sprinted along the gray linoleum with only one thing in her mind: not the late Erick Weir or his psychotic assistant, Art Loesser, not the brilliance of the fire illusion at the Cirque Fantastique. No, all she thought was: Am I in time?

Down the dim corridor. Footsteps pounding on the floor.

Past doorways closed and doorways

open. Hearing bits of TV and music, hearing farewell conversation as families prepared to leave at the end of Sunday visiting hours.

Hearing her own hollow footsteps.

She paused outside the room. Inhaled a dozen deep breaths to steady her voice and, more nervous than she'd ever been going onstage, stepped into the room.

A pause. Then: "Hi, Mum."

Her mother turned away from the TV. She blinked in surprise and smiled. "Why, look who it is. Hello, dear."

Oh, my God, Kara thought, looking at the bright eyes. She's back! She's really back.

She walked over and hugged the woman then pulled the chair closer. "How are you?"

"Fine. Little chilly tonight."

"I'll close the window." Kara rose and pulled it shut.

"I thought you weren't going to make it, honey."

"Busy night. I'll have to tell you what I've been up to, Mum. You won't believe it."

"I can't wait."

Excitedly Kara asked, "You want some tea or something?" She felt a fierce urgency to pour out all the details of her life in the

734 / Jeffery Deaver

past six months, to ramble. But she told herself to slow down; gushing, she sensed, could easily overwhelm her mother, who seemed immensely fragile at the moment.

"Nope, not a thing, dear. . . . Could you shut the TV off? I'd rather visit with you. There's that control. I can never get it to work. Sometimes, I almost think, somebody sneaks in and changes the buttons."

"I'm glad I got here before you went to bed."

"I would've stayed up to visit with you."

Kara gave her a smile. Her mother then said, "I was just thinking about your uncle, honey. My brother."

Kara nodded. Her mother's late brother was the black sheep of the family. He'd gone out west when Kara was young and never kept in touch with the family. Kara's mother and grandparents had refused to talk about him and his name was verboten at family gatherings. But, of course, the rumors flew: he was gay, he was straight and married but he'd had an affair with a Roma gypsy, he'd shot a man over another woman, he'd never married and was an alcoholic jazz musician. . . .

Kara'd always wanted to learn the truth about him. "What about him, Mum?"

"You want to hear?"

"Oh, you bet—tell me some stories," she now asked, leaning forward and resting her hand on the woman's arm.

"Well, let's see, when would it've been? I'd guess May of seventy, maybe seventy-one. Not sure of the year—that's my mind for you—but I know it was May. Your uncle and some of his army buddies had come back from Vietnam."

"He was a soldier? I never knew that."

"Oh, he looked very handsome in his uniform. Well, they had a terrible time over there." Her voice grew serious. "Your uncle's best friend was killed right next to him. Died in his arms. A big black fellow. Well, Tom and another soldier got it into their heads that they'd like to start a business to help their dead friend's family. So what they did was they went down south and bought a boat. Can you imagine your uncle on a boat? I thought it was the strangest thing ever. They started a shrimp business. Tom made a fortune."

"Mum," Kara said softly.

Her mother smiled at some memory and

shook her head. "A boat. . . . Well, the company was very successful. And people were surprised because, well, Tom never seemed too bright." Her mother's eyes sparkled. "But you know what he used to say to them?"

"What, Mum?"

" 'Stupid is as stupid does.' "

"That's a good expression," Kara whispered.

"Oh, you would've loved that man, Jenny. Did you know he met the president of the United States once. And played Ping-Pong in China."

Not noticing her daughter's quiet crying, the old woman continued to tell Kara the rest of the story of *Forrest Gump,* the movie that she'd been watching on TV a few moments before. Kara's uncle's name was Gil but in her mother's fantasy he was Tom—presumably after the film's star, Tom Hanks. Kara herself had become Jenny, Forrest's girlfriend.

No, no, no, Kara thought in despair, I didn't make it in time after all.

Her mother's soul had come and gone, leaving in its place only illusion.

The woman's narrative became a garbled

stream that moved from the shrimp boat in the Gulf to a swordfish boat in the North Atlantic caught in something called a "perfect storm" to an ocean liner sinking while her brother, in tuxedo, played the violin on deck. Thoughts, memories and images from a dozen other movies or books joined real memories. Soon Kara's "uncle," as well as all semblance of coherence, vanished completely.

"It's somewhere outside," the old woman said with finality. "I know it's outside." She closed her eyes.

Kara sat forward in her chair, gently resting her hand on her mother's smooth arm until the old woman was asleep. Thinking: But she *had* been in her right mind earlier. Jaynene wouldn't've paged her if she hadn't.

And if it happened once, she thought defiantly, it could happen again.

Finally Kara rose and walked out into the dark corridor, reflecting that, as talented a performer as she might be, she lacked the one skill she so desperately wanted: to magically transport her mother to that place where hearts stoked with the fuel of affection burn warmly for all the years God assigned them. Where minds retain perfectly every chapter in the rich histories of families. Where the apparent gulfs between loved ones turn out to be, in the end, nothing more than *effects*—temporary illusions.

Chapter Forty-nine

Gerald Marlow, a man with thick, Vitalis-crisp hair, was head of the NYPD's Patrol Services Division. His deliberate manner had been forged walking a beat for twenty years and tempered by spending another fifteen at the far-riskier job of supervising officers who walked similar beats.

Now, Monday morning, Amelia Sachs stood more or less at attention in front of him, willing her knees to ignore the arthritis that dug switchblades into them. They were in Marlow's corner office high up in the Big Building, One Police Plaza, downtown.

Marlow glanced up from the file he'd been reading and eyed her impeccably pressed blue navies. "Oh, sit down, Officer. Sorry. Sit down. . . . So, Herman Sachs's daughter."

Sitting, she noted a faint hesitation between the last two words of his sentence. Had the word "girl" been quickly replaced?

"That's right."

"I was at the funeral."

"I remember."

"It was a good one."

As funerals go.

Eyes on hers, posture upright, Marlow said, "Okay, Officer. Here it is. You're in some trouble."

It hit her like a physical blow. "I'm sorry, sir?"

"A crime scene on Saturday, by the Harlem River. Car went into the water. You ran it?"

Where the Conjurer's Mazda took out crack-head Carlos's shack and went for a swim.

"Yes, that's right."

"You placed somebody under arrest at the scene," Marlow said.

"Oh, that. Not really arrest. This guy went under the tape and was digging around in a sealed area. I had him escorted out and detained."

"Detained, arrested. The point is he was in custody for a while."

"Sure. I needed him out of my hair. It was an active scene."

Sachs was starting to get her bearings. The obnoxious citizen had complained. Happened every day. Nobody paid attention to crap like that. She began to relax.

"Well, the guy? He was Victor Ramos."

"Yeah, I think he told me that."

"*Congressman* Victor Ramos."

The relaxation vanished.

The captain opened a New York *Daily News.* "Let's see, let's see. Ah, here." He lifted the paper and held up a centerfold, which featured a large picture of the man in cuffs at the scene. The headline read: "TIME-OUT" FOR VICTOR.

"You told the officers on the scene to put him in *time-out*?"

"He was—"

"Did you?"

"I believe I did, sir, yes."

Marlow offered, "He claimed he was looking for survivors."

"Survivors?" she barked, laughing. "It was a ten-by-ten squatter's shack that got clipped when the perp's car went into the river. Part of a wall fell over and—"

"You're getting a little hot here, Officer."

"—and I think a bag of goddamn empties got ripped open. That was the only damage. EMS cleared the shack and I sealed it. The only living things left to rescue in that place were the lice."

"Uh-huh," Marlow said evenly, uneasy with her temper. "He said he was simply making sure anybody living there was safe."

She added with uncontrolled irony, "The *home owners* walked out on their own. Nobody was hurt. Though I understand one of them later got a bruised cheek when he resisted arrest."

"Arrest?"

"He tried to steal a fireman's flashlight and then urinated on him."

"Oh. Brother . . ."

She muttered, "They were unharmed, they were stoned and they were assholes. And those were the *citizens* Ramos was worried about?"

The captain's grimace, containing shreds of both caution and sympathy, faded. The emotion was replaced by his rubbery bureaucratic façade. "Do you know for a fact that there was any evidence Ramos destroyed that would've been relevant to collaring the suspect?"

"Whether there was or not doesn't make a bit of difference, sir. It's the procedure that's important." She was struggling to keep calm, keep the edge out of her voice. Marlow was, after all, her boss's boss's boss.

"Trying to work things out here, Officer Sachs," he said sternly. Then repeated, "Do you know for a *fact* that evidence was destroyed?"

She sighed. "No."

"So his being in the scene was irrelevant."

"I—"

"Irrelevant?"

"Yessir." She cleared her throat. "We *were* after a cop killer, Captain. Does that count for anything?" she asked bitterly.

"To me. To a lot of people, yeah. To Ramos, no."

She nodded. "Okay, what kind of firestorm're we talking?"

"There were TV crews there, Officer. You watch the news that night?"

Nup, she thought, I was pretty busy trying

to collar a murderer. Sachs chose a different answer: "Nosir."

"Well, Ramos was prominently featured, being led off in cuffs."

She said, "You know the only reason he was in the scene in the first place was to be filmed risking his goddamn life to look for survivors. . . . I'm curious, sir: Ramos running for reelection anytime soon?"

Even *confirming* comments like that can get you early retirement. Or no retirement at all. Marlow said nothing.

"What's the . . . ?"

"Bottom line?" Marlow's lips tightened. "I'm sorry, Officer. You've washed out. Ramos checked on you. Found out about the sergeant's exam. He pulled strings. He got you flunked."

"He did *what?*"

"Flunked. He talked to the examining officers."

"I had the third highest exam in the history of the department," she said, laughing bitterly. "Isn't that right?"

"Yes—on the multiple choice and the orals. But you need to pass the assessment exercise too."

"I did fine on it."

"The preliminary results were good. But in the final report you flunked."

"Impossible. What happened?"

"One of the officers in the exercise wouldn't pass you."

"Wouldn't pass me? But I . . ." Her voice faded as she pictured the handsome officer with the shotgun stepping out from behind the Dumpster. The man she'd snubbed.

Bang, bang . . .

The captain read from a piece of paper, "He said you didn't quote 'display proper respect for individuals in a supervisory position. And she exhibited disrespectful behavior with regard to peers, leading to situations of endangerment.'"

"So Ramos tracked down somebody willing to dime me out and fed him those lines. I'm sorry, Captain, but you really think a street cop talks that way? 'Situations of endangerment'? Come on."

Well, Pop, she thought to her father, how's this for sticking in the craw? Feeling heartsick.

Then she looked carefully at Marlow. "What else, sir? There *is* something else, isn't there?"

To his credit he held her eye as he said,

"Yes, Officer. There is. It gets worse, I'm afraid."

Let's hear how *exactly* it could be worse, Pop.

"Ramos is trying to get you suspended."

"Suspended. That's bullshit."

"He wants an inquest."

"Vindictive . . ." The "prick" didn't get spoken as she saw in Marlow's gaze the reminder that it was this sort of attitude that had gotten her into trouble in the first place.

He added, "I have to tell you that he's mad enough to . . . Well, he's going for suspension without pay." This punishment was usually reserved for officers accused of crimes.

"Why?"

Marlow didn't answer. But he didn't need to, of course. Sachs knew: to bolster his credibility Ramos had to show that the time-out woman who'd embarrassed him was a loose cannon.

And the other reason was that he was a vindictive prick.

"What'd the grounds be?"

"Insubordination, incompetence."

"I can't lose my shield, sir." Trying not to sound desperate.

"There's nothing I can do about your flunking the exam, Amelia. That's in the board's hands and they've already made their decision. But I'll fight the suspension. I can't promise anything, though. Ramos's got wire. All over the city."

A hand rose into her scalp. She scratched until she felt pain. Lowered her hand, feeling slick blood. "Can I speak freely, sir?"

Marlow slumped slightly in his chair. "Jesus, Officer, sure. You have to know I feel bad about this. Say what you want. And you don't have to sit at attention. We're not the army, you know."

Sachs cleared her throat. "If he tries for suspension, sir, my next call'll be to the PBA lawyers. I'll light this one up. I'll take it as far as I have to."

And she would. Though she knew how non-rank cops who fought discrimination or suspensions through the Patrolmen's Benevolent Association were unofficially red flagged. Many of them found their careers permanently sidetracked even if they won technical victories.

Marlow held her steady gaze as he said, "Noted, Officer."

So it was knuckle time.

Her father's expression. About being a cop.

Amie, you have to understand: sometimes it's a rush, sometimes you get to make a difference, sometimes it's boring. And sometimes, not too often, thank God, it's knuckle time. Fist to fist. You're all by your lonesome, with nobody to help you. And I don't mean just the perps. Sometimes it'll be you against your boss. Sometimes against their bosses. Could be you against your buddies too. You gonna be a cop, you got to be ready to go it alone. There's no getting around it.

"Well, for the time being you're still on active duty."

"Yessir. When will I know?"

"A day or two."

Walking toward the door.

She stopped, turned back. "Sir?"

Marlow glanced up as if he was surprised she was still there.

"Ramos was in the middle of my crime scene. If it'd been you there, or the mayor, or the president himself, I would've done exactly the same thing."

"That's why you're your father's daughter, Officer, and why he'd be proud of you." Marlow lifted his phone off the cradle. "We'll hope for the best."

Chapter Fifty

Thom let Lon Sellitto into the front hallway, where Lincoln Rhyme sat in his candy-apple red chair, grumbling at construction workers to mind the woodwork as they carted refuse downstairs from the repair work currently going on in his fire-damaged bedroom.

Passing by on his way to the kitchen to fix lunch, Thom grumbled back, "Leave 'em alone, Lincoln. You couldn't care less about the woodwork."

"It's the principle," the criminalist replied tautly. "It's *my* woodwork and *their* clumsiness."

"He's always this way when a case's over," the aide said to Sellitto. "Have you got some really thorny robbery or murder for him? A good pacifier?"

"I don't need a pacifier," Rhyme snapped

as the aide vanished. "I need people to be careful with the walls!"

Sellitto said, "Hey, Linc. We've got to talk."

The criminalist noted the tone—and the look in Sellitto's eyes. They'd been working together for years and he could read every emotion the cop broadcast, especially when he was troubled. What *now*? he wondered.

"Just heard from the head of Patrol. It's about Amelia." Sellitto cleared his throat.

Rhyme's heart undoubtedly gave an extra slam in his chest. He never felt it, of course, though he did sense a surge of blood in his neck and head and face.

Thinking: Bullet, car crash.

He said evenly in a low voice, "Go on."

"She washed out. The sergeant's exam."

"What?"

"Yup."

Rhyme's hot relief turned instantly to sorrow for her.

The detective continued, "It's not official yet. But I know."

"Where'd you hear?"

"Cop radar. A fucking bird. I don't know.

Sachs's a star. When something like this happens, word gets out."

"What about her score on the exam?"

"*Despite* her score on the exam."

Rhyme wheeled into the lab. The detective, looking particularly rumpled today, followed.

The explanation was pure Sachs, it turned out. She'd ordered somebody out of an active crime scene and, when he wouldn't leave, had him cuffed.

"Bad for her, the guy turned out to be Victor Ramos."

"The congressman." Lincoln Rhyme had virtually no interest in local government but he knew about Ramos: an opportunistic politico who'd abandoned his Latino constituents in Spanish Harlem until recently, now that the politically correct climate—and size of the electorate—meant he could push for Albany or a spot in Washington.

"Can they wash her out?"

"Come on, Linc, they can do what they fucking want. They're even talking suspension."

"She can fight it. She *will* fight it."

"And you know what happens to street cops who take on brass. Odds're, even if she wins, they'll send her to East New York. Hell, even worse, they'll send her to a *desk* in East New York."

"Fuck," the criminalist spat out.

Sellitto paced around the room, stepping over cables and glancing at the Conjurer case whiteboards. The detective dropped into a chair that creaked under his weight. He kneaded a roll of fat around his waistband; the Conjurer case had seriously sidetracked his diet. "One thing," he said softly, a whiff of conspiracy in his voice.

"Yeah?"

"There's this guy I know. He was the one cleaned up the Eighteen."

"When all that crack and smack kept disappearing from the evidence locker? A few years ago?"

"Yeah. That was it. He's got serious wire all over the Big Building. The commissioner'll listen to him and *he'll* listen to *me.* He owes me." Then he waved his arm toward the Conjurer case evidence boards. "And, fuck, lookit what we just did. We nailed one hell of a doer. Lemme give him a call. Pull some strings for her."

And Rhyme's eyes too took in the charts, then the equipment, the examining tables, books—all devoted to the science of analyzing the evidence that Sachs had teased or muscled out of crime scenes over the past few years they'd been together. "I don't know," he said.

"Whatsa problem?"

"If she made sergeant that way, well, *she* wouldn't be the one making it."

The detective replied, "You know what this promotion means to her, Linc."

Yeah, he did.

"Look, all we're doing is playing by Ramos's rules. He wants to take it down a notch we'll do the same. Make it a, you know, even playing field." Sellitto liked his idea. He added, "Amelia'll never find out. I'll tell my guy to keep the lid on it. He'll do it."

You know what this promotion means to her. . . .

"So what do you think?" the detective asked.

Rhyme said nothing for a moment, looking for the answer in the silent forensic equipment surrounding him and then in the green mist of spring buds crowning the trees in Central Park.

● ● ●

The scuffs on the woodwork had been scrubbed away and all traces of the fire in the bedroom had been "vanished," as Thom had put it, rather cleverly, Rhyme thought. A rich scent of smoke lingered but that reminded Lincoln Rhyme of good scotch and was therefore not a problem at all.

Now, midnight, the room dark, Rhyme lay in his Flexicair bed, staring out the window. Outside was a flutter of motion as a falcon, one of God's most fluid creatures, landed on the ledge. Depending on the light, and their degree of alertness, the birds seemed to shrink or grow in size. Tonight they seemed larger than in the daylight, their forms magnificent. Menacing too; they weren't pleased with the noises radiating from the Cirque Fantastique in Central Park.

Well, Rhyme wasn't very happy about them either. He'd dozed off ten minutes ago only to be awakened by a loud burst of applause from the tent.

"They should have a curfew on that," Rhyme grumbled to Sachs, lying beside him in bed.

"I could shoot out their generator," she replied, her voice clear. She apparently hadn't gotten to sleep at all. Her head was on the pillow next to his, lips against his neck, on which he could feel the faint tickle of her hair and the smooth cool plane of her skin. Also: her breasts against his chest, belly to hip, leg over leg. He knew this only by observation, of course; there was no sensate proof of the contact. He relished that closeness all the same.

Sachs always adhered to Rhyme's firm rule that those walking the grid not wear scent because they might miss olfactory evidence at crime scenes. But she was off duty at the moment and he detected on her skin a pleasant, complex smell, which he deduced to be jasmine, gardenia and synthetic motor oil.

They were alone in the apartment. They'd shipped Thom off to the movies with his friend Peter and had spent the night with some new CDs, two ounces of sevruga caviar, Ritz crackers, and copious Moët, despite the inherent difficulties in drinking champagne through a straw. Now, in the darkness, he was thinking again about music, about how such a purely mechanical system of tones and pacing could consume you so completely. It fascinated him. The more he thought about it, the more he decided that the subject might not be as mysterious as it seemed. Music was, after all, firmly rooted in his world: science, logic and mathematics.

How *would* one go about writing a melody? If the physical therapy exercises he was doing now eventually had some effect . . . could he actually press his fingers on a keyboard? As he was considering this he noticed Sachs looking up at his face in the dim light. "You heard about the sergeant's exam?" she asked.

A hesitation. Then: "Yep," he replied. He'd scrupulously avoided bringing up the matter all night; when Sachs was prepared to discuss something she would. Until then the subject didn't exist.

"You know what happened?" she asked.

"Not all the details. I assume it falls into the category of a quasi-corrupt, self-interested government official versus the overworked heroic crime scene cop. Something like that?"

A laugh. "Pretty much."

"I've been there myself, Sachs."

The music from the circus kept thudding away, engendering mixed responses. Somehow you *felt* you should be irritated that it was intruding but you couldn't resist enjoying the beat.

She then asked, "Did Lon talk to you about pulling some strings for me? Making calls to city hall?"

Amelia'll never find out. I'll tell my guy to keep the lid on it. . . .

He chuckled. "He did, yeah. You know Lon."

The music stopped. Then applause filled the night. The faint yet evocative sound of the MC's voice followed.

She said, "I heard he could've made the whole thing go away. Bypassed Ramos."

"Probably. He's got a long reach."

Sachs asked, "And what'd you say about that?"

"What do you think?"

"I'm asking."

Rhyme said, "I said no. I wouldn't let him do it."

"You wouldn't?"

"No. I told him you'd make rank on your own or not at all."

"Goddamn," she muttered.

He looked down at her, momentarily alarmed. Had he misjudged her?

"I'm pissed at Lon for even considering it."

"He meant well."

He believed that her arm around his chest gripped him tighter. "What you told him, Rhyme, that means more to me than anything."

"I know that."

"It could get ugly. Ramos's going for suspension. Twelve months off duty, no pay. I don't know what I'll do."

"You'll consult. With me."

"A civilian can't walk the grid, Rhyme. I have to sit still, I'll go crazy."

When you move they can't getcha. . . .

"We'll get through it."

"Love you," she whispered. His response was to inhale her flowery Quaker State scent and tell her that he loved her too.

"Man, it's too bright." She looked toward the window, filled with glare from the circus spotlights. "Where're the shades?"

"Burned up, remember?"

"I thought Thom got some new ones."

"He started to put them up but he was fussing too much. Measuring and everything. I threw him out and told him to do it later."

Sachs slipped out of bed and found an extra sheet, draped it over the window, cutting out much of the light. She returned to bed, curled up against him and was soon asleep.

But not Lincoln Rhyme. As he lay listening to the music and the cryptic voice of the MC some ideas began to form in his mind and the opportunity for sleep came and went. Soon he was completely awake, lost in his thoughts.

Which were, not surprisingly, about the circus.

Late the next morning Thom walked into the bedroom to find that Rhyme had a visitor.

"Hi," he said to Jaynene Williams, sitting in one of the new chairs beside his bed.

"Thom." She shook his hand.

The aide, who'd been out shopping, was clearly surprised to see someone there. Thanks to the computer, the environmental control units and CCTV, Rhyme was, of course, perfectly capable of calling someone up, inviting them over and letting them inside when they arrived.

"No need to look so *shocked*," Rhyme

said caustically. "I *have* invited people over before, you know."

"Blue moon comes to mind."

"Maybe I'll hire Jaynene here to replace you."

"Why don't you hire her as *well* as me. With two people here we could share the abuse." He smiled at her. "I wouldn't do that to you, though."

"I've handled worse."

"Are you a coffee lady or a tea lady?"

Rhyme said, "Sorry. Where *were* my manners? Should've had the pot boiling by now."

"Coffee'll do."

"Scotch for me," Rhyme said. When Thom glanced at the clock, the criminalist added, "A small shot for medicinal purposes."

"Coffee all around," the aide said and disappeared.

After he'd gone Rhyme and Jaynene made small talk about spinal cord injury patients and the exercises he was now pursuing fanatically. Then, impatient as ever, Rhyme decided he'd been the polite host long enough and lowered his voice to say, "There's a problem, something bothering me. I think you can help. I'm hoping you can."

She eyed him cautiously. "Maybe."

"Could you close the door?"

The large woman glanced at it, rose and then did as he asked. She returned to her seat.

"How long have you known Kara?" he asked.

"Kara? Little over a year. Ever since her mother came to Stuyvesant."

"That's an expensive place, isn't it?"

"Painfully," Jaynene said. "Terrible what they charge. But all of the places like ours, the fees're pretty much the same."

"Does her mother have insurance?"

"Medicare is all. Kara pays for most of it herself." She added, "As best she can. She's current now but she's in arrears a lot of the time."

Rhyme nodded slowly. "I'm going to ask you one more question. Think about it before you answer. And I need you to be completely honest."

"Well," the nurse said uncertainly, looking down at the newly varnished floor. "I'll do the best I can."

• • •

That afternoon Roland Bell was in Rhyme's living room. To the soundtrack of some enticing Dave Brubeck jazz piano they were talking about the evidence in the Andrew Constable case.

Charles Grady and the state's attorney general himself had decided to delay the man's trial in order to include additional charges against the bigot—attempted murder of his own lawyer, conspiracy to commit murder and felony murder. It wouldn't be an easy case—linking Constable to Barnes and the other conspirators in the Patriot Assembly—but if anyone could bring in convictions Grady was the man to do it. He was also going for the death penalty against Arthur Loesser for the murder of Patrol Officer Larry Burke, whose body had been found in an alley on the Upper West Side. Lon Sellitto was presently at the officer's full-dress funeral in Queens.

Amelia Sachs now walked through the doorway, looking frazzled after an all-day meeting with lawyers arranged through the Patrolmen's Benevolent Association about her possible suspension. She was supposed to have been back hours ago and, glancing at her face, Rhyme deduced that the results of the session were not good.

He himself had some news—about his meeting with Jaynene and what had happened after that—and had tried to reach her but had been unable to. Now, though, there was no time to brief her because another visitor appeared.

Thom ushered Edward Kadesky into the room. "Mr. Rhyme," he said, nodding. He'd forgotten Sachs's name but he gave her a second nod in greeting. He shook Roland Bell's hand. "I got your message. It said there's something more about the case."

Rhyme nodded. "This morning I did some digging, looking into a few loose ends."

"What loose ends?" Sachs asked.

"Ends I didn't know were loose. *Unknown* loose ends."

She frowned. The producer too looked troubled. "Weir's assistant—Loesser. He hasn't escaped, has he?"

"No, no. He's still in detention."

The doorbell rang. Thom vanished and a moment later Kara stepped through the doorway into the room. She looked around, ruffling her short hair, which had lost its purple sheen and was now ruddy as a freckle. "Hi," she said to the group, blinking in surprise when she saw Kadesky.

"Can I get anybody anything?" Thom asked.

"Maybe if you could leave us for a minute, Thom. Please."

The aide glanced at Rhyme and, hearing the firm, troubled tone in his voice, nodded and left the room. The criminalist said to Kara, "Thanks for coming by. I just need to follow up on a few things about the case."

"Sure," she said.

Loose ends . . .

Rhyme explained, "I want to know a few more details about the night that the Conjurer drove the ambulance bomb into the circus."

The young woman nodded, flicking her black fingernails against one another. "Anything I can do to help, I'd be glad to."

"The show was scheduled to start at eight, wasn't it?" Rhyme asked Kadesky.

"That's right."

"You weren't back from your dinner and radio interview yet when Loesser parked the ambulance in the doorway?"

"No, I wasn't."

Rhyme turned to Kara. "But you were there?"

"Yeah. I saw the ambulance drive in. I didn't think anything about it at the time."

"Where did Loesser park, exactly?"

"It was under the box seat scaffolding," she said.

"Not under the expensive seats though?" Rhyme asked Kadesky.

"No," the man said.

"So it was near the main fire exit—the one most people would use in an evacuation."

"That's right."

Bell asked, "Lincoln, what're you getting at?"

"What I'm getting at is Loesser parked the ambulance so that it would do the most damage and yet still give a few people in the box seats a chance to escape. How did he know exactly where to park it?"

"I don't know," the producer responded. "He probably checked it out ahead of time and saw it was the best location—I mean, best from his point of view. Worst for us."

"He *might've* checked it out earlier," Rhyme mused. "But he also would be reluctant to be seen doing reconnaissance around the circus—since we had officers stationed there."

"True."

"So, isn't it possible that someone on the *inside* might've told him to park there?"

"Inside?" Kadesky asked, frowning. "Are you saying somebody was helping him? No, none of my people would do that."

"Rhyme," Sachs said, "what are you getting at?"

He ignored her and turned again to Kara. "I asked you to go to the tent to find Mr. Kadesky about when?"

"I guess it was about seven-fifteen."

"And you were *in* the box seat area?" She nodded and he continued, "Near the exit row?"

The woman looked around the room awkwardly. "I guess. Yeah, I was." She looked at Sachs. "Why's he asking me all this? What's going on?"

Rhyme answered, "I'm asking because I remembered something *you* told us, Kara. About people who're involved in an illusionist's act. There's the *assistant*—the person that we know is working with the illusionist. Then there's the *volunteer* from the audience. Then there's someone else: the *con-*

federate. Those're people who are actually working with the magician but seem to have nothing to do with him. They pretend to be stagehands or volunteers."

Kadesky said, "Right, lots of magicians use confederates."

Rhyme turned to Kara and said sharply, "Which is what *you've* been all along, haven't you?"

"What's that?" Bell asked, his drawl more pronounced in his surprise.

The young woman gasped, shaking her head.

"She's been working with Loesser from the beginning," Rhyme said to Sachs.

"No!" Kadesky said. "Her?"

Rhyme continued, "She needs money badly and Loesser paid her fifty thousand to help him."

Desperate, Kara said, "But Loesser and I never even met before today!"

"You didn't need to see him in person. Balzac was the intermediary. He was in on it too."

"Kara?" Sachs whispered. "No. I don't believe it. She wouldn't do that!"

"Wouldn't she? What do you know about her? Do you even know her real name?"

"I . . ." Sachs's troubled eyes turned toward the young woman. "No," she whispered. "She never told me."

Tearfully the young woman shook her head. Finally she said, "Amelia, I'm so sorry. . . . But you don't understand. . . . Mr. Balzac and Weir were friends. They performed together for years and he was devastated when Weir died in the fire. Loesser told Mr. Balzac what he was going to do and they forced me to help him. But, you have to believe me, I didn't know they were going to hurt anybody. Mr. Balzac said it was just an extortion thing—to get even with Mr. Kadesky. By the time I realized Loesser was killing people it was too late. They said if I didn't keep helping him he was going to give my name to the police. I'd go to jail forever. Mr. Balzac would too. . . ." She wiped her face. "I couldn't do that to him."

"To your *revered* mentor," Rhyme said bitterly.

With a look of panic in her brilliant blue eyes the young woman shoved her way through Sachs and Kadesky and leaped for the door.

"Stop her, Roland!" Rhyme shouted.

Bell sprinted forward and tackled her. They tumbled into the corner of the room. She was strong but Bell managed to cuff her. He rose, panting from the effort, and pulled his Motorola off his belt, calling in for a prisoner transfer down to detention.

Looking disgusted, he put the radio away and read Kara her rights.

Rhyme sighed. "I tried to tell you earlier, Sachs. I couldn't get through on the phone. I wish it weren't true. But there you have it. She and Balzac were with Loesser all along. They gulled us like we were their audience."

Chapter Fifty-one

Whispering, the policewoman said, "I just . . . I don't see how she did it."

Rhyme said to Bell, "She manipulated the evidence, lied to us, planted fake clues. . . . Roland, go over to the whiteboards. I'll show you."

"*Kara* planted evidence?" Sachs asked, astonished.

"Oh, you bet she did. And she did a damn good job too. From the first scene, even *before* you found her. You told me that *she* gave you that sign to meet her in the coffee shop. They set it up from the beginning."

Bell was at the whiteboards and as he pointed out items of evidence Rhyme would explain how Kara had tricked them.

A moment later Thom called, "There's an officer here."

"Show 'em in," Rhyme said.

A policewoman walked through the doorway and joined Sachs, Bell and Kadesky, surveying them through stylish glasses with a look of curiosity on her face. She nodded to Rhyme, and in a Hispanic accent, asked Bell, "You called for prisoner transport, Detective?"

Bell nodded to the corner of the room. "She's over there. I Mirandized her."

The woman glanced toward the corner of the room at Kara's prone form and said, "Okay, I'll take her downtown." She hesitated. "But I got a question first."

"Question?" Rhyme asked, frowning.

"What're you talking about, Officer?" Bell asked.

Ignoring the detective, the officer sized up Kadesky. "Could I see some identification, sir?"

"Me?" the producer asked.

"Yessir. I'll need to see your driver's license."

"You want my ID *again?* I did that the other day."

"Sir, please."

Huffily the man reached into his hip pocket and withdrew his wallet.

Except that it wasn't his.

He stared at a battered zebra-skin billfold. "Wait, I . . . I don't know what this is."

"It's not yours?" the cop asked.

"No," he said, troubled. He began patting his pockets. "I don't know—"

"See, that's what I was afraid of," the policewoman said. "I'm sorry, sir. You're under arrest for pickpocketing. You have the right to remain silent—"

"This is bullshit," Kadesky muttered. "There's some mistake." He opened up the wallet and stared at it for a moment. Then he barked an astonished laugh, held up the driver's license for everyone to see. It was Kara's.

There was a handwritten note inside. It dropped out. He picked it up. "It says, 'Gotcha,'" Kadesky said, narrowing his eyes and studying the policewoman closely, then the driver's license. "Wait, is this *you?*"

The "officer" laughed and removed the glasses then her cop cap and the brunette wig beneath it, revealing the short reddish hair once again. With a towel that Roland Bell, now chuckling hard, handed her she wiped the dark-complexion makeup off her face and peeled away the thick eyebrows and the fake red nails covering the black glossy ones. She then took her wallet back from the hands of the astonished Edward Kadesky and handed him his, which she'd dipped when she'd plowed into him and Sachs in her "escape" toward the door.

Sachs was shaking her head, too astonished to react. She and Kadesky were both staring at the body lying on the floor.

The young illusionist walked into the corner and lifted the device, a lightweight frame in the shape of a person lying on her stomach. Short reddish-purple hair covered the head portion, and the body wore clothing that resembled the jeans and windbreaker Kara'd been in when Bell had cuffed her. The arms of the outfit ended in what turned out to be latex hands, hooked together with Bell's handcuffs, which Kara had escaped from and then relatched on the phony wrists.

"It's a feke," Rhyme now announced to the room, nodding at the frame. "A phony Kara."

When Sachs and the others had turned away—misdirected by Rhyme toward the chart—Kara had escaped from the cuffs, unfurled the body frame and then silently slipped out the door to do the quick change in the hallway.

She now folded up the device, which compressed into a little package the size of a small pillow—she'd had it hidden under her jacket when she'd arrived. The dummy wouldn't have passed close examination but in the shadows, with an unsuspecting, misdirected audience, no one had noticed it wasn't the girl.

Kadesky was shaking his head. "You did the whole escape *and* the quick change in less than a minute?"

"Forty seconds."

"How?"

"You saw the effect," Kara said to him. "Think I'll keep the method to myself."

"So the point of this is, I assume," said Kadesky cynically, "that you want an audition?"

Kara hesitated and Rhyme shot a prodding glance toward the young woman.

"No, the point is, this *was* the audition. I want a job."

Kadesky studied her closely. "It was one trick. You have others?"

"Plenty."

"How many changes've you done in one show?"

"Forty-two changes. Thirty characters. During a thirty-minute routine."

"Forty-two setups in half an hour?" the producer asked, eyebrows raised.

"Yep."

He debated for only a few seconds. "Come see me next week. I'm not cutting back my current artists' time in the ring. But they could use an assistant and an understudy. And maybe you can do some shows at our winter camp in Florida."

Rhyme and Kara exchanged glances. He nodded firmly.

"Okay," the young woman said to Kadesky. She shook his hand.

Kadesky glanced at the spring-loaded wire form that had fooled them. "You made that?"

"Yep."

"You might want to patent it."

"I never thought about that. Thanks. I'll look into it."

He looked her over again. "Forty-two in thirty minutes." Then nodding, he left the room. Both he and Kara looked as if they'd each bought a very nice, very underpriced sports car.

Sachs laughed. "Damn, you had me going." A glance at Rhyme. "Both of you."

"Wait up here," Bell said, feigning hurt. "I was in on it too. I'm the one hog-tied her."

Sachs shook her head again. "When did you think this up?"

It had started last night, Rhyme explained, lying in bed, listening to the music from Cirque Fantastique, the ringmaster's muted voice, the applause and laughter from the crowd. His thoughts had segued to Kara, how good her performance at Smoke & Mirrors had been. Recalling her lack of self-confidence and Balzac's sway over her.

Recalling too what Sachs had told him about her mother's advanced senility. Which had prompted Rhyme's invitation to Jaynene the next morning.

"I'm going to ask you one more question," Rhyme had said to the woman. "Think about it before you answer. And I need you to be completely honest."

The query was: "Will her mother ever come out of it?"

Jaynene had said, "Will she get back her mind, is that what you're asking?"

"That's right. Will she recover?"

"No."

"So Kara's not taking her to England?"

A sad laugh. "No, no, no. That woman's not going anywhere."

"Kara said she couldn't quit her job because she needs to keep her mother in the nursing home."

"She needs to be cared for, sure. But not at our place. Kara's paying for rehab and recreation, medical intervention. Short-term care. Kara's mom doesn't even know what year it is. She could be anywhere. Sorry to say it but all she needs is maintenance at this point."

"What'll happen to her if she goes to a long-term home?"

"She'll keep getting worse until the end. Just the same as if she stayed with us. Only it wouldn't bankrupt Kara."

After that, Jaynene and Thom had gone off to have lunch together—and undoubtedly to share war stories about the people in their care. Rhyme had then called Kara. She'd come over and they'd had a talk. The conversation had been awkward; he'd never done well with personal matters. Confronting a heartless killer was easy compared with intruding on the tender soul of someone's life.

"I don't know your profession too well," Rhyme had said. "But when I saw you perform at the store on Sunday I was impressed. And it takes a lot to impress me. You were damn good."

"For a student" had been her dismissive response.

"No," he'd said firmly, "for a *performer.* You should be onstage."

"I'm not ready yet. I'll get there eventually."

After a thick pause Rhyme said, "The problem with that attitude is that sometimes you *don't* get there eventually." He glanced down at his body. "Sometimes things . . . intervene. And there you are, you've put off something important. And you miss it forever."

"But Mr. Balzac—"

"—is keeping you down. It's obvious."

"He's only thinking what's best for me."

"No, he's not. I don't know what he's thinking of. But the one thing he's *not* thinking of is *you.* Look at Weir and Loesser. And Keating. Mentors can mesmerize you. Thank Balzac for what he's done, stay friends, send him box seat tickets for your first Carnegie Hall show. But get away from him now—while you can."

"I'm not mesmerized," she'd said, laughing.

Rhyme hadn't responded and he sensed she was considering just how much she *was* under the man's thumb. He continued, "We've got some juice with Kadesky—after everything we've done. Amelia told me how much you like the Cirque Fantastique. I think you should audition."

"Even if I did, I have a personal situation. My—"

"Mother," Rhyme'd interrupted.

"Right."

"I had a talk with Jaynene."

The woman had fallen silent.

Rhyme'd said, "Let me tell you a story."

"Story?"

"I headed the forensics department here in New York. The job had the typical administrative crap, you can imagine. But the thing I loved most—and what I was best at—was running crime scenes, so even after I was promoted I still got into the field as often as I could. Well, we had a serial rapist working in the Bronx a few years ago.

I won't go into the details but it was an ugly situation and I wanted that man nailed. I wanted him bad. I got a call from patrol that there'd been another attack, just a half hour before, and it looked like there was some good evidence. I went uptown to run the scene personally.

"Just as I got there I found out my second in command—and a good friend of mine—had had a heart attack. A bad one. Big shock. He was a young guy, in good shape. Anyway, he was asking for me." Rhyme had pushed down a hard memory and continued, "But I stayed and ran the scene, filled out the chain of custody cards and then went to the hospital. I got there as fast as I could but I was too late. He'd died a half hour before. I wasn't proud of that. It still hurts me after all these years. But I wouldn't've done it different."

"So your point is that I should put my mother in some shitty home," she'd said bitterly. "A cheaper one. Just so I can be happy."

"Of course not. Put her someplace that'll give her what she needs—care and companionship. Not what *you* need. Not a rehab center that's going to bankrupt you. . . . My point? It's that if there's something you know you're meant to do in life, that has to take priority over everything else. Get a job with Cirque Fantastique. Or another show. But you have to move on."

"Do you know what some of those homes are like?"

"Well, then your job is to find one that you're both comfortable with. Sorry to be blunt. But I told you up front I don't do well with delicacy."

She'd shaken her head. "Look, Lincoln, even if I decided to, do you know how many people'd die for a job at Cirque Fantastique? They get a hundred résumés a week."

Finally he'd smiled. "Well, now, I've been thinking about that. The Immobilized Man has an idea for a routine I think we should try."

Rhyme now finished telling Sachs the story.

Kara said, "We thought we'd call the trick the Escaping Suspect. I'm going to add it to my repertoire."

Sachs turned to Rhyme. "And the reason you didn't tell me before was . . . ?"

"I'm sorry. You were downtown. I couldn't get through."

"Well, it might've worked better if you'd told me. You could've left a message."

"I. Am. Sorry. There. I've apologized. I don't do it very often, you know. I'd think you might appreciate it. Though, now that you brought it up, I don't really see how it could've worked *better.* The look on your face was priceless. Added to the credibility."

"And Balzac?" Sachs asked. "He didn't know Weir? He wasn't really involved?"

Rhyme nodded at Kara. "Pure fiction. We wrote the script, the two of us."

Sachs eyed the young woman. "First you get stabbed to death when I'm supposed to be looking out for you. Then you turn into a murder suspect." The policewoman gave an exasperated sigh. "This could be a difficult friendship."

Kara offered to run up the street to get some more Cuban takeout, which they'd missed the other day, though Rhyme suspected it was just an excuse for her to pick up another one of the restaurant's sludgy coffees. But before they could decide on the order they were interrupted by Rhyme's ringing phone. He ordered, "Command, answer phone." A moment later Sellitto's voice came on the speakerphone. "Linc, you busy?"

"Depends," he grumbled. "What's up?"

"No rest for the wicked. . . . We need your help again. We got a weird homicide."

"Last one was 'bizarre,' if I remember correctly. I think you just say things like that to get my attention."

"No, really, we can't figure this one out."

"All right, all right," the criminalist grumbled, "give me the details."

Though the translation of Lincoln Rhyme's gruff demeanor was simply how pleased he was that boredom would be held at bay for at least a little while longer.

Kara stood outside Smoke & Mirrors, seeing things she'd never noticed in her year and a half working there. A hole in the upper left-hand corner of the plate glass from a BB or pellet gunshot. A tiny swirl of graffiti on the door. A dusty book on Houdini in the window, opened to the page discussing the type of sash cord he preferred to use in his routines.

She saw a flare inside the store—Mr. Balzac lighting a cigarette.

A breath. Let's do it, she thought and pushed inside.

He was by the counter with that friend of his who'd been in town this past weekend, an illusionist from California. Balzac introduced her as a student and the middle-aged man shook her hand. They made small talk about how his performance had gone last night, other people appearing in town . . . the typical gossip performers everywhere engage in. Finally the man picked up his suitcase. He was on his way to Kennedy airport for the flight home and had stopped at the store to return the props he'd borrowed. He embraced Balzac, nodded to Kara and left the store.

"You're late," the magician said to her gruffly. Then observed that she wasn't putting her bag behind the counter as she always did. He glanced at her hands. No coffee cup. That was, of course, the giveaway.

A frown. "What?" he asked, drawing on his cigarette. "Tell me."

"I'm leaving."

"You're . . ."

"I talked to Ed Kadesky. I've got a job with the Cirque Fantastique."

"Them? Kadesky? No, no, no—it's all wrong for you. That's not magic. That's—"

"It's what I want to do."

"We've been through this a dozen times. You're not ready. You're good. You're not great."

"That doesn't matter," she said firmly. "What matters is getting up onstage. Performing."

"If you rush it—"

"Rush it, David? Rush it? When would I be ready? Next year? In five years?" Normally she found it difficult to hold his eye; today she looked straight at him as she said, "Would you ever let me go?"

A pause, while he ordered papers, slapped them down on the scuffed, cracked counter. "Kadesky," he scoffed. "And what'll you be doing for him?"

"Assistant at first. Then some winter season shows of my own in Florida. Then who knows?"

He stubbed out the cigarette. "It's a mistake. You'll be wasting your talent. What he does, it's not the kind of illusion I taught you."

"I got the job *because of* what you taught me."

"Kadesky," he said again contemptuously. "New magic."

"Yeah, it is," she said. "But I'll be doing your routines too. Metamorphosis, remember—the old becoming new."

He didn't smile though she could sense the reference to his act pleased him.

"David, I want to keep studying with you. When I'm back in town I want to take lessons. I'll pay for them."

"I don't think that would work. You can't serve two masters," the man muttered. When Kara said nothing he said grudgingly, "We'll have to see. I might not have the time. I probably won't."

She hitched her purse higher on her shoulder.

"Right now?" he asked. "You're leaving now?"

"Yeah. I think it's best."

He nodded.

"So," Kara said.

The illusionist said a formal "Goodbye then" and stepped behind the counter, offering nothing else.

Struggling to keep the tears at bay, she walked to the door.

"Wait," he called as she started outside. Balzac stepped into the back of the store and then returned to her. He held something in his hand and thrust it into hers. It was the cigar box that contained Tarbell's three colored silks.

"Here. Take these. . . . I liked the way you did that one. It was a tight trick."

She remembered the praise she'd received for it. *Ah. . . .*

Kara stepped forward and embraced him fast, thinking that this was the first physical contact they'd had since she shook his hand when she'd met him eighteen months ago.

He gave her an awkward hug in return and then stepped back.

Kara walked outside, paused and turned to wave but Balzac had vanished into the dim recesses of the store. She slipped the box of silks into her purse and started toward Sixth Avenue, which would take her downtown to her apartment.

Chapter Fifty-two

The homicide was indeed a weird one.

A double murder in a deserted part of Roosevelt Island—that narrow strip of apartments, hospitals and ghostly ruins in the East River. Since the tramway deposits residents not far from the United Nations in Manhattan many diplomats and U.N. employees live on the island.

And it was two of these individuals—junior emissaries from the Balkans—who'd been found murdered, each shot in the back of the head twice, their hands bound.

There were several curious things that Amelia Sachs had turned up when she'd run the scene. She'd found ash from a type of cigarette that wasn't in the state or federal tobacco database, traces of a plant that wasn't indigenous to the metropolitan area and imprints of a heavy suitcase that had been set down and apparently opened next to the victims after they'd been shot.

And strangest of all was the fact that each man was missing his right shoe. They were nowhere to be found. "Both of them the *right* shoe, Sachs," Rhyme said, looking at the evidence board, in front of which he sat and she paced. "What do we make of that?"

But the question was put on hold temporarily by Sachs's ringing cell phone. It was Captain Marlow's secretary, asking if she could come down to a meeting at his office. Several days had passed since they'd closed the Conjurer case, several days since she learned about Victor Ramos's action against her. There'd been no further word about the suspension.

"When?" Sachs asked.

"Well, now," the woman replied.

Sachs disconnected and, with a glance and tight-lipped smile toward Rhyme, she said, "This's it. Gotta go."

They held each other's eyes for a moment. Then Rhyme nodded and she headed for the door.

A half hour later Sachs was in Captain Gerald Marlow's office, sitting across from the man, who was reading one of his ever-present manila files. "One second, Officer." He continued reviewing whatever so absorbed him, jotting occasional notes.

She fidgeted. Picking at a cuticle, then at a nail. Two grass-growing minutes went by. Oh, Jesus Christ, she thought and finally asked, "Okay, sir. What's the story? Did he back down?"

Marlow marked a spot on the sheet he was reading and looked up. "Who?"

"Ramos. About the sergeant's exam?"

And that other vindictive prick—the lecherous cop from the assessment exercise.

"Back down?" Marlow asked. He was surprised at her naïveté. "Well, Officer, that was never an option, him backing down."

So that left only one reason for a face-to-face—an understanding that came to her with the sharp clarity of the first pistol shot at an outdoor range. That first shot . . . before your muscles and ears and skin grow numb from the repeated fire. Only one reason for her to be summoned here. Marlow was going to take possession of her weapon and her shield. She was now suspended.

Shitshitshit . . .

She bit the inside of her lip.

Easing the folder closed, Marlow looked at her in a fatherly way, which unnerved her; it was as if the punishment to which she'd been sentenced was so severe that she needed the buffer zone of paternal kindness. "People like Ramos, Officer, you're not going to beat 'em. Not on their turf. You won the battle, cuffing him at the scene. But he won the war. People like that always win the war."

"You mean stupid people? Petty people? Greedy people?"

Once again the genetic makeup of a career police officer stopped him from even acknowledging the question.

"Look at this desk," he said as he did just that. It was awash in paper. Stacks and piles of folders and memos. "And I remember when I used to complain about all the paperwork when I was a portable." He rummaged through one of the stacks, apparently looking for something. Gave up. Tried another pile. He came up with several documents that weren't what he wanted either and took his own sweet time reorganizing them then resuming the search again.

Oh, Pop, I never thought a suspension'd really go through.

Then, within her, the sorrow and disappointment formed into a rock. And she thought: Okay, that's the way they're going to play? Maybe I'm going down but they'll *hurt.* Ramos and all the little prick Ramoses like him're going to lick blood.

Knuckle time . . .

"Right," the captain said, finally finding what he wanted, a large envelope with a piece of paper stapled to it. He read it quickly. Glanced at a clock in the shape of a ship's wheel on his desk. "Darn, look at the time. Let's get on with it, Officer. Let me have your shield."

Heartsick, she dug dutifully into her pocket. "How long?"

"A year, Officer," Marlow said. "Sorry."

Suspended for a year, she thought in despair. She'd imagined three months at the worst.

"That's the best I could do. A year. Shield, I was asking." Marlow shook his head. "Sorry for the rush. I've got another meeting any minute now. Meetings—they drive me crazy. This one's about insurance. The public thinks all we do is catch perps. Or thinks we *don't* catch perps, more likely. Uhn-uhn—half the job is business bushwah. You know what my father called business? 'Busy-ness.' He worked for American Standard for thirty-nine years. Sales rep. B-U-S-Y-ness. True about our job too." He held out his hand.

Dismay pooling around her, drowning her, she handed him the battered leather case containing the silver shield and ID card.

Badge Number Five Eight Eight Five . . .

What could she do? Be a fucking security guard?

Behind him the captain's phone rang and he spun around to answer it.

"Marlow here. . . . Yessir. . . . We've got security arranged for that." And as he continued to talk to the caller, something about the Andrew Constable trial, it seemed, the captain placed the interoffice envelope in his lap. He pinched the phone in the crook of his neck, turned back to face Sachs and continued his conversation as he unwound the red thread that was twisted around the clasps to keep the envelope sealed.

Droning on about the trial, the new charges against Constable and others in the Patriot Assembly, raids up in Canton Falls.

Sachs noted the man's perfectly nuanced, respectful tone, how he played the deference game so perfectly. Maybe he was talking to the mayor or governor.

Maybe Congressman Ramos.

Playing the game, playing politics. . . . Is this what policework is really about? It was so far from her nature that she wondered if she had any business being a cop.

No busy-ness.

That thought tore her apart. Oh, Rhyme. What're we going to do?

We'll get through it, he'd said. But life isn't about getting through. Getting through is losing.

Marlow, still pinching the phone between ear and shoulder, was rambling on and on in the language of government. He finally got the envelope opened and dropped her shield into it.

He then reached in and extracted something wrapped in tissue paper.

". . . don't have time for a ceremony. We'll do something later." This latter message was whispered and it seemed to Sachs he was speaking to her.

Ceremony?

A glance at her. Now another whisper, his

hand over the receiver. "This insurance stuff. Who understands it? I've got to learn all about mortality tables, annuities, double indemnity. . . ."

Marlow unwrapped the tissue, revealing a gold NYPD badge.

Back in his normal voice as he spoke into the phone: "Yessir, we'll stay on top of that situation. . . . We've got people in Bedford Junction too. And Harrisonburg up the road. We're completely proactive."

Whispering again, to her. "Kept your old number, Officer." He held up the badge, which glistened brilliant yellow. The numbers were the same as her Patrol ID: 5885. He slipped the badge into her leather shield holder. Then he found something else in the yellow envelope: a temporary ID, which he also mounted in the holder. Then handed it back.

The card identified her as Amelia Sachs, detective third-grade.

"Yessir, we've heard about that and our threat assessment is that it's a handleable situation. . . . Good, sir." Marlow hung up and shook his head. "Give me a bigot's trial any day over insurance meetings. Okay, Officer, you'll need to get your picture taken for your permanent ID." He considered something then added cautiously, "This isn't a chauvinist thing so don't take it the wrong way but they like it better with women's hair pulled back. Not down and all, you know, well, *down.* Looks tougher, I guess. You have a problem with that?"

"But, I'm not suspended?"

"Suspended? No, you made detective. Didn't they call you? O'Connor was supposed to call you. Or his assistant or somebody."

Dan O'Connor, the head of the Detective Bureau.

"Nobody called me. Except your secretary."

"Oh, well. They were supposed to call."

"What happened?"

"I told you I'd do what I could. I did. I mean, let's face it—there was no way I was letting you go on suspension. Can't afford to lose you." He hesitated, looked at the tide of files. "Not to mention, it would've been a nightmare to go up against you in a PBA suit or arbitration. Would've been ugly."

Thinking: Oh, yessir, it would've been.

Real ugly. "But the year? You mentioned something about year."

"That's the *sergeant's exam* I was talking about. You can't take it again until next April. It's civil service and there was nothing I could do about that. But reassigning you to the Detective Bureau, that's discretionary. Ramos couldn't stop that. You'll report to Lon Sellitto."

She stared at the golden shield. "I don't know what to say."

"You can say, 'Thank you very much, Captain Marlow. I've enjoyed working with you in Patrol Services all these years. And I regret I will no longer be doing so.'"

"I—"

"That's a joke, Officer. I *do* have a sense of humor despite what you hear. Oh, you're third-grade, you might've noticed."

"Yessir." Struggling to keep the breathless grin off her face. "I—"

"If you want to make it all the way to first-grade and sergeant I'd think long and hard about who you arrest—or *detain*—at crime scenes. And, for that matter, how you talk to who. Just some advice."

"Noted, sir."

"Now, if you'll excuse me, Officer . . . I

mean, *Detective.* I've got about five minutes to learn everything there is to know about insurance."

Outside, on Centre Street, Amelia Sachs walked around her Camaro, examining the damage to the side and front end from the collision with Loesser's Mazda in Harlem.

It'd take some major work to get the poor vehicle in shape again.

Cars were her forte, of course, and she knew the location, as well as the head shape, length and torque, of every screw and bolt in the vehicle. And she probably had all the ding-pullers, ball-peen hammers, grinders and other tools she needed in her Brooklyn garage to fix most of the damage herself.

Yet Sachs didn't enjoy bodywork. She found it boring—the same way that being a fashion model had been boring and that going out with handsome, cocky, bang-bang cops had been boring. Not to put too much of a shrink's spin on it but maybe there was something within her that distrusted the cosmetic, the superficial. For Amelia Sachs the substance of cars was in their hearts and hot souls: the furious drumbeat of rods and pistons, the whine of belts, the perfect kiss of gears that turned a ton of metal and leather and plastic into pure speed.

She decided she'd take the car to a shop in Astoria, Queens, one she'd used before, where the mechanics were talented, more or less honest and had a reverence for power wheels like this.

Easing now into the front seat, she fired up the engine, whose gutsy rattle caught the attention of a half-dozen cops, lawyers and businesspeople nearby. Pulling out of the police lot, she also made another decision. A few years ago, after some rust work, she'd decided to have the factory-black car repainted. She'd opted for vibrant yellow. The choice had been impulsive, but why not? Shouldn't whims be reserved for decisions about the color of your toenails, your hair and your vehicles?

But now she thought that since the shop would have to replace a quarter of the Chevy's sheet metal and it would need repainting anyway, she'd pick a different hue. Fire-engine red was her immediate choice. This shade had a double meaning to her. Not only was it the color her father always said that muscle cars ought to be but it would also match Rhyme's own sporty vehicle, his Storm Arrow wheelchair. This was just the sort of sentiment that the criminalist would appear wholly indifferent to but that would privately please him no end.

Yep, she reflected, red it would be.

She thought about dropping the Chevy off now but, on reflection, decided to wait. She could drive a beat-up car for a few more days; she'd done that plenty in her teen years. At the moment she wanted to get back home, to Lincoln Rhyme, to share the news with him about the alchemy that had transformed her badge from silver to gold—and to get back to work unraveling the thorny mysteries that awaited them: two murdered diplomats, alien vegetation, curious imprints in muddy ground and a couple of missing shoes.

Both of them right.

ACKNOWLEDGMENTS

My thanks to Jane Davis, who practices her own brand of unparalleled magic in overseeing my website, to my sister and fellow author Julie Reece Deaver, to my dear friend and thriller writer extraordinaire John Gilstrap, and to Robby Burroughs, who accompanied me to the performance of the Big Apple Circus at which the idea for this story was born.

I also found the following sources extremely helpful in the writing of this novel: *The Creative Magician's Handbook,* Marvin Kaye; *The Illustrated History of Magic,* Milbourne and Maurine Christopher; *The Magic and Methods of Ross Bertram,* Ross Bertram; Magicians and Illusionists, Adam Woog; *The Annotated Magic of Slydini,* Slydini and Gene Matsuura; *The Tarbell Course in Magic,* Harlan Tarbell; *Houdini on Magic,* Walter B. Gibson and Morris N. Young, eds.; and *Magic in Theory,* Peter Lamont and Richard Wiseman.

ABOUT THE AUTHOR

Former journalist, folksinger and attorney Jeffery Deaver's novels have appeared on a number of bestseller lists around the world, including *The New York Times, The Times* of London and the *Los Angeles Times.* The author of eighteen novels, he has been nominated for five Edgar Awards from the Mystery Writers of America and an Anthony award, is a two-time recipient of the Ellery Queen Readers' Award for Best Short Story of the Year, and is a winner of the W. H. Smith Thumping Good Read Award in the United Kingdom. His book *A Maiden's Grave* was made into an HBO movie starring James Garner and Marlee Matlin and his novel *The Bone Collector* was a feature release from Universal Pictures starring Denzel Washington and Angelina Jolie. His most recent novels are *The Stone Monkey, The Blue Nowhere* and *Speaking in Tongues.* He lives in Virginia and California. Readers can visit his website at www.jefferydeaver.com.